Three Ruined Realms

Hallowed Wars series

Ann W.T.

Winter Tales

Three Ruined Realms is a work of fiction. Names, characters, places, incidents and events are the product of the author's imagination or are used fictitiously. Any resemblance to an actual person, living or dead, events, locales, is entirely coincidental.

Edited by Anne-Marie Rutella

Book design by DHMC45/Dahmcee

Illustrations by Lya Alves

Map Illustration by Ann W. T

ISBN 978-1-7383426-3-1

ISBN 978-1-7383426-5-5

CONTENT WARNING

This is an adult novel targeted to mature audiences. Some content presented in this book may be upsetting to some readers such as adult themes, violence, strong language, and graphic descriptions. Readers' discretion is advised.

Contents

To my Grandfather; my second dad.

You wouldn't have understood the story or even liked it that much. Yet you were and will continue to be, always, my number one fan.

White Mountains
North Raevich
East Kingdoms
West Raevich
Raevich
East Raevich
South Raevich
West Kingdoms
Carnarbur
Centrion
Galmion
Albaron
Qirion
Haste Mountains
Necrosis Hurst
Trymion

PART I

The Divine Order

CHAPTER I

To ward those below and secure those above
To shield our hearths and embrace our lands
To protect the realm and maintain its faith
To bring light and sustain hope
To never falter be it Bless or Gallows
To fight for honor and sustain life
This oath I take binding heart and soul

- *The Divine Oath,* created by the Divine Order of Orphys Knights' founders.

Bedtime Tales, Wartime Cries

Fall of Night

It happened in a time long past, a time when men's blood drenched the very soil they fought on and the air was weighted with a stench of war and despair. In the West, three great kingdoms lived in dismay, stuck in a battle that held no promises to ever end. Carnarbur, Raevich, and Albaron, the most powerful kingdoms where only peace was away from their grasp.

"Why did they fight so, Nana? Were they mad with each other? Could they not apologize and hold hands?"

If a good reason ever existed for the everlasting bloodshed, it had long been forgotten. No matter if it was greed, betrayal, misunderstandings or covetousness, a point was reached where the war's single purpose was to exist and prevail. On every chance the kings would attempt to end the devious thing, yet on each chance a corruption would appear, tainting their hopes of harmony. To all it felt as if the Divines had abandoned the realm, leaving their fates to their own demise.

"Why would the Divines do so, Nana? Aren't the great Divines supposed to help us in our time of need?"

None can truly grasp the reasoning of the Divines nor Their intentions. What mattered was that hunger ailed the kingdoms and Death delivered its kiss from Wake till Gallows, marking those times with nothing but darkness. But there came a day when one of the three kings fell ill and a hope emerged from the depths of their tainted war for it was the ill king's wish to see an end to that calamity before he passed. However, on a frightening Gallows—

"The firstborns! They all died at the same Gallows, isn't that so, Nana?!"

All three firstborns were found in their beds, murdered in the cruelest way, blood neither warm nor cold, pure horror in their eyes. No kingdom claimed guilt yet all fingers were pointed. A new grief covered every village and every house, for people knew their hope had died alongside the three heirs that night.

"Who killed them? Did the Divines punish them, Nana?"

To this day, the real perpetrator is nothing but a mystery. No trails were left behind except the blood of the ones who perished and like so, the war prevailed. It was on the first full moon of winter, on the day of the First Snow with the wind whispering and the trees cowering, that ten noble knights reunited in secret. They were all desperate to end such a cursed war, fearing for the fates of their kingdoms. So, a plan was made and before winter came to an end, all ten knights were facing their kings with soldiers and citizens by their side. The ten knights threatened the three kings, swearing to end the war one way or another.

"They are the Divine Order's Knights! They were the ones that founded the Order, right Nana?! It *is* them!"

"Do you wish for me to finish the story, little one, or do you wish for me to blow out the candle and put you to sleep?" the young woman asked with a smile touching her lips.

The child widened their eyes while shaking their head with passion.

"Please, no! Finish the story, Nana! I will keep my words, I swear." The child tugged and pulled the young woman's sleeve, begging with their eyes, their face, and their voice. The woman laughed, caressing the small one while speaking with warmth in her words.

"Then listen with care, little one."

The knights' audacity could be a reason for punishment. The kings could have their lives right at that moment, yet it was the ten knights' bravery and determination that moved all the kings to their cores and souls. It is said that light poured down the windows as if the Divines Themselves were blessing the knights and with that sight, one by one, Raevich, Albaron, and Carnarbur abandoned the cruel everlasting war. The ten knights were not only praised but rewarded lands, with songs and tales being spread not only in the West but on the whole Tërnya. It was decided not long after that their comradeship and strength should not be ignored, for the realm needed them still. It was then that the great Divine Order of Orphys Knights was created, fortifying the bond between the kingdoms and bringing many other knights under their wing, making the oath to forever protect Tërnya and our mortal realm.

"Is that really true, Nana?! Not even one small lie?"

The child's eye glimmered by the candlelight, the young woman's reply being the very same as every other time the same tale was told.

"Not even a single one."

The child's smile grew brighter and was filled with glee, the candle's flame trembling as the little one moved and jumped on the bed.

"Did they really meet in a secret room and plot against their kings?! How did they convince the others? Did they promise sweets and horses to whoever would aid them?"

The woman tried to control her laugh, holding the child still on the bed while attempting to give a disapproving look. "I was not there, little one. But this is how the story goes, so we can only guess and imagine. Now it is time for you to sle— "

"I shall be the next leader, the Order's greatest champion! I will convince all knights to aid me and create the best world our kingdom ever saw!"

The lady smiled and laughed, defeated by the child's claim. Inside, her heart felt warm and filled with butterflies and joy as she watched the child's dreams flourishing and growing.

"I wish I could make your wishes come true, little one, yet our world demands struggles and hardships. Inside the Divine Order there is a group of ten knights— "

"The ten Orphys Knights!"

"—that are not easily chosen by mundane disputes and tournaments. The leader is one of those knights, the most challenging to pursue."

The child at last sat on the bed, bulging eyes and a mouth open in disbelief.

"What do you mean? Nana said so herself that to become a knight in the Order one just needs to win the Great Tournament! You lied to me!"

"Yes, I did say so, and I did not lie," the young woman said with haste, the child already pouting with their lips and tears burning in their eyes. "However, the Orphys Knights are special. Nine are chosen by the leader and all Knights must belong to one of the three great West kingdoms. The trial to become the leader comes only every ten years and once chosen, there is nothing else to be done but wait ten more. This is their only way," the lady explained while wiping the child's tears away, kissing their cheeks and nose with words spoken in a calm and soothing voice.

"But—wah, that's not fair! Why would the Orphys Knights need to belong to one of the three big kingdoms?! There are so many others, with villages and small homes. They cannot do that! Nana, would I be able to change that? It is not fair!"

The young woman sighed, once again laying the child into bed, pulling the covers, and adjusting the pillows. "Now, now, the sun is asleep and so should you be. Do you wish to stay awake during Gallows?"

The child's lips trembled, tightening as they shook their head in one slow motion.

"I thought so. Tomorrow, I shall tell you more tales and hear all your words and doubts—*if* you behave and go to sleep when I say so. What do you say, little one? Can I trust you with this task?"

The woman tickled the child until a smile appeared on their face, the fear and sadness leaving their eyes with a weak giggle. "I promise, Nana! I will do so."

"Then I shall bid my farewell for this Fall." The young woman kissed the child before blowing out the candle and turning her head one last time before closing the door. The small child waved their hand and she waved back, whispering a last prayer inside her heart as she held her medallion close to her heart.

May the Divines' bless your dreams, my dear child.

A Dark Eye from the Gallows

Fall of Night - East Raevich

THE HOODED MAN STEPPED into the tavern with mud on his boots and blood in his mouth—one he could hide well.

Water ran down his clothes and hair followed by the foul smell of wet rats and dogs that came from the streets behind him. Maybe it came from him as well, it was not easy to tell. The scarce warmth provided by all those bodies and fire was quite welcome, although his presence was ignored for the most part as if he was nothing but a sly rat hiding from the rain. It was pouring like Ancient times. The Divines must have been pissed with something that Fall for that rain was enough to punish all simple mortals from Raevich for their foolish mistakes. Which, if he could be honest, was a stupid thing to do. One would think that after the third attempt the Divines would learn that, be it pouring or raining daggers, humans were humans. Rotten to their core.

The hooded man walked around until he found an empty table, picking off the pieces of bread on the chair—he was a bit hungry after work. They were kind of stale, but he would forgive them for that.

"Ancient rains are one of the worst omens you could see these days—it's what my mama used to say to me." The bald man at the table in front of him spoke with such caution, one could swear he was afraid to wake the dead. Someone had to tell the poor soul it was not Gallows yet.

As the hooded man glanced over that table, he saw five men: Fat, Bald, Somber, Drunk, and Ugly. Well, they were all ugly but there was one that really caught the eyes.

"Every time with those foolish superstitions! One should know when to stop talking and start drinking, so just go on with it, you stinky fool!" said Ugly. The others laughed, Drunk laughing way too hard with his red cheeks and teary eyes.

The hooded man waited a little more and when he realized he would not get any alcohol so soon he snatched one from another table. The cup was almost full.

"Perhaps his sweet mama was right." The laughs from the others diminished as Somber spoke, a shadow passing through his eyes while he looked at the other four as if they were the dead Bald was afraid to wake. "I heard the news. Dark Eye left another body at the river, another gold-plated."

"Dark Eye?!" Drunk almost choked on his own drool, punching Somber in the shoulder. "You don't *actually* believe this fiend exists, do you, mate?"

"Now, we have his mama and his *news* to think about while we drink!" They all laughed, Fat choking on a piece of meat.

The hooded man felt his pride being tainted. That drink was bad enough to taste even more to swallow. How could they sell that thing with a straight face? He had been so happy when he saw the cup was almost full, realizing how naive he had been. *Oh*, the pain one must face in East Raevich's taverns.

"You all can laugh while you can, drink and eat while you can." Their laughs still echoed at their table but that did not steal the shadows from Somber's eyes. "I caught a glimpse of this fella and I swear, it was Death that looked back. Dark Eye is as real as I am, a demon with flesh and bones." The laughs got weaker but were not gone.

"Now our man talks about demons."

"Maybe his mama made him believe them," said Ugly and Drunk, yet the hooded man could almost smell the fear that grew between them.

That only motivated their good friend Somber, as all joyfulness and drunkenness from other customers faded into another room, another world. "Seen it with my two good eyes—a scene I will not soon forget. A man covered by shadows with evil in his eyes, killing three armed men with his bare hands. If that is not the work of a demon, then I don't know what a demon would be." Somber looked at his own palms, a shiver passing through his shoulders and body. "This is a night with bad omens, so watch your backs for Dark Eye may tire of hunting only gold-plated. We could be next."

The hooded man was quite offended to be called a demon with such ease, even though not even he was sure the things existed.

He had killed them with a *dagger* after all.

"Go tell those stories to your lady, keep her scared enough to warm you in bed." And with Fat's words the laughs and choking returned, tears falling from their eyes.

Not that any of them had any lady to warm them on that cold night, much less do anything else. Men who had nice wives and nice kids and were not that fond of Death would not walk into such a place, in a weather like that. Only sad men, the worst kind of scum, and the trashy bastards would be found in taverns like that, after all who else would be able to drink and eat their nasty foods? They had spit roasting *rats*, for Divines' sake. And something told him they were not the clean ones.

And oh dear, was that an eye inside his cup?

"Go on, keep thinking I am a liar— "

"A shitty snotch, that's what you— "

"Dark Eye is now the greatest and most vile killer in this cursed kingdom. If your laughs and insults brush past him, you may all consider yourselves dead to never again share any warmth with anyone."

Bless the Divines, it was just a meatball. Maybe that was the reason it tasted so bad?

"Now, why won't you stop babbling before you lose your teeth? Unless you want to share the warmth of my fingers," said Ugly, his eyes lowering with a "threat" filling his words. Ugly *really* thought he was scary, huh?

And *definitely* not. The hooded man had taken another cup, no meatballs this time, from the next table and the taste was the same. Maybe that was why the Divines were punishing them.

Shitty drinks.

"I think you could use something to warm your brain—it must be dead cold in there." Then there was some fist here and there, some moans, chairs falling, drinks spilling, and just like that everything was back to normal. It was good to enjoy some late-night amusement after a rough workday.

The chair in front of the hooded man suddenly moved, and a boy sat right by his side. The hooded man did not look up to see who it was, playing with the drink in his hands. His eyes followed the scroll that was passed right beside his hand.

"A present so soon? Have I been such a good boy to deserve such a noble gift, I wonder?"

The newcomer did not smile back nor did he reply, his dark skin attracting enough attention that made him cover his face after a few seconds. Yet the hooded man could only see impatience and annoyance in the newcomer's eyes.

Which was quite rude.

"You know all too well how *noble* this gift is. I am always the one who has to carry the damned thing to you, *every* time," the newcomer whispered with harsh words, some anger following them in his voice.

"Well, I *know* that." The hooded man sighed, staring at the ceiling with bored eyes. "You still cannot take a joke whenever you are, Lee. Still too worried for your own good."

"Since worry is a lack in you, I guess I feel obliged to compensate for us both." The seriousness filling the boy's golden eyes almost made him laugh.

"Am I not alive, still? If anything will kill me, it will be this thing over here," the man said, while he pointed toward his drink, finishing the damn thing while he had the guts. A shiver went down his spine, a joyful smile touching his lips. "Drink it yourself! See how bad it tastes, you won't regret it."

Lee did not blink or give a reply, his face frozen on a blend of anguish and a terrible stomachache. Maybe he had already drunk it?

"Relax, for the sake of all Divines! I'm only joking, I care enough for you— "

"Master!" Lee shouted while slamming both hands on the table. That was loud enough to attract a few good looks, making the hooded man roll his eyes as he stood up and grabbed the scroll, putting it inside his leather pouch.

"You are such a bore sometimes." The man turned around, taking another cup from the next table, finishing the thing in one go. It tasted horrible, but it was alcohol all right. His throat was burning. "We are done here, Lee. Great to see you!"

As he moved toward the door, the hooded man felt a hand grab his shoulder, a stranger's voice reaching his ears.

"You are not done with *me*, you piece of shite!"

Oh wait, that was Ugly. And may it be possible or not, Ugly was even uglier with a pissed face. How could the Divines allow such a face to be born into that world? It was as if someone had molded eyes, mouth, nose, and cheeks and mashed everything together after putting in some broken bones.

"Have I ever started something with you?" the hooded man asked with a sweetened voice and pleading eyes.

"Your sorry ass did! I paid for that drink, you fucking maggot!" Ugly was a big man. He could even be an ugly man who thought he was scary. But before that, he was an unlucky man.

"My condolences, good sir. To know you, willingly, chose by your own free will to pay for such a poor and hideous drink does bring tears to my eyes. That is why I felt obliged to free you from such a burden and suffering. You can welcome me later for carrying such a kind heart in me." He then looked past Ugly, toward his fellow men, giving them a pitiful smile. "If you wish, I can end your suffering as well."

All four men stood up, most laughter and drunk noises gone. That alone made the hooded man *so* much happier. He could feel his heart race, the blood pumping in his veins spreading a euphoric feeling that would fulfill his soul for the next five minutes: sweet happiness and bloodlust.

"Stop this instant, brother!" Another hand grabbed him by the other arm.

His gaze followed that voice as the blood froze inside him. That hand belonged to Lee.

Look at that, a soon-to-be dead man.

"I already told you to not leave our home when Dad is away. May Säh and the Divines help you, brother, have you got no sense at all?!"

Lee pulled the hooded man away from Ugly and his companions, bowing to the five men.

He could see Lee's sweat, the trembling of his lips. "I sincerely apologize to you, gentlemen. My brother is ill-minded and tends to lose his good senses whenever our father is away. Forgive his lack of decency."

Lee should realize how close he was to taste death by the finest hands, at that point. Lee just had to hold him still for some more.

"Your retard brother stole my drink, half-breed! You think your damned apology will do shite for me?! You are not in the East, bastard!" Ugly said, while sinking his finger on Lee's chest.

The hooded man said nothing as he watched Ugly's fat finger touch Lee, letting the dagger slide to his hand while the demon whispered in his ears. Maybe there could be a finger inside a cup soon.

"I believe this will compensate for your trouble." Lee threw a small pouch filled with silver coins—*his payment for that night's work*—while hurrying to the exit. "Excuse us."

The next seconds were a complete madness, with the five men punching and colliding against each other to grab the blooded money, but soon all the shouts and curses were muted by the heavy sound of the rain as they stepped outside.

Lee took him to the middle of the street, no soul to be seen. None would be insane enough to be walking with Gallows approaching, during that rain. And that was all that Lee managed to do.

Take him to the middle of the street.

"Please do not kill me, master." Lee's whisper was almost lost as his face paled while his frightened eyes said enough. The hooded man had his dagger on Lee's neck, his mouth twisted in a smile.

"Now, why wouldn't I do that? Apparently, I am ill-minded so I guess I want to go for a killing spree." The rain kept washing away the blood that ran down Lee's skin making the red trail disappear completely. He could almost feel Lee's heart through the dagger, the blade pulsing. "Who said you had the right to *touch* me?"

The dagger went a little bit deeper. Lee drew a deep and shaken breath before opening his mouth. "Master, please forgive me. I needed to help."

"I had no need for help," the man answered in a cold, dead tone. He wondered if he would be able to feel his heart as well, with that cold blade.

"Help the *others*, master." Even as blood ran from his body, his golden eyes pleading and begging him, there was still kindness in Lee's eyes. Almost a sense of blind loyalty.

Trust.

The hooded man lowered his dagger, feeling tired all of a sudden. Maybe that drink would be the death of him after all. Lee's shoulder relaxed, his hand going to his neck and flinching as he touched the small cut.

"Next time you feel the urge to help someone I will break your neck and feed you to the rats. Keep that in mind." The man touched Lee's shoulder, whispering close to his ear so the boy could hear every word. Lee nodded without ever looking away, but there was fear in his eyes. Concern.

Dark Eye felt sick.

"Please hear my words, master. *Please...*" As the man didn't answer, the boy continued to speak even louder to be heard in the rain, "You know I truly care about you! I worry for you." When he began to walk away, Lee followed him like a pitiful dog.

Really, such a *tiring* night.

"Please, don't accept this contract, master! It's like no other, it will cost your life this time! You have plenty already, you can live by yourself in a good home, be free from this life. Just don't do it, master. *Please*. You will put your life at ris— "

"My life is *always* at risk, Lee!" the man shouted, turning to face the young boy once more, opening his arms to welcome the Gallows and the cursed rain. "If I shall perish by accepting this contract, then so be it. Maybe then my life will be useful for someone." His heart pounded in his chest, or maybe it was a demon knocking to let him in. "If you plan to convince me with those arguments, give up. You are wasting both our time."

Before he could leave, Lee grabbed his shoulder. There was no malice, no anger or hate as he was used to. Only kindness. Only a friendly gesture, followed by sad and hurtful eyes from a pitiful, loyal dog.

Which was so much worse.

"I beg you, master, in Säh's name and light, refuse this contract. Live your own life. I beg you not as your servant; as a friend." For the first time that night, the hooded man took off his hood. The rain fell on his head as if it thought it could clean him.

"My life is worth nothing for me to risk it. I thank you for your words, but you should know better after so long—I have no friends."

Dark Eye did not stay to see Lee's face. He did not stay to say his goodbyes. He put his hood on once again and walked away. Had he any sorrow or regrets left, he let the rain try to wash them away, together with all his worries. Gallows was there to embrace him as it always had, darkness welcoming him like his oldest lover as he felt the demon knock faster and faster. There was no warmth. All he could see at every window, every puddle, every drop of rain, was his eyes. An abyss so dark it could swallow him whole and drag him to the deepest despair.

That, the rain could never wash away.

But he did wait.

He prayed.

Ten Stars in Blackened Skies

Haze of Dawn - The Divine Order of Orphys Knights, Haste Mountains

That room had always been too cold for Sean's taste, yet that day was even colder. The tapestries that hung from the walls looked dull after so many years, and the painting of the Orphys constellation that stared down at him made it feel like they were all in a poor, empty church. After all, there was only one big table in the middle of the room with a few shelves and chandeliers spread out for "decorative" purposes. Also, why keep all twenty chairs when there were only ten of them? Sure, the grand marble table was beautiful to look at, even its heavy chairs, however all it did to that Polaris Chamber was make it seem shallower with its tall pillars and stone floor.

For the past year, the nine Knights had felt the change of seasons all the same, except for one single thing. They all knew the Last Bonfire would bring not only autumn to their doors but also a pristine new leader for the Order. A leader that could choose to keep them as Orphys Knights or change their ranks completely, back to being unit commanders, squad captains or even lower, like Ruby knights. Since he was a great listener, Sean knew they all felt that weight. The man knew their fears, their hopes, their passions—and their lies.

It was a change that was fated to happen, one that most Knights were not quite prepared to face. Among those Knights, Clarice was the one showing her frustration with the most...passion.

"Is this what will become of us, then? Nothing but fallen Knights inside isolated mountains, being no more than a source for mockery and cruel words?!"

"Clarice, please, we all knew this day would come— "

"I am no stupid woman, Rowan! This has *nothing* to do with our position as Knights!" The petite woman shoved the Red Knight's hands, circulating the room with heavy steps. Their colleagues fell in silence as they watched, unsure of what to say to her. Being from Raevich, even without one drop of noble blood, her eyes as dark as her hair, she managed to make almost every Knight flinch and avert their gaze. "The Order has become nothing but a joke! *We* are nothing but a joke, after doing our best for those useless idiots for ten bloody years! By Säh's brightest light, we sacrificed *everything* for them!" Clarice slammed her hand on the pillar beside her, her voice failing while her words burned more by the second.

"There is nothing to be done after we lost the Ancients' aid— "the Red Knight started to speak, passing his fingers through his long red hair when Clarice cut his words before he could even blink.

"How can you even think that, Rowan?!" She turned around to face the fellow Knight once again, rage flaring from her eyes.

Sean covered his mouth as if in thought, hiding the smile that he could not control. That woman had always been far too emotional for her own good after all.

"To say that those monsters were anything but demonic spawns and that we should weep about the fact that we finally got our freedom? Preposterous!" Clarice's dark braids fell from her shoulders, moving and raging alongside her as she finally returned to her seat.

"Clarice, the Ancients were the ones that gave the Divine Order their power and respect back. You can't possibly have forgotten such a fact?" At least someone else joined the discussion, one of the Qirian twins, trying to reason with her as all others watched from their seats.

Sean touched Säh's pendant on his chest, glancing toward the closed doors. *He should be here by now—this is getting tiring.*

"A fake glory followed by a war we cannot even prove because *no one saw it happening.* The Ancients aided us to fight *demons*?!" Clarice laughed as she looked at Rowan and the others as if they were all poor ill-minded souls close to their damnation. "Those are all *lies*, Ritta. We assumed our posts after this

' war ' and never got a glimpse of those things and all that we conquered these past years we conquered on our own, without any help from those beasts. Every single Knight who was once master of *them* is either dead or gone without a trace. What does that tell you? "She rested her back on the chair, showing a smile filled with nothing but irony and disgust. "That those Ancients are *evil*, vile creatures we should not even consider crossing paths with, and that one thing done right by our ancestors was making sure every single one of those creatures was exterminated."

Finally, the doors opened, stealing the attention from all of them. Sean almost clapped after waiting so long, tired from listening to the same speech from Clarice they had heard throughout the year since the Great Tournament had begun. As soon as the Knights recognized the man that walked into the room, they all stood from their chairs, the space filling with nothing but silence. Alexander had held the title of leader for one whole decade and it showed, not only on his hair but on his face. The fine lines and wrinkles, the gray tainting his short hair—even if the man chose to wear his fancy, youthful clothes for their last supper as Knights, like the rest of them—he could not cheat his own age. He was way past his prime.

"Why the somber faces?" Alexander asked with a smile, the words spoken calmly and serenely. "An entire week of preparation for one last celebration before the final duel and I find all of you here debating history?" The man glanced toward Clarice, furrowing his brows. "I thought we were all over this, Clarice. It is pointless to try to change the past when not even the future is set in stone."

The woman clenched her jaw, holding the same pendant Sean carried on his chest with a clenched fist. "I cannot see how changing leaders and the Knights will do our Order any favors when its walls are already crumbling from the inside. We are only entertaining and useful to them when there are duels and tournaments to watch, but no one supports us anymore, Alex."

The man walked toward her, giving the woman a hug. Clarice's body was stiff as a block of ice and she did not reciprocate at first. "I know...I know."

That was all Alexander said but somehow it was all she needed to hear, biting her lips as if to keep the tears at bay. After a moment, Alexander took a few steps back, staring at them all while sharing a sad smile.

"I can see you are all worried about the Order. I shall not lie to any of you—the Divine Order is not in a pleasant situation. Our funds are low and this year we had fewer than eleven new recruits." Alex walked closer to Rowan, grabbing his shoulder for a few seconds before continuing, "However, we cannot lose hope. In the end, that is why the Divine Order exists. To provide hope when there is nothing but despair left."

No more words were spoken until Rowan himself took a deep breath and smiled, looking at their colleagues and friends. "As Alex said, we cannot let one week of preparation go to waste. Let us go to the Grand Hall and eat and drink until the sun is down and have a great night's rest!"

That was hardly enough to motivate them but their gazes lowered as one by one the Knights left the room. Sean waited a little longer, until Clarice passed through the door and their distance grew, to speak his words to his leader.

"I was quite disappointed by your final speech, Alex. I thought it would be more emotional."

Alexander continued to walk without sparing a glance to Sean. "I believe it was enough."

"Was it though?"

"Are you implying som— "

Sean smiled, giving a shrug. "I am just saying that perhaps more could have been done. That is all."

Nothing more was spoken between them, however, deep down both of them knew.

Tomorrow would be a *grand* day.

Ties Shackled by Blood

Wake of Day - Reliquary Room, Haste Mountains

Kayden stared through the window without being able to feel the wind brushing against his skin. His heart was restless, yet at the same time it was as if there was a wall of mist surrounding it as Kayden gazed into the distance, watching the forest below him awake with the sun. Behind him there were whispers, sounds giving him words he did not wish to understand, for that was a day that demanded more than he could possibly provide.

How long had it been?

He hoped the child inside him was smiling, glad that day had finally come, yet that was all that could be done for that child. Hope. Wish.

Kayden was waiting for the call inside the Order's Reliquary Room, waiting for the moment that would forever change his life and the things he was fighting for. Apart from the book-filled shelves that covered most walls and some glass cases that displayed ancient artifacts and scrolls, what held his attention was one thing. The beautiful mosaic that showed the three great kingdoms' crowns like a stone gaze, weighing on him every time he glanced toward it. Blue jewels for Carnarbur, green and gold for Raevich, and deep purple and silver stones for Albaron.

He had battled and fought with participants and champions from all these kingdoms, completing task after task, the entire past year. Kayden was finally standing between the grand finalists, yet he was unsure how to feel. Proud? Sad? Anxious? Would any of those feelings matter, in the end? His hand went for the moon medallion on his chest, feeling once again the metal against his skin. The mist around his heart got thicker, spreading through his body as if it was searching for something inside him. Something that could, perhaps, make that cloud go away.

The past year, he had faced so many creatures, from small boars and great bears to trolls and Skürs. Even at that moment, Kayden could not recall the last trial without shivering, the one that saw the most losses by far.

Bring the remains of an Ancient creature.

There were places known as Primal Tombs, where with a bit of luck and some backbone one could stumble upon some "exotic" bones and carcasses. Yet those places carried enough perils to send a whole army back to where they came from. Death's presence was so dense and thick it was hard to walk on those paths without noticing Its scent. Those were sterile, dead lands, forsaken by the Divines, and all things that the Divines did not touch were fated to perish in the most horrible ways. Kayden had been fortunate, *blessed* one could say. Blessed to watch other competitors take their last breaths, hearing their screams fade like a forgotten promise that got carried away by the wind. Blessed to come back alive, with the Ancient's remains on his back.

Blessed to have a chance to become Order's next leader.

"It *was* you, I see it now."

Kayden stopped in his thoughts, the mist becoming a silent wave that began to drag him deep beneath its waters. He could not breathe—he could not think. There was an invisible knife stabbing his guts as he began to drown simply by staring at those eyes.

"Father." Kayden's whisper got lost, a word that not even he could hear.

Felix Faeryl stood at the entrance, the light covering his eyes and nothing more. His dark hair hung loose just above the shoulders, and his beard was somehow longer than Kayden remembered, the mustache thicker. However, one could see in the man's eyes the same feeling he always showed his heir every time he laid his gaze upon Kayden. Contempt.

His father came close, his trembling hands reaching out for him while his words were filled with thorns and poison.

"Do you have *any* idea of what you've done? Of the actual consequences of your *imbecile* acts?" The older man spoke with a low voice, yet his words burned enough to restrict all movement and thought Kayden could ever make. Kayden tried to take a deep breath, however he almost choked as his father approached, standing so close to him that Kayden could sense the heat, the rage coming out of him. "I thought that your distance and avoidance of the Tournament's tasks were the result of my words getting through to you, at last. Now I see I've been foolish. Were you not my own blood and kin I would have you *arrested*."

"Father, I broke no rules nor have I been unjust in this Tournament," Kayden found his voice again, yet it was shaken, weak. There was no confidence, no authority, nothing that he could stand on apart from fear. "I will not answer to your reasonings."

"You will answer to *me*. If you once believed your position in the kingdom makes you exempt of punishment, you shall rethink your childish plans."

Kayden clenched his fists, taking a step away from his father while tears burned his eyes due to the man's anger. "I place my beliefs neither in my position nor yours! I trust only myself and in what I can do as a person, as you taught me so *diligently*. If you will excuse me, I have a duel to prepare for and no visitants shall bother the participants before their tasks."

There was a great silence as his father looked down on him, piercing his gaze as if the man hoped it would scar Kayden's flesh. Then the older man turned around with the same grace he had presented himself before, without looking Kayden in the eye.

"I cannot stop this Tournament as it is beyond my power to do so. But I *will* show you what it takes to defy me. If you think you can become a high-ranking knight or even their *leader*, reality will teach you where you should stand."

The door closed with a loud noise and to Kayden it felt as if the water surrounding him fell helplessly on the floor, finally allowing him to breathe. He rested his arms on one of the displays' lids to prevent himself from falling on his knees while his sight returned to normal, the darkness fading. Kayden kept taking deep breaths until he managed to regain control, until the mist returned inside him.

Why do I still let him affect me so?

Kayden closed his hand on his medallion, the metal hot against his fingers, trying not to let his thoughts wander toward his father and how he knew Kayden would be there. Kayden let out a shaken breath, his heart still once again.

Should he feel proud? Sad?

Desperate?

The knock on the door came before he reached an answer, one of the Tournament guides at the door.

"Sir Keith, it is time."

Kayden gripped the medallion once more before the words left his mouth.

"Indeed, it is."

A Sight Too Bright to See

Wake of Day - Sun Arena, Haste Mountains

After dreaming and imagining it so many times, the arena was not at all what Kayden expected. It was no small place, the circle in which the participants would fight being quite wide and spacious, but Kayden knew it was not the Order's biggest space. There were nine rows of benches that followed the circled arena on an elevated space, with two passages from which the visitors could enter. However, one of them was solely for royalty and the ten Orphys Knights.

There were nobles and their prestigious ones spread throughout the benches, some Houses that Kayden could spot with ease like the Argyris and Bertram from Raevich, as well as the Allison and a few more from Albaron. For a moment Kayden thought he would never find him amid that crowd, yet how could he not? The knight could feel his father's presence like knives on his back, as whispers followed the man's gaze while Kayden fought to avoid it.

The other three competitors were scattered at the other extremities. Two of them belonged to Carnarbur—twins—with light brown hair and light eyes with tanned skins, while the other had Raevich's golden-and-green emblem shining on his chest armor, its pauldrons molded after a lion's face. His hair was a very light blond—a distinctive trait of Raevich's noble Houses and royalty, which explained how the man had gotten himself such expensive armor. Carnarbur's knights wore a simple gambeson armor that with one glance Kayden could tell it was not of great quality, making the status between Raevich's noble set and theirs as clear as the Wake. The only thing from Kayden's armor that was noticeable enough to be of a greater quality was his hooded cloak that hid his face alongside the mask that covered all but his eyes. Apart from that, his dark leather armor set was dull to the eyes, even though Kayden had spent a good amount of coins to put some pads on his shoulders, elbows, and knees. As the Great Tournament's rules dictated: *all contestants must provide their own gear and equipment.*

All four competitors had brought swords for the duel, as previously arranged, but only Kayden had chosen a rapier. Raevich's knight had a two-handed sword while Carnarbur's had brought simple longswords. People looked at Kayden's rapier with smirks and chuckles, glancing over to Raevich's two-handed sword as if to show how pointless their combat would be. If there was one thing that Kayden *was* proud of, it was his footwork and defense. After years training his rapier's skill, it would be ungraceful if he felt otherwise.

Kayden could not say he remembered anything exceptional from Carnarbur's knights, however Raevich's champion would be a problem. It was not his size—taller than the benches' elevation—that got Kayden apprehensive but his physique. Kayden had never seen him tired or exhausted after strength tests; while Raevich's had been the first participant to climb the White Mountains and get the flag during the third task, Kayden had placed sixth. He was already used to fighting while wearing a mask, but that alone was a hindrance. Rapiers were perfect for duels due to their range, weight, and flexibility. However, to fight someone who possessed far more endurance without being able to exchange full blows would be a challenge. That was no fencing duel—it was a succinct, controlled war.

"I welcome you all to our blessed home! May the Divines shine Their wisdom upon us in this Wake as the next leader for our Divine Order of Orphys Knights is born."

The man that spoke in the middle of the circle was not Alexander. The current leader watched everything along with his fellow Knights, in front of the royals. The spokesman was a jolly man with reddish cheeks, his long hair braided on his back like Narturers, a distinguished group who lived on Centrion Island in Carnarbur. It was odd to see a Narturer as an Order's knight since Narturers were pacifists at heart and soul.

"The Great Tournament has finally come to its grand end after four seasons. It started with the first harvest and after a year of memorizing complete collections of treasured scrolls, hunting Ancient remains, and fighting deadly creatures, four champions shall take their last stand to reach their prized goal. Today, the Great Tournament to choose the Order's next leader comes to a conclusion!"

"Wasn't this the small one that brought one of *those* creatures' bones on the last trial?" Kayden could hear the voices above him overlapping with the Narturer's words, certain he would find fingers pointing his way if he turned around.

"I heard he got hold of an entire skull!"

"I do wonder how he managed to find out. Certainly he did not kill it, bless Säh."

"Only way he got one is with a load of coins stuffed up his arse, that's how." It did trouble him so to hear such scorn in the woman's words, yet the lack of courtesy on the man's side removed all respect Kayden could ever feel toward them. Säh followers with such level of speech meant they were only present due to luck and favors.

"We congratulate our final four competitors!" Kayden's attention went back to the man in the middle of the arena, praying to keep his hands dry and steady. "Sir Corey and Sir Daniel from Carnarbur. Sir Thurstan from Raevich. Sir Keith from Albaron."

As each participant was named, cheers and howling could be heard, residents of all kingdoms mixed and spread through the benches. Both knights from Carnarbur seemed confident enough, looking at each other as if they were making a silent vow. As for Thurstan, little could be said from his expression alone, his stance relaxed while the grip on his sword remained strong. But when the man met his eyes Kayden felt a chill, whispers being carried by the wind as if they belonged to the dead, making his insides quiver while a cold spread through his body. "...and wish to them all the luck they can carry! May the last trial begin!"

People cheered as the Narturer walked away, going to his reserved spot at the entrance of the arena. Seconds passed, yet no participant took even a small step, abiding by the ninth rule of the Great Tournament: *the tasks commence by the ringing of the bell*. Kayden tried to get a better hold on the rapier's handle, his skin damp as he tried to control his breathing.

Something was not right.

Kayden could feel the lightness in his head, the bitter taste spreading inside his mouth. His gaze started to run in all directions, trying to focus on whatever it was that had made him feel that way. Not the Narturer, not his father, not even someone in the audience. He prayed to be wrong, prayed to *Them* it would not happen. Then he felt it. A light so hot and fierce burning inside his head as if it wanted to melt his entire brain while images and voices overlapped each other, fighting to be noticed while Kayden felt himself being sucked inside a dark hole in the cold ground while losing his senses.

He could feel it crawling on the walls and dragging on the ground, such a menacing and hideous future that its strength was like poison on his skin. By the time Kayden finally got control over his body once more, being able to discern what he had seen, the signal had already been given. A loud bell echoed through the arena while Kayden's feet stuck as if they had created roots that sank into the ground.

Before he could blink his horror away, Thurstan had closed the distance between him and one of Carnarbur's knights, the smaller one called Corey. The young man did not have the time to react as Raevich's knight thrust the heavy sword into his stomach, holding young Corey almost as if he was pulling him for a hug. Blood spilled from Corey's mouth, eyes frozen. Thurstan lifted the body while holding the sword a few centimeters above the ground before tossing the young knight aside, the smell of death spreading like heated iron. Silence befell the people like a thick veil, gasps and murmurs stuck in people's throats. Kayden could hear his own heart, his mind fighting to believe what was unfolding in front of him. *Why?* It was the question that echoed inside him.

The other Carnarbur knight, Daniel, was the first to break free from the shock. His scream was one filled with loss and grief, painful enough to tear Kayden's own soul apart. Tears ran down his face as the knight charged against Thurstan, giving clean hits against his enemy's sword time after time, the blades colliding against each other in an aggressive song. However, no matter how Kayden looked, it was

as if Daniel was hitting a stone wall that moved along with him. Thurstan's sword was heavier and, although he had a defensive stance, one could notice how at ease Raevich's champion was blocking every attack without showing a single drop of sweat. Kayden tried to move his body, yet it was as if his limbs held no life, his gaze following the knights against his will. It was like stones were being poured into his heart, the fate shown to him looming over his head, drying his tears before they could even fall. *Why? Why are they needed in the Divines' plan?*

Thurstan ducked and deflected Daniel's every move, the swords' clash echoing inside Kayden's ears like Death's knell. There was nothing in the duel's rules that forbade killing or inflicting severe injuries on other participants, however they all knew this task was supposed to be nothing but a simple spar to finally choose the winner.

Then why? Kayden tried to glance at his father, haunted by the whispers that spoke back. It couldn't be, not that, not something like that.

It was a sudden cry that made Kayden bite his lips, his muscles aching as he fought Them to no avail. Thurstan's movements changed, his pace getting faster and faster, his blows getting stronger and harsher, making Daniel recede at every strike. Daniel's hand began to move alongside his lips, Kayden recognizing the arcane movement though the knight didn't even get to finish. Choosing to divide his attention to manipulate energy cost him dearly, a slight drop in speed was all that Thurstan needed. The man faked from the right, hitting Daniel's face from the left in one violent movement with his head. Blood gushed from Daniel's nose and while the knight still recovered his senses, Thurstan swung his sword with all his might.

The sturdy blade cut the knight's head off in one blow, his body standing still for a few moments, arms hanging loose at its side as it dropped the longsword. And then, just like that, it fell like a doll. The head flew, rolling nonstop until it hit the circle's wall at Kayden's feet. He could not tell if some people had screamed, fell sick, or cried. All he could hear was his own heart breaking while Daniel's eyes stared back at him.

Face wet with tears and for only a second his mouth twitched, Death's kiss coming far too early for both knights. *Why?*

Kayden clenched his fists, his blood boiling, his veins pulsing as he took his stance. The Divines' power over his body was gone, and Thurstan still held his two-handed sword in a relaxed position on the other side of the arena. Kayden waited until the man was right in the center of the circle, closing their distance in seconds. Thurstan was looking down on him and for that the man would pay dearly.

Kayden dodged the first impact by moving to the side, and while Thurstan desired to close the distance between them, he had no rush. He overshadowed Kayden by height, his muscles were bigger, and his blows more powerful. But Kayden made sure Thurstan's blade would never even grasp him. A shallow cut was made on Raevich's champion's arm since only his chest and shoulders were covered by the plate armor, however Thurstan paid no mind as he aimed for Kayden's legs. The only sound that could be heard was Thurstan's swords cutting through air and the sound of their steps even when his movements changed with the blows getting faster and stronger, the same tactic Thurstan had used with Daniel. To his opponent's misfortune, Kayden was not Daniel. But he shared his grief.

The bigger man could not seem to follow his footwork, striking whenever he got the chance but meeting nothing but air. Kayden could not pierce Thurstan's chest armor, however every spot his armor did not cover was a clean hit. Raevich's champion was bleeding slowly from small cuts over his arms and legs, but still paying them no mind. On Thurstan's following blow, Kayden tangled the man's sword in his cloak and twisted the weapon in his opponent's hand, throwing the blade meters away the moment Thurstan let go of the sword. Kayden felt the punch before he saw it coming, a hit in his ribs the moment Thurstan closed their distance.

Kayden bit his lip as pain shot through his body, using his rapier's pommel to hit Thurstan on his chin before the man gave another blow. Kayden took a few steps back as Thurstan shook his head and wavered for a few seconds before reaching for one of the twins' longswords that was not that far from him.

Thurstan charged with speed, ready to give a powerful strike that was aimed at Kayden's waist. Two steps back, one to the side, and Kayden had his adversary's sword stuck on the rapier's pommel. He twisted Thurstan's hand, making the man drop his weapon, kicking him in the chest to push him enough to take him off balance and create a little more distance. Kayden pushed the longsword with his feet and threw it behind him and that was when Thurstan made one single mistake. And it did cost him.

The man raced toward Kayden without a weapon, ready to knock him with his weight and shoulders. Yet Kayden was faster. He had sworn to himself he would not use the arcane arts, that he would only trust his Way. However the anger and contempt that grew in his heart were enough to make Kayden reach for his core, manipulating the air's energy to increase the power and speed of his blade. The rapier sliced both ankles almost with a thirst of its own, cutting right through the tendons and that time it was Thurstan's scream that echoed through the space as he fell on his knees. He used one hand for support, breath uneven, while the champion clenched his jaw. Kayden gave a full blow with his handle on Thurstan's back, making Raevich's champion gasp and fall. Kayden rolled the man with his feet so he could see his face.

It would be simple to sink the blade into his throat and watch Thurstan drown in his own blood. Raevich's knight had only followed someone's orders, Kayden *knew* that, but foremost Thurstan had been the one to accept them. *Why?* His foolish choice had taken the life of two bright young knights, and Kayden could not hide the disgust in his eyes. To kill such a thing would be simple, easy. Deep down, he knew others would not condemn Kayden for the act, most would even praise him. Yet he could not.

Kayden lowered the rapier, stepping aside. He walked over to Daniel's head, picking it up with utmost care, taking it back to where it belonged. Kayden knelt, placing the head in its rightful place, closing the boy's eyes before taking off his cloak to cover the body. Were it not for the shock and dirt on his face, Daniel almost looked asleep, no more need to stare at death any longer. Kayden stood up, locking glares with the spokesman while he waited still on the spot.

It was sad to see the Narturer after the duel, his face pale and sickened, arms and legs shaken as his braid swung from side to side. The Narturer cleared his throat a few times before looking down at Thurstan, his face twisting with loathing. "Can Sir Thurstan continue the fight?" he asked louder, his words surprisingly steady.

"I. Cannot," the knight spoke with clenched teeth, Kayden almost tasting the humiliation drenching Thurstan's words as he spoke before shifting his gaze to Kayden.

"You forfeit this battle, then?" Once more the Narturer spoke aloud, crowd cheering the spokesman while some cursed at Thurstan.

"Yes," Raevich's knight replied through his teeth as if the words were bleeding.

"Then I announce Sir Keith, knight of Albaron, as the winner of the Great Tournament!"

Everyone rose from their seats, apart from some of the royal families, whistles and howls louder than their clapping. Should Kayden feel proud?

Should Kayden feel happy?

"Why not kill me?" Thurstan asked among the cheers, his words being heard only by Kayden and the braided Narturer, his eyes red and dry. Kayden did not glance over toward the fallen man, his own eyes trying to get lost in another world and time.

"Death for you would be too kind. You do not deserve a kind future, Thurstan of Raevich." Upon hearing Kayden's voice, Thurstan's expression changed slightly, confusion filling his eyes.

That was one of the first times Kayden had ever spoken to any of his competitors. His presence in the Great Tournament had been lacking in many ways, never speaking unless he had to, never staying more than he had to, never interacting more than dictated.

"Above all else, I cannot make someone carry the weights of my own actions, whether they have some blame for them or not." When Kayden spoke his words once again, Thurstan widened his eyes with a question he had no need to ask.

"Who..." The word was lost in the air, forgotten amid the crowd's noises. Kayden glanced toward the bodies, toward his own weapon. Was it worth it? Was the child inside him happy to fulfill their dream? Would Nana be proud of the outcome, proud of Kayden's actions?

Should I be happy?

"People of Tërnya, you hear my words!" Kayden's voice surpassed the sounds that filled the Sun Arena. The words were strong and impactful enough to steal the attention and to silence their victory cries and applause. Perhaps due Kayden's tone or by the way the fallen knight and the spokesman held their breath with stunned expressions, the air shifted and changed around them as if people knew something was coming.

Kayden took off the mask and the cap that covered his head and face, hearing gasps and curses from the crowd. It was clear who recognized Kayden and even those who had never seen his face could take one glance at Felix and they would be able to tell. Kayden held no resemblance toward his late mother after all. Kayden watched as Felix remained in his seat, arms crossed with a gaze that seemed to want his only heir gone. Waiting for Kayden to end the farce in front of everyone.

The long hair fell from his shoulders, reaching the middle of his back and the bandages that bound his chest had never felt so tight, making it harder to breathe by the second; Kayden had to finish that trickery, all those lies.

"I stand here as a knight and as Kayden Allis Faeryl, the only heir and daughter of Felix and Cyrenne, Albaron's king and late queen. Here, with victory still fresh in my hands, I stand before you all as the Order's future leader."

Was *she* supposed to feel free?

Chapter II

The Ten Tournament Rules

I - The new leader shall be decided through a series of tasks and the selection shall last a year

II - Each task shall have a set of rules that must be obliged

III - No contestant shall receive any aid from outside sources

IV - All contestants must provide their own gear and equipment

V - All contestants must be from one of the three great West kingdoms

VI - Misconduct and uncalled-for violent acts shall receive appropriate punishment

VII - Any contestant that fails to complete a task shall be disqualified

VIII - No sponsors shall be accepted after the beginning of selection

IX - The tasks commence by the ringing of the bell

X - Any contestant that fails to uphold these rules shall be disqualified

Envies From an Old Soul

Bless of Day - Carnarbur's Heart, Carnarbur

Orion wandered the halls with the long, starry cloak dragging on the floor along his steps. The osprey that lay on his shoulder could almost be mistaken for a stuffed bird if it refrained itself from blinking and tilting its head from time to time. The child could scarcely comprehend why *he* had to be the one to deliver these types of messages to the king. Fred was one of their fastest birds, yet it was not the osprey tasked to carry the news since Fred could not speak, and Orion envied that. The king would certainly hear the news sooner than later, so why should Orion be bothered? Weren't counselors supposed to talk and advise *after* their kings heard things? Orion had important studies and tasks being neglected at that very instant, his apprentice's return from the small journey nearing the clock. Time was never to be wasted. And by thinking of the amount of time Orion would lose with his king's lectures about duties and responsibilities were he *not* to share the news firsthand...Orion shivered with such thoughts. He sighed, his legs heavy, yet he forced them to go with haste. Such a bothersome deed should be taken care of sooner than later.

Sometimes being the king's counselor was tiring.

King Gregory was, per usual, in his private room. Maps, telescopes, and books were scattered all over the place however this time the king had a visitor as well. A young man, a resident from Qirion Island judging by his light and loose clothes. Orion entered the room, standing at Gregory's side as the osprey flew over to the king's shoulder. A pity Fred couldn't talk. King Gregory, even by suffering the passage of time, was a man with kind features and gentle blue eyes. One could spot his age by seeing the white hair blending in his dark beard, but apart from that, Carnarbur's king had a young soul. Gregory spoke with a certain enthusiasm with the visitor, gesturing with his hands nonstop while the Qirion resident kept nodding with an awkward, shy smile.

Maybe that was no visitor at all, but a simple wanderer who had crossed his king's path at a very wrong time. Orion could imagine the boy getting dragged along without being able to have a say in the matter while Gregory got lost in thoughts and speculations. Sometimes the king would forget things, like his robe, his glasses, and his boots. That particular day, Orion noticed, he had forgotten his belt. His pants were sliding down bit by bit, yet the king was so absorbed in the conversation he didn't even notice the bird landing on his shoulder, caressing Fred's head as if in a trance.

Orion did not have the time for that conversation to end.

"I ask to speak my words, Your Majesty," Orion spoke as he stood by his king's side, tugging the man's sleeves with care.

It took almost six seconds for Gregory's gaze to lower, almost two for his smile to brighten. "Orion! There you are—I was talking to our small Ian here about that theory of ours! About how the sun and moon influence the sea and the land together with the Divines' energies flows. Yes, you could show him your notes. I believe it would be the most wonderfu— "

"Your Majesty, I bring news from the Great Tournament." Orion knew better than to let the king speak. He knew all too well, and he knew how much time he was willing to waste.

There was a very small hint of annoyance in King Gregory's eyes, yet he continued to smile as he pampered Fred. "Oh, *so* you bring. Tell me, Orion, were the Divines merciful with us this time or did Felix snatch the Order for himself once again? I do not recall the last time our Divine Order belonged to any other kingdom."

"Pardon my insolence, my king, this is why I came," the visitor Ian spoke with hesitant words. "My brothers were among the competitors. I was likely to hear some news faster if I came to you, my king, since our parents are most excited to know if our Danny and Corey were successful on their journey." A bright smile burst onto the visitor's face, his eyes lighting up as he spoke with pride filling his words. "It was even said in their previous letters that, even though they were not confident enough to win the Tournament, their positions as Diamond knights is almost guaranteed! One of the Orphys Knights said so herself!"

The king gave the boy a warm smile, his eyes joyful and kind as he grabbed small Ian by his shoulder. Orion thought for half a second the king was going to hug the poor boy.

"But of course! It must have been a great honor for your family, getting this far in the Tournament. Even if they did not succeed, a Diamond rank is still an incredible feat! I shall congratulate them both the instant they arrive."

"Your actions are far too generous, my king." The visitor bowed, touching his heart with his right palm. King Gregory switched his attention to Orion, a smile still too bright and innocent, his concerns with Albaron already in a forgotten past.

"Now, Orion! Speak your words."

Why couldn't Fred speak? Why couldn't Orion transform into a bird instead?

"Unfortunately, I do not have news on Carnarbur's knights. I believe you will find your luck at the port, where most posts are. You are fated to find at least one bird wandering with the news you seek." The young mage spoke as he stared the boy Ian in the eye. There was a faint frustration, but the boy soon smiled with a brief nod.

"Of course, I shall go there at once. Thank you both for your time and generosity. My King." The young man bowed briefly toward Gregory, turning to face Orion after. "Counselor. May the Divines' bless and brighten your paths."

The king's smile waned as Ian left the room, eyes no longer joyful or warm. The king also knew Orion well. Gregory sighed, his gaze staring at the maps and tools on the tall table as if he was afraid to ask. It took him almost nine seconds to speak his words again, not daring to meet Orion's eyes.

"Will I need to sit, my dear friend, or can my old heart take the news you are about to share?"

That was precisely why Orion was so envious of a single bird. More often than they would like, the news would not be kind.

"Your heart will not stop its beating, if that is your worry. However, you will not be pleased, Your Majesty."

The older man finally turned his head, facing the counselor with a new weight in his eyes. His words left his mouth with something Orion could only describe as acceptance. "Speak, Orion."

As the contents of the letter were revealed, King Gregory did take his seat without ever averting his eyes from the young mage. Fred was one of the fastest ospreys Orion had ever seen, yet it would not take long for all Tërnya to know about this year's outcome. It was not at all uncommon for noble families to participate in the Order's tournaments, especially the Great Tournament that chose their leaders. However, no royal had ever enrolled their heirs—the idea of a king or queen entering the competition was absurd. No kingdom would take this news lightly. And Orion had little idea of how Felix would be able to counter others' reactions.

"Who... How... How did they die? Not even once was it said they should fight until death." The king's voice was heavy with loss, his words trembling and weakened.

"I shall only say that they suffered brutal deaths by the hands of Raevich's knight." As Orion spoke, Gregory rose from his seat, going toward the open window. He had his back to Orion, yet the mage could see the thoughts that crossed the man's eyes.

"What about the perpetrator?"

"It was said that Raevich's knight will never again be able to walk properly."

"Good." There was a ruthless coldness within the king's words, enough to make the air between them change. "What of Princess Kayden?"

"Knowing her, she will soon return the bodies for a proper burial."

Almost seventeen seconds passed before the mage heard His Majesty's words again. "I hear you, Orion. You may go. I would like some time alone."

"As you wish, Your Majesty."

Orion returned to his chambers with haste, knowing full well he would later need to discuss matters with Gregory. But until then, his door would remain locked.

The Lion's Roar

Bless of Day - Harvest Hall, Haste Mountains

Inside the Haste Mountains, thousands of men and women trained, slept, and ate every day, for it was the place where one could find the hearth and official site of the Order. Inside the perilous mountains, there were three arenas, four dinner halls, and far too many chambers to count with passages connecting the three mountains to one another. The true builders of the Haste Mountains palace were unknown, yet most believed it had been built in the Ancient times before the Divine Order even existed. It was the first leader who found the wonders inside the Haste Mountains after they received the lands from the three kings. Not long after, the Order established itself inside the Haste Mountains not only for their grand proportion but also for their position. At least, that was what was told to every knight upon their arrival at the Order.

The Haste Mountains should never be crossed with fleetness or without ware. Its passages were too narrow, the ground too unstable. Unwise would be the ones who chose to cross the Haste Mountains with no care and no poise, for one misstep would cost a life. Composed of three mountains, their name was a warning for every wanderer and adventurer who was too quick to judge and act. The three mountains were named spiritedly after the stars found in the Maiden Heart constellation. They were Red Heart, Dawn Star, and Ice Draco.

It was Harry's first time in the Harvest Hall, which resided in the middle mountain, the tallest among the three, Dawn Star. Harvest Hall was the main dining hall, where suppers and the Wake meals were served, but it had been closed for a few years since the Order's number were dropping and their meals were served elsewhere. Yet for that day, there was a special feast for all guests and knights who had chosen to stay for the next day's ceremony. The tables and benches were filled with plates, cups, and people. At first the knight was excited, yet all his joy faded by seeing the supposed *feast*. There was hardly any meat, even fruits were withered and unappetizing, with no cheese, no nuts, no nothing. Many guests had left without delay as soon as the duel ended and more left as they entered Harvest Hall, disappointed and probably hungry.

"If you said that to me a few seconds before the duel, I would have slapped you in the face and called you mad. Can you truly believe it? Princess *Kayden* won the Tournament!" Harry avoided the "food" on his plate, trying to engage in conversations with other knights to forget his hunger. His companion seemed to pay no mind to the food's poor quality.

"I wonder how she managed to hide it for so long. Never mind her face—have you ever seen her breasts? It would be nice to grab them once." The other man spoke with a full mouth, making Harry widen his eyes.

"She could have your head for those words! This is no way to speak of a lady!"

The other knight shrugged, drinking the ale in one go. "Nay, she's not my princess." As soon as he finished his words, the man burped, hitting his chest a few times.

Apparently, Harry had made a poor choice on the right person to talk to. "You do realize that starting from the next Bless she will be our leader, hence she can stab you right in the heart if she wishes, and rightfully so, may I add."

The other knight blinked a few times, looking down at his cup. "I realize I must get more ale while I take a piss." He then got up, soon to be lost in the crowd.

Harry bit his apple, regretting it the following second. After wiping his mouth, his eyes wandered until he spotted the big man in front of him. For some reason the knight did not notice the different food on the stranger's plate, only his noble clothes standing out for a brief moment. For some reason, the knight thought he could be someone polished and cultured enough to talk to.

"What about you, my friend? What do you think about the princess winning the Tournament?"

The big man said no words, continuing to eat in silence. His lines were harsh and strong, yet the knight could not see the stranger's eyes. He knew the big man was from Raevich though.

"There was never a leader of the royal lineage—no one ever attempted so! Don't you wonder what will become of the Order now? With the princess as our leader, will we knights work along with Albaron's royal guard? Will the Order finally become part of Albaron or— "

The big man rose from his seat, a man who could be two meters tall with ease, and as he stood up, the knight felt like he was staring at a wood troll who had just been awakened from its sleep. For the knight, that scene was the last thing he would witness before his death, for only when the stranger stood up and looked at him in the eye did the knight see the bigger man's eyes and chest. Right there, hanging from his neck on a small chain; the insignia of a lion. It shone against the candlelight, the silver creature's ferocity captured by the metal in a beautiful and fearful way with its teeth and eyes in sight.

The knight cowered even more, choking on his words as if they could spare his life. "Fo-forgive me, Lord Argyris, I d-did not know who you were n-nor your— "

"If I wasn't clear enough with my silence, I shall be clear with my words. I hold no care for your thoughts, you brainless fool." His voice was not deep, it was low and powerful as if it carried a whole tempest inside, its words made with thunder and lightning. It made the hair on the knight's neck stand up, made his empty stomach turn upside down, the fear feeding and filling his veins.

"I b-beg your pardon, my lord, I— " Why couldn't he remember how to speak? His mind went completely blank, a cold reaching him from head to toe. The man in front of him was an Argyris, and if the silver lion didn't give his identity away, the man's features would. Dark coal hair, silver blue eyes, pale skin. The Argyrises were one of the most powerful noble Houses in Raevich, controlling almost every mine and foundry at the North. The Argyris were known for their Way of Sword, their weaponry, their steel—

Their mercilessness.

"You will cease your speech now, for I do not wish to spend more of my time hearing words of some ludicrous knight from a fallen and decadent Order, especially one that fails to know his proper place." The dark-haired Argyris spoke with such strength and loathing the knight could swear by the Divines' blessing that the liquor in his mug trembled. He was terrified, but still the knight could not look away from those piercing blue eyes.

He had heard something similar from his cousin Jeremy years before, and not even time could make him forget his cousin's words. Jeremy had told him in the Gallows, right before Haze, about how he had come close to take Death's cold kiss yet somehow escaped its lips. Jeremy told him he had been out for a few weeks and was coming back home when he came face-to-face with a Skür. It was not only odd but almost impossible to think a Skür would be so far from the Necrosis Hurst, making most people who heard Jeremy's words doubt him in a matter of seconds. Yet his cousin did not doubt him, for the knight could always tell when the man was speaking with mischief and lies. Skürs—nasty, dreadful creatures they were. And Jeremy had not only seen one, but escaped it with a beating heart. He had told his cousin that when he saw the creature's eyes, even knowing he would be a dead man if he did not start running at that same second, he became powerless.

They know your fear of them, Harry, and that's what makes them so fearsome. They use your own fear against you so you cannot look away. You cannot run. That's when you die.

In the end Jeremy bit his own tongue, freeing himself as he ran faster than his feet could bear. He was blessed by the Divines that day, lucky the Skür did not follow him.

And that was what the knight Harry felt at that moment. As if he was staring at a Skür right in the eye, trapped by his own fear, waiting for Death's kiss to reach him.

"Yet since you asked, even with the most disrespect and futility, I shall be kind today and answer your foolish questions," the Argyris's expression remained blank without even a scornful smile playing on his lips.

Knight Harry felt the size of a worm, wiggling as Death came to him.

"To become a mere puppet in this *Order* of yours is the most aggravating humiliation a man such as myself could feel. I could not care less about its future leader, much less if it's a kingdom like Albaron that holds its title once again. The fact that a royal won changes nothing about Albaron's decadence and the only thing that could really save this pathetic organization would be if it ceased to exist. True warriors do not need some make-believe group to save others from perils. We can do that on our own, and perfectly better as well. Now, if my answer sufficed, you may take your leave to see if there are any fools who would like to share their opinions on such a ridiculous topic."

Harry the knight could not even remember standing up or walking away. He suddenly found himself on the other side of the hall with a few friends holding his arms and tapping his back while giving him some water to drink. Was that water? He could not taste it well. The only thing he was able to feel was his body, cold and shaken. And later, the vomit in his throat.

A Divines' Call

Bless of Day - Dawn Star, Haste Mountains

From the window she could see the wind shift, making the trees dance in a slow rhythm with no control over their leaves. Kayden stood still watching the wind shift and the trees dance, wondering if the trees took pleasure in their dance or if they resented the wind instead. Kayden had ordered a few knights to prepare the twins' bodies. She knew people from Carnarbur had very specific and particular ways to handle their burials. There were two Qirians among the current Orphys Knights, so they were perfect to deal with the fallen twins.

Were those the consequences of her actions? It was the thought that was trapped in her mind. For an entire year Kayden had performed trial after trial, arranging meetings that matched the Tournament's tasks, making sure no living person would be aware of her deceit, her father above all else. It had been exhausting, yet she had done so for her kingdom. Her people. For *Them.*

King Felix had left that room hours ago, yet his words still haunted her. He came to meet her as soon as she was alone, after dealing with the turmoil that followed the duel's end. Kayden was waiting for him, her ribs aching from the earlier blow, her heart throbbing due to his gaze. It felt like four walls surrounded her, her muscles rigid as she waited for her father's words. Kayden would close her eyes and remember everything again, hear everything again.

"You cannot fathom how you make me feel. No words could even express it." He spoke with a low, shaken voice, words carrying emotions so vile it made her sick just by standing close to him. Although they were alone, Kayden felt herself standing in front of a battalion, weapons pointed at her with disdain and scorn.

"Father, I—"

"Do not call me father!"

Her body did not flinch, the invisible walls so close to it she could barely move. Yet there were no walls surrounding her heart, only a dense mist, and it did flinch. It ached, it bled. "Then I shall speak with my king!" Kayden's words carried her will, the one thing that was giving her strength at that moment, the reasons for her actions, the foundations of her choices. She would not let them falter. "I won the Tournament with nothing but fairness and I shall not *step down from my position as leader. I have proved myself over and over. I* am *qualified and fit to stand where I stand today. It is my right—"*

"You will talk to me about rights? *You will speak to* me, *after all you have done, about* rights?! *How dare you?" Felix circled the room without glancing toward her, his body trembling like his voice.*

"How dare you, *Father!" Kayden's voice mirrored the sadness in her heart, a voice that was struggling to reach a man who would not even come close to her. "How can you not see that Albaron is dying and you are doing nothing to prevent it? To avoid our fall?!" There were tears in her words, tears she could not shed herself as her father stood upright a few meters away from her. "The entire council hates you, our people admonish and demonize you from the time they wake till they sleep. What are you waiting for?! To be poisoned, beheaded or worse—"*

"These matters do not concern you, foolish child! I *am the one who rules over the kingdom and* you *should have kept with your studies as you were supposed to, not chase after some child's tale. How could I be stupid enough to believe you had grown?!"*

His words hurt not only as her father, but as her king. She raised her voice, a new emotion emanating and filling her sentences. Rage.

"Perhaps you have forgotten, Father, *but your own blood runs through my veins. That makes everything concerning Albaron my concern as well. Regret it until the last day of your pathetic life, as long as I have your blood I am still the future queen of Albaron and I shall do everything in my power to save* my *kingdom."*

Felix began to laugh, arms on his waist, shaking his head. The next moment he looked at her, Kayden's blood froze inside her veins. He spoke with whispers, in a way that made her nausea worsen, made chills go through her body, made her light-headed. "You expect to save Albaron with the Order?" Felix's laugh echoed in his voice as if he was mocking her on every future choice she would make. "I thought I had taught you better yet your lunacy makes me sick."

Kayden could barely speak. "I am aware of what I can and cannot do and I assure you that with the Order, I know—"

"You. Know. Nothing." With each word spoken her father got closer, hands raised toward Kayden's face, but the princess could not step back. There was a wall behind her, intangible as it was. His hands were like claws, his feelings daggers with poison, his words wounds. "You cannot fathom what your decisions caused, the true weight *of your actions. You fool yourself, believing you understand what you have done. Yet you. Know. Nothing."*

Felix then whispered one word in her ear, one word that made her heart stop and the air leave her lungs. With nothing more to be said, King Felix left. Back to a kingdom that welcomed him no longer.

A knock on the door was all it took for Kayden to pull herself away from those memories. The air in the room shifted as that person came in, her muscles relaxing, her breathing lighter. Kayden had no need to see who had arrived. She felt it.

"Dorian. I was wondering how long it would take for you to find me." Kayden still glanced through the window, the wind still. Birds flew across the forest, traveling distances as they so desired. The day was bright and beautiful, the Divines blessing autumn with its sun across the lands. Did Their blessings have a cost? She wished to know.

"You lied to me." He spoke with no resentment or sadness.

"Yes. I would do it again." It was all she replied, her gaze still following the flying birds.

"I know. But you could have confided in me."

"Yes...I know." Kayden turned around, locking gazes with him, feeling her heart small after missing him so much after so long. "And I cannot apologize for it."

"Kill me if I ever dared to ask for your apologies." Dorian closed their distance in a heartbeat, kneeling in front of her as his armor reflected the blessed sunlight. He gave her a smile, a warmth spreading inside her, making Kayden forget the coldness in her memories. "The fact I was not there by your side throughout the past year hurts me so, my lady. That is all."

"Until when you will persist in calling me as such when we are alone?"

"It's been more than six years, so I shall push my luck a bit more if you so allow it. My lady." The mischief in his eyes was enough to bring a smile to her face, as she wrapped her arms around him as soon as her Ward stood up.

"I have missed you, Dorian," Kayden whispered, feeling some weight leaving her chest. The man said nothing, yet Kayden felt his relief, his joy, as if it was a sun rising on a starry sky. As her Ward, Dorian could never have accompanied her during the Tournament without risk of exposing her. She had lied by stating she would be receiving more classes on the arcane arts with her teacher, against her father's wishes. And for all those months, Dorian covered for her.

His brown hair was longer than the last time she saw him, almost passing his ears, yet all the rest remained just the same. Kayden had missed the sight of him. The Färküh Wards insignia on his cape, the full set silver armor he would never remove, the soothing feeling that would wash over her every time she glanced at his gray eyes. The sound of his voice. Looking at him at that moment, Kayden could hardly contain the smile on her face. If she wore a dress instead, they would make the perfect pair of a Ward and their royal.

"I heed at your call, my lady. One word from you and I shall be at your side." Dorian held her tighter for a brief moment before letting go. Yet at that second the whispers intensified, hands that were not really there touching and grasping her skin. Kayden pushed the heavy air before she spoke, stealing the golden light from Dorian's eyes.

"Where do I stand now, Dorian? Before meeting Alexander, I need to know the situation."

He straightened himself, his hand grabbing his sword's handle at his waist. "Few Houses stayed, only a few representatives remain. The few that stayed could prove to become trusted allies in the near future, so it is something to pay some mind."

"Which Houses?"

"The Argyris and Goldwich chose to stay, along with some prestigious ones from Carnarbur. That being said, many knights resigned and returned to their kingdoms."

"What about our ranks?"

She was not at all surprised when Dorian answered within a heartbeat. "There are currently no high or unit commanders—it would be wise to appoint them after the ceremony. For captains, there are a few left, but the squads themselves must be reassembled. Most Ruby and Diamond knights left, so those that remain in the Order are basically— "

"Rankless knights...I see." It was hard to see a good side on that news. If Carnarbur's prestigious ones stayed, that meant they did not resent her for the tournament. But to have most high-ranking knights resign was a loss that would be difficult to take. She could only pray that some would change their mind. "Have you heard anything from Rowan?"

The Red Knight was not only one of her oldest friends, he was also one of the most esteemed Knights in the past decade. To gain some clarity on the former Knights' thoughts was something she needed quite desperately, and Rowan could provide that information with ease. There were a few Säh followers who would not be the least pleased, and in order to achieve her goals, Kayden needed the Knights' collaboration. If they refused, she would be obliged to nominate new Knights.

Dorian shook his head, closing his eyes briefly. "I apologize, Kay, yet I came to you as soon as I could. The king obliged me to stay by his side until the moment his carriage left my sight, so I did not have the time to look for our old friend."

"No need to apologize, Dorian. His words could be of value, that is all." Kayden kept her silence for a few more seconds before grabbing the book she was reading before. "I will make my way to the Polaris Chamber, then. I must talk to Alexander and the Orphys Knights before talking with the guests and knights in the Hall. I believe until I'm done they will still be at the feast, or at least that is what I hope."

"Most of them must be waiting anxious in their seats, waiting for a chance so see the beautiful princess who won the Great Tournament."

Kayden shook her head, glancing toward the Ward. "I am hardly that interesting to keep them in their seats, with such a poor feast being delivered to them."

"I beg to differ, my lady." Dorian spoke with a light voice, the warmth from his words spreading inside her. However, before Kayden could reply, it happened again.

The whispers grabbed her, light blinding, burning her mind as her muscles turned into ice while lightning struck her until Kayden could feel nothing but her body depleted of any strength. A water curtain opened before her eyes, as she saw only pure white light surrounding her, revealing a whole new world before her very eyes. Showing her numerous possibilities and endings and images blending together in all sorts of despicable and unspeakable ways. Kayden could feel her limbs being cut down over and over; she could smell blood and ashes at the same time as she could feel the sun warming her skin and smell the sweet scent of summer flowers. There was a voice that tried to speak with her, screaming and whispering at the same time but in no way could she understand their words. There were so many sounds, so many voices that showed far too many outcomes and paths making it impossible to discern one from another. The vision ended abruptly and only when all her muscles relaxed, her true sight slowly returning to her, was Kayden certain that she had control once again.

Dorian had the princess in his lap, holding her hand as Kayden still fought to breathe. The look in his eyes made her heart feel like weak glass, so easy to scratch and break.

"What have They shown you?" he asked while covering Kayden with his cape, her body cold. The princess only noticed she was shaking after watching her trembling hands.

"I'm not sure yet," she whispered, her words weak and cracking. "Yet it scared me, Dorian. Scared the demons out of me."

Beware of the Gallows

Gallows of Night - Woods, Haste Mountains

THE CLOAKED MAN HELD his fists together, heart racing with each step he took inside the darkness, his breathing becoming erratic. He still could not believe all the past events that had unfolded right before his eyes. She had ruined *everything*. All those months, all the money he spent.:. Wasted. Ruined. He crumpled the note in his hand, a bitter taste spreading inside his mouth as he felt sick, nauseated. *Let her bask in glory, let her plan her changes*. He would set things right again. *He* would make everything right again.

Meet me at the usual spot at Gallows. Don't keep me waiting.

Those were the words written on the note, however wasn't that the funniest thing? The note clearly said that, but wasn't he waiting at that vicious rain in the haunting Gallows instead of the stink rat that had sent him the note? It was, indeed, *so* funny. And why, by the Divines, a man like *him* should wait for a drain rat? The rat had proved his skills more than once, he was obliged to admit. For once, the man didn't have the slightest clue of how that note had ended up inside his pocket. It was almost like "magic" and one thing he was certain was that his drain rat was not an arcane one.

He was a dirt one.

"Beware of your wrinkles, it makes you look older."

His first reaction was to jump and get ahold of his sword. Although the voice had come from behind, nothing could be seen. The trees were tall and rain polluted his sight, yet it was the darkness that dominated, even with his lantern. One would never be unwise to avoid the Gallows, was what everyone said. The Gallows were the hours where blood was spilled, where Death ran free and lawless, the time the dead would whisper and touch. One could feel it in the air, the cold that brushed against the skin, hear the whispers lost forever in the night. And the man could hear them. Could feel the cold that was neither brought by the rain nor the chill of the wind. *Cursed be, that rat!*

"Reveal yourself now, filthy! I am done with your feeble tricks!"

Laughter filled the night, empty and mischievous. A laughter that carried the souls of the dead away from their bodies, to blend along with the merciless Gallows.

Never unwise to avoid the Gallows. The man shivered.

"Relax your muscles, uncle. Is that any way to treat your laborer?"

The cloaked man could finally see the rat, hanging from a tree right behind him. The assassin was seated in one of the branches, his chin resting in his right hand while a dagger spun in his left. Nothing could be seen apart from his smile, yet there was only darkness in that gaze.

"You should be done by now! The champion still lives while the ceremony will be performed at Fall as soon as the sun is asleep! Why should I be happy with your performance?! This is *not* what we negotiated." The man had to scream to make his voice overcome the rain, feeling his words vibrate with all his frustration, all his anger. Yet, for some reason, the rat's voice didn't change its tone.

The assassin spoke with calm, unsettling words. A void opening in his voice, teeth appearing from Gallows' shadows ready to reach him. "Oh, you are indeed right, my good sire! Things *did not* happen as it was prior agreed. You see, I was supposed to kill the Divine Order's future leader, but that's when things get blurry... The contract never said anything about the future leader being a royal. It changes things, uncle."

"It changes nothing," the man replied with clenched teeth.

The rat suddenly jumped, surprising him by the abrupt movement as the man's muscles froze in place for a few seconds as that darkness continued to surround him, nothing to be seen but shadows. He kept moving the lantern, trying to light up the dark, heart pumping against his chest. Then, just as suddenly, a voice came from behind his shoulder.

Death comes in the Gallows.

"Oh, but it changes everything, you see." He felt the pressure of the dagger in his ribs, the gloved hand touching and tightening on his shoulder.

Avoid the Gallows.

"I do not see why!" The man's voice trembled, taking a moment for him to regain control over his own words. "You are still getting rid of a single person, one that shall become the Order's new leader. Our contract remains intact." For once he was glad there was rain.

"Then let me spell it for you, *uncle*." The assassin's words were hotter, fiercer, like a heating blade pressuring itself on his skin. "If it was a mere stable boy we were referring to, there would be no problems. And *why o why grand sire,* you will ask me. Well—" The hold on his shoulder got tighter, the pain making the cloaked man flinch as the dagger pressured deeper on his back. "A mere stable boy cannot rule a kingdom. He cannot start wars, he does not wear a crown on his dirty head nor does he sign papers with his shitty hands that could either send people to their deaths or give them freedom. If I were to kill a mere stable boy, or any insignificant nobody, there would be no more complications. *Oh no, the leader was killed*, people would gasp and cry and that would be all."

The dagger was going deeper into his skin, the pain so sharp the man thought it would cut through his flesh and reach his organs.

"You can see my point now, can't you? I will not be killing a mere nobody anymore. I will be killing an *heir*. *Oh fuck, our future queen was killed,* see why it changes things from my side, uncle? See why I can't let our business be left untouched after everything that I saw today?"

The assassin pushed him, making the man stumble on his feet while fighting to maintain balance while holding the lantern and having a sword on his waist.

"Well, what do you want, then?! I did not wish for *any* of that to happen! I would snap that little wench's neck, would burn and step on her ashes." The man spoke through his teeth, heat coming to his face. At last he was right in front of the rat, Raevich's most infamous and discredited assassin. Dark Eye.

"Isn't it obvious what *you* can do, uncle? Price has changed. Fourfold all the gold you have given me until now, plus a small bonus of two hundred silver coins since your target is a woman. Hide it below that tree behind you by Wake. If even a coin is missing, I can guarantee you will never see me again."

"Fourfol—*You are insane*! Where would I find that amount of gold by the Wake?! And what does it matter her being a woman?" He almost dropped the lantern, his hand and legs shaking and trembling.

It happened so fast; the man did not even see the movement. He only felt the sting. Touching his cheek, he felt the cut's sting looking over his finger. Blood was washed by the rain in a few moments, the dagger stuck on the tree behind him when he turned his head around. *Death always awaits in the Gallows.*

"I am not fond of killing women. You may say it's to clear my conscience." The assassin smiled, walking close enough that the man could see the other's face. *Death always awaits.* "Now, I know you have your resources. You are the big boss around here, aren't you, uncle? You are smart enough to figure it out." There was another sudden movement, this time by Dark Eye's hand. The man had barely any time to move before the metal clashed against the glass lantern, the fire dying out a few seconds later.

You have until Wake, uncle. Do not forget.

Dark Eye's voice was carried through the Gallows along dead's whispers, getting lost in its darkness. Spirits that would never again find their peace.

For they were not wise, and they ventured on the Gallows.

Eighteen Hours Until The Ceremony

CHAPTER III

"The Battle of Nähsur was the Divine Order's greatest accomplishment and its greatest shame. It was a secluded battle that left thousands dead, where men and demonic creatures fought against each other due to one king. No one apart from the Divine Order's Knights knows where it happened or when it started, yet all Tërnya would notice the sudden disappearance of the Order's greatest triumph: its Ancient creatures. In a war witnessed by none other than its Knights, where demons erupted from the ground, the Divine Order lost the power to command the great Ancient creatures, beginning their grand descent and fall."

- *The Battle of Nähsur's Mystery*, Author Unknown

Ten Stars in Clouded Skies

Midday - Dawn Star, Haste Mountains

One Day Until The Ceremony

It was something she realized only after walking inside those halls for a while, the ease in which her feet found their way through those mountains. One could argue it was her Sight, the Divines' twisted gift, that aided Kayden to find her path. Yet only those that truly carried the Divines Sight could say, could *feel* what it was to live in a life where spirits spoke through whispers and divine beings delivered messages unruled by time. Even before the Great Tournament began, the Divines were already showing her visions, images, voices, and sounds, all pointing toward one single path. A path she was obliged to follow, for it was a path blessed and lightened by the Divines' will, a path showed by her Sight. Then a few nights before the last duel she had a dream, not a vision but a real dream that bore the Divines' scent.

Kayden stood in front of the Polaris Chamber where all Knights should be gathered, trying to feel the air fill her lungs yet failing in doing so. The whispers were louder inside that room, urging the princess with a pull of their own. Like claws and chains wrapped around her core.

"Is something amiss, Kay?" Dorian asked as he entered her field of vision again, his gray eyes searching for answers Kayden hadn't found yet.

"I wish I knew, Dorian. Wish They could show me..." Before her Ward could speak again she opened the doors, bringing into view the cold Polaris Chamber.

It was one of the few rooms at the top of Dawn Star mountain, where only an Orphys Knight had the permission to enter. Antique tapestries decorated the walls, organized in a way as if a tale was being told, with Ancient creatures beautifully sewed among stars and the faceless Divines. On the ceiling was a painting of stars that resembled a great sword; the constellation of Orphys, shining among others and helping to create the feeling that in that room all Kayden had to do to touch the skies was stretch her hands. How many times had Nana spoken of that room, of that mountain? How many times had Kayden begged for Nana to tell the stories again, even after her father forbade it?

Whispers dragged her attention to the table, where all Knights stood away from their chairs. Alexander, their current leader, appeared to be the one talking right before Kayden walked into the room, the air shifting as Kayden felt an animosity so strong it made her waver for half a second, but from whom she could not tell. The princess was glad to spot Rowan amid them, at least.

"What is *she* doing here?! She has no right—"

"Clarice, am I right?" Kayden's words were followed by a brief smile as Dorian closed the door behind her, staying only a few steps behind the princess.

The woman that had first spoken had a smaller frame than the rest, with two short braids dividing her hair. Kayden remembered her well, after an entire year knowing the current Orphys Knights and completing their trials. The only thing that bothered Kayden was Säh's pendant hanging from Clarice's neck, making the burn on the woman's words stronger.

"I may not be Raevich's heir, yet I am above every single one of you, as the future leader and as Albaron's future queen. You shall refer to me with due respect." As Kayden spoke, her words unwavering, Clarice clenched her fists, eyes burning with a raw anger while Rowan waved secretly as if supporting her words. The other Knights shifted uncomfortably in their places.

"Forgive me, *princess.*" Clarice did not even try to hide the scorn from her voice, however Kayden would waste no more time with that woman.

"As long as you learn where we stand, there will be nothing to forgive." She approached them, her feet leading her closer to Alexander. "I am sorry to disturb your meeting, however my words are words of importance. I wish the Orphys

Knights' cooperation to perform the ceremony tomorrow at Fall and we are already behind the preparations."

"I beg your pardon, Your Highness?" Alexander furrowed his brows, exchanging glances with the other Knights before he could continue. "The Blood Ceremony has been performed the same way for generations. It's one of our most sacred traditions, performed on the Bless of Day inside our Dawn Star mountain. Everything is already set so I cannot understand your concerns—"

"I am aware of the ceremony performed at Bless, Alexander." But that was not the one that was being blessed. "It has come to my knowledge there was once another tradition that lost itself in time, a ceremony that was quite complex and distinct in its ways."

Whispers were being carried by the Knights themselves, the former leader at a complete loss at what Kayden wished to say. "Well, yes, I've heard of an old ceremony, yet there is nothing wrong with the way we perform it now, Your Highness. Why should we change it now?"

The answer was simple, with no way to be countered. However, there was a reason why the Sight was a devious secret, one that could never be shared unless their carrier wished for Death's cruel kiss. "I have not come to the Divine Order to maintain things as they are. The Order is weakening and something must be done to regain its power. Changes must happen and the truthful Blood Ceremony shall be where we start."

Even Clarice lowered her eyes and clenched her jaw. They should all know her reasoning was sound and truthful, they should see that it made *sense*. Kayden approached the stone table, placing a single book on top of it.

"I believe you are not very acquainted with it, so I brought this book from the Order's own library. Since I've spent most of my time reading it and already copied the parts I need in some scrolls, feel free to use this book to make the proper preparations. I shall meet you later this night to discuss the steps that shall be performed in private, Alexander. There cannot be mistakes." Before Alexander could answer, Kayden shifted her attention to the others, focusing more on the two Qirians Knights while giving a side glance to Rowan. "There is something we require in order to perform the ceremony that you Knights can aid with, however you must provide it by tomorrow at the first sign of light."

"What would that be, Princess Kayden?" one Qirian spoke, taking one step closer.

"I need the remains of an Ancient creature."

They all gasped, widening their eyes. The whispers surrounded her, louder and colder as if affected by her words, suffocating Kayden for a brief moment, completely shaken.

Clarice laughed, crossing her arms as she shook her head. "Do you take us for fools, *princess?* If this ceremony of yours shall be performed tomorrow, how, by Säh's light, do you expect us to bring you such a rarity?"

"What do you mean by *bringing it to me*? I already brought it to *you.*"

"The last trial!" Rowan's voice surprised them all, the red-haired man trying to hide the smile on his lips. "It was quite an uproar when you brought that skeleton's head to the judges, indeed. I believe our curator would be quite upset if the whole thing was to be destroyed, but it can be done."

"A tooth will suffice, hold no worries." Kayden concealed the smile and the urge to hug an old friend, although their relationship paled compared to his friendship with Dorian. "I need the bone to be turned to dust. I believe you two Qirians can do it with ease, especially since it is already part of your custom."

The women were a little startled at first, yet they soon shared a warm smile and nodded, the smaller one placing her palm on top of her chest.

"We still owe you for what was done to our kin. It will be our gratitude to perform this task for you."

Kayden's heart ached as once again the vision flashed inside her mind, memories of blood and death that refused to fade.

"Please do not thank me. What I did was nothing that shouldn't be done. I failed to do more." *I failed to save them.* For the Divines were not kind. Kayden brushed away those feelings, taking a deep breath while the Divines' grasp still held her on that spot. "That should be all for now. I do appreciate the aid. Rowan can collect the bone dust once it's ready and bring it to my chambers."

The princess looked at Alexander one last time, seeing him blink a few times before speaking his words. “I have things I need to attend while I still have the time, so you can meet me at the Reliquary Room at Fall, Your Highness. In the meantime, I shall read the book and prepare.”

Kayden smiled in reply, leaving the Knights to their new tasks. Dorian followed her, his eyes asking the same thing every moment he glanced at her. “I am fine, Dorian. I just need a small rest before I can continue the preparations.”

“Are you truly fine, Kay?” he whispered, sharing the comfort and intimacy she shared with no one else.

Kayden replied with a smile.

The Great Demonic War

Lull of Afternoon - Dawn Star, Haste Mountains

One Day Until The Ceremony

When Dorian entered the room after knocking, there were more than five books spread on the table. The man held a cup of hot tea, the scent reaching Kayden from afar. When he placed the tea on the table, the princess closed one of the books in frustration, the noise almost startling the man.

"There is *nothing*, Dorian. Nothing relevant about Nähsur's battle. All accounts from knights are nothing but mumblings filled with fear and the Orphys Knights that survived and wrote something did little to detail anything!"

Dorian covered her with a blanket and she wrapped her arms around it without thinking while opening a journal.

"Here, right here, it says *'The man was no demon, yet the beasts followed him as if he was their liege, obeying his every word. No mortal should grasp the demonic powers with such ease, yet Kih Nähsur mastered it, making something new.'* That is *all*. It is one of the few depictions of the king's power and the demons, but we need *more*." Her words were anxious, desperate as her heart beat against her chest again and again as if by the next heartbeat Kayden would have all the answers to soothe it. She had been in that study room for hours, surrounded by as many books and scrolls as she could find, piling a few on the ground when the table became full. Yet with every page she turned, her heart became more unsettled.

After talking with the Orphys Knights, she paid a short visit to the guests that still remained inside the Order, notifying them of the changes for the ceremony while hoping most would choose to stay. The princess even apologized for the scarce feast since it had been provided by Albaron, where most crops had died in the past months alongside their cattle. That was all her kingdom could provide at the moment. However, once back in her chamber, she found no comfort whatsoever.

"The demonic realm has been a mystery to us for *decades*, some not even believing its existence. It is said that arcane arts have little to no impact against demons unless it is of the highest arcane level. Yet we know few mages that are able to manipulate that much energy, with such proficiency. I believe there must be less than one hundred who possess such an ability and I am talking about one hundred in all Tërnya! How would we be able to fight millions of demons with only one hundred mages without the Ancients' aid? The Order would be found at a complete loss, Dorian, worse than what happened decades ago, and if we cannot find powerful mages and increase our numbers somehow, we will—"

"Kay."

She ceased her speech, lost for a moment as Dorian knelt at her side holding both her hands while speaking with a serene, soothing voice.

"Breathe, Kay."

It took her a few seconds to realize the state of her breathing, her chest going up and down in an erratic and fast pace. The princess took a deep breath, holding the air inside for a few seconds before breathing it out, repeating the process twice more before Dorian could give her the tea.

Seconds passed before her Ward spoke again, this time with a concerned gaze. "It is not usual for you to lose control in such a way, Kay. The Divines have showed you something, isn't that so? Something to do with that war, the Ancient ones... Are you to bring them back?"

Kayden let out a shaken breath, holding his hands tighter. "We will lose without them, Dorian. I know we will. I believe that, perhaps, the Blood Ceremony can help me locate the ones that survived. The Ancients that are still hiding."

Dorian had always known better than to ask things related to her Sight, but there were times she knew he could not help but try. "You think he will come back? Kih Nähsur, the Shadow King?"

She shook her head, whispers surrounding her in a cold embrace. "I do not know, Dorian. I really don't... But I know something will come, something that does not belong to this realm or the Divines. If we are not prepared, everything will be lost."

"Kay, you are the Order's leader now. You finally achieved your dream, the thing we have talked about since we were children. If there is anyone that can search for ways to prevent this thing from happening, it is *you*."

Kayden gave him a smile, desiring to believe his words more than anything the whispers would ever say to her, brushing her fingers on her medallion. "My father did everything he could to make this dream as impossible to reach as he could. Even when he found out I was one of the finalists, he came to me, trying to make me give up, threatening me." A chuckle left her mouth, holding things that had been choking and tearing her from within as they remained stuck in her throat. Images she wanted to forget flashed inside her mind, things that had been shown to her right before the twins' death, things far too cruel for her to believe to be true. Yet they were.

"Kay?"

A tear fell from her eye, her lips trembling as Kayden fought to keep the other tears inside, whispering words that ripped her heart out. "He did that to them, Dorian."

"What do you mean?" Dorian came a little closer, his hands sharing a bit of warmth. Kayden shook her head, holding the medallion as if it would make everything go away.

"Right before the duel, I received a vision. It was one so strong I was unable to move a single muscle."

She was back at the arena, feeling her legs rooted to the ground, the Divines' will so strong she could do nothing but abide. "It showed me a man that was paying Thurstan to hurt the twins. He said he should kill them or at least hurt them enough so I would cower in fear." Tears kept falling, words struggling to leave her mouth. "And when Thurstan asked what should be done to me, the order was that my legs should be shattered so I would never walk again. Then I saw. Their deaths, their blood—I could feel all the hurt and pain Daniel felt when he saw his brother fall dead on the ground. I could feel his fear when he realized he would never go back home." Kayden looked straight into Dorian's eyes, his face twisted in a way that made her cry even more. "My father was the one who paid Thurstan. *I* am the reason those two boys lost their lives, Dorian. And even when I saw what would happen to them, the Divines would not let me move. *I killed them.*"

He pulled her into an embrace, brushing her hair as Kayden sobbed and trembled. She held him closer, tighter, wishing it would make the pain go away, yet it did not.

"People are right, Kayden," he whispered to her, his words breaking her. "The Sight *is* a curse."

Winds That Flow Adrift

Toll of Evening - Dawn Star, Haste Mountains

Three Hours Until The Ceremony

THE BLOOD CEREMONY WAS one of the most sacred traditions in the Divine Order, for it was how the former leader passed their power and memories to their successor. Upon completing the ritual, the old leader would transfer everything they knew to the new leader and, soon after, forget everything they had once known. It was the way the Order had kept the Ancients' secrets within their grasp, alongside their own. Since all Knights were bound by a pact, once the former leader stepped down all nine Orphys Knights would pledge their fidelity to the successor, in order for the pact to be renewed. Although on some occasions the new leader would demand a new selection, even if the Orphys Knights could hold their position for ten more years. That was the tradition since the foundation and pact with the Ancients, although no one could tell why it had always been so.

Yet what most said was that the tradition seemed to have lost its purpose since the disappearance of the Ancients. For a long time, the Blood Ceremony had been performed in the Draco Hall where all important Houses and guests could attend. There, the two leaders would make a small cut on their palms and hold their hands together, performing the memory transference. Upon its completion the new leader would drink a cup that held small droplets of an Ancients' blood, ending the ceremony. Yet to find such blood was becoming even more of a challenge as time passed, which called for minor changes.

However, that was not the one Kayden had planned.

The moon should be high in the sky, its form full and bright. A circle should be drawn on the ground, where no one other than the leaders would enter. There were incantations to be said while drawing the circle, the blood of its speaker to be dropped every ten steps. A chalice from Ancient times, which the Order had plenty, would hold a ceremonial drink, making it all possible for the memory transference. Kayden read the scrolls in front of her time and time again, the incantations and steps already scarred in her mind. The medallion felt hot against her skin, her hand holding the metal with shaking fingers. If Nana saw her, would she be proud of her? Would she smile and embrace Kayden, saying how happy she was? Answers like these were never given by her Sight.

There was a knock on the door, followed by familiar words.

"May I come in, my lady?"

She took a deep breath before letting go of the medallion. "I am already dressed, Dorian. You may."

Dorian closed the door quietly, staring at her for a few seconds before making a short bow. "You are stunning, my lady. I am sure every person will have their eyes on you."

"That certainly would be a problem, Dorian. It is not my wish to bewitch others with my wardrobe."

"I can assure you that would not be the cause." There was a hint of warmth and kindness in his words, but when Kayden met his eyes she felt like his thoughts wandered through dark places, emotions the Ward fought to ignore already emanating from his skin. She shivered, a cold air following the whispers.

"What troubles you, Dorian? Have you seen or heard something?"

He walked toward the small window behind her, sparing a brief glance toward the bone dust Rowan had brought early that day. To Kayden, it was as if he had not heard her words.

"The wind is different today. It's drier, colder... It feels like it's running through the woods to warn us."

Kayden walked near him, trying to see what Dorian was seeing through the glass. Not even one tree was moving. Yet Dorian could sense the shifts in the air better than anyone she knew.

"Warn us from what peril, do you think?"

He shook his head, meeting her gaze. "Not a peril, my lady. But a change. I am not sure if it is something I will enjoy."

A change... Kayden had been dreaming for weeks, dreams that had the touch and scent of the Divines. Some were like strange lullabies, hinting the same notes again and again but never with straight words. Others were a compilation of images and sounds that would overlap each other far too fast for Kayden to understand. Yet they all had one thing in common: a melody, a note that shared the same tune. The Blood Ceremony.

The Divines never allowed an intervention on things that were attached to Them in any way, yet They were the ones providing those signs. As if the Divines were rushing her, *urging* her to act. Why though? The Sight only gave the knowledge of things that did not belong in the present. Yet when the power of Sight was a strong one, the person could not only see or hear through the visions but also feel the physical and emotional sensations in the moment. Kayden's Sight was too strong for her own good and even then, she noticed how active it had been the past year. What were the Divines demanding of her? To locate the Ancient creatures? Change the Order, fight demons, fight a new Shadow King—what?

What did *They* want?

"I have spoken with Rowan." Dorian had always been quick to change the subject whenever Kayden seemed to be too troubled by her thoughts to reply to him.

She gave him a weak smile, getting away from the window. "Is that so? Did our friend make any remarks that got your interest?"

Dorian sighed, his armor shaking as he leaned on the wall. "As a matter of fact, he did. Not joyful ones, I might add."

"It would feel strange if it started now." Kayden smiled, her fingers brushing the medallion on her chest, the metal warm.

Dorian stared at her in silence, lowering his gaze as his hand reached for the sword's hilt.

"Some of the Knights were not that pleased with your attitude on yesterday's visit, Clarice and the other Säh followers being among them. Alexander did spend the rest of the day reading about the new ceremony, so that may soothe you. However, some guests and knights are not so favorable toward you either. Apparently, the only reason most decided to stay was to witness the forgotten Blood Ceremony you spoke of."

"It could be worse." Kayden's words earned her an angry frown from Dorian, making her chuckle. "All is well, dear friend. It would be foolish of me to expect to win their favors so soon. I hope to bring new changes with the new ceremony, so we shall wait and see." She touched his arm while meeting his gaze, yet Dorian averted his eyes, staring at the window once again.

"Is this new ceremony...dangerous, in any way?"

Kayden was caught by surprise by his words, taking a few seconds to reply. "I...believe not."

Dorian met her gaze, his eyes darker than usual. "Have the Divines shown you anything regarding this ceremony? About you getting hurt, or what could happen after it?"

"No, but—"

Her Ward pulled her away in one sudden movement, clenching his fists as he held his breath.

"Kayden—"

A knock on the door stole his words. Kayden's eyes took more than a few seconds to leave Dorian's gaze, her voice weaker than she wished for.

"You may come in."

A knight opened the door, giving a full bow before stepping into the room. "Your Highness, pardon the intrusion."

"All is fine. You may speak your words."

The knight gave one brief nod. "Alexander sent me to pass a message—the preparations for the ceremony have started in the place you showed us. It will soon be ready for the guests."

Kayden smiled, her heart racing against her chest. "I thank you for the message. I will soon go down to meet you all."

The knight bowed again, making a brief salute. "May the Divines' bless your ways, Your Highness. Färküh Dorian."

"Yours as well." Dorian and Kayden replied at the same time.

The door closed soon after, silence covering them like a cold blanket.

"Is there anything else I can aid you with, my lady?"

Kayden glanced toward Dorian, his eyes unmoving. She could feel his anguish through her Sight, yet there were no words she could speak to take it away.

"That would be all, Dorian."

"Pardon me, my lady." In a matter of seconds, he was gone.

Kayden kept staring at the door for a long time, her hand grasping the medallion.

It felt cold.

A Pretty Punch in The Jaw

Toll of Evening - Dawn Star, Haste Mountains

Less Than One Hour Until The Ceremony

He hid in the trees. They were always good friends, trees. They never asked, just stood still. If one were not in the mood to share their sweet darkest secrets, trees would let them be. And well, one could suppose a famous assassin had a secret or two. He looked over toward the sky, for once putting his mind off the royal assassination Lee was so determined to make him reject. Yet what could be done, the payment was nice. Maybe he should have asked for more gold? In any case, he was enjoying the last sunlight of the day as he watched some knights prepare the ground for the ritual or whatever would happen, the people carving things on the ground and removing the leaves. He had seen the glade—had to analyze all his escape routes, after all—and thought it was actually quite a lovely place. Not that many flowers, a lot of tall trees, some moss-covered rocks here and there, and quite a pleasant stream by the side. Truly a beautiful location to end the life of a princess.

The breeze was quite refreshing up in the trees, smelt like wood and wet leaves, though a bit chilly since his clothes were not completely dry from last night's rain. He needed to make sure he wouldn't end up sick. What could be worse than an assassin sneezing and sniffling? Especially a famous and overpriced one. If he was going to rob them blind, he had to do it with some class. Otherwise, it would be rude of him, and Dark Eye was many things—a polite killer was one of them.

Although, he was starting to feel his throat a little dry...

There were sounds coming from below. The assassin quickly shifted his position on the branch so he would be better hidden in the shade. And who would've thought he would have such a well-dressed target right before the kill! Dark Eye had killed plenty of those golden pigs, women and men from noble Houses, prestigious ones that wanted to believe they were nobles, all the shitty trashes that loved to show their rings, silk dresses, and big jewels on their necks. He even kept some for himself as a well-deserved souvenir, though he would sell most of those. Even gave some to Lee, who would usually complain and ask if the owner had been breathing when Dark Eye took their belongings. He could not see why such useless information would matter, but Lee seemed to care for the useless information.

The woman who walked below him was nothing like any noble he had ever seen. She did not have any charisma in her, but she was stunning. Yet not in a polite way. Her face was not delicate—it was strong and impactful, as a nice punch in the jaw that could knock out someone in seconds, making them dream about the stunning and strong punch that hit them. Not people like Dark Eye, though. He was perfectly balanced in the tree's branches and it would take a whole lot more to knock him out of his senses, even with a pretty soon-to-be-dead princess.

However, he could acknowledge the Divines' fine work at blessing the woman, could he not? Beautiful things were created to be appreciated, like the beauty inside the Gallows. The princess's long, wavy cinnamon hair was braided into a crown, shining against the last rays of sunlight alongside the red jewels that decorated her head. The wardrobe choice of the soon-to-perish target was a dress of a deep red, a little darker than blood, which he loved. It had long sleeves that reached her middle fingers, made of the same fabric that covered the dress's upper body with golden threads that matched some decorations embroidered on the lower half. Oh, those nobles and royals always fancying luxurious clothing.

Dark Eye's gaze followed the princess as the long train dragged on the ground, which was a terrible waste of good material, in his opinion. But who was he to ponder? He didn't have any shiny swords or fancy dresses. How *would* he look in a beautiful tail dress, thinking about it? Probably not that handsome, his hair was way too short and his frame would not fit a dress with enough grace. And it would make a terrible outfit for running and climbing. In any case, he had never seen such a well-dressed contract! That night, Tërnya would lose one of its beauties. Although why did the princess look so sad? Had someone spoiled the surprise about him killing her?!

"Already nervous?" A voice came from behind her, a man with a blue velvet vest and dark linen pants. *That* resembled a lot of the golden pigs Dark Eye was used to slaughtering—*oh my*, that was a strong word. He meant kill with tenderness.

The princess continued to watch the forest in quiet contemplation without turning her head toward the blue vest man. "Why would I be? As long as I've done everything I needed, I know things will go as planned."

Oh, princess, if only you knew. Wait, that meant the surprise hadn't been spoiled! *Oh*, the relief. The young assassin would never tire himself of pleasant surprises.

"But of course, I could not agree more. May I question, though, why are you already here when the preparations are not yet finished?"

Finally, she turned to face the man, giving her back to Dark Eye. That was so rude of her, being a princess and all; he *was* still watching.

"I must say, Alexander, you seem unexpectedly calm about this situation. Have you studied and read properly all the incantations and steps for this Blood Ceremony?"

"With all due respect, Your Highness, I spent the night reading the scrolls you sent to my chambers. You may trust me."

Dark Eye could not tell if Alexander's smile was genuine or not, though his words did seem kind enough. Maybe it was fake. Maybe the assassin could never take a man wearing velvet clothes seriously after so many tears and pledges done by others wearing the same vests.

"I really hope so, Alexander. People cannot fathom how important they are, even one misspoken word could risk all of our lives."

The breeze suddenly got cooler up there in the trees. Their leaves trembled and danced with the wind, forcing Dark Eye to retreat even deeper into its foliage.

"I beg your pardon?" Alexander, or rather, the pig in the blue vest, seemed quite distressed after all. Wasn't that a fun sight? "Where did you even find such a thing?" The man gave a nervous chuckle, his words a mix of incredulity and tension. Or he had a bad stomachache.

The princess gave him a gentle smile, tilting her head a bit. "I thought I should not doubt your abilities and have faith in you, Alexander. By such remarks, you make me believe you are not prepared at all."

"Of course, I am!" he spoke too loud all of a sudden, clearing his throat and continuing his speech with a more controlled and assured voice, "Of course I am prepared, Your Highness. You just need to understand how new all of this is. Such a ceremony has not been performed in *decades*. Maybe only the founders of the Order truly performed this Blood Ceremony in such manner. Many important steps and information could have been lost, so my remarks are justified."

"One could suppose, yes. However, for these same reasons we should double our efforts to make everything perfect. We are dealing with an Ancient arcane ritual after all. We can never know what could happen."

Dark Eye suddenly decided he quite liked her voice. It was soothing, pleasant, and had that smooth depth to it like a missing treasure hiding inside an underwater cave. Or a nice warm meal. It also didn't sound like a dying bird but one that could actually sing. Worst thing was to kill women with such a voice, their sole dying purpose had to be to make him deaf.

In any case, velvet man was quite speechless that time. How proud Dark Eye was of his contract. If he died trying to kill her, he would die happy knowing she dressed well and made velvet users speechless. Though she was a *royal*.

Suddenly there were rustles and snaps—someone who was far too noisy to ever make it as an assassin. As the noises took shape, Dark Eye saw; by the look of his armor and brooch, this man was a Ward. Also, a side note: Who would subject themselves to wear a cape? Did that Ward have any idea how ineffective capes truly were? Although he had to admit, Ward man looked pretty fancy: armor was silver, cape was black, brooch was gold. The colors of the Färküh Wards, quite elegant. They were the noble and royal families' "protectors", so the least they had to muster was a lavish look.

The Ward had one hand resting on the sword's hilt while the other held a very old and, likely, boring book. "My lady, pardon the interruption. The preparations are almost ready."

"I really appreciate it, Dorian. I must get ready, then. We shall start at Fall."

"Also, as you asked, Rowan brought the book."

Dark Eye could see as the princess brought the book into her hands, flipping through the pages.

"Here is the book that not only details the incantations we shall perform but also explicitly says how dangerous it could be to make a mistake while performing the Blood Ceremony. I was going to revise before we started, but maybe you want to read instead, Alexander."

The man did not say a word. He had a blank expression on his face, not calm but not exactly anxious either. Dark Eye was already guessing it, the man wanted to shit. "If reading more will cease your worries, Your Highness, it shall be done." He then made a bow, taking the book into his hands with care, and walked away into the woods. Oh yes, indeed reading was great to make the bowels move.

It didn't take long for the Ward to speak to the princess. "Alexander does not seem very pleased with the changes to the Blood Ceremony," the Ward spoke without ever taking his hand off the sword's hilt. The assassin wondered if it was a golden or a silver one.

"I don't think most of them are, Dorian. Save the Qirians and Rowan, most Knights felt my demands to be quite...intrusive to their tradition. It was one of the rare occasions I was actually glad of my royal title."

Sure she was. How often did these *rare occasions* happen, he wondered. The princess sighed, speaking so low Dark Eye almost didn't hear her.

"You know, Dorian, sometimes I wish for a simple life. Not one weighted by a crown but by my own destiny."

"It is you who builds your own destiny, Kay. You must know it is not about royalty or about what the Divines want from you; it can be about what *you* want."

Sweet intimacy, how close *were* they? Was the Ward with the shiny silver sword *Princess Kay's* lover?! Did they share more than intimate names, some covers, and pillows for a night or two perhaps, a jar of juice in the morning with some sweet and wild berries, picked by some dumb servant? So many possibilities. Oh, maybe it was a *golden* sword! They were quite popular with nobles those days; he had even stolen some—they were not as effective, he had to say.

"I do not believe it is mine alone to build. I have a kingdom to protect, since my father seems...lost." The princess rested her back on the nearest tree, sighing. "Our people are in need, Dorian. *My* people. And on top of that, I can feel something coming for me."

Uh-oh. There goes the surprise. He was never there—it was all a scam. He won that money gambling.

"Kayden, whatever may happen, know that you have my heart and my sword to protect you and to stand by you. You can always lean on me."

Yeah, maybe the great assassin was not *that* interested in seeing the Ward's shiny sword, be it silver or golden. He didn't like to kill more than he had to, bound by the contracts and all, since only *planned* corpses meant income. Ward-man could pose a real challenge. However, if the situation asked, well—

He wasn't *infamous* for nothing.

"I really thank you, Dorian. Your words mean a lot, truly." The princess looked up, and for some reason Dark Eye did the same. The light was coming to its bitter end, it seemed.

"Should we go now, my lady?"

"Yes, my dear friend. I must stop by the stream for a few minutes, then all shall start."

Dark Eye stayed even after the night had fallen, only hearing the sounds of his friend the mighty darkness, wondering if that would be the night he died. Would he see the Divines, or even Säh, being condemned for not following His path of truth and blessings? Would They frown due to his life on the Gallows, with nothing but bodies in his shadow, with so much blood on his hands? Would he plead, cry, and beg like those golden pigs he had killed for the sole sake of his salvation?

Nay.

Dark Eye did not beg. He only killed.

And that night he would see if Kayden Allis Faeryl would either beg or cry.

A Sight Too Blind to Miss

Fall of Night - Woods, Haste Mountains

Blood Ceremony

Even if she had never dreamed about that place, she would know the spot. It had to be there and no place else. A few knights had taken the task to prepare the ground and the space, bringing torches and drawing the first symbols on the earth. It should be done with robust and firm branches to leave distinctive marks on the ground since later the marks would be filled with the stream's gravel.

Kayden felt her muscles relax when she saw the work well done, the glade well lit with torches around it, and the small trail that led straight to the stream. She could hear the water, the stillness of the night with no birds or animals daring to make a sound. The guests were the ones talking and whispering, their murmurs filling the space in a way that made her even more anxious. The trees were tall and majestic with moonlight passing through their leaves, and the scent of the woods carried by the wind soothed her mind. The moon shone beautifully, the sky clear as if the previous rain had never come before that day, as if the Divines had set it just for that moment. Kayden fought the desire to hold the medallion.

"I believe everything is ready, princess."

That voice triggered her Sight. She lost her breath for a few seconds, a sudden sharp pain running through her side between her ribs. There was a blinding light inside her mind, burning and throbbing. The world became a single shade of white, bright enough to make her head spin.

"Is everything all right, princess?"

Kayden managed to look in the voice's direction. She blinked a few times praying that there would be no strong glow in her eyes.

"Yes. Thank you for the concern."

An arm wrapped itself around hers, taking less than two seconds for her to recognize that touch and warmth.

"I shall take you there, my lady." Dorian tightened the hold on her arm in warning, his words unfazed. She could not thank him enough for approaching her at that moment. Dorian walked a few steps before speaking close to her ears, his words lower than whispers. "Are you all right? Has the Sight overcome you again?"

"I cannot see, Dorian." Kayden tried to keep the desperation away from her voice yet she could not. "There is light everywhere. It feels like my head will be torn in two. I do not know how long this will last—it's so strong. I will require your aid to guide me through the circle." The air got colder around her, the voices that followed her so loud she wanted to shout for them to disappear and leave her be.

"I thought no one could enter the circle apart from you and Alexander."

Kayden took a deep breath, the pain on her side stealing her breath. "You can't, but you can guide me. I did not have a chance to see the stone table before it happened. Is the table in the middle of the circle?"

"Yes."

"Describe what is on top of it."

"There is the dagger you asked for on your left, the glass chalice in the center, and the bone-dust bowl on your right. The symbols are surrounding the table in three separate circles like rings, just like in the drawings. The gravels inside the markings highlight the symbols, like you asked. Alexander is waiting so that you can both enter the circle together."

"Perfect. How many steps until I reach him?"

"Fifteen at most."

Her heart was beating so fast Kayden thought it would burst and bleed. The Sight was so strong Kayden almost couldn't feel her legs. She couldn't breathe, could hardly think. One misspoken word and she could condemn them all. And to whom could she pray when it was the Divines' blessing that befell her? Demons? Her father? Nana? If anyone found out about her Sight Kayden would hang, burn or worse, so why would her Sight trigger in such an abrupt way, in such an important event?

A sudden thought crossed her mind. "Dorian, who was that person who was with me? Before you arrived to aid me just now."

"Just some knight that volunteered to help with the—"

"I believe we can start the ceremony now, my princess."

Kayden smiled, letting go of Dorian's arm as she heard Alexander's voice.

"Certainly, we can." Kayden smiled as she stared at a white wall.

"Were your eyes always so vividly green?" Alexander asked.

She felt sweat run down her spine. "It is this beautiful full moon above us, Alexander. There was a good reason why *this* night was chosen. Let us make haste."

The knights and the guests, she was starting to *sense* them behind her, waiting, the same way she could sense Alexander and the stone table in front of her. Everything was covered in a pulsing white light, yet for some reason the symbols on the ground were easier to "see", as if they were watermarks in her mind, and the people around her emitted an energy Kayden could feel with all her senses.

She walked toward the table, passing her finger on its border to guide her, gazing toward the guests. The only luck on her side was all her experiences with the Sight, having to talk with nobles and royals without being able to see a single thing. Kayden knew how to fake it, she knew how to hide the pain, how to hide her Sight. She was just praying this time she would be able to hide it as well.

"Thank you all for joining us tonight. It is a great pleasure to hold this old tradition, forgotten for decades, on such a special night. I must ask all of you to keep your silence, for Alexander and I will need the most absolute concentration and focus for the steps ahead." She made a longer pause every time she had to take a quick breath, glad that at least the pain in her ribs was subsiding as the seconds passed. "I thank you all for the consideration."

By the end of her brief speech the murmurs and whispers had completely ceased, a new tension covering the glade like a chilling and rough blanket. As if even the stream and the wind were afraid to make a sound, the breeze that caressed her skin becoming more gelid as it prickled her skin. It was as if all her other senses were heightened; Kayden could hear Alexander's nervous breath as the man scratched his hands, she could scent the cheap colognes worn by some guests as well as the sweet perfumes chosen by others. But above all else, she felt every nerve within her body reacting to her Sight, the pain crushing her.

Kayden made a little nod in Alexander's direction, following Dorian's direction to reach for the dagger. She closed her eyes, the white light that burned her sight getting brighter and even more intense. The princess counted to three and begun the incantations. Her voice started low, whispering the words with care, yet as Kayden spoke she felt an energy spread through her entire body. It started as a low hum, as if the trees themselves were vibrating and reacting to her words. When Kayden made a deep cut on her palm, letting the blood drop inside the bowl with bone dust, it got louder, as if the energy of every particle surrounding them was being affected by the ritual.

Alexander took the dagger from her hand, chanting his words in reverse to Kayden's, a new energy spreading at a faster pace with a burning power being carried along; it made her skin burn, her throat dry.

Although she could not see, the princess could sense and hear Alexander walking over the symbols, dropping the blood from the fresh cut on his hand without ever missing the words beat. While he drenched the soil and gravel with his blood, Kayden did the same with the bone dust, letting her blood run and drip inside as long as she could. The crowd gasped altogether, making her wonder what had happened, for even Alexander's voice failed for half a second.

Those words, when Kayden first read them, were depleted of meaning. Those incantations had been written in a lost language, not even used that frequently in arcane arts. Yet at that moment Kayden could hear an echo in her words, words she could actually comprehend as if it was her mother language, the sentences leaving her mouth with ease.

With the power of blood these words will bind
The souls of the ones who shall define
The purpose of Sun, Moon, and Stars

Her palm burned, the cut deeper than she had intended, yet her blood had to flow until Alexander had circled all three rings and all marks on the ground. It took a few moments, but she sensed him coming and when he reached her side, Kayden took her hand away from the bowl as Alexander returned the dagger to her. She used the blade to stir her blood with the bone dust, the bowl getting hotter with every word they spoke. The princess was able to hear the metal scraping the bowl as if they were inside her ears, sweat running down her neck and temples. When the incantations changed, Alexander chanting the same words alongside her, the bowl began to cool.

Through bones there's death, with blood a life
Three halves, two cores, one light

The energy that was spreading through her body was at that point unbearable, and the vibrations and humming surrounding the glade were so loud it made her body shake and tremble. Kayden felt dizzy and sick. She continued with the incantations unconsciously as the wind around them got stronger, harsher, shaking the trees and their leaves. Kayden felt the energy pierce and reach her skull, almost making her pass out, ceasing her chanting. She could not say if the blood had been properly mixed so she simply poured the liquid into the chalice, blending the two quarters of blessed wine with her blood. When she felt another piercing in her skull, she dropped the bowl, the sound of its fall almost deafening.

She started the incantation again, holding the glass with her good hand while giving the other to Alexander, their cuts overlapping each other. Their blood burning, blending.

Sun, Blood, Fire
Sacrificed eyes and lies

Masked in corporal beasts
Rise the souls in hopes to die

Kayden raised the chalice, letting the moon pour its light on it. She could almost see the moon for a second, full, bright, and mesmerizing. As moonlight was poured into the chalice, the princess heard and sensed as the energy within the object moved, blending with her own blood and the Ancient's remains. She felt her hand tingle, her fingers getting numb as if her skin was absorbing poison.

Then she drank it all.

At first she was glad she tasted the wine, but soon she dropped to her knees fighting against herself to keep that thing down. When the sickness passed, she screamed for it burned, it burned as if she was turning into coal, her skin and flesh melting her veins and becoming tempered iron. She screamed and screamed only waiting for her heart to explode and open a hole in her chest. Somewhere the sound of the chalice breaking reached her, yet Kayden's head was searing as if it was going to rip itself open, skull, scalp, all of it. Then she could not move. It was as if she had been buried alive inside a mountain, its weight crushing every bone in her body, suffocating her as she fought to breathe.

Alas, she saw it.

Images, sounds, whispers, everything she had ever felt yet more. More vividly, more intense, more tragic. She was there when Ancient creatures first appeared, when the Knights made cuts on their bodies and received inside their cores the Ancients' blood. She was there when demons tore their wings and bit chunks of meat with their black teeth, feeling her own flesh being chewed and swallowed. She was there when Kih Nähsur killed one of the Knights with his own hands, opening a hole inside his chest and crushing his heart with his fingers, feeling her own burst and die.

Kayden was also there in another war, another chaos, with thousands of lives being crushed and lost. She could hear the realm tremble and its depths collapse while people drowned in a never-ending darkness. And then the guests were screaming and panicking, their voices echoing in her ears as if they belonged to another time, another world that was so far away from her. Kayden could feel the forest around her shake, the earth grumble and shatter while her blood boiled and burned and it hurt. The pain, the chaos inside her head, that light—

It hurt.

Stop stop stop please stop!

She cried over and over inside her mind, not sure of what was happening in the past and what was happening in her present.

And then it did stop. Everything. The pain, the burning, the light, the images, the voices. Kayden felt cold and lonely—she felt weak.

It was at that moment she heard a roar. The darkness the light fought so hard to keep away found her, consumed her, dragging Kayden to a world of nothingness while the whispers told her a name. A name so old it had long been forgotten.

An Ancient's name.

Chapter IV

"After decades upholding their values and beliefs, it is unknown to many how the Divine Order prioritized their traditions and ceremonies. The famous Blood Ceremony, said to hold the power of the Ancients, had already been changed more than once since their creation so it is safe to say that the great Divine Order of the Orphys Knights are as keen to uphold and know their origins as they are to keep their records straight. One might ask in the future if their war with Nähsur was a delusional side effect caused by their lack of professionalism and conscience or simply a well-deserved punishment from Those the Order took its name from."

- *The Fall of the Haste Mountains: The Order in Itself*, Ibha Kaminer

Curse Through Ancient Blood

Fall of Night - Woods, Haste Mountains

It was cold. It felt like Death was playing with her lips, holding her still while burying her in snow as the flesh of her body turned into a stone of pure ice. There was something attempting to speak to her, trying to reach her, yet Kayden could not even manage the strength to open her eyes. That voice was distant, echoing in mist so far away from her. How long had she stayed like that? Minutes, hours, days? Kayden did not know how much time had passed until she felt her numbed fingers, a warmth pushing the cold away in a slow, steady pace. Sounds became closer, screams and shouts that she could hear with more clarity, however it was one word that kept repeating inside her mind like a spell, fighting to wake her up. Her name.

"Who—" She attempted to speak, feeling a desert in her throat as her voice cut its way out.

"It is I, my lady."

The warmth spread more, allowing Kayden to feel his arms around her as she tried to open her eyes. The first thing she saw was the clear sky, the moon shining above them. Then she saw him.

"Dorian—"

"If I may, my lady, I would urge you to recover as soon as you can." Dorian spoke with cautious and slow words.

Kayden noticed his eyes locked on something else. She felt his fear, a dangerous aura weighing in the air around them. The Ward was pale, sweat running from his face as he held his sword in a defensive stance.

“What is happening, Dorian?”

“Can you stand, my lady?” It was almost as if he was begging her, his gaze focused and trembling.

“Please, try to not scare it! The leader needs to regain her consciousness. She will be able to explain the situation to us.” That was Alexander’s voice.

“You do it yourself! I want to live—”

“Do not panic! It is not engaging in an attack, if we simply remain calm—”

As soon as Kayden started to force her muscles to stand Dorian supported her, staying in front of the princess like a tall and wide shield. But even if briefly, Kayden saw it.

No.

She saw *her*.

“Antrühriel...” The name slipped from her lips in a whisper, the word itself carried by the wind like a feather. Time seemed to stop and everything else vanished from sight. The new leader felt a power pulsing, running through her like pure lightning and divine light, the Ancient creature staring right into Kayden’s eyes. And she could *feel* her. Standing with her back legs in the stream and bending a tree beneath her body meters away from all the guests. An Ancient taller than the trees, claws bigger than a wagon, a body wide and strong.

A white dragon.

She had an angular face with two long delicate horns growing from the sides. The nostrils were almost imperceptible, yet even within the dark glade Kayden noticed the strength within her muscles, the sharpness of the dragon’s claws. Kayden lost her breath, eyes wide and incredulous. Her heart seemed frozen in her chest, so why did it feel like it was racing?

“Kayden!”

She was not sure who called her and she was not sure she said anything back. The Ancient creature, Antrühriel, stared at her with silver eyes without paying any attention to the humans below her feet, moonlight reflecting off her white scales in silver and purple hues that shone in a mesmerizing way. The white dragon held this serene air around her, even as water splashed on all sides with the bent tree blocking the stream and the crowd panicking beside her, her white mane moving together with the wind.

Kayden's gaze was overflowing with awe and admiration, words stuck in her throat while a burst of light spread on her chest. That was it. What the Divines wanted, the thing that could save them. The leader kept walking toward the Ancient, the creature pulling her with those silver eyes alone. Commanding her, binding her.

"It is dangerous, my lady—"

"All is well, Dorian. Tell the knights to back away."

Though Dorian's words were desperate, the Ward said nothing else. Kayden saw swords lowering and steps retreating out of the corners of her eyes. When she reached the dragon, blood oozing from the fresh cut on her hand, Antrühriel moved, crushing the tree with her claws, approaching Kayden while bending her head in a graceful bow. The princess blinked, heart pounding as she approached the dragon's head with a shaking hand. Was it fine? Was that what was supposed to be done? The mane appeared to be softer than any wool, silk or cotton, the scales glowing under the moonlight and Kayden could hear the dragon's breath, hot air coming out of her nostrils. Antrühriel was still looking at her, the Ancient's gaze piercing her own.

Kayden touched her.

Wind blew on her face, hot and cold at the same time, circling Kayden as if it was playing with her. The white dragon closed her eyes and golden light escaped from Kayden's wounded hand, the one that still touched the Ancient's skin, the light getting brighter and stronger by the second. A sharp, intense pain shot through her hand, her wrist burning and aching. She felt her blood being drained in a strange, uncomfortable way. It felt like minutes, yet only a few seconds passed before the pain disappeared. Then all of a sudden, the wind stopped, the light died out, and when Kayden stared at her hand...there was no more cut.

The dragon raised her head, roaring at the skies. All guests and knights covered their ears as Antrühriel's roar echoed through the Fall like thunder and Kayden *knew* that roar was no warning. It was a victory cry.

She felt a hand reach for her arm, meeting her Ward's gaze.

"I am well, Dorian," Kayden answered the question in his eyes before turning her attention to the crowd that cowered and stared at the Ancient dragon. The creature that had been hunted since Ancient times for all the destruction and chaos they had brought into the realm, a creature that was, for all their knowledge, extinct. A creature that was, once again, bound by the Orphys Knights. "As you all can see, the bond we Orphys Knights possessed with the Ancient dragons has regained its strength! The white dragon is bound to *me*. No harm will come to any of you as long as the Divine Order and the Ancients' pact remain intact, and it shall be for a long time."

There was still some reluctance in their gazes, fear emanating from their bodies. The leader looked at the dragon, asking her for aid. Antrühriel walked away from the stream, the people moaning and cowering as the dragon moved and sat on the ground close to Kayden. "Antrühriel has been asleep for decades. She, alongside the other Ancients, has been waiting for the day we Knights would strengthen and revive the pact once more. It was shown to me through our bond that it is the Ancient creatures that shall choose the next Orphys Knights, not myself. This is the moment for our Divine Order to regain once more its former glory, working together with the Ancients to fight the perils that ravage Tërnya. This is the moment to change!"

The former Knights, the guests, the knights, none of them seemed relieved to hear her words. They eyed the creature with skepticism and doubt. None of the knights had put their swords away, and one former Knight in particular felt such strong disgust toward the creature it even reached Kayden, almost making her sick.

"How could you be sure? Isn't it suspicious enough this *thing* appeared together with *you*?" Clarice's words were harsh and spiteful, attracting the dragon's gaze.

Kayden felt annoyance from the creature, a low grumble coming from Antrühriel.

"You all must see how odd this is!" the woman shouted as she turned to the others, some nodding while most remained in silence.

Kayden glanced toward the dragon, her teeth showing along with a furious frown. The leader was about to open her mouth when the air inside her lungs froze and disappeared. A Sight. It showed a dark energy, sleek and dense with not an ounce of warmth around it. Kayden felt nauseated, her gaze jumping from guest to knight to prestigious one, searching. That energy came from an arcane practitioner, however there were no licensed mages among the guests or former Knights. It was one of the first things Kayden did when she won the Tournament, search for mages inside the Order, and she found none. Yet that energy came from a vile, despicable source. Who was its caster, the person who had triggered her Sight?

"...supposed to happen."

Kayden felt the energy from the words before she heard them, focusing on the same spot they were coming from. There was a man with his face down, clenching his fists so hard she could see his whitened knuckles. Shadows were gathering around his hands.

"Why?" Kayden asked in disappointment, the dragon's rage hitting her like waves.

"...it was not supposed to happen." The shadows around the man's fists got darker, thicker.

She glanced at Dorian at her side. He nodded once.

The leader looked around, spotting the dagger used to cut their hands during the ceremony on the ground a few meters away from her. "Stop this nonsense before others get hurt, otherwise you *will* regret it." Kayden's voice alarmed the others, the air weighing on them as it got colder, suffocating.

The man in the blue velvet vest looked up, face twisted with anger and veins popping out on his forehead as he bared his teeth at her. "You ruined *everything*, you wench!" Alexander shouted, throwing the shadows at Dorian as the Ward came from behind. Dorian was sent away until he collided with one of the trees, its branches breaking with the impact. Antrühriel roared at the same time as the others screamed. The dragon was already moving to strike however Kayden raised her hand, commanding her to stay still.

Do not engage! she shouted in her head, the thought immediately reaching the dragon. The others had to see that the Ancient creature could be controlled, that she obeyed Kayden.

Alexander had his sword in hand, launching toward Kayden, the knights and guests getting away from them with haste. All former Knights stood frozen in their places, Rowan, Clarice, the Qirian sisters, all nine of them. The princess could sense a dense energy around them, something that kept spreading toward most of the guests, something sickening and vile. What kind of energy *was* that?

Kayden rushed toward the dagger, cursing the heavy dress and train she wore, grabbing the weapon and turning soon after. The dagger blocked Alexander's sword while the shock reverberated through her arm. Alexander's smile twisted and curved, a laugh crawling out of his mouth.

"You should have stayed in your castle, princess. *You should have stayed put.*" Alexander moved the sword away, ready to make another strike.

Kayden kicked his chest to gain some distance.

He charged again, his movements erratic as he swung the sword toward her. Kayden ducked, sinking her elbow into his stomach. Alexander gagged, yet his blade still moved in an attempt to hit her. Kayden cut the train from her dress, thanking the fact the fabric was cut with ease, feeling lighter. The white dragon roared, spreading its wings and sending a powerful gust of wind toward them. Kayden turned her face in time to see Alexander's sword above her head, the wind taking away his balance and making the blade escape from his hands. Kayden had time to glance toward Antrühriel with a grateful smile before Alexander jumped on top of her, hands around her neck.

"Fucking rotten whore! You ruined *everything!"*

Spit fell into her eyes as he choked her, the man's eyes covered in shadows. *Fool.* Kayden sank the dagger between his ribs. The man screamed and removed his hands from her throat, giving enough of an angle for Kayden to hit his jaw with the dagger's pommel. Alexander fell and staggered to the side, smiling like an ill-minded man. Kayden stood up, walking away from him as she looked over to Dorian. Her Ward was still unconscious.

"You were supposed to be *dead* before this day even started, *dead!* And *I*, I was supposed to be a *hero*!"

Shadows gathered around his fists in seconds. He threw the shadows with haste, forcing her to use her own weight to send her body to the left to dodge the attack, yet the shadows grazed her shoulder. It felt like thousands of frozen needles piercing her skin, burning cold. Kayden bit her lip, her hands moving as she felt and touched the wind's energy, opening her core to it while sending a blast that hit Alexander straight in the chest. The man flew, spinning in the air before colliding and knocking the stone table.

Kayden was drained, arms hanging loose beside her as she took deep breaths and wiped the sweat off her face. Her core was not vast enough to manipulate that much energy, especially after performing the ceremony. She waited, prayed, yet the man stood up again laughing and shaking with blood dripping from his mouth.

"The wench can play as well! Look, everyone, she knows *the arcanes*!" The insane man spread his arms, the shadows dancing and spinning around his sword while he spoke with nothing but mockery. "She is as great as we thought!"

Antrühriel looked at the man from above, the desire to crunch him and pierce him with her claws so strong it almost clouded Kayden's thoughts. *You already aided me. I can deal with him, so let me.* Air came out from the Ancient's nostrils as the dragon pierced the man with her gaze, unmoving. Kayden recomposed herself, watching Alexander walk around the fallen table, getting closer to her. Blood tainted his vest from the cut on his side, his body limping. The vile energy came back stronger, shadows flying with haste toward his hands as he accumulated them in one single attack.

"Begone, filth!" His voice was almost deformed by the insanity that weighted his words.

Before Alexander could throw the shadows, something hit the former leader and sent him to the ground. A metallic figure that could not stop shaking, white breath coming out of his mouth, wearing an armor that reflected the moon's light. Dorian. He kicked Alexander in the face more than four times, kicking the very same spot Kayden stabbed him with the dagger again and again. Alexander kept shouting, as if he wanted to speak, however Dorian did not stop hitting him. The Ward only stopped when Alexander's voice faded and his body became still. Dorian moved away from the man, glancing at Kayden as his body shook nonstop. She rushed toward him as Dorian's knees failed, the man collapsing on the ground.

"Someone bring me a torch here!" Kayden shouted, hiding the fear inside her words, looking around toward the former Knights and guests with widened eyes. "I need a torch *now!*"

Rowan watched the scene with frozen eyes, along with all the former Knights. Not even one guest moved a muscle, shock covering their faces. That vile energy was still looming around their bodies like a dark fog. Kayden was about to shout, use the arcane arts again if she had to, when warmth suddenly spread against her back.

"Here, princess."

That voice struck her—it was the same voice that had triggered her Sight before the ceremony started. The leader glanced toward the white dragon, her silver eyes glowing for a brief second as she nodded just once.

"You have my gratitude. What is your name, knight?"

The young man blinked a few times, clearing his throat before answering with the torch in his hand. "You can call me Bash, dear princess."

The knight Bash was so pale she could see his veins on his hands and neck. By his accent, Kayden could tell with ease he was from Raevich, maybe the East or West side. He had delicate features and a small build, eyes and hair as dark as the Gallows itself, which could only make her wonder how difficult it had been for the knight to fight his way into the Order, given Raevich's usual approach to its class system. His hair was messy with bangs that almost reached his eyes and a length that almost passed his ears. And with one glance toward his clothes she could tell he was still a rankless knight.

"I thank you, Bash," Kayden said with a smile as she took the torch, focusing her attention on Dorian who laid in her lap. With the torch in her hands, she whispered soft, warm words against the flame, capturing its light with her free hand. The flame burned without its bright and shine while Kayden held the fire's heat. With slow motions, she spread its heat through Dorian's body by touching the cold armor, his arms, shoulders, chest, face, and legs, warmth melting the cold from his skin. As seconds passed the color returned to his face, his body stopped trembling, and the man's breathing returned to normal—steady and calm.

Dorian opened his eyes, sorrow escaping from his gaze. "Forgive me, my lady. I should have been faster."

"You should ask for my forgiveness for putting yourself in harm's way like that." She touched his forehead, removing the hair from his eyes. Dorian let out a trembling sigh, his breath white at first but soon it got warmer.

"That was, well, quite remarkable. How you do that?" It was Bash again, looking with a sort of fascination toward her and the torch.

"I transferred the fire's light and heat to his body."

The knight Bash remained with a puzzled look, nodding his head as if he understood. "Sure, sure—quite amusing."

"Shadow energy is filled with cold hate, its caster being able to control their emotions and transfer them into their own shadows. It is a dangerous, vile arcane art since it can easily consume its caster's sanity."

Bash blinked again, nodding a few more times. "Cold. Fire light. Makes a lot of sense, sure. That was quite educational, princess. I thank you for the quick lecture." The knight smiled before taking the torch back from her. When Dorian attempted to stand, the young knight helped the Ward while removing some leaves that had been stuck in his armor and cape.

Kayden felt depleted. She had no more energy or strength to spend. The white dragon stared at her from above while the guests and knights stared at her from below. She turned around to face the crowd, their eyes frightened and shaken. That energy had finally dissipated.

"I beg for your forgiveness, all of you. It was not my intention to put you all in harm's way. By Wake we will question the former leader, so we can decide what shall be done with him."

The next seconds were filled with chaos.

As the guests started to whisper and mumble among themselves, Kayden saw a silhouette out of the corners of her eyes. She saw it before Antrühriel roared or Dorian shouted. Kayden had not remembered at all, the detail escaping her thoughts completely. She forgot how it was possible for Shadow casters to drain and use shadows of living things to regain energy. Kayden saw the dagger in Alexander's hand, wondering with a shock when she had dropped it and the memory failed her. Her legs did not move. Dorian, Kayden, Bash, no one did a thing, not even Antrühriel. However, before the blade pierced her Alexander coughed blood, spilling it over her face. His eyes dropped, his finger touching the tip of the sword that crossed through his chest. The man looked up again, his eyes locking with hers.

There was betrayal in them. Loathing. "It should have been *you*."

And then he collapsed, light vanishing from his eyes.

"By Säh's eyeballs, *am I dreaming*?" Bash whispered under his breath. A dark-haired man stood beside them, looking at the blood on his sword with disgust. One glance at the man's necklace and face and Kayden knew who he was. The only member of the House that had come and chosen to stay for the ceremony. Leander Argyris.

"Why did you kill him?" was all that Kayden asked him.

Leander removed a cloth from his pocket, wiping Alexander's blood from the blade without looking at her. "Not even his blood is worthy of my sword. The ones who attempt to strike their enemies from behind while hiding in the shadows... The world has no need for that kind of scum." Leander stepped away from Alexander's body as if the corpse was carrying a plague. "Disgusting."

"How *dare* you?!" Clarice stormed toward Leander, her sword blocked with one swift movement of his arm. He did not seem the least surprised. Tears streamed down her cheeks, her face twisted with anger and grief.

"You should mind yourself with whom you are speaking. Such a low *Knight* as yourself should not even see a glimpse of my sword, much less touch it with your poor blade.“ He pushed her sword with his own, the other Knights holding Clarice together as she struggled and fought her way out.

"Murderer!" she screamed, dropping her sword while falling on her knees.

The former Knights looked at each other at last. A few of them cried along with Clarice, others stared at a void.

"How amusing of you to say that, when this *man* tried to murder his own future queen. However, there is not much to expect from one of his *students.*" Leander's words carried the coldness and sharpness of a blizzard, a glare that pushed others down with a powerful force.

Kayden looked toward Rowan, the only former Knight that met her gaze with some strength in his eyes.

"Please, take everyone back to the mountains. This was an arduous night for us all—a long rest is needed. We shall hold a proper burial at Bless, after all is resolved."

Rowan nodded, signaling all guests to follow him.

When the other knights saw Rowan, some began to move and help him with the guests. A few could not even walk properly, their legs shaken and weak. As the guests and knights left the glade almost every person stopped to stare at the Ancient, their last steps slow and reluctant. The white dragon met each one of their gazes.

As the glade emptied, one of the Qirian tried to help Clarice up, yet the woman slapped her hand.

"Do not *touch* me." Clarice stood up on her own, looking toward Kayden and the white dragon with a vile gaze. "You can bury him now. I will not attend to whatever you perform. I will be leaving at Wake."

"Clarice..." the other Qirian knight spoke, her eyes sad, her voice cracking.

"He is already *dead*. It will not matter what happens to his body. It has already begun to rot. As long as I'm not here when it does, I do not give a care." Then she walked away, leaving her sword on the ground with no more words. The former Knights glanced toward Kayden, their eyes reluctant to meet hers.

"Princess, I can start digging a proper grave." It was Bash who made the offer, touching her shoulder slightly. None of the former Knights made any comments, their heads down.

Kayden sighed. "Yes, I appreciate it, Bash."

It was Antrühriel who sensed it first, signaling Kayden with her visions. The leader blinked a few times, feeling her head light and dizzy.

Kayden turned toward the Argyris, the man ready to leave. "For you, Leander Argyris, I am also grateful. Were it not for you, only the Divines know what could have happened. You have my appreciation." Kayden raised her hand, waiting a few seconds before the nobleman shook it briefly, feeling her skin tingle and burn even after the nobleman had left the glade.

Kayden approached Dorian, feeling the knot in her chest dissolve as she saw her friend was fine. He sensed her intention, closing their distance so she could whisper in his ear. Words that would bring change. "The Argyris and the young knight, Bash. They shall not leave the mountains."

Farewell, Great Gallows

Haze of Dawn - Woods, Haste Mountains

WHAT.

A.

Night.

Not even in his wildest and darkest dreams did he ever expect something like that. Dying was something he was almost willing to bet for—make some money on his post-life, see? However, insane magic, treason, and *dragons*? Well, treason he saw coming. After all, Dark Eye was hired by the man. He had offered plenty of ideas on where and how to kill the sweet princess, yet Alexander-man was set on making a public execution. The assassin was not stupid, he knew what velvet man would've done to "become a hero". He certainly would not be the first one who would've tried. But *gasps*, velvet man was the one who died instead?! Oh, the irony! It must have been quite the show for everyone else watching. Yet, a dragon?! Lightning struck him twice with Säh's burning hands; he was shaken.

It had been a fun night.

He realized something big would happen the moment the marks on the ground started to shine, when his contractor bled on the symbols. It was a beautiful bluish light that only kept growing as the incantations went on and on, the princess's words being almost sung, a sweet lullaby. He almost killed her that moment, but then he thought, *so pretty o glowing lights*, that he decided to wait. He felt a certain peace, hearing the princess's voice, watching the blue light covering the glade. It was so poetic. It touched his blackened heart.

Then the princess drank her own blood.

That was utterly disgusting. Dark Eye had tasted blood, too many times to count, and found it was not pleasant at all. Once he received a punch that cut his gum and the thing wouldn't stop bleeding for minutes—it was nauseating. And sure, blood smelled fine, texture was fine, but to drink it of their own will?! Insanity. Yet the princess gulped it all down, a strong soul indeed. At that moment Dark Eye thought, *yes, now the time has come to offer Death's kiss to the well-dressed princess.*

But then she begun to levitate, in the middle of the air, which only reaffirmed Dark Eye's wisdom: stay away from odd blends in drinks. Well, he said that because it would usually be poisoned, but it fit the moment quite well. But of course, Dark Eye was a dedicated assassin! He wouldn't let a flying target get in his way of finishing his job!

But then blue light exploded and blinded everyone, including him, and a dragon showed up right after.

There was nothing in his contract mentioning murderous winged demons, so he called it a night. Well, he *did* stay to watch the whole drama with blue vest man and the princess. It was *majestic*. All he did was fake some surprise and shock and no person ever thought he could be there to murder their leader.

People! They could be so trusting. He did not fancy when some people shite their pants and threw up. Smelled terrible and ruined the mood—it lost some of the fun.

Still—

Great night! His contractor was dead, his target had a new exotic pet, he still got his money, bless all Divines and kiss Them on the face.

Did he have a great story for Lee.

Talk in a Haze

Haze of Dawn - Dawn Star, Haste Mountains

SOMETHING WAS OBVIOUSLY WRONG. The sun was not even awake yet, the princess was clearly tired, and the winged creature was nowhere to be seen. The real wrong thing, however, was *his* presence in the room. Bash should not be there. He was a nobody, a rankless knight that only stayed in the Order to see the dandy fresh ceremony so he could bail the day after. That was what he was doing.

Leaving. Forever. No turning back, would find his happiness elsewhere—then the Ward blocked his passage and dragged him to that room. A higher room, inside the mountain, with one door and one window.

Why...?!

He cleared his throat before speaking, praying he would soon be out of this place. He had to be. "I am here, per your request, dear Lady Faeryl." Didn't know how the mighty princess fancied being called, did he? Nothing safer than *dear* and *lady* mashed together. It usually worked with other nobles around the place, at least. People from noble Houses could be quite nasty. How should he know how royalty would be? Oh, dear Säh, Bash hoped she wouldn't cut his fingers. Nobles had threatened him with that thrice already.

"I can quite see that, young man. You said Bash was your name?" The princess spoke without looking in his direction, too "occupied" reading some scrolls in her comfortable chair. Right, as if he had never seen *that* before.

"Yes, Lady Faeryl." At least he was right with the *lady* part.

"Kayden is fine." Säh be damned. "What is your family name?"

"Just Bash, Lady—Kayden, I mean Kayden." Perfect, the princess knew he had no family name and was nothing but a low class knight. Bash was so stiff he could feel the muscles on his feet stretching and his hands sweating. All he wanted was for them to spare his fingers. Oh, and his toes. Actually, no...he had changed his mind. Bash could live without intact and whole hands, but he cared for his feet. He used them to run a lot. So, the princess could have his hands, may she at least spare his feet.

Kayden glanced toward him. "I see."

Ten more seconds passed without either of them saying anything. He bit his lip, flexing his hands. "I was just wandering why would you call for me, a rankless knight, at such a time." After all, it was Haze. Better than Gallows, certainly, but still—they were meeting *during the Haze.*

"There is a matter I would like to discuss with you." Her eyes still passed through the scrolls, as if he wasn't *really* there.

Yet Bash was. His heart was thumping and hitting against his chest stronger by the second, the bastard wanting to rip a hole in Bash's body and run away before they were both dead.

"May I know what this matter addresses?"

"In a moment."

Then there was silence again. The *princess* wanted to talk to him. The new leader wanted to discuss a *matter* with him. In the Haze. People didn't do pleasant talks in the Haze, people cheated and did *shady business* in the Haze.

Bash could already see a reprise of his life, all its major events that somehow shaped him into the person he was. He couldn't say he had a *good* life, yet in some memories he could see his limbs, fingers, and toes so well it almost brought tears to his eyes. So many years that he managed to keep those things alive and well made him so proud. There were also some pretty decent meals he ate along the way, some with a lot of running involved—see that was why Bash loved his feet—and even his brief journey in the Order had been somewhat entertaining. His life had been quite mediocre, yet it had some nice moments.

He just hoped the princess would make his death as mediocre as he so rightfully deserved.

Then the door behind him opened and someone passed right beside him. Good quality vest, nice leather boots, soft dark hair, sword on a scabbard on his back—Oh, an *Argyris!* Those folks were quite uptight, owned some mines, had a poor reputation with their employees—yes, Bash disliked them very much. If he had a last wish before kissing Death's sweet lips, it would be to slap that man just one. No, twice. One for each cheek, that would do it beautifully. Wait, wasn't that the man who killed the previous leader?

Säh blessed his feet and fingers twice, he would have to ask the princess to remove the Argyris's sword before Bash slapped him.

The Argyris noticed Bash staring at him, yet the man turned his face away. Well, there you had it. Argyrises, no gentlemen.

Suddenly, a thought hit him as Bash stared at the caped Ward, the royal leader and the Argyris to keep his mind distracted from whatever awaited him. Was he... The smallest in the room? The nobleman was a giant tree compared to him. Bash barely reached the man's shoulder. The Ward was not exactly on the low scale, they could almost see eye to eye, but even then... Säh be damned, he felt like a lost child and he did not like it. At least he was a bit taller than the princess, if that would soothe his heart.

"At last you are both here," Kayden spoke, finally leaving the table and old scrolls behind. Bash was not so sure anymore if he was glad of that.

"If you can make haste with your words, Lady Faeryl. I cannot delay my plans."

Oh, ho ho, someone could lose their fingers with that.

"I must be at my wagon before Wake and I already spent more time than planned," the Argyris spoke again.

Oh wait, *Leander!* Bash had remembered his name. Still, the knight was quite in awe of how someone could speak like an imbecile without looking like a horrible scumbag. Maybe it was the hair or the fancy accent from the North.

Who was he kidding? It was *definitely* the hair.

"Wasn't the place to your liking? I am sure you had one of the best chambers among the guests," the princess asked as if she already knew the answer.

He bet noble sire had the best chamber, since the Argyris *paid* for it.

"The settlements were fine, for what I expected. However, it bothers me so to spend so much time in this...*Order* of yours. My sword needs proper cleaning and my pride is being tainted by staying here for so long. So, I would ask you once again to make haste with your words, Lady Faeryl."

Kayden smiled. "Of course. I shall be as blunt as I can be, then, seeing both of you are in such a hurry."

Both who? *Bash*? Bash was in no hurry, he simply didn't want to *be* there.

"How familiar are you with the pact?" the princess asked at once, and Bash's mind split in two. One part sent blessings and sunshine through his body, a sea of relaxation and beauty.

The other aimed daggers at his heart.

"You are referring to the pact..." As Bash let the question float in the air, he prayed the new leader would answer with anything, *anything at all*, but what he was thinking.

"The pact that bonds the Ancients and the Orphys Knights, yes," the princess finished his sentence, the daggers closer to his heart.

A laugh made its way out of him. "Oh, I see. Well, I'm not. Familiar in any way, I mean, never even thought about the matter, forgive me. That being said, I believe I can—" Was he still smiling? Bash felt like he was actually crying.

"Let me explain to you both, Bash. The pact is something that binds the dragons to the Order—"

"Had I wished to learn more about this pitiful organization, I would—"

"Many believe it is the leader who binds the Knights to their dragons." Oh, it did feel good to witness an Argyris being ignored like that. Maybe Bash *was* smiling. "However, that is not quite right. The Ancient creatures always played a key role in the choice of the ten Orphys Knights; it was simply never made clear in the registers."

The princess was wearing comfortable clothes at that moment. It reminded him that there was a window behind her and that Bash still had his legs. After all, Bash could be poor, rankless, a non-noble and live in East Raevich yet Bash was not stupid. He saw the end of that talk.

He would rather lose his toes.

"This means no volunteers?! For Säh's desperate eyes, Dan will be devastated!" There was no Dan. "I must leave at once, princess, so the poor man can have his time to grieve—"

The Ward blocked his way as he turned to face the door.

Well, fuck.

"If you could spare me and go straight to the point, Lady Faeryl." Leander Argyris spoke with some new rumbling inside his words. It seemed the Argyris was not stupid either.

"Congratulations on being chosen. You both will become Orphys Knights."

Leander started to laugh like a maniac. Bash felt the daggers piercing his heart and being aimed at his brain. Clearly, one of them was not in their right mind.

"I had really considered giving you a chance, Lady Faeryl. You seemed earnest enough as well as you proved yourself to be a warrior of honor. However, a grown woman such as yourself should know the time to stop playing child's games."

Bash could make a sprint and break through the window. He still had his legs—it would be simple. He had to aim, run, and break. Only three steps to it, quite a solid plan.

"Oh, this is no game at all, Leander. I am quite serious, and so should you be. Their marks are already on you both—now it is just a matter of time. You cannot leave these mountains."

There were plenty of trees down there, he just needed to calculate his speed well enough, maybe grab something to protect him in the fall, and he wouldn't die. Probably.

"I *will* leave this place and no one will have a say in the matter, Lady Faeryl. If any of your *knights* believe you can keep an Argyris here against their will you shall be—"

The voices gradually disappeared. Everything faded into a nonexistent state. Was he a joke to them? First, they had called for him when the sun was not even awake, without saying a word. He thought they were going to kill or punish him for whatever reason, but then it turned out to be something even worse than losing his life. They were demanding him to become an *Orphys Knight* when he was not even a proper knight. Maybe that was why the Argyris could not stop laughing. That was funny.

Fucking hilarious.

And what? A dragon? A real Ancient creature that was still referenced as spawn of demons, bringer of destruction, had *chosen* him?

Ha.

No no no. Bash was quitting—he was a *quitter*. Their man here was bailing with his tail between his legs when the armored Ward got to him. Alexander held a big title for ten years and look where it got him! Very much *dead* and disturbed. That minus a dragon, mind them. Why would Bash want something like *that*?! He lived in East Raevich; if he was hungry he ate, if he was poor he stole, if he got caught he ran. No dragons. No attachment. Free life. Good, mediocre life. What more could he ask for, for Säh's undergarments' sake?

Oh, that was real serious business right there, Ward-man? Not playing games. If Bash resisted, the man would go for blood, he was sure of that. The princess had a dragon, that was all he needed to say. That only resorted to one thing: he had to jump through the window. There was no other choice. Die as a free, honorable man. Wait, no, he had to scratch the honorable bit.

There was a sudden bang that made Bash jump with his two legs while reaching for an invisible weapon that was just not there. His eyes made turns, bulging in Kayden's and the Ward's direction.

Bash looked behind him, taking a few seconds to put the arrow and the apple together. The Argyris, the pride lion, had just left, leaving Bash all alone and worst of all—

He had completely ruined his surprise bail! Oh, the nerve! *May Säh eat that Argyris's eyeballs with a very tiny spoon. And very slowly.* All the focus was on him again, curses and ashes! Before he would make four steps toward the window the Ward would grab him by the neck and spit on his face while cursing his entire family tree, including the dogs. No, wait...that was how they did it in taverns. The Ward may be more polite than that, maybe just grabbing him by the neck.

"So, priorities first, dear leader Kayden. You see, my family is insanely poor. My grandmother has to take care of my bedridden mother and my father died on a haunting Gallows trying to bring some food to our home. They are all I have left and one must take proper care of their family." His words were filled with outrageous lies, although him faking sadness in his voice was truthful. However, the despair in his eyes was very real. "I just received a letter the last day, from my dear grandmother, begging me to return home to take care of them. Since I am a young lad, I can find some job in the mines, you see. That is why I must humbly reject your fine offer, my leader."

Maybe he could still make it through the window if the sick momma card didn't play off well.

However, Kayden smiled, her words carrying warmth and kindness. "How unfortunate, Bash. I really feel sorry for you family. This is no offer of *mine*, but I guess explaining would just be tiring. You can go."

Bash blinked a few times. Apple, arrow, hit a mark.

Oh, blessed joy.

Had he died? Had Bash actually jumped and got pierced by some pointy branch and was imagining how things would have been different had Kayden just let him be? Wait, no, his heart had stopped, but it was beating again. He lived!

"*Gracious Divines*, you will never regret that, princess! I thank you for all the costless food and bed and may the crown be always heavy and shiny on your head!"

He then shook their hands without being able to control his grin, walking through the *door* in a *straight line* rather than falling through a window.

That was the best day of his life.

Stale Winds

Haze of Dawn - Dawn Star, Haste Mountains

"Why did you let them both leave with such ease?" Dorian spoke with pure confusion in his words. He could not understand his princess at that moment.

"Who said I let them leave?" Kayden was reading the scrolls again, not even an ounce of worry on her. Dorian furrowed his brows.

"The Argyris's wagon is already waiting for him and unless we send a search party at this instant we will lose that knight in the forest. If they are who you say they are, why would you..." His voice died as the princess looked at him, making Dorian curse his own stupidity and ignorance.

For a second the Ward swore a roar was carried by the wind, reaching him.

"It is *them*," he said while glancing at the window, afraid he would actually see something.

"They will not be able to leave this place as long as the creatures are here."

"What can be done for now, my lady?" Dorian asked.

"For now—"

We wait.

Blood and Stones

Haze of Dawn - Ice Draco, Haste Mountains

Half an Hour until Wake

LEANDER WAS AMAZED. WITNESSING idiocy and lack of common sense was something he was far used to, therefore it bothered him no longer. Yet to see and *hear* fanatical, foolish nonsense from the mouth of someone like Lady Faeryl herself... He was obliged to laugh, otherwise others may think he was encouraging her behavior. There was a limit as to how much of that gibberish someone like him could take in a Haze.

However, there was something serious and problematic that involved Albaron's heir—her role in the Ancient's return. How many years had it been since those creatures were no longer in Tërnya? Thirty, forty years? Perhaps more. His father had sent him to Haste Mountains to watch and report anything of value, since only a brainless fool would not think it strange the Order's past five leaders were either born and raised in Albaron or had some connections with the kingdom, three of them with Felix as its king. Were it not for the decaying state of Albaron, those situations would not bother the House Argyris that much yet one glance at the "feast" provided by the kingdom said plenty. Leander was fortunate that the man had brought a meal of his own, otherwise he would have no choice but to hunt his food. Although Leander did not care for such tedious state affairs, his father and uncle did; the return of Ancient dragons was something the entire family would ponder.

Leander had sent a report back to his father after Lady Faeryl's delusional remarks, so all that had to be done was gather his belongings and leave the place at last.

His chambers were located at one of the most isolated rooms in Ice Draco, occupying almost the entire floor. The Ice Draco was the Order's restricted mountain where only a few distinguished guests and their "special Knights" could access. His father had paid a comfortable amount to Alexander so Leander could stay in one of their best accommodations when Leander would rather stay put at home. The man wanted to train for the next hunting season and finish his training with the new sword his uncle forged; not play *spy* for his father's political conflicts.

Still, he had to admit to the beauty found in the natural rocks inside Ice Draco's walls, rocks that possessed their own glow whenever darkness appeared. Leander had heard that a bit of sunlight was enough to charge the mountain's rocks, and the mountain was filled with small fissures and windows to provide sunlight just so. At least it was something to enjoy on that tedious trip.

The chamber given to him was spacious, walls and floor made from the mountain itself, with rocks merged within. A wide window provided quite a splendid view of the woods, yet that was all Leander could compliment. It lacked decoration and color. No curtains, tapestries or vases. Nothing to improve the worth and status of the place but a few glowing rocks on the ceiling and even the weapons at show were old, their blades dull and neglected. Leander never expected much to begin with, so he was not surprised, only tired after spending an entire week in the place. Albaron's princess could speak whatever words she wished to. He had had enough of that child's playground. It was time to get back to the real world.

Leander had sent their prestigious ones back to their house the day before, since he would rather do things on his own and lacked the patience to deal with their servile behavior. He was about to put away his swords when his body shook for one brief second.

That was strange. What was that feeling? Was he *sweating*? Impossible, it was not even warm outside. It was autumn and inside those mountains the air was chilling, cold. Then why did Leander feel his body aflame suddenly, as if a disease had stricken him after the long week, sweat running down his face and neck? His head was getting heavier somehow and his senses weakened. What in Säh's name was happening? Water, he needed water. There was still a jar at the bedside table, he just had to drink it. The Argyris took a few steps, his legs and body heavier than they had ever been, his head unable to stay still as if it was filled with lead, a sickness washing over him. His hand finally managed to reach the jar, arms trembling as he poured the water into a cup. His mouth and throat were dry, hot. Leander took the cup to his lips, unable to hold the object properly, when a sound echoed in the distance.

A roar. It was such a powerful and fierce sound, Leander screamed as he dropped and broke the glass at his feet. It was like claws piercing and tearing his skull open, going deeper into his head.

What in all the Divines' name—

There was a second roar, louder, even more powerful than the last. The Argyris cried out, falling to his knees, cutting his hands and legs on the broken glass although the man could not feel that pain. His body burned, sweat dropping to the floor as he gasped and fought for air. He clenched his fists, glass penetrating his skin deeper between the fingers and on his palm. Had that pitiful princess poisoned him to imprison him? A poison to make his body crumble, his mind hallucinate just so he could entertain her delusions?! How could he, an Argyris, fall into such a pitiful *trap*?

Suddenly a third roar reached him and that time Leander felt blood running down his nose and eyes. The pain, that heat... The woman did not want to trap him, she wanted to kill him. How could he die in such a meaningless, useless way? How could he—

Leander's heart stopped. The Argyris glanced toward the window, the entire view was blocked as a devilish yellow eye stared right at him. It had an eerie glow, a vertical pupil like a snake's. The room was as hot as a furnace. Leander could hear a low growl, a sound that was different from the roars from before. Only then he realized his own mistake, as those roars were *in* his head. That growl, that sound, was coming from the beast *outside*. The entire mountain trembled and shook as Leander fought for air, choking and gasping. Then he was covered by glass and rocks as the whole window exploded, a hole being opened in the mountain by the creature's mouth. The beast roared again, right at Leander's face as if it were challenging him.

A dragon. *That* was a dragon.

Leander's body trembled, yet he still turned toward the bed where he could see a glimpse of his sword's hilt. He just needed to grab it. The man tried to stand, not one leg possessing enough strength to sustain him, his stomach hurling, his world spinning. It was less than five steps—Leander just had to grab the weapon and fight. He *had* to fight it!

The Argyris felt the dragon's teeth sinking and crunching his bones, both of the man's legs shattered with the strength of its bite as blood gushed out of the wounds. Leander saw his vision blurring, too weak to scream.

His consciousness faded as he felt the beast pick him with its mouth, a monster of chaos and death.

Decaying Freedom

Haze of Dawn - Woods, Haste Mountains

Less than One Hour until Wake

Bash felt great. He was alive, he had all his ten fingers and toes, the princess had let him go, and he hadn't fought with the Färküh Ward. For Säh's luck charms, it felt good to be alive and free! He had a fake grandmother and bedridden mother to take care of, after all. What would they do without their flesh-and-bones relative? Oh, maybe Bash could create a small sister as well to keep with all the drama. Not that he planned to see that princess again, nor even come close to those mountains. For he was a new man, filled with hopes and dreams!

Dreams of liberty and blissful freedom with hopes of a new tomorrow. Or at least, a new day. The past week had been quite turbulent and all he wanted to do was rest. He could stop at a lone village on his way—they were great for people like him since lone villages were independent from other kingdoms. No nobles and heirs to get on his nerves, small enough to have a good amount of trusting and reliable families and, if he hit big, everything he needed to spend a few days. Those villages had deals with other kingdoms to gain resources they lacked and all that for the price of some taxes and raw material or whatever.

Bash didn't really understand how the whole thing worked. They had the stuff. That was what mattered.

Maybe Whitepoddle was nearby! It was on the frontier of South Raevich and Albaron, so that meant he had to go north. He quite liked Whitepoddle. It was named after a small lake that always had this milky water. Children loved that lake, adults recalled the times *they* loved it, and Bash just thought it was a fun lake. Tried to drink once to see if the flavor would resemble milk. He spit it out and never got that thing close to his mouth ever again. However, the lone village was still quite pleasant. The inner conflict between the Quinnies and the Johnsons were always a delight to see—they fought over *fishnets*. In any case, Bash had to choose his lone villages with care since from time to time he *would* come across some nasty, bitter folks. Who names their village after an old sick goat, anyway? He was hungry, the animal was dying, *someone* would profit from it either way. People could be *so* rude. Also, Pádraig was a terrible goat name.

Wait, he didn't have actual money with him.

Oh well, he would just have to borrow again.

As Wake neared the horizon, Bash felt the wind get chillier, the woods quieter. It was autumn, yes, but why did he feel so unsettled? He looked at the sky, seeing not even a single cloud. That wasn't impossible, so maybe it wasn't the sky...

The silence in the woods was quite strange. He couldn't even hear the birds and there were always birds singing during the Haze. It was literally their thing. Bash stopped walking, his eyes searching his surroundings. No bear. No monster. No...nothing really. Was he imagining it? Wait no, something *was* strange, his body...was it shaking? Chills ran down his spine and a sudden pain spread through his chest, going down and up his arms, legs, and head. He started to cough, leaning his back against the tree as his vision darkened. That was not good, that was not good at all. Had someone hit him with a poisoned needle? Did he step on or touch something he shouldn't have? He could barely see anything at that point, but he didn't remember suffering any bruises or injuries, so how...

Bash bent over, feeling as if his eyes would pop out and his heart would rip out of his chest and bail. Maybe his stomach had already exploded and he was dying. He grabbed his shirt as if that would make his heart stay still, but that pain did not go away—it got worse. He could taste the bile going up to his mouth, burning his throat along the way as sweat dropped on the ground. There was no sunlight and the air was cold—how could he be sweating?

Maybe it was death sweat. He *was* dying.

Bash grabbed one branch before he fell, the entire world spinning and bleeding inside out. No, wait, that was his head. And his insides. Bash was going to finally receive Death's kiss and it would not be by jumping through a window. No more freedom, no more hope. Maybe that wasn't so bad after all. But dear Säh, that *pain*—couldn't he die in a more boring way? Less painful? Someone could give him a knife; one cut through his throat and that was it.

He heard something. It was not so far away, but Bash had definitely *heard* something. A single thought crossed his mind, the side of his mind that kept pointing daggers at his heart to feed it with despair. No, no, no, it couldn't be. That sound...he had heard it the night before, before that *thing* had showed up. If he could, he would laugh. Ain't no dragon insane enough to choose him to be an honorable Knight. Dragons should be smart.

Another roar, so loud and powerful Bash thought Säh had sent lightning inside his head to punish him. He gasped, air running away from his lungs in haste. For all the bloody Divines, that *hurt*. Bash looked above the trees and green leaves, shutting his eyes many times before he could admit to himself what he was seeing. There was a giant shadow in the sky, roaring once again even louder than before, making Bash grovel on his knees as a guttural sound echoed inside his mind.

"I already heard you, you fucked winged demon!" Bash screamed with every ounce of strength he had left and that was enough to make him collapse hard on the cold ground, the world becoming as dark as the Gallows as gusts of wind hit him again and again. He glanced once more, not sure if what he saw was a hallucination or Death coming for him. He was afraid it was real.

"Eat me before I get cold, rude bastar..." Bash could not finish his sentence. He could taste blood and feel death.

Yet his last thought was of an apple. It had been some time since he had had one.

Influx Winds

Haze of Dawn - Woods, Haste Mountains

Less Than Ten Minutes Until Wake

"How much longer we must wait, my lady?" Dorian asked, something inside him knowing the answer.

"Not much at all, Dorian."

Kayden waited beside the white dragon. It seemed alert, watching the horizon with careful eyes. Moments ago, they both heard screams and roars being carried by the wind. Kayden was also staring at the horizon.

"They will arrive soon."

Chapter V

Journal Entry, Autumn

Haze, after the ceremony

Most of my companions decided to leave the Divine Order after Alex's betrayal, Clarice among them. Although I sympathize with their choice, I cannot force myself to do the same. Something tells me Princess Kayden will need all the support she can find and what is an Orphys Knight but someone who helps those in need? I may not hold this title any longer, however as a former Knight I must provide any aid I possibly can.

I still cannot meet my own reflection, due to what occurred at the ceremony. Shame haunts my every thought.

I will talk with Clarice one last time before she leaves. Convince her in some way, even if I know how impossible this seems. What worries me the most is that I have not seen Sean since the ceremony. For what I have asked, no one saw him return to the mountains. Did he truly know about Alexander's plans?

Why did Alex even do this to us?

Reawakening

Haze of Dawn - Woods, ???

?? Minutes Until Wake

There was a calming sound coming from below. A warm breeze caressed his skin, carrying the scent of wood and moss. Oh, was that a river he heard? It felt so relaxing. So much joy and peace. He had his eyes closed, yet that felt great. It was as if he was dreaming, a soul traveling through the wild with no care in the world, wandering and contemplating nature in its most natural beauty. But then he started to fall. No, not fall. He was thrown onto the ground like a half-eaten spoiled apple. He rolled one, two, three times before banging his head on a tree. How did he know it was a tree? He got moss and wood stuck between his teeth. Also, he opened his eyes and saw—wait for it, *a tree!* Another lesson learned; moss did not taste any good.

The pain ran from his legs to his torso. For a moment, he thought his consciousness would fade again, fall into a silent void, yet it was the pain that dragged him back from the darkness, waking him as the desire to live pulsed stronger within him. He clenched his fists as the scent of blood and burnt flesh reached him, daring the man to open his eyes and see for himself as water ran through his hair, face, limbs, and clothes. He was in a stream, yet he did not dare to open his eyes when his hand touched his legs. The man did not open his eyes to see the warm blood that stained his hand, he did not open his eyes to search for a sword he knew wasn't there. So he screamed, his lungs burning and his throat aching. The man opened his eyes then, to know where *it* was. To face it.

Bash could say, with no great amount of certainty, that his brain was a good brain no more. As he stood up, it felt like he was bleeding and oozing, a sickness still gripping his poor stomach as he rested his hands on the mossy tree. Bash sensed that gaze before he even turned his head, gagging and choking when he faced at last the shadow that waited in the corner of his eye.

That—

Was a very mean-faced, scary, irate looking dragon with eyes the color of blood, skin like ashes, and scales that looked dry and rough. The creature was the same size as the white dragon, yet no matter how Bash looked at it, bloodshot-eyes buddy did not seem happy. Its face was shaped like a reverse triangle, six small horns covering its head with two sharper and longer ones at the top of its head. Yet he could rest assured, there were thorns on its legs too. They seemed to be made of bones sharp enough to behead him, so those were *great* news.

The Argyris could not raise himself—there was no strength in his body, no way to move his legs. He could feel his bones shattered, crushed, the wound pulsing and throbbing and the man knew that the moment he glanced at his legs a part of him would die. No physician in that realm would be skilled enough to mend his legs, make him able to walk and run again. There would be no more place for him within the Argyris, no more place for him as an honorable warrior, no way to carry the Way of Sword his family cherished. Leander gritted his teeth, eyeing the soul responsible for his state, a beast he had a burning desire to obliterate and destroy even with the cost of his life.

The demon showed its teeth a few meters from him, gazing at Leander from above with bright, glowing yellow eyes, filled with menace and preeminence, its face narrow and slim with a sharp nose. The scales resembled coal, black rocks that would glow as if they were aflame whenever it moved or breathed, sharp and rough edges emanating such heat it made his exposed flesh ache even more, a rigid reddish mane going down the beast's neck. He *would* obliterate it.

"Look, I taste no good. I am spoiled, you must know that already, right? So you can, you know, fly away back to wherever you came from, pick another knight, do whatever you want. I can give you directions, so you won't get lost." *Just leave, please.*

At first, Bash feared the creature could not understand one dot of what he was saying, which would make Bash look like an idiot. However, the creature roared almost as if to tell him to stop talking—he didn't know how he knew that, he just did. It had very sharp teeth and some awfully long wings attached to his front legs with some very sharp elbows and claws. The young man felt his heart beating fast once more, this time not from pain. Just his old friend desperation.

"I am right in front of you, so you don't need to scream at me!" Bash knew for a fact he was dead anyway, so why not die happy for getting into an argument with an Ancient creature? He could go down in *history*.

"You finally got my attention, demon. If it is blood you so desire come closer! I will battle you even without a proper weapon, so show me *your* dignity!" Leander shouted as hot tears refused to fall from his eyes, the inferior creature unmoving from its spot. If he had to crawl in order to face the vile creature, that was what he would do. The man would rip his own legs off if he had to, if that meant a quicker death.

Unwanted memories from the past haunted him, crawling inside his mind and body. Leander would not allow his death to be so meaningless, so weak and pathetic. For an Argyris to face their final moments without even a weapon by their side was a disgrace, his heart beating with contempt and rage. He would not succumb before a proper duel.

"Taking your opponent in such a cowardly, preposterous way...you know *no* shame." The words dragged themselves from his mouth, weighted by his ruined legs.

The dragon snorted, *it actually snorted*, lying on the ground as it broke one or two trees. Then it turned its face away from him! Bash stared at the creature with his mouth open, refusing to believe what he saw as the words slipped from his mouth of their own volition.

"That is so fucking rude!" Would others believe the nerve of that thing? Beheadings? Sure. Pure chaos and destruction? Say no more. But childish pouting? Nay. They would laugh at Bash before he could speak any other words. Yet the dragon was still there, ignoring Bash's own existence. The young man glanced toward the horizon, seeing the sun slowly wake, feeling that maybe that was the cue for his disappearance. Step by step, Bash began to retreat.

Then the dragon raised its head and roared at him with raging eyes, making Bash jump and raise his arms like a criminal. "Sorry, sorry! Didn't think you would miss me, with *that* behavior. Maybe you could be just a little bit more—"

The creature snorted again, rolling its eyes before resting its head on its claws.

Seriously?! Bash gasped. "You are mean!"

Leander grabbed a rock from the stream, throwing it as hard as he could, watching as the beast smashed the rock with its teeth. Leander screamed, throwing rocks again and again, many missing and falling too soon while others were crushed and dodged with mocking ease.

"Face me! Come right here and face me, low demon. I'm right *here!*"

The beast did not move or even blinked. Was Leander such an insignificant man to it? Was he not worth a fight? Had the Argyris possessed his sword with him, would things be different? If he still had his legs? His hands closed around the mud and rocks from below the stream, his cuts stinging as blood flowed from the wounds. Would this really be his end? Bleeding to death, like a powerless and weakling fool, without even being able to fight for his own life? *That* would be the culmination of his entire life, the thing he was entitled to? A paltry death?

Leander felt hot tears finally escape from his eyes, running down his face in pure shame. "Face me or kill me at once..." The prideful lion that hung on his chest got heavier and heavier, ready to snap his neck and claim his life. Then something changed.

That splitting headache was coming back to him, which was *not* great, especially because Bash did not know what to do. More than one step away from the creature would result in a roar—an angry one—forcing him to go back. Yet if Bash spent too long in the same spot the dragon started growling and flashing its bare teeth. Bash sighed, wanting to cry and die at once. There was one thing he hadn't done yet because he didn't want to. He had a *reason* for avoiding it.

He let out a silent cry, biting his lip before taking one step closer to the dragon. No reaction. For Säh's tight treasures, the suspense would be the death of him. Bash took another step, yet that time the creature tilted its head in his direction. Blooded rains and stinking rats, he would just get it over with. The young man walked all the way to the stream, looking at the water with a sad gaze.

"No chance of working this out with me in a dry state, is there?" There was not even a blink that time. Bash let out a moan, going knee-deep into the stream, toward the gray dragon that stared at him with bored eyes.

A weak light emerged from the water suddenly, a light that at first did not have any form or texture; it was simply there. Then the light compressed itself, as if invisible hands had started to mold it, give it a shape—a human form. Soon there was a slender man with delicate features and round eyes, wearing loose clothes facing him. Leander could not tell the color of his eyes, his hair or his skin for all he could see was the light's glow. The Argyris held his breath, something inside him knowing what that was. At plain Haze, the spirit of dead. At first there was confusion in the spirit's eyes until it locked eyes with Leander himself.

"Oh, I see you now. I was right in leaving something behind, this is good." His words were so far away, yet so close. Like an echo lost in his head that was not so sure how to reach his ears, belonging everywhere and nowhere. "You are the new chosen Knight, isn't that so?"

How the spirit of a dead man could interact with Leander was beyond him, however what mattered was what would be addressed to him. He knew and clenched his teeth, blood running down his mouth.

"The only choice bestowed upon me is of my own reasoning and liberty! I will not succumb to some rubbish tale and foolish delusions from that woman. From no one!" The spirit exchanged glances with the dragon, no words spoken between them.

"You *really* want me to get near you. I mean, *really close.* Is that it?" If Bash wanted a reply, that dragon had bad news for him. Bash took a long, deep breath, getting only a few meters apart from the great beast. *That should be enough, right?* When the dragon moved, raising itself in one single motion, Bash fell on his arse in the stream. So much for not getting too wet.

The Ancient creature roared into the skies, bringing all the headache and pain from the whole Tërnya right into Bash's skull. Yet at that time, something was different. There was a pull. Something that attached itself onto his wrist, stretching in a forceful, *painful* way. Bash had to walk closer, as if he would only be able to breathe and be released from that pain if he did so. Yet the closer he got, the stronger the pull was, to a point where he could not even control his own steps anymore. Bash was simply being dragged. It was not a pleasant feeling. Was he sweating again? But how could he be sweating if his body would not stop trembling? That being true, why was his body trembling that much—better yet, since when was he so cold? By the time Bash was standing in front of the beast, the young man could barely feel his fingers or move his muscles, as if he had stayed a whole night naked at the top of the White Mountains in the middle of a blizzard yet survived in exchange of his limbs. Just when Bash thought he would be able to keep his fingers and toes. Life was cruel.

"Have you not realized what is happening here?" The spirit spoke, something weighing on his words, his face frozen and untouched by years. "Refuse to accept, of your own free will, to form the bond and you *will* die. Amträh is the only one who possesses the power to heal your wounds."

Leander would guess *Amträh* was the vile beast, eyeing the creature with bitterness spreading in his mouth. "I would rather die than have this thing aid me."

The spirit sighed, passing his hand through his hair. When he spoke next, desperation and tiredness filled his words. "I do not think you can fathom the situation. A fragment of my soul was left inside Amträh, for I *knew* what awaited Tërnya." The spirit moved two steps to the right, gesticulating with his hands in

a slow pace. "If you were chosen, that can only mean you possess what it takes, within your capabilities, to become a Knight. To become the one that can fulfill this role in my stead and the ones that came before. However, if you prefer to die in such a way, be gone at once. I may have some power left to search for a less suitable person." The Argyris felt his blood rushing inside him, silence overtaking him.

"W-was there any chance you have some goodness inside your heart to light up a small fire, good friend?" Bash could not even speak, the words poorly leaving his lips while sweat ran down his face as if he was bathing in the sun. The dragon looked at him satisfied, yet Bash kept getting weaker and weaker. He would leave the stream and drag himself through the ground if he had any strength left in his legs, however he couldn't move anymore. Maybe...

That was the day Bash would finally die. At last. With a mean, rude creature draining the life out of him so Bash could meet Death one last time before finally letting it take him with a sweet kiss. Wait, was that the sky? Since when was Bash lying on his back? He could not even tell if he was still in the stream or on the riverbed. All the young man could say was that the day was actually quite beautiful. He could see the sun waking, its light spreading through the skies, red and warm hues and for a very brief moment, Bash could swear he felt some kind of warmth grow inside him. Was that Death? He thought it would be colder. That was weird. He suddenly could not feel anything anymore.

It was as if Leander had to make a choice: either die by fire or frost. Which one would be the fastest, which would be the most painful? Which would he choose? "How did you meet your end, then?" he spit the words, watching the spirit's reaction closely. Upon hearing that question, the light grew stronger and darker like the glow of death.

"It has been a very long time since this memory crossed my mind. Should I resent or thank you, warrior?" The dragon behind him growled, anger filling the beast's eyes, yet that was an anger that was not aimed at Leander. "We had already lost one of our own, right at the beginning. My fiancée, Elora. She was the bravest woman I had ever known, yet her death was futile. Meaningless, the first of us to die in our own home. That day I wanted to see that man's eyes as I crushed his heart with my own hands, just as he had done to my Elora."

Leander was set aback as the spirit's feelings and emotional words flowed through him, making his heart ache and throb. The grief, the pain, the desire for vengeance—it was all so unbearable and dense the Argyris lost his breath for a brief moment.

It was quite weird, that place. There was no light and no warmth, yet somehow he could see a mist covering the ground without ever spreading farther than his knees. Most of all, Bash was all alone, yet he could still hear voices and whispers coming from all places. What *was* this place?

"Hello?" Bash's words echoed, welcoming a great nothingness as they got lost in the air. The whispers and voices continued, not bothering to answer him. "Could someone at least tell me if I'm dead?" Once again, his voice echoed through the empty place without reaching anywhere, his words blending with the whispers and voices that refused to give their reply. Maybe he had died at that stream, with the dragon laughing at him, showing not even the courtesy to bury him. Life sure could be very cruel, and rude, sometimes. It was at that moment that Bash noticed something from a distance. Was that...a light?

It was!

Bash started to run, seeing nothing on his way, no rocks, leaves, people, animals, or trees, only a complete blackness and mist that almost seemed to slow down his pace. It was weird that he was running, since dead people had no need to rush, yet he couldn't explain. He *had* to. When he finally reached the light, he took one step back. That...was quite a peculiar light, in so many different ways. Too strong, yet it didn't blind him. Hot as foundry iron, however it kept sending chills over his spine. It had no physical form at all, but Bash knew it was *someone* waiting for him. That was the moment he just wanted to make sure he was, indeed, very, *very* dead.

"Yet in the end it was all just some childish game to him..." the spirit whispered and Leander swore he saw Death in the man's eyes. "That monster wanted to see our struggle, he wanted to see our pointless dedication as he murdered us one by one. One could see so in his eyes. I was a fool to believe I had a chance to avenge her." The light got darker, colder, sending a shiver down Leander's spine as the spirit continued to speak, "Right before I received Death's kiss I looked into the man's eyes and saw. How fruitless our efforts had become, how pathetic we truly were. And, for just a glimpse, I saw his real self. His actual power."

The spirit looked straight at Leander then, his gaze so powerful and desperate it froze the Argyris on the spot. It made Leander feel something he had never felt, something he hadn't come across even in his most daring moments as a warrior, something that could freeze and rot his own bones and flesh and even steal a star's light. True fear.

"You cannot even fathom what I saw, warrior. You cannot even grasp with your limited mind and narrow eyes the power I saw inside that man. The demons we ridiculed and made little out of it are something we mortals cannot destroy with pure strength, things we cannot control or overpower. Yet that man does—he controls them." A name crossed Leander's mind and the spirit nodded as if he had heard his thoughts. "The king bestowed upon me the same death he gave my betrothed, carved a hole in my chest and burned my heart with his bare hands. I felt my whole body burst and burn, and it was then that I saw the other realm. What awaited us in a distant future."

Death was coming for Leander, its lips almost reaching him. He felt cold, his eyes with no more strength to remain open. He saw blood run down the stream, his body becoming weightless yet heavier than it had ever been.

"You must choose now, young warrior. Die in a pitiful state or seal your pact with Amträh. Do not forget that the weight of your life and this realm is the same as comparing a grain of sand and a mountain. So, choose wisely, for there is a wrong answer."

Leander had made his decision some time ago, upon knowing that name. The spirit's gaze pierced him, as the Argyris was already losing his consciousness to the darkness.

"Uh, hello. Could you tell me where I am? Have I died? Is this what the afterlife looks like?" If it was, he pitied those Säh followers. The light blinked and trembled and for some reason Bash could understand what it was saying. "I am *not* dead? How could this be?! I felt Death and everything, accepted my fate and all that nonsense. This is so frustrating!"

The light sparked, sending Bash three more steps away from it.

"Wow, forgive me, I shall speak no more." The light calmed, a gentler and warmer glow emanating from it. Then it starting moving away, asking to be followed. Bash was smart enough to comply. How it would make any difference the spot where they were in such a place, he had no clue. It all looked the same. Yet the sparks were quite frightening in their own way, so he decided to follow along even if they never reached the place. However, a few steps after, the light stopped blinking and twisting so that Bash would look at the ground.

"There is only mist on th—" and the mist parted in half, revealing a stone with mold and strange marks written all over it. Bash could not understand a thing. The light trembled, showing its frustration, flying over the rock and shining on it. In a blink there were words, yet the moment Bash read them they vanished from the stone.

Problem was Bash understood them, and remembered them still. He let a loud cry.

"Oh no, no. I can't. I mean, I feel honored, truly, for being bestowed with such an honorable task. However, I'm definitely *not* your man. You should know that I'm not really a knight, only someone pretending *really* hard at it." Bash swore that light was staring at him with bloodlust, right then.

The dragon shifted in its place, the earth rumbling as its feet moved on the ground. The light started to go back to its original color, shining dimly against the rising sun.

"I see. Remember you will carry this choice forever, even after your last breath. And forever is longer than it seems." When the light vanished, Leander felt Death placing its cold, hard lips against him. He felt a cold embrace, darkness wrapping itself around him as he wished it all to end. Then, there was pain. The man screamed as he felt his legs moving on their own. No, not moving.

Healing.

It was like getting his legs crushed all over again yet in reverse, with the bones and flesh returning to their original state. The Argyris glanced at his limbs, watching as his flesh sewed itself, the bones cracking into place, blood rushing back to his veins. It burned, it ached, and it made him sick. When it was finally over, Leander turned to the side and vomited, a taste of blood and raw meat, almost making him sick again. Something pulled his gaze. He did not have any control over it, his head turning on its own toward the creature that gazed upon him victoriously. Leander could do nothing but crawl in its direction, Death and darkness far away from that place.

The man cursed under his breath, feeling an unknown force pull him, drag him. As if he had been drugged, the world around Leander danced and laughed at him while the noble Argyris stood on his knees and stared deep into the dragon's eyes. There was a burning on his right wrist, spreading through his body like melted fire, drying the air in his lungs. For one second Leander thought his heart would burst, kill him in one second as all those images, sounds, and scenes flashed inside his mind. After it was all over, he turned his head to face the dragon, a bitterness spreading in his mouth.

Amträh—no...

His name was Amträhfar.

The light sent sparkles, getting hotter and hotter, cursing Bash with the most profane words until it stopped abruptly, twitching in the air.

"What? You think it can be *fun?* To train alongside an Ancient creature?! *Are you mad?"* The light exploded in sparkles, swirling angrily around him. "Hey, hey, sorry! I am just...not your man. You should simply find someone else." As an answer, the light got darker, ice-cold.

Images, memories began to pass right across his eyes, making Bash let out a shaken breath. The light then flew right in front of his face, pulsing with energy.

"Fine, I hear you. Can't find someone else, use my own memories against me, who doesn't love to relive their traumas, I hear you. But that doesn't make me good for the job." Bash was hit in the forehead. Then he snapped. "*Fuck!* Well, that's it! Still want me? *Fine*, you have my entire body to do whatever you please! You won! But don't *dare* come at me when all goes to shit because *you* chose poorly!"

The light got brighter and even hotter than it originally had been, urging Bash to touch the stone. For some reason he was unsure about doing it. However, when the light began sending the angry sparkles he did it anyway, and it was like getting struck by lightning while using narcotics and vomiting his own guts out. The. Worst. Sensation. In that whole damned world. It felt like forever had passed until he was able to open his eyes with a gasp, finding himself drowning in the stream.

After a few minutes of coughing and recovering his breath at the riverbed, he glanced toward the creature. The dragon was waiting, with a very annoyed look.

"Well, good Wake to you too, you rude and hypocrite boy." Bash knew *his* name. He just wanted to piss him off for all the dragon had put him through that morning. When the creature pushed him in the stream with its front leg, Bash knew his plan had been a success.

And that his back hurt.

The Legend of Kih Nähsur

Fall of Night - A Moment in The Past

On nights like those, when it looked as if the stars were hiding and cowering and the moon refused to shed its light, people used to say the Divines were neither joyful nor pleased. They were nights when the Gallows passed slower, colder, nights when one could sense Death's presence just by closing their eyes. During those nights, the woman would carry three candles to the child's chambers to keep darkness at bay and leave at least two lit in the room, for those were nights not blessed by the Divines.

"Nana..." The child spoke with a mellow voice, her eyes speaking more than her words.

"Say your words, little one." The woman was more tired, her body demanding rest, yet she already knew what the child would ask and knew she would oblige.

"Could you tell me one story before you leave? I promise it will be only one." The child took out one finger under the blankets as an oath, winning a smile from the young woman.

"Which one you desire to hear?"

"Could you tell me the story about the Shadow King? *Please!*"

The woman furrowed her brows. "Your father made himself very clear about this matter, little one. Anything related to the Divine Order is abolished. You must devote yourself to your studies."

The child removed the covers sitting on the bed with haste, speaking so fast she even lost her breath. "Papa said that 'a great ruler must know the history of their people and their kingdom, as well as the land itself'. The Battle of Nähsur is an event that impacted our kingdom and Tërnya, even if most grownups do not believe it really happened, so there should be no reason why I shouldn't learn more about the war's perpetrator." The child lost her breath, cheeks flustered as her eyes stared at the ground.

She was but the child's nurse, replaceable and unimportant. Even when her situation diverged from most, if Felix heard of her insubordination... The woman met the child's pleading eyes and sighed, caressing the little one's head with gentle fingers. She glanced at the candles, seeing all three lit, her heart easing some of its worry.

Long ago, rumors begun to circulate Tërnya. They were dark, vile rumors that told the story of a cursed man, born with the power to bewitch monsters and devils, a power that could bring real demons to our realm. The tales called him Kih Nähsur, a man who had been deserted by the Divines. It was said Kih Nähsur ruled over the Gallows and terrorized the Bless, that his servants could walk among men be it Wake or Fall and that no living being was safe under the Divines' bless for he was Their unravel. At first, people paid those rumors no mind, using them to scare their children and frighten their friends close to the Gallows. To all Tërnya, Kih Nähsur was a myth born from blather and nothing more.

Then other rumors began to spread, fearful whispers that stated demons had been spotted. Beasts with a thousand eyes and no legs, creatures that spilled fire with five clawed hands, actual monsters that followed only one voice and obeyed but one man's words walking beside us mortals. The rumors grew and grew until the Divine Order could ignore them no longer. However, it was not its ten Knights that found the man who ruled the demons, but Kih Nähsur himself that appeared at the Order's door. The evil king challenged and humiliated them, starting the war that would change everything for the Divine Order.

"The Order lost its dragons..." the child whispered.

The woman nodded slowly.

The war lasted no more than five days. That was all it took for Kih Nähsur to obliterate them and kill the Ancient creatures that fought beside their Knights, yet even though it lasted so little, it felt like a thousand days had passed for the Order's Knights. In ways that no one knows, the Divine Order managed to purge

Kih Nähsur back to the realm of demons, saving Tërnya from a future it would never again recover from. However, the price the Order paid for their peace was far too great, losing not only hundreds of their own but the Ancient creatures that for decades had been aiding them on their sacred and holy quest. With the passing time, the Divine Order's power weakened, its prestige and influence waning as no kingdom truly witnessed what took their most prized companions. Rumors about Kih Nähsur and his demons became a legend, tales to frighten and nothing more, no traces to be found.

The child was silent, her eyes glowing with the candle flame. "Do you believe it, Nana?"

"I believe the time has come for you to sleep."

"But Nana—"

"Hush, hush now. I want to hear no more complaints, if the king finds out I told you this story I will never be allowed to enter your chambers again."

The child widened her eyes, biting her lower lip with sadness flooding her eyes.

The woman gave her a warm smile, touching the small one's cheek. "Forgive me, little one. I would stay more if I could."

The child laid on the bed, pulling the covers and blanket all the way to her chin. "Promise me you will come back tomorrow."

"You have my word."

The woman kissed the child's forehead and stood up from the chair.

"Nana."

"Yes?"

"Do you think Kih Nähsur is still alive?"

The young woman felt a cold entering her bones, a chill brushing her skin. She stared at the child for a long moment, unsure of what to say. "I cannot say, dear. He could be nothing but a myth—"

"What if you knew he was real? Do you believe he really got trapped with the demons?" There was fear creeping inside the child's gaze, something that left the young woman unsettled. Why would the child be asking her those questions?

Why were her hands trembling?

The shadows in the room shook, their forms waving for a moment as the light dimmed. The woman glanced at the candles, seeing that there was only one still lit. She felt a shiver go down her spine.

"No one can know the answer to that, child. Let us sleep and rest now."

She lit the two other candles with shaking hands, touching the child's head once before leaving toward the door. The young woman turned around, only once, to see if the candles were still lit.

Two of them were.

A Fool's Covet

Bless of Day - Dawn Star, Haste Mountains

It all felt like a cruel joke. A joke people would hear at funerals right before burying their dead that would set eyes aflame, for it was no time for jokes or funny business. Bash was unsure if he was the poor soul being buried or the foolish one who had told the joke, yet he could feel Death thriving still, holding his head so his eyes would not wander from all the stares, from all those gazes that were fixated on him.

To be fair, he was standing on a stage at one of the Order's fancy dining halls. He was at the back, the tables arranged in a way that an open path laid in front of him, as if at any moment someone would drop a red carpet for him to run away in all his glory. In those gazes the young knight could see a lot, for he knew those feelings too well. At that moment he was standing next to a noble, the dainty lion who, for Bash's displeasure, shared the frustration he felt himself. Neither wanted to be standing there, yet *there* they were. To be standing side by side an Argyris was enough to make his stomach sick and the weight in all those staring eyes made it worse. He should be down there, just another random knight looking up toward the shining Knights with wishful thoughts.

Yet a princess called him a shining Knight, the most royal of bloods he dared to approach, and was speaking those words for the whole Divine Order to hear.

"—disappearance after Nähsur's battle decades ago, it has now fallen to the great Ancients to make the choice of who shall be worthy of the title of an Orphys Knight. We were blessed by our Divines to have received not only one but two worthy men of such position..."

Her voice would come and go, an echo that spoke words far too frightening for him to pay close attention. Yet those eyes, all those gazes—those he could not run from. He saw them all, felt their envy, their fear, their covetousness. Weren't they fools, to covet such a thing? To envy a dead man's grave?

Poor, fortunate bastards basking in ignorance.

Bash envied those grand houses. The warm, delicious food nobles such as the Argyris beside him would eat as many times as they wanted, the fine clothes and beautiful jewelry they wore so that people like him would always know where each of them stood in the world. The ones fated to yearn and the ones fated to gloat. There was where he belonged, together with the eyes that stared not down but up toward the royals and the shining Knights, coveting, trying desperately to find faults in the ones above, trying to justify why they deserved better.

"Straighten your posture." The words were carried by a slow whisper, almost failing to reach Bash's ears. The Argyris still looked straight into the crowd, eyes unmoving. When no movement was made, his words left his mouth once again with a bitter annoyance filling their spaces. "You are, from this day onward, a Knight. Behave as such."

Bash felt the smile inside him, a maddening irony that mocked him as he did just as the Argyris ordered. A *Knight,* a shining Knight with the great Ancient's power at the tip of his finger, a majestic beast that would bend to his every will and stare down at all those below him. Yet that was just an elaborate lie. Give a castle to a farmer and he won't become a king, give a token of honor to a burglar and he won't become honest. So why would changing his posture turn him into a *Knight?* That was a joke that at first had been funny for its absurdity, yet soon it became tiring and cruel.

"What will happen now that the Order possess these...beasts?" That was some random voice that belonged to a random pair of eyes that stared at Bash from below. They were in a grand hall, which he did not know—hadn't paid attention. The Order's knights were seated on the chairs with meals untouched on their plates. Princess Kayden, her Ward, Bash, and the Argyris stood on some sort of platform with a wide window behind them. To Bash, it felt like a stage. He was the dying man being buried and Kayden was the person telling the story of how he came to be in that hole, as if it was the funniest story in the entire world. All those knights listened to her as if she was telling a hero's tale, envying him.

Bash was crying and laughing inside. *Oh, those poor,* damned *lucky bastards.*

"Nothing will change. All knights shall continue with their designed tasks and obligations. A list will be posted tomorrow with all your schedules. Trainings shall be ministered by our former Red Knight, Sir Rowan, while any knight that possesses knowledge or affinity with the arcane arts can meet me at my office as soon as this meeting is done; exams will be held to find new captains and Diamond knights. The Ancient ones and their Knights will receive special training sessions starting as soon as possible."

Bash's entire body felt weird. Ever since that Wake the young knight felt the presence of the winged beast inside his mind, prying eyes and an uninvited touch brushing against his private thoughts and darkest memories, while a power pulsed and wriggled within his veins and soul, something he was afraid to touch or get anywhere near. His body was not his own anymore and Bash was not fond of that feeling. Even worse—

CHILDREN'S THOUGHTS. NO AMUSEMENT IN PRYING.

Can I silence you remotely, or do I have to be near you?

EVEN REASONS LIKE CHILD.

The dragon—*his dragon*—laughed inside Bash's mind with a condescending tone. The young man could not even explain how he knew the Ancient creature was laughing; he just *felt it.* And Bash's dragon—

Was incredibly rude. He was nineteen years old, for Säh's damned sake! In East Raevich that usually meant one had already lost their purity, innocence, morality, and were betrayed at least three times. He was practically an old man.

A MAN CHILD.

Well, you were the one who chose this man-child. What does that say about you?

Bash could feel the dragon's annoyance as his own, the scent of wet pebbles mixed with the woods. If he concentrated hard enough, Bash could actually hear the stream and feel the wind and sunlight against the dragon's dark skin. Vührähkam was in the woods, in the river where they—officially—first met. So romantic. Every time he focused on the Ancient, that power inside him would move, spread, and flow through him. All those knights, they envied *that? That* was giving him bowel problems. Also, apparently he had a jewel attached deep into his wrist, a sort of welcome gift from the dragon. It *did* look like crystallized blood with some dark hues, so it was actually quite amusing. But since he could not remove it and sell it, what was the point?

"Are there any more questions?" The princess's voice was loud and clear, bringing Bash back to her speech with a scare. He hoped she would ask no questions regarding that meeting later, for he would not be able to remember much of it. The younger knight glanced toward the Argyris. The man's face was the very same anytime he looked at it. Those fancy nobles sure were something, if there was not even an ounce of fear glowing in his cold blue eyes.

A sudden thought crossed Bash's mind, a realization as he went from knight to knight seeing the same glances and stares he had been receiving since the very beginning. There had been no change. *She hasn't told them.*

As the knights went back to their meals, some leaving the hall, the air in the space didn't shift. There was no fear in their eyes, no desperation or fright. Kayden hadn't told those poor ignorant souls one of the most significant pieces of information—what the two new pristine Knights had been tasked to do, what *all* Knights had seen as they made that devilish pact with the Ancient creatures. They didn't know that all their lives depended on *Bash,* on whether *he* succeeded in stopping those visions from coming true. He turned his head, finally meeting his new leader's gaze. Kayden saw him—it almost felt like she saw *through* him. What Bash was thinking, what he was fearing. The princess smiled, yet he saw her real answer within her eyes. Bash was not entirely sure how he knew what the princess meant—he just did.

They don't need to know yet.

Sure, they didn't need to know about their impending death and the utter destruction of the world. If he had to be honest with himself, he wished to be back to his old, blissful ignorant self. Yet as Bash turned to watch the knights, sensing the weight of their gazes on him, flooding him with their greed, coveting his position in the high, nice stage, all Bash could do was smile.

Those fool bastards. They were coveting Death while he was the one who couldn't even choose in which hole he would be buried.

Ha, Death's jokes were cruel—even to him.

The Weight of Choice

Midday - Ice Draco, Haste Mountains

"THE FATE OF THE mortal realm is permeated in death and, for some reason known only by the Divines, the sole duty to prevent the fall of Tërnya was tasked upon the Orphys Knights of the Divine Order." Those words alone were enough to strain every muscle in his body. Lady Faeryl's voice somehow managed to conceal their true weight, the real meaning behind those dooming, ill-fated words.

Leander was not a man to succumb to nightmares and fear, for he was raised as an Argyris. He had earned that title and one did not earn the Argyris family name by showing and dwelling in weakness. Yet when the Ancient beast showed him the future that awaited them, visions of things that could come in a few decades or a few months without them knowing, for the first time since he was a nameless child the noble felt a sense of dread befall him. Deep inside, the man still did not believe, for only the Divines possessed the power to reveal times that had yet to come to pass. However, that lingering feeling, the possibility of *any* of those visions coming true no matter how small...

That made Leander Argyris's bones tremble.

He tried to focus on the room, its dim and old furniture and the poor tapestry that hung on the walls as if it wanted to tell a depressing tale. He tried to recall the comfort of his own chambers, all his conquests in sight that would never fail to remind him who he was and what he did to stand where he stood. Not a Knight but a warrior. One that would become part of history, equal to no other.

"How can you guarantee that any of it is true?" He did not hide the coldness in his words.

The princess glanced his way and if Leander was of a simpler mind, her eyes would've been enough to convince him. "I can guarantee you nothing, Leander Argyris. After all, how could I prove that what we saw is truly the future? I am but a human living in the same time as you." Beside him, the other Knight shifted in his space, his eyes staring at the hardwood floor. Leander did not trouble himself to remember the dark-haired man's name. "However, there is one proof I can provide you both."

The two Knights focused on the leader's face, Princess Kayden's voice showing a trembling weakness for the first time since they formed their pacts with the beasts. That was the second proof Leander needed to know where Lady Faeryl had put her faith. As she spoke, he finally noticed the Färküh Ward behind her as the man shifted and placed his hand around the sword's hilt on his waist. If not by that Leander would have mistaken him as the princess's own shadow, one that shared the terror in their leader's eyes.

"I can feel Antrühriel's fear as my own, flowing stronger than my own blood inside my veins. For an Ancient creature, dragons that powerful, to feel such a fear... How could mere humans like us ignore such a threat?"

Their *bond*.

Leander could feel the Ancient's mind just as he could his own. The beast's feelings and raw emotions came to him without him desiring them, a violation of his basic rights that set an annoyance far too great for the dragon to ignore. The Ancient knew how the Argyris felt about everything, yet the beast did not care in the slightest. Their positions were clear as day; the one that held the power was not the *human* Leander. As soon as he was healed, the noble found a jewel sewed into his wrist, a precious stone that shone as if it was made with liquid fire and burning ashes that would throb and burn with the Ancient's will and power.

Did you show me transparency, beast? If I shall aid you, I must know.

BELIEVE WHAT YOU WILL. NOT MY REALM.

Leander clenched his jaw, averting his eyes as if he spoke with the dragon face-to-face. Never a straight answer or interest. How he could work alongside such a creature was beyond him. However, he had been deprived of any choice.

"What will happen now?" There was a quiet despair Leander could notice coming from the other Knight, an emotion that almost made the young man's voice tremble. "I mean, do we wait for it to happen? Do we stay here and...I don't know, train and play fetch with the dragons until it happens? I never even had a dog."

Leander scoffed at the words of the younger Knight, yet the princess spoke with a calm and strong voice. "We must strengthen our bound. Our connection with the Ancient ones is far more complex than we can imagine. Both of you must learn how to harness their power and fortify your skills. I did not speak frivolously in front of the knights when I said we would begin our training as soon as possible."

The Argyris saw fear fill the princess's green eyes, his own hair standing up against his wishes.

"I do not know how much time we have, Bash. Yet we must assume it is not much."

Leander wanted to argue with his new leader, anything to make that conversation less ridiculous. What was the use of a Knight's title when he was already a successor of the current family chief? When he sought the greatness of warriors and champions? However, there was one thing during that whole conversation that he could feel every time he breathed, something that could not be concealed by any means. Amträhfar, the Ancient beast bound to his soul, could not hide his fear. Nor could Leander hide his.

"When do we start?" The Argyris did not ask because he wanted to. At that Wake, Leander Argyris had sold his freedom and life to a single purpose: to become the first Argyris to ever confront a ruler of real demonic beasts, the King. And due to that choice, there was but one path he could walk until that day finally came, even if the walk would be lamentable. The path of an Orphys Knight.

Kayden smiled at the Knights, glancing toward the window behind her. "Right now."

The Sound of the Realm

Fall of Night - Trymion Island, Carnarbur

Two Nights After The Blood Ceremony

The scholar was finishing his studies in the classroom, writing his last report on how to manipulate energy in order to move and control fire. If he failed the next exam, he would not be able to get his license until the next year. Beside him was a young woman who tutored and aided him with his notes.

"No, that is not quite right. You *pour* your core's energy into the natural flow of the world, you have to feel the flow in your core before you can manipulate its energies."

"My core energy...?"

The woman sighed. "The world's—look, maybe this type of manipulation is not for you if you keep struggling this way. You accomplished a lot more in Herbalist Studies than Flow Manipulation. You could still get your license as an herbal physician—"

"No! I need to do this." The scholar spoke with closed fists, crumpling the paper in his hands. If he failed again, his family would disown him and stop paying for his studies. "I-I can do this. I only need to get the theory right."

The woman sighed again, shaking her head with slumped shoulders. "Fine."

"I will also attend some special classes before the exam. Professor Orion's apprentice will also give a small lecture. I will do it. I just need to get the theory, right?"

The woman eyed him with doubt, shrugging as she went back to page one. "You should be careful with anyone associated with Professor Orion. He is not well liked here in the academy and he is not the one administrating the exams this term. If you take too many classes from different teachers, it might confuse you even more. Here, it is not really that hard once you get the idea and the concept."

As the woman explained and showed him her own notes and illustrations, comparing with his own, his anxiety worsened. *Would he* do it? Would he be able to pass that exam and get his license as a licensed mage?

The scholar got up from his chair suddenly, gazing out of the window with bewildered eyes. The woman jumped from her place, staring at him with panic growing inside her words. "*What*?! You scared the demons out of me!"

He stood still for a few more seconds before walking toward the window. Air rushed into the room in a nice, cool breeze.

"You didn't sense it?" he asked almost in a trance.

The young woman furrowed her eyebrows. "I didn't sense anything. Now, could you *please* sit down again so we can finish this? We still have plenty to cover and your exam is in a few days, isn't that so?"

The scholar stared outside for a few more seconds before closing the window with an uneasy feeling spreading inside him. He must've imagined it, then.

"Of course, forgive me."

Yet from time to time, he would glance toward the window, where he felt that ominous and dense energy from afar. Someone with his skills, it was unlikely to be anything of importance.

He could not even manipulate his own core after all.

CHAPTER VI

Journal Entry, Special Classes #1

I attended the special classes ministered by Professor Willow and also a small seminar taught by Professor Orion's apprentice.

Where Willow focused on a dense theory about all the possible paths on flow manipulation using our cores to connect to the world's, I found Apprentice Saranm easier to understand and assimilate. She explained in a more practical way how to harness the energy from our own cores to manipulate the world's energy, without going into details about all the paths we can follow once we do so.

It is unfortunate that my fate lies in Professor Willow's test, if I will pass the subject and acquire my license or be fated to be just another student with a physician license. I must do my best to learn all the different paths on flow manipulation before the exam tomorrow.

I managed to understand the core's theory and feel it on my own.

Only twenty-three paths to learn now.

In a New Tomorrow

Lull of Afternoon - Woods, Haste Mountains

Dorian was throwing pebbles at the water on a small lake close to the mountains, the stones sinking on every try. The Ward gazed at the sun's reflection on the lake's surface, feeling the chilling wind on his skin. It felt like months had passed since the Order received two more Knights, months since a small celebration was held where no one seemed joyful or happy enough yet it had been but hours.

Kayden had given her first official speech as the new leader, promising to bring better changes while the Divine Order started anew with the Ancients' aid, yet even then a good number of knights resigned and returned to their homes. The Order was, at that moment, in desperate need of more captains and high-ranking knights; however even then toward his lady, his dearest friend, Dorian could not feel more pride. She had achieved her dreams, brought back the Ancient creatures, and there was hope for whatever future she had seen, even when the visions the Ancients showed them promised devastation.

Dorian was certain that if anyone could save them from damnation, that person would be his lady, yet there was an ache in his heart, a knot in his chest that didn't want to go away. It followed him no matter the time of day, if he was asleep or with eyes wide open, it was always there and even though he tried to control his thoughts, prevent them from wandering places they should not go, the Ward kept failing time and time again as his thoughts sank into a dark bottom that would never provide him with light or answers.

What was that loneliness he felt? What was the cause of his lady's fading smile? Why did he feel so distant to her when he was always two steps behind her?

Why did it feel like their worlds were no longer the same?

Another pebble sank into the water until no more trace could be seen of it. *Better changes, wasn't that so?*

"Do my eyes mislead me or is that our leader's grumpy Ward that I see?!"

Dorian turned around, surprised to recognize that voice when he knew it for such a short time. The new Orphys Knights were both there. Dorian furrowed his brows with a sigh, his quiet moment ruined. Three mountains, more than thirty knights, an entire forest, and *still* they met.

"I have a name, Sir Bash, one I appreciate people using." Dorian averted his gaze, continuing to throw pebbles at the lake. Was their training already over? Only when Dorian glanced toward the sun did he realize the time. How long had he been there?

"Don't be like that! We are all companions now—we can be closer than that! Isn't that so, Leander?"

"I do not recall allowing you to be so informal toward myself." The Argyris words were as dry as they could be.

Dorian listened as their steps got closer to him. Why did he feel as if the Divines' blessing had left him?

Another pebble sank, yet he thought it almost skipped the water.

Bash sighed, resting his arm on Dorian's shoulder. The man immediately stopped with the pebbles, eyeing the young Knight with troubled eyes. "Säh help me, what a tedious crowd! One is a boring lion, the other a dying dog."

A dog?

Dorian removed the Knight's arm from his shoulder as the Argyris knelt in front of the lake. "Are you both here on Kayden's orders?"

The Argyris clenched his jaw, his eyes fixed on the water. "I cannot see why we *should* partake in such ridiculous tasks. We already spent the day dealing with these beasts, now we must waste our nights as well?"

"Oh, he is just sour since our princess leader had to give him a serious talk of why he was still questioning his new friend," Bash said with a gleeful smile on his lips, a bitten apple in his hand. "She told us to try to ride them, to see if that would strengthen our friendship power or something."

Leander stood up in one fast movement, eyeing Bash sideways. "A ridiculous task with no real purpose. My relationship with the Ancient beast should matter to none but myself." The noble turned his gaze toward Dorian once before turning back to the lake. "It may be of your interest, Ward, to know that your princess received a visit from Carnarbur's counselor. *That* should be something to keep your attention on."

Dorian blinked, taken aback by the Argyris's words, yet before he could reply the man entered the lake until the water was above his knees. The light and air bent for a brief moment while the water moved and waved beside the noble. In less than a mere second, a dragon stood in the lake, looking at them from above. Dorian stumbled on his feet, the pebbles almost falling from his hands as he took many steps back, nearly losing his balance. Even from there he could feel the heat that emanated from the creature's body, its eyes glowing in a way that made the Ward uncomfortable as they seemed to pierce his own. Leander climbed the creature with ease, not even glancing back at them as the Ancient dragon spread its wings and flew away from there, wind gushing along with some water in Dorian's face and clothes. The Ward had seen the creature before, right after the Argyris and the younger Knight met Kayden at the stream after they made their pacts with the creatures, yet the sight of them still frightened him.

"Do you both understand what must be done from now on?" Kayden asked the Knights when they arrived with their Ancients, right before her speech. Both averted her gaze, their eyes staring down.

"Yes, dear leader."

"Yes."

"Do you understand what is at stake? What your role is within the Order, your duty with this realm?" Kayden spoke again, her voice stronger.

"Yes." They both answered.

Dorian did not. He wished to.

"Can you do it?"

That time they both looked up to meet her gaze. Dorian felt the air shift then, it stopped completely as its weight got heavier and colder. None of the men answered, making the Ward's heart palpitate, race against his chest as he felt something enter and freeze his bones. The three of them shared something that Dorian could not be a part of, not entirely, and he was unsure if he would regret knowing even though he ached for it.

"No way, that is complete horseshit!" Bash's words dragged him back, surprising Dorian when he saw on the other side of the lake a gray dragon lying on the riverbed. "The blooded noble gets to *ride* his scary-ass dragon and you won't even let me *pat* you?! Wasn't *that* noble scum being scolded by the leader due his relationship problems?!" The Knight's shouts echoed through the space, yet the creature did not even flinch. "Oh, I see how it is now! Gold-plated *sires* get whatever they want, but gutter rats such as myself can go fuck themselves in their—oh no, hey! Don't even think about it—I'm talking to you, *mister!*"

The dragon began to spread its wings, standing up and flying away from the place while leaving the younger Knight shouting.

Dorian blinked a few times, uncertain of how he should feel about what he had just seen. So, he tried to leave.

"For Säh's cursed ashes, can you believe him?! Leander's dragon looks way crueler than Vühräh, yet that bastard keeps giving me the low treatment! He put me in his mouth, drowned me, forced me into making that shitty pact—and I don't even get *one* fun ride? What about fair trade?!"

Dorian held his breath, staring at Bash without knowing what to say. What was a *Vühräh*? It could be the Ancient yet...

And in what world would stand on top of an Ancient be a *fun ride?*

"Now he flies away, saying all those rude things to me. Would you believe the balls of this fellow?!" Bash exclaimed while turning his attention to Dorian, pure indignation flooding his dark eyes.

Dorian was unsure of what he could say, so he asked something instead. "Does it *have* balls?"

That question gave the young Knight a pause. Bash turned his gaze and stared toward the horizon, where the gray dragon had disappeared, shaking his head as his eyes focused once again on Dorian.

"Don't dragons lay eggs? Could male dragons lay eggs? I never felt his balls. Well, I didn't try to focus on his balls to actually feel them. Would they need balls to lay an egg?"

How in the Divines' names was he having that conversation? "I am not sure. My lady would probably know the answers, however."

Bash sighed, kicking the pebbles at his feet, throwing some into the water. They sank slowly. "That is fine, I suppose. Not that I expected much from him, even though I am *the best choice* to form the pact or something. It just felt somewhat random, you feel me? As if it wasn't really supposed to happen this way, such a change with *me* in it." The young Knight talked to Dorian as if they were long-lasting friends, yet that did not bother him. His words did.

Change. The world around Dorian kept changing and turning, yet he always felt as if he stood in the same place, as if the world shifted *without* him. Places became unreachable, situations out of his control, people unreadable. A world where he could not make any difference.

"How come you and the Argyris are fine with staying in the Order? You were desperate to leave before any of this."

The Knight gave him a twisted smile, fingers brushing his black hair. "I do not think we had much of a choice. Not sure about Leander's reddened pet, but Vühräh would drag me back to these mountains if I ever tried to leave."

Something in the way he spoke told Dorian the boy had already tried.

"Princess Kayden has great expectations for you both. You'd better live up to them."

"Take your treasures off and burn them like crispy rats, Sir Ward, there was no need to depress me so," Bash cried out, sitting on the ground as he played with the pebbles and threw them in the lake. A stone bounced on the water two times before it sank. "I am already competing with *sire mighty lion* and trying to please a smug Ancient. I am in need of a hug."

The Knight threw another pebble. It bounced three times before sinking.

Dorian stared at those dark waters for a long time before he dared to speak again, trying to hide the shaking in his words. "What did you see?"

Bash froze in his place, his arm still raised to throw another stone. He exchanged glances with Dorian before sending the pebble into the middle of the lake, a shiver passing through the boy's eyes. "When everything was over, and you and Princess Kayden came to us, the moment I saw her eyes I knew." Bash seemed lost in his memory of that day, as if Dorian was gone, leaving the young Knight alone with his thoughts. "She had this calm thing around her body, as if she was relieved the pact had been made. Yet not in her eyes. There was fear and despair in those green marbles and I know this because I had the same look."

Bash turned to Dorian, dread being carried by his voice. A dread Dorian could feel in his stomach, reaching for his guts.

"I do not know what our lady Kayden saw, nor even what that noble saw. However, the things that were shown to me made the child inside me cry and shit his pants. And believe me, that kid hasn't cried for a long time."

Dorian could feel the stillness in the air. Almost a weird scent to it, being carried by the wind as if it was not there at all, being some odd thing that one would get used to on the first time sensing it. Yet in Dorian's heart he could feel the force needed to keep that air still, the energy used to make that scent spread. *Something is coming. Something is changing.*

"What were the things you saw?" Dorian asked more firmly then, because somewhere inside he was trying not to break.

The young Knight smiled but in his gaze the Ward saw only shadows. "Trust me, you don't wish to know. Yet if the images are true, if Kayden is right and we fail, I don't think it will take that long for you to find out."

Dorian clenched his fist, the pebble in his hand scraping and hurting his skin. The Ward threw the pebble into the lake, never taking his eyes off it.

It bounced six times on the water.

And sank.

Three Realms, Three Pillars

Lull of Afternoon - Ice Draco, Haste Mountains

"Are you certain you have no desire to rest until Toll? It is quite a journey from Carnarbur to the Haste Mountains."

It always felt strange to meet her old tutor after years had passed and see he looked the exact same, appearing to be a seven-year-old boy. Although from time to time Kayden would send the mage letters with questions and doubts, they would not meet each other often. The princess poured licha's flower tea, being the mage's favorite, as she sat on the chair in front of him. She was quite exhausted after training alongside the Knights and the Ancients, yet she could never disregard Orion's visit.

"There is no need for such trivial things, Kayden. I am well used to being out of bed for long hours and what we must discuss is far more important than a mere rest." Even as the child said so, Kayden could see the dark circles under his eyes as he yawned.

Kayden was spending her time at the leader's office and until that point she had not gotten used to it. She felt out of place, staring at things she had dreamed to see with her own eyes since she was a child. A chandelier, where five dragon's mouths held the mountain's rocks, their glow spreading in the room. A table made from Oliban trees, a tree that grew only in extremely cold regions, its wood dark and robust. Tapestries that hung from the walls, made with fabrics found only in the East Kingdoms, with breathtaking illustrations as its threads seemed to shine like precious stones. Tapestries that showed Ancient creatures and their Knights, events that brought the Divine Order together, and the story of generations being told on those walls. Yet Kayden could only think of how much the Order's past would aid her in the future and how much her Sight and the Divines would aid her to make sure there would *be* a future.

"How is Gregory? I only pray that the commotions I caused did not trouble him much." Kayden spoke before taking a few sips of her tea, watching as Orion tried to fill his second cup, the table barely reaching his chest.

"He is very grateful for your efforts in providing the brothers a proper burial. Their family was thankful."

Kayden helped him with the kettle, her words attempting to distance themselves from her heart. "I did the bare minimum. I do not believe I deserve any sympathy or gratitude from their kin."

"The Divines did not let you interfere, isn't that so?" Even though it was a question, it was said with such certainty and assurance she did not even respond. Orion was the only person apart from her Ward that knew of her Sight. He discovered when they met for the first time, however the princess only came to know of it when he began to teach her the arcane arts, when she was fourteen.

Orion tried to grab the kettle once again, his cup empty a second time. Kayden helped him pour the tea.

"What intrigues me most is why would the Divines forbade my intervention. The visions I've been receiving are odd. They are more frequent and more—"

"That is one of the reasons I am here, Kayden," Orion interrupted her, his third teacup already half-empty. "Since I had to thank you in Gregory's name and congratulate your new position, I thought it would be beneficial to come here and do all at once while discussing some pressing matters."

Kayden raised her eyebrows. "Which would be?"

As the mage finished drinking the tea, he searched inside his robe for a few seconds, revealing a small pile of notes and scrolls tied together with a ribbon. "Forgive their current state. I didn't have the time to organize my notes properly." The child stretched his small hand, pushing the notes and scrolls toward Kayden. She gave them a brief glance, a numbness reaching her fingers before she could even touch them.

"When did you write these? I would presume before the ceremony."

Orion yawned again, nodding as he reached for more tea, the kettle almost empty. "I've been observing for some time. Far too many coincidences, you see? Of course, I was right to suspect."

Kayden turned back to Orion, staring at him. The child had a bored and tired expression, however she could sense his angst slowly crawling to the surface. For Orion to be afraid of something... She did not dare to finish her thought.

The mage lowered the teacup, empty once again. "The dragons had to return; it was eminent, however there is much that must be done if you wish to succeed."

Kayden could see the knots on her hands, her veins, the trembling of her fingers. Were the Divines *controlling* that as well? She took a few pages, her eyes passing over their content as confusion swarmed within. "But what is this? All of this, I mean—it is not about the dragons. This is something else."

Orion sipped more of the tea, his face a unique blend of tiredness and awareness. "I assume you remember our lessons? About the flow manipulation's fundamentals, the arcane path and so on?"

Kayden nodded. "Although I never studied hard enough to get a license as a mage, I always relied on the notes I took in our classes. Your teachings aided me greatly the past years."

"Oh, you can burn those notes. I lied." Orion's teacup was, once more, empty.

"Excuse me?" She failed to hide the astonishment in her words.

When the child saw the kettle was at last empty, he pushed the teacup aside. "That was the last one. So, let us finally start."

"What are you—"

Orion raised his index finger, looking right into her eyes. "I didn't lie about everything. All the fundamentals I explained to you, how to reach your core's energy and manipulate the world's flow, all is correct. However, when I explained how the arcane arts divide in paths, I was not quite accurate."

Kayden could only ask one thing. "But *why?*"

The child sighed. "Most mages use one 'school of thought' that is completely wrong, but none of them believe me. Since it got bothersome to keep justifying myself in classes and fighting their academic strife, I started using their most accepted lessons and theories and distanced myself from them. All they enjoy is creating a thousand divisions and paths so they can fail their students on the exams and tax more for a retake. It's tiresome and annoying, so I am a part of their faculty no more. As if mages weren't rare as it is, they *insist* on making it almost impossible for our young to graduate."

It was rare to see Orion so genuinely frustrated, the emotion palpable in his words. Kayden was never allowed to enroll in Carnarbur's Academy, yet it was well-known how many students failed to get their licenses due to devilish exams.

"The truth is, there are only three different pillars, whose systems work in completely different ways. The Natural, the Demonic, and the Archaic pillar. What changes is basically two things—how we humans extract and manipulate the energies and how the energy affects its surroundings."

Orion began to draw on the table with his fingers, a bright blue light leaving its own marks on the dark wood, its glow never fading. Kayden felt nostalgic. He drew three pillars, each with a symbol of its own. One of them Kayden knew all too well, yet the remaining two were nothing she had ever seen.

The boy continued to speak as fast as she recalled. "What I taught you was the Natural pillar, it is what most know as arcane arts. It is the flow manipulation licensed mages use, the one taught on Trymion, which draws the energy directly from the caster's core. Humans give their energy in order to manipulate the world's own energy."

"Yes, this is what I remember from our classes."

"Good." He then drew two simple humans, one with a small oval form inside and the other with a greater one. "Then you should also remember what I told you about people's cores. They are filled with their own power, the one that connects our energies with the world around us, and core sizes are determined at birth. Only those with greater cores can manipulate greater energies, if a person depletes their core at once, they can easily die. That being said—" Orion passed his hand across the table, clearing the drawings before making new ones, the symbol he had used for the Demonic pillar.

"The demonic arts do not belong in this realm. Humans should have never had any contact with their power; demonic energy is lethal to us. However, somehow a long time ago, someone got a hold of how to explore and use demonic energies to create a new kind of manipulation. Hence, the Demonic pillar was born. Then we have the Archaic pillar, also known as Ancient arts." The third symbol was drawn, together with trees, birds, rivers, and fire. "This is energy in its rawest form. It is the one that exists with or without humans, that shall exist as long as our realm remains alive. It's the energy from everything surrounding us, from the air we breathe to the rain that falls, the energy that maintains the balance in our world." The other two pillars' symbols appeared suddenly, each one shining brighter than before.

"However, to perform Ancient arts the caster does not use their core's energy, they take from the world's. There is no fair trade, so anyone could manipulate Ancient energy as long as they knew how it worked. The Blood Ceremony you performed manipulated a sort of Ancient flow, however it used blood as a balancer for blood is also a life force for us."

All the drawings disappeared, a silence stretching between them. Kayden knew he was just waiting for her to ask.

The notes weighed heavy in her hands, her face turning pale. "The incidents that have been happening all around Tërnya...the diseases, the crops, the animals—"

"One thing about practicing arcane arts is it doesn't interfere with the world's balance. We use our own power to manipulate nature's energy, yet we don't *steal* it, we *mold* it. Although some mages blend arcane with Ancient arts to meddle with energies that should be left alone. You had a recent encounter with a Shadow caster, correct?"

She nodded once.

"That is a perfect example of how Ancient arts can disrupt our surroundings. Although I do not agree with the term, Shadow casters use Ancient energy to steal and manipulate the world's shadows and their own, while using their own desires and emotions as a balancer. Yet this type of exchange does not work; desires and emotions are not a life force to us—you saw the results yourself."

As she listened to his words, Kayden glanced over her teacher's notes while holding her breath.

"Now, demonic arts bring demonic energy into the realm while Ancient arts draw energies from our world. Both cause an imbalance, both cause instability and open the door to chaos. Albaron is not the only kingdom that has been suffering, Kayden. As you can read, even in the East Kingdoms there have been reports of droughts and floods, diseases and disasters."

Her heart was beating faster, the words written on the notes haunting and crawling in her mind, dominating her thoughts. She was not frustrated with her former tutor for lying to her, she was not angry or anxious. She was terrified.

"Orion... These notes... How long have you..." The words left as ghosts from her mouth, fearing things that would still come to pass.

"That's the real problem, princess." His voice was exhausted beyond his years, carrying wisdom that far surpassed her own. "Our world's balance has been broken for a *long* time. We are simply seeing its effects now. Not only that, but someone or something has been increasing the demonic energies in the realm *and* stealing its energies. If this continues, Tërnya will be gone."

The white dragon reached her, their bound strong and tangible. The leader could sense all things that surrounded the Ancient, the breeze, the grass, the sun. It was not common for Antrühriel to open her mind to Kayden. Through their connection, they could share thoughts, feelings, and visions. At that moment Antrühriel revealed to Kayden how she sensed the world, its flow and core, and only then could Kayden feel how sick it truly was.

For months the princess had been wondering and asking herself what the Divines wanted from her. With the Order, with the Ancients, how these things related to the Shadow King, Kih Nähsur. Kayden never imagined how much the truth would frighten her.

"What can be done?" the leader asked with a whisper, to both of them.

Both answered.

"The ten Ancient dragons must be reunited. I am still not sure why... I'm failing to see their connection within all of this, yet you *must* reunite them. Along with all their Knights."

REUNITE US.

"To fight Kih Nähsur?"

Orion shrugged, resting his back on the chair. “To save all of us.”

TO SAVE MORTAL REALM.

A Sight Too Strong to Hold

Toll of Evening - Ice Draco, Haste Mountains

The Ward found his princess in the leader's office. The cool wind ran inside the halls with moans and small cries, passing through doors and cracks with ease yet the new leader did not seem to be bothered by the cold air. As Dorian entered the room, he saw how exhausted his lady was, the paleness of her skin, the look in her eyes, the position of her body. How many times had he seen Kayden like that? It was something that should bother Dorian no longer, especially since he could seldom aid his lady. Yet one glance he spared at her and Dorian could already feel his heart getting smaller, breaking and aching for her. Even when he knew it was all but a lost cause, he walked toward her and knelt beside her, speaking words that were fated to be ignored the moment they left his mouth.

"Kay, you should rest."

"I cannot do that right now, Dorian. I need to read Orion's notes once again. There's so much written in here, so many events and tragedies we were not even aware of..." Her words trailed off, her anxious gaze skimming through the pages.

His muscles tensed as he stood, his hand reaching for the sword's hilt. He closed his fingers around it with a tight grip.

"I heard that Orion's apprentice also came. Was there a reason for it?"

Kayden met his eyes for a brief moment before returning to the notes. "Tomorrow I will have a meeting with the Knights. Orion and his apprentice will participate as well. I suppose we could call it the Divine Order's first official business. We must find the remaining Ancient creatures if we wish to stop whatever is happening."

Dorian watched her for a few more seconds before sitting next to her, glimpsing toward the notes. His lips curved in a smile. "Orion still remains a very odd man. Do you believe he got any better from when he used to teach you?"

Kayden chuckled, lowering the papers in her hands. That sound was enough to warm just a bit of the cold air in the room. "If by better you mean more impatient, then I must agree. He said he lied to me because most people don't agree with his 'school of thought' and it was too bothersome to convince others, can you believe it?! Sometimes I swear, he is worse than an old man."

"An old, *childish* man, you mean?"

Kayden stared at him before she laughed, making him laugh with her. Dorian saw light flood in her eyes and the hard, tired lines on her face softened just enough. Just enough so he could find her again, the Kayden he knew. Not the one bound by a crown or Ancient creatures but the one sworn to her own heart. The one he would fight and die for.

Then, as fast as it appeared, he saw the light fading from her eyes while a shadow ate the joy from her, leaving a fear strong enough to freeze the air around them and make the wind still. "Dorian, I do not think I will be enough." Kayden's words were shaken, her hands trembling above the notes. He reached for her hands, trying to share as much warmth as he could.

"Why would you say such a thing?"

Kayden squeezed his hands harder, staring at him with green eyes that glowed like waves. Dorian often wondered how something could be so beautiful but bring so much tragedy to someone. "The Sight is stronger than before, Dorian. I can hear the whispers if I just pay enough attention to them. I can feel what others feel if I let myself get close enough—" Her words failed for a moment and Kayden shook her head as she continued to speak, "Antrühriel can communicate with me through sensations and feelings, sometimes even short sentences. I can feel her whenever she is, the things she is thinking. She is *afraid*, Dorian. An Ancient creature is afraid of our future." Dorian felt a pit open in his stomach, a dark void where his heart fell inside as his entire body froze.

"You believe it could be Kih Nähsur? That demons would return, that we will have to fight them?" For all the Divines, may it be something else. Not demons or an evil King but earthquakes, hurricanes, and giant waves—things they could see and understand, even if poorly.

Yet Kayden's eyes said the thing he feared most. Words that had no need to be spoken, feelings that had no need to be shared. "What I saw, what all Knights saw... It was calamity itself. And I am afraid I won't be enough to save us, Dorian. I fear I will be what dooms us."

Her eyes trembled with tears that still refused to fall and the Ward could hear his heart tear itself apart and bleed. He grabbed both her arms, trying to keep his voice steady and strong, for he knew Kayden could feel him crumbling from the inside. "You said we must reunite the dragons, so that is what we shall do first. After we do that, we will worry about the things that can or cannot be done. Know yourself before you know your enemy—wasn't it you who taught me that?"

Kayden let a weak laugh escape her lips, one tear trailing off her face. "Indeed, I taught that. I am surprised you remember it after studying so many years with the Wards."

"As if I could ever forget something you taught me yourself, my lady." He wanted to caress her face yet his hand remained put. His princess smiled, even if fear still permeated her eyes and voice. "This is also a great time to start recruiting new members for the Order, isn't that so?"

She let go of his arms, a small hint of light returning to Kayden's eyes. "I can announce small tournaments in each kingdom for whoever wishes to apply. We still have a few more experienced knights and they could make a good evaluation of the participants."

"I will send word for them as soon as I can, my lady."

"Also, we may be able to find new mages in Carnarbur! Or at least ones with a gift good enough to be trained. Orion could appoint someone he trusts to teach them the Three Pillars the right way; perhaps if he taught me the fundamentals well enough I could minister their lessons."

Dorian smiled as he watched Kayden, the air around her lighter, even if just a little. He stood by her side as she wrote down dates and separated a few knights that would be able to judge and travel. He even made suggestions here and there, from what he had observed since their arrival. Yet when Kayden mentioned the Red Knight, Dorian's smile faded just a bit. Just enough to make his lady's own light dim as well, the pen lowering in her hand.

"What really brought you here, Dorian?"

A word almost passed through his lips, something his soul had whispered with the foolishness of a child. Yet Dorian was a Ward. He had sworn an oath to his lady, one he would fulfill until the end of his life.

"Rowan wished to talk to you, my lady. Although he did say you should come at a time that suited you best, I believe it is quite urgent."

She nodded once, taking a deep breath before saying, "Then we shall meet him at once."

For the rest of that day, not even once did the light in Kayden's eyes return. Nor Dorian's.

The Lion and The Snake

Fall of Night - Dawn Star, Haste Mountains

Leander hit the target once again in its chest, the wooden doll absorbing the force of the attack. The sword had to move like his third arm. It had to become a part of him and even more, possess its own eyes, its own mind; he had to understand its mind and its movements better than he understood his own. Those were the first teachings of the Way of Sword the House Argyris taught their children from the moment they could hold the weapon. As every Way, by each generation it was improved and incremented, as the most notable warriors created their own techniques and forms, making sure the Way of Sword would never die and instead would ever evolve.

Leander was training in order to create his own technique, a completely new form that would forever shape the Way of Sword of the Argyris, something not even his father had accomplished. Yet being in the Order was nothing but an impediment, a wall on his way. What use would an Ancient creature be in the Way of Sword? To improve his own worth as a dignified warrior? Leander had made his choice; to survive in order to have a chance to fight the King and that man could not only prove Leander's worth but make him go down in history in the House Argyris. The greatest chance to show them his sword, to face an unbeatable force, and to preserve the balance in the realm not as a Knight, but as a true warrior. As an Argyris.

The sword continued to move in a constant dance, hitting and striking the targets with ease. Arms, head, legs, chest, then arms and legs again, yet it was still not good enough. Leander was missing the beat, the sword in his hand was moving faster than his eyes, moving on its own. They had to be one and the same.

From within, the Argyris could sense the creature in his mind, watching through his eyes, analyzing him, judging his movements, however it remained silent. As if that was the dragon's way to show his respect, only waiting for Leander to finish his segment to make his comments about the man's form and ability.

IS GOOD. YET NO GOOD ENOUGH.

Amträhfar's voice reached him the moment he lowered his sword, making the noble clench his fist.

I do not need your opinion or your aid. I know where I stand.

THEN DO BETTER.

With a shout Leander moved his blade in an arc, cutting the head off one of the wooden dolls making it roll a few meters away. He would rather give that beast back to Lady Faeryl and be done with it.

"Why so much anger?"

The voice reached him from not far ahead, his head turning with haste to find its source. There was a woman seated atop some metal bars, eyeing him with a mischievous, amorous gaze. Leander did not need to ask to know that woman had been born in the East Kingdoms. She had golden eyes that seemed to capture the sun's glow, skin darker than bronze that shone and reflected the rock's glow. Yet he did not fancy her attitude.

"Who are—"

"Your anger shifts the air, makes it more anxious and nervous. That is not a good air to be around, handsome."

The woman remained still in her place, staring at him from a few meters away. It took Leander a few moments to notice the single braid that almost touched the ground. He chose to ignore her last word. "As far as I am concerned it is not polite to spy on others, much less refuse to identify yourself when asked."

She smiled even though there was irritation in his words, walking away from the metal bar and closer to him while moving her hips. What surprised him the most was the fact the woman almost reached his height.

"I felt it would be even ruder of me to speak out of turn when you were so clearly focused. That was a nice blow with the sword." When Leander said nothing in reply, she pointed toward the headless doll. "The wood on their necks are quite thin, yet I would assume it is difficult nonetheless to cut it with a weapon like yours."

"I know what you meant," he spoke with cold words, having a better chance to see the woman since she was close to him.

The clothes she wore were of good fabrics, yet they were too loose and simple for a noble. It was one single piece, the sash on her waist almost made it seem she was wearing separate trousers and a long-sleeved shirt, which was an odd choice for most families that could afford something like that. She did not have any earrings to indicate she currently lived in the East Kingdoms, nor did her accent indicate such a thing. However, there was something quite familiar by the way she spoke, the mannerisms from Carnarbur were strongly present.

Was she a *mage*?

"What brought you here?"

The woman got closer, crossing a line Leander was not comfortable with as she closed their distance. "Princess Kayden called for me; I was following the energy from the Ancients. I guess I forgot you Knights also possess the same scent." She spoke her words with amusement, touching the marks his sword had left on the wooden dolls with the tips of her fingers. A smile flourished on her lips then, her words being carried with longing and fervor. "But who would've thought the scent would've brought me such a treat? Say, handsome, would you care to keep me company this Fall?"

The warrior ignored the tone and the woman's words, his attention focused on one single thing. She *was* a mage.

Pathetic.

"What would *our leader* want to discuss with someone like you?"

Her gaze met his and, for a second, he thought he saw something flash in her eyes, a fiery glow before dying out. Yet the stranger's sensual smile remained. "If she has not told you, then I believe it is not the place for someone like myself to share with you. Yet we could share other things if you wish, warrior."

His heart skipped a beat, a new annoyance growing inside him as Leander attempted to control his words. "I have nothing to share with those of your kind."

The woman laughed, the sound piercing his ears like a burning melody carrying poison. "I see. That is unfortunate, handsome. I was looking forward to some company on this cold night."

It happened so fast Leander could not react in time. The woman only moved her hand to the side as if she was trying to slice the air itself when the man *heard* the air around them freezing as it cut all the remaining heads, the four pieces falling to the ground with loud noises. The tips of their necks were frozen as a cold wind passed among them.

Leander gripped his sword stronger, eyeing the woman with the blood pumping and running through his veins with haste.

She passed beside him, daring to touch his shoulder as she whispered next to his eyes before walking away. "Forgive me for ruining the dolls. I guess my *kind* has a temper."

Leander refused to turn his head to watch her leave, the anger building up inside him, so he simply prayed to all Divines he would never again see that woman in front of him ever again.

The place her fingers had touched him still burned.

Stigma of a Red Knight

Toll of Evening - Ice Draco, Haste Mountains

Although the Red Knight was an Orphys Knight no more, Rowan was the only one of the former Knights that had decided to stay. The man was moving from Ice Draco to where all the other knights resided, the Red Star. The leader was surprised to see the amount of weapons, relics, and art spread out in the man's room, noticing a few bags already full. However, what surprised Kayden the most was the man's state. It was unusual to see his hair loose and unkempt like that, and not even the brightest smile would be able to conceal the dark bags under his tired eyes. Even then, the cheeriness and joy in the Red Knight's voice remained the same.

"I see you have made quite the collection," she said while looking at the aged knives and small axes atop one of his tables. They were in quite good condition, she noticed. There were from small knives and daggers to spears and claves, all shined with care and meticulously sharpened—she could really feel the man's dedication and pride to them.

"Years traveling on small quests and expeditions. Most of the times I traveled alone and it is amazing the things you can find when you just dig a little into the dirt and cut some vines." Rowan gave Dorian a golden dagger with spiral drawings in its blade. "I would like to give this to you."

Dorian took the dagger, feeling its weight and grip. "For what reason?"

The Red Knight shrugged, a smile touching his lips. "It's been years since we last saw each other—consider it a birthday and graduation gift. A Färküh Ward, huh?! You *did* it."

Kayden could feel the pride of the knight as if it was her own, the warm feeling spreading inside her like a pure, gentle light. "Also, I believe I will not be able to display all of them in my new room. If most will be kept in wooden chests, at least I can share some with one of my dearest friends." Rowan gave Dorian a gentle push with his shoulder, bringing a smile to the Ward's lips.

"I shall accept, then. Thank you, Rowan."

The knight smiled back, yet that warm light began to fade, turning colder and darker as his emotions shifted and filled his hazel eyes.

"I am grateful for you coming here, Your Highness. I wished to talk to you both about a matter that has been bothering me for the past few days."

"Is it about the former Knights?" Dorian's words carried the same concern the Red Knight shared as Rowan nodded in silence.

"It is strange. Ritta and Felicia were set on staying here as well."

"The Qirians sisters, correct?"

"Yes." Rowan looked at Kayden as he replied, "They said they would pay the twins' family their respects back at Carnarbur and come back. Yet I've lost contact with them, *all* of them. Their rooms, empty. No letters sent, or even replies to the ones I sent them. I cannot help myself but wonder if Sean—" Rowan stopped cold in his sentence, closing his fists as he averted his gaze.

Kayden took two steps toward the knight, a chill going through her skin. "What about Sean?"

Rowan sighed, his body stiffening while he passed his fingers through his hair. "From time to time I cannot sleep, so I often wander the halls, go for a walk and train, until I can return to bed. Yet before the Tournament's last duel, I saw something I should not have seen." Rowan then looked straight at Kayden, a shiver going down her spine, whispers growing inside her mind. "I saw Alexander and Sean talking, and Alex was *not* happy with whatever Sean was saying. I swear, after years together I can count on one hand the times I saw that man mad with anger filling his eyes. Yet that night, I swear to all Divines... For a second, I thought he would kill Sean right there. However, since the Tournament was coming to an end and Sean and Alexander had never had a great relationship I thought...I do not know what I thought! I should have *known*."

That time Kayden could not only feel the pain and guilt coming from him, she could hear it in his voice, see it in his eyes. It made the hair on her arms rise and a coldness go down through her throat, all the way to her feet.

"It was not your fault, Rowan. There was nothing any of you could have done that night—"

"There was!" Even Dorian was taken aback as the former Knight shouted, his following words shaken and weak. "You cannot be this blind or naive as to believe that nothing could be done, princess. We could have done *so much!* Something about Alex that night was not right, the air around him, his voice, it was as if something was lurking *inside* him. And when he attacked, I..." Rowan closed his eyes, covering his face with both hands as he let out a trembling breath. "We were all petrified, we did not move a muscle and all those people could have been hurt or worse. All I could think of was how I needed to do something, *anything,* yet my feet would not move and I could barely feel my body."

Kayden wanted to say that there was, probably, a reason why the former Knights were unable to act. That vile and sickening energy that kept circling around them and the guests that night...something *was* causing that. Yet would it make him feel better? Daniel and Corey had died before her eyes, due to the Divines' own will, yet the leader still felt the weight of their deaths on her soul. Their blood on her hands and heart. In the end, she knew that for both herself and Rowan, those excuses would not matter. Their failure would forever haunt them.

The Red Knight's words left his mouth like heavy rocks, sinking at his feet before even spreading through the room. "I kept asking myself over and over, how could Alex betray us like that, how could he hide that he was an arcane caster, *why* he was doing such things, yet even with all that was happening I could see clear as day. Sean, just a few steps beside me, was *smiling.*" The red-haired man laughed with disbelief, his eyes not focused on that room anymore. "That bastard was smiling as if he was having *fun*, not even an ounce of surprise on seeing Alex raise a sword against the princess, nor to see him using the arcanes. As if he already *knew* that would happen. And also—"

Rowan searched his pockets, taking out one wrinkled note that he passed to Dorian.

"I found this in Alexander's chambers. After his attack, I went to his room..." His words got lost, yet Kayden understood what the man was trying to say. She *felt* them.

Dorian opened the note, his expression stiffening as he read its content. Kayden approached him, not even asking for the note before Dorian himself gave it to her.

"I wish I could kill that man again," he whispered under his breath, the anger in his words so strong it made the princess dizzy.

If you think I can kill the target without entering these mountains of yours, you are more foolish than I thought. Give me access to the final Tournament. I don't care how you do it. Also, I would like a nice welcoming.

I am one of the greatest assassins, after all.

D.E

Kayden was not at all surprised as she read the note, in fact, she thought it was funny. Her reaction seemed to upset Dorian, however.

"We must find the assassin at once, my lady." The raw anger that reached her almost made her choke. The anxiety built up inside her friend as he grabbed Kayden by her wrists in an urgent manner. "I can fetch the horses and send a small party to search the woods. As long as this assassin still breathes—"

The leader smiled, touching the Ward's shoulder while locking gazes with him. "The assassin is long gone by now, Dorian. You do not need to worry. He will pose no harm to us. I *know* this." She spoke her words low, more to ease her Ward's worries than anything else. If Rowan suspected anything from her words, if he heard them, he said nothing.

The Red Knight gave a weak laugh, staring at the ceiling as some rocks shone their light on them. "I believe Sean knew from the beginning what Alexander planned to do. The arcane arts, the assassination, he knew it all. Yet Sean neither said nor did anything and now he is gone while the former Knights are missing.

What I wanted to say is...be careful, Kayden. For I do not think the worst has come to pass."

Before Kayden could say anything else, something appeared. She felt a shiver go through her spine, darkness covered her vision with nothing more to be seen, and her body trembled from the inside out. Then she sensed it, something *staring* at her. A gaze so strong and powerful it took her breath away as one forceful gasp. For a split second, the leader thought Death would take her right at that instant, kiss her and steal her soul, throw it into the frozen darkness. Then, it was gone. The eyes, the darkness, the trembling, as if it was nothing but Kayden's own fears playing tricks on her. That scared her. It was nothing like the Divines' touch on her mind; it was more invasive, more savage.

More terrifying.

"My lady, are you all right?" Dorian asked with a concerned gaze.

Rowan looked at her with worry as well.

The leader shook her head, holding her hands together so they would stop shaking.

"I am not sure, Dorian." Kayden took a deep breath and searched the room, finding nothing that could justify her fear. "However, Rowan is right. We must do something about the former Knights. Rowan, try to reach their relatives, anyone that they might have had contact with."

The Red Knight's eyes told her that was something he had already tried. "What if it is to no avail?"

Kayden saw the fear that creeped inside the former Knight. She felt shivers going through her skin like worms that crawled in the dirt, a mirror of the Red Knight's heart. Kayden felt her own heart heavy as they both clung to a hope that had everything to fail them. "I was planning on doing this anyway, so this could just be the perfect timing. I want you to be one of the Order's new high commanders. With that, not only do you have my permission but also the authority to gather a small search group and look for them, guarantee their well-being."

For almost an entire minute, Rowan did not seem to know what to say. He closed and opened his mouth a few times, before bowing to Kayden with so many mixed feelings it gave her a headache. There was relief, fear, joy, sadness, and frustration. Yet above all, there was hope.

"I cannot thank you enough for this opportunity, Kayden Faeryl. I give you my word, I shall do my very best to support you; to find them."

Within the room, Kayden could sense hints of despair. It was faint, yet it was there. She was not sure if it came from the Red Knight, her own Ward or herself. All she knew was that Rowan was right.

The worst was yet to come.

Chapter VII

"Many dedicate their lives to a quest to find artifacts from Ancient times, the first objects to be infused with the arcane arts and the Divines' blessings. It is unknown why those artifacts present higher powers in their forms than the ones created in our current days, yet researchers struggle with their studies since so few artifacts from Ancient times have been recovered. One of the most prestigious noble families from Raevich, House Argyris, dedicates a part of their fortune to search for some artifacts that once belonged to their ancestors, yet until the day of this recording no artifact was ever found by the family."

- *A Visit to Ancient Träh*, Bailoch Möhke

"The Sacred Sword of Three Thousand Soldiers is one of the most sought-after artifacts to this day. It is said that its blade possesses the power to burn an entire army as well as the power to entrap the souls of those it kills. The Sacred Sword is last mentioned in the poem "Three Thousand Vengeances" *written by Laish Argyris, where it tells the fate of Ishalär's final battle."*

- *Artifacts of Old*, Trilby Wand

"Little is known of its creator and the great warrior that last possessed it. However, the House Argyris claims ownership of the artifact without any solid proof of their kinship with the Sword apart from a single poem that never indicated any involvement between the Sacred Sword and the Argyris."

- *The Divines' Truth on The Ancient Quests*, Ibha Kaminer

Child's Play

Bless of Day - Albaron's Castle, The Past

THE SUN WAS HIGH and awake, burning the tears that wet his face, the sweat making his arms and legs damp. Nothing was fair in his life. All things stank worse than horses and the communal lavatories. He had been scolded *again* by the big-nose lady and his father got angry with him *again*. It wasn't his fault his dad's position in the castle stank. It wasn't his fault his dad wasn't a strong knight or part of the king's guard. Also, why would it be his fault that the horse ran away when he was playing? Nobody told him to watch them, that was his father's job. His father was the horse man. Also, it wasn't *his* idea to stay near the stables—his father told him to. He was bored and had nothing to do since there was no one to play with him and everything was suddenly his fault. Why did *he* get the blame for everything? Why did everything in his life have to stink so much? Nothing was fair. The world was not fair, and it stank. Everything stank.

"Hello!"

It took less than two seconds for the child to jump and even less for his anger to appear. "Who are you? Go away, leave me alone!" he said before hiding his face. The child had taken small solace under a tree, and even then there were no shadows to comfort him from the blazing sun. Yet the new person who had arrived somehow managed to block the sun from his face, making him grateful for just a second. However, he didn't want to thank that person—he was mad at his dad and the big-nose lady and everything that stank in the world. Also, why should he let a stranger see him cry? If people saw him crying, they would laugh at him.

"Have you been crying? Is something wrong?"

He got up very quickly, using his hand to wipe the tears. He tried to make sure his voice wouldn't betray him. "Why would I?! I am no weakling, I am strong! Stronger than my father. And I will become way better than him, I will become a knight so no one will scold me ever again or get angry with me! *And* I will play whenever I want!" The boy bit his lip, for the tears were coming again. All the frustration, the sadness, and the anger were all mixed in a very unpleasant feeling and worst of all, in front of a stranger. Others would know he was a weakling and that his life stank worse than horses and he would get scolded again for no reason because they stank. Just like his dad. And the lady with the big nose.

"You will become a knight?"

For the first time since the stranger had appeared he paid more attention to that voice, noticing the excitement and joy in their words. He managed to give a side glance, more to confirm if there was any laughter or pointing fingers yet he only saw a girl looking at him. She had very long hair. The boy sniffed, blocking the view of his face once again. "Of course I will. I will become a very strong knight. And I will never set my feet in a stable ever again or smell the horses. I will have my own horse and his name will be Lyon because he will be the best horse ever!"

The boy did not even know why he was talking so much to the stranger. Maybe it was something in her voice or the fact that he didn't want others to think he was a weepy weakling who hid in the trees and cried all day because his life stank. But it could be because he had liked her voice.

"*Really*?! Then we can be friends!"

He finally looked over to the girl, his eyebrows frowned. She was dressed nicer than him and there was also a sweet fragrance coming from her, which meant her life didn't stink like his. Why would she want to be friends with someone like him? Probably to make fun and point at him later. His life was not fair at all.

"Why would I want to be friends with you?! I already said I will become a strong knight; I won't have time to play with others."

The girl smiled and got very close to him, so close she was actually whispering in his ear, making him feel something weird and warm inside. It was weird—he was not that angry anymore. But that girl was odd. She was really, really weird.

Maybe the others made fun and pointed at her, so that's why she went to talk to him. Maybe he *could* play with her.

"That's fine. I'm going to be a knight too." The way she told him, whispering her words with such secrecy and excitement, it was as if the girl was sharing with him her darkest secret. Something that would make a lot of people mad at her and scold her. The boy widened his eyes, turning his head just enough so he could stare at her. She had green eyes, a cinnamon hair and he could swear that for a moment her eyes glowed and he thought that it was so pretty. She was kind of pretty. Well, looking closely, she was very pretty, but he wouldn't say something like that to get scolded again.

"How will you become a knight? People say it's actually really hard, you know." Somehow those were the only words he could manage to say that would make him seem smart. Or at least that were his thoughts. His foot tried to take a step back, however the rest of his body stood still as if he could not get away from her. The girl let out a devious laugh, stepping aside and reaching her hand toward the skies.

"If it is my dream, I will fight and reach for it!" She then mimicked a sword fight, ducking and slashing invisible creatures that maybe only someone like her could see. "Even if I shall need to slay a hoard of demons, nothing will stand in my way to become an Orphys Knight! I will be the Order's next leader, you know?"

She said that in such a natural way, like a simple fact that everyone knew. Even if the boy thought that girl was weird and wore fancier clothes than him, he believed her. He knew she was saying the truth. Although he knew demons weren't real. "How will you become the leader? I heard only the strongest knights can make it."

She suddenly stopped, lowering her invisible sword while gazing at him with an odd expression. "Then I will just have to become the strongest knight." She then grinned, a joyful glow passing through her eyes as she closed the small distance between them and held his hands. The boy was taken aback, almost pulling his arms out of her reach, however his heart was beating louder than his thoughts and he could barely hear anything inside his head. His hands were sweaty. "I know!

Let's become the strongest knights together! That way, we can be friends *and* be the Order's leader together!"

"I-why, why would I want to be friends with someone like you?" The boy could actually feel his face burn and the sweat on his hands, still trying to look smart with the best answers he could think of, yet every time he opened his mouth to talk back he was not even sure of what he was saying. The girl's shoulders dropped, the joy in her green eyes fading as it took away their glow.

"You don't want to be my friend?"

The boy was confused.

All he could do was stare at her while glancing at her blue dress. It was so pretty, he could see the small stars embroidered in very dark red all over the dress's skirt. She had to be at least some cousin of an important person, but he was a nobody. Why would *she* want to be friends with him? Maybe to order him around and then complain to her parents how he wasn't doing what he was told so that the big-nose lady would scold him again and then make fun of him.

Or maybe...

She could be his first friend ever. The girl looked younger than him so maybe he could become a Knight first and be so incredible she would get jealous of him afterward and say how he was far smarter than anyone else she knew. Maybe being her friend wouldn't stink. And also, seeing her face like that made him feel something weird in his chest. He felt somehow guilty and...sad.

"I-it's not like I said I didn't want! I only asked—"

"Great! We are friends now!" And then she jumped and hugged him, her head barely reaching his chest. He felt hot all over, his heart beating so hard the boy thought for a second he would die. Wait, was he dying? No, that wouldn't make sense. Only grown people died like that; he was still too small.

Was his heart dying?

There were some shouts coming from the castle far ahead. They were just outside its walls after all. The boy wasn't mad enough to wander too far. The girl looked over her shoulder with a troubled expression.

"I have to go now. Otherwise, I will get into trouble." She looked back once more before running away, smiling as her green eyes glowed. And it was all so pretty. "Let's meet here again, tomorrow at Wake! Until then!"

And just like that, she was gone.

It was only after he walked all the way back into the stables and then back into his room, when he laid on his bed still in a daze, that he remembered...

He didn't ask her name.

Promises of The Wind

Wake of Day - Dawn Star, Haste Mountains

"Are you sure, Kayden? You know that once chosen, you cannot change their path."

"I'm certain, Orion."

Dorian opened the door, trying to control the guilt that grew in him as he heard Kayden's words before entering. "Forgive me, my lady. I heard you called for me."

Her lines softened for a brief moment before her muscles tensed again. "Yes. There is something that must be discussed at once. The others shall arrive soon."

Dorian walked toward her, giving a small nod toward the mage. Orion simply held his teacup higher before finishing the tea, acknowledging him, setting it aside right after. "It may not be simple to convince the others, Kayden."

"I am aware." The words left her mouth in whispers.

The Ward was still confused about what his princess would address. He took a glance toward the opened map on the table, a wind reaching his neck and sending a chill down his spine. He grabbed the sword's hilt stronger. Orion's words to his princess still echoed in his head, the tone in his voice something that shifted the air, made it colder and sharper. He didn't want to know the promises they held.

It took a few minutes for the two Knights to arrive, however one entered the room with his mouth first.

"A great Wake to you, dear leader! Tell me, would you happen to know where I could find a post here? I heard some knights talking about it. I wish to send some letters to my old employer, give him some news about why I am never returning."

Bash chuckled, turning his gaze toward Kayden, the mage, and Dorian, his smile quickly fading from his face. "Oh my, did anyone die?"

"I believe you called, Lady Faeryl," the Argyris spoke as he stood a few meters away from Kayden and the table. The Knight Bash chose to sit, sparing a few of his seconds to gaze toward the counselor. Dorian wished the mage was not present in that room, as if that would make the problems go away, make his lady joyful again. Yet there was no warmth in Kayden's eyes.

"This is Carnarbur's counselor and licensed mage, Orion. He has brought to my attention two pieces of information that may prove to be keys to prevent the dark future that awaits us."

Bash raised his eyebrows toward Orion while the Argyris barely moved.

"Licensed mage?"

"I know who he is." They spoke at the same time, yet only one continued, "Tell us, then, perhaps in this way my role within this poor organization will not present itself to be so meaningless and wasteful."

Dorian took a deep breath, keeping his emotions under control. His place was behind his lady.

Kayden's following words were spoken with grace. Dorian felt as if the woman was trying to convince the men with her voice alone. "First, I would like to announce that we will be holding new tournaments across the kingdoms to whoever may wish to join the Divine Order. This means we may see an increase in our number soon, hopefully."

The Argyris seemed unimpressed at best, his blue gaze hinting his annoyance. "And what of the news brought by Carnarbur's counselor?"

Dorian felt the air around his lady still, losing its warmth and strength. Yet it lasted only a couple of seconds, the feeling gone as soon as she continued to speak.

"To ensure we will have a chance, all Ancient dragons must be united. After Nähsur's battle, most of those who survived chose resting places so they could regain their strength. We must find the Ancients in those places in order to connect them with their Knights since there is no way for us to know what makes an Ancient choose their Knight. Each dragon possesses their own...requirements. Antrühriel was the one who warned me about you two, since both Vührähkam and Amträhfar were awakened together with her and they communicated their will."

"How delightful." There was not even an ounce of joy or warmth in the nobleman's words.

"However, for the others, I am completely blind." Did the others notice how her voice trembled with those last words or only Dorian could see her lips shaking? Did that mean that even the Divines would not aid his lady with this quest, that her needs would once again be left aside for Their own will and agenda? "That being said, by reuniting all seven remaining Orphys Knights and their Ancients, we might have a chance."

The nobleman laughed with a cynical smile, crossing his arms. "We *might* have a chance, you say?"

Dorian glanced toward the younger Knight, his face becoming even paler with lost eyes. He tried to ignore the faint sounds within the wind, a premonition he didn't wish to know.

Kayden's voice became stronger, a hint of anger in her words. "Yes. *Might.* I hope you did not forget what we saw, Leander Argyris, as I also hope you do not believe you could stop something on that scale with your abilities alone."

The man's voice became a bit harsher, a certain intensity appearing in his words. "I hope you at least called us here because you know their locations, otherwise I have no use for this information at the moment."

The little mage, Dorian noticed, was drinking another cup of tea.

"Thanks to Orion, we know the location of one of them." Kayden's words were filled with confidence and assertiveness. However, the Ward knew for a fact that Orion was not the one who shared the location.

"Then send your other Knight on this mission, alongside the Red Knight you seem so friendly with. I don't see why you would need my intervention."

Bash's eyes lightened up a bit when he was mentioned, however Kayden stared at Leander with a fierce conviction, something that made her gaze burn. Dorian felt his heart racing against his will, something unsettling growing inside him.

"This dragon is guarding the Sacred Sword of Three Thousand Soldiers." The moment those words left Kayden's lips, the air around them changed.

Bash appeared to be even more confused, while Dorian saw all color being drawn from the Argyris as pure shock filled his eyes. The Ward also recognized that name, his heart beating faster and faster against his chest. What was Kayden planning?

Even though the Argyris smiled, there was a unique sharpness within his voice, "You can't possibly know the Sword's location. My family has been searching for its whereabouts *for years*! We have never found *anything* related to it, only fake rumors and silly songs pointing toward wrong directions." Anger burned the man's words, his eyes bright and hostile.

Dorian took two steps forward, hand on his sword, yet Kayden touched his shoulder.

"I suppose your family did not possess Ancient creatures aiding them on their blessed quest; isn't that so, Leander Argyris? Are you that surprised that it took an Ancient to find another?" she asked with a smirk, one of her fingers pointing at the map.

Dorian felt the chill again, his body shaking from the inside as he looked at the map. And he was not the only one.

"By Säh's hidden pockets, what sneaky little bastards those fellows can be," Bash whispered almost to himself, his eyes widening as he saw where his leader was pointing. "Are you sure you are pointing right, princess? I mean, sometimes maps can be devious little things." Bash's voice was nervous and anxious, yet Leander's reaction was more of the same.

"That is *impossible*. My family has been to the White Mountains more times than I can count and there was never any hint about the Sacred Sword there, much less Ancient creatures." The silver necklace that held the Argyris emblem shone with an eerie glow, reflecting the fireplace's light. For a second, it almost seemed alive.

"The White Mountains cover more than Raevich's borders. I highly doubt they explored its whole extension during your expeditions. Above all else—"

"You got no *magic*, handsome." The voice surprised Dorian yet it appeared to have surprised the Argyris the most. A woman stood by the fireplace, her long hair loose apart from a few braids. She wore dark clothes yet even Dorian was shaken by the fact that he had not noticed her at all.

The noble kept his gaze on the woman, his face a twist of anger and perplexity.

Orion's voice reached them suddenly, his teacup empty. "This is Saranm, my apprentice. And she speaks the truth—only someone with good eight senses could feel the presence of the Sacred Sword or an Ancient."

The woman glanced to Leander, her eyes calm and her smile inviting. "And sadly our mighty warrior has no talent, his core is so shallow I wonder if one could even dip their toes inside."

"Saranm possesses one of the greatest eight senses I have ever seen. She can read and track auras and energies with ease." Orion's words were almost far away as the air around the Argyris shifted and became more aggressive, denser.

"Pardon me, dear leader, let me get the reasoning right. There's no grannels unless we get someone with a great aura sense to be a flesh-and-bones, breathing compass. Have I got it right?" Bash suddenly spoke, his tone anxious and doubtful.

Grannels?

The Argyris scoffed, a vein pulsing in his forehead while Bash shot him a dirty look before speaking again when no one replied. "No grannels as in, there are no guarantees we get the golden treasure unless we got a mage. Is that right?"

The younger Knight's speech confused him.

"Yes, Bash, you are correct. In order to find the dragon and the Sword they are guarding we need someone with good arcane senses. Which is why—"

"No."

Leander's word was so strong, so final, it made not only Dorian but everyone in that room look at him.

"What do you mean?"

Before Kayden had even finished her question the words were already leaving the Argyris's mouth. "It is not going to happen, *leader*. You want me to go to the White Mountains alongside *her?* No. Find someone else to do this job for you."

A wind barged through the window, the air spinning and circulating between them. Orion was the only one who was unfazed. Dorian already felt his blood rush in his veins by watching the neglect on the Argyris's face. Yet the Ward could not stop his eyes from locking on his lady, the wind even colder and stronger around her as if she was dominating it.

"You don't have the word here, Leander Argyris, to decide if anything will happen or not. Your role is to obey and respect my orders. You said so yourself—you have already been to the White Mountains, therefore you must know how to survive and venture their trails better than any of us."

The man clenched his jaw. "I am sure a person such as yourself could—"

"A person such as myself cannot waste her time on a quest that her underlings can perfectly accomplish on their own. I am the leader of a whole organization that is not supported either by you or your family. I have knights I must care for, duties that go beyond your responsibilities as an Orphys Knight, and a battle to worry about; I do *not* have time to concern myself about you not wanting to perform your role accordingly."

"I could teach Bash how to—"

"Bash will go on a different quest, alone." Kayden elevated her voice and Dorian felt her words like lightning, a tempest being created above them.

"Wait, Bash will what now?" The younger Knight's words were ignored completely, almost making Dorian pity him.

The Argyris eyed Kayden with both hands down, clenching his fists as he held his breath. "Does our leader already know us so well to send us on missions accordingly to our skills? If I am not mistaken, we have known each other for mere days."

"Kayden, what is the Bash-solo-quest thing again?"

"Do I need to, Leander? How many lives were already lost to the White Mountains perils? You may teach Bash how to walk backward on those mountains, but there is no guarantee his physique is prepared for their environment as yours would be, especially after spending months training on those grounds yourself."

As the Ward watched their argument, the other man took two steps back while the fire that burned in his eyes was replaced by something distant, a bafflement.

"How do *you* know that?" There was no more strength in the Argyris's voice, the words getting lost on the wind that still circulated them with its cold, lonely air.

However, even weakened, Dorian could almost taste the dark lurking on the Argyris's tone.

"Is it not a tradition in your family?" Even Dorian was surprised by his princess's words, unsure if she knew that due to her training as a royal or due to her cursed Sight. "As soon as the children complete their eleventh year they are sent to the White Mountains for three months. It's quite an old tradition that already raised quite a few controversies among other Houses, which is why it was abolished in recent years. However, it is known to me you completed this tradition nonetheless."

Leander Argyris froze. After a few more soundless seconds, the wind dissipated as if it had never been there, leaving them to the warmth and crackling noises of the fireplace.

Yet the silence was quickly broken. "So, just to be certain princess, am *I* the Bash you were referring to? Is there no other knight here who shares my name?"

The princess sighed, averting her eyes toward the map. "I shall explain the details to you in a moment, Bash."

Kayden placed both hands on the stone table and only then did Dorian notice she looked somewhat thinner and a few of her nails were broken. He felt a dark cold embrace his heart.

"I want to send you on your missions as soon as possible. I believe one month should be enough to prepare, yet more time could be provided if needed. Orion gave permission for Saranm to accompany you, Leander, so you may teach her whatever you can about the White Mountains. There is a lot at stake, so I hope you will all give your best. You are dismissed. Bash, you can stay."

The Argyris said nothing more and looked at no one else. He simply turned his back and left the room.

A few seconds later, Saranm approached them to stand beside Orion. The mage slid down the chair, not looking at them as he spoke.

"I will stay here for a few more days. I trust Saranm as I would trust my king, so you can believe she will do well at your side, Kayden." Something in the child's voice seemed odd, yet Dorian did not know what. Saranm gave Kayden a polite bow before following Orion, both leaving the room. The counselor eyed Dorian for a brief moment right before closing the door.

He saw how exhausted Kayden was, when it had been less than a couple of hours since the sun had awakened, and Dorian *knew*—he just knew—the princess needed to rest. The Ward felt his heart shrink inside his chest when he realized not only Kayden looked tired, but it was almost as if she had lost strength. Why did she look so exhausted so early in the Wake? He saw a shiver pass through her, a faint glow in her eyes right before she focused her attention toward the younger Knight and his heart ached. Should he curse the Divines himself to receive Their "blessing" or should he try to take Kayden's to ease her pain?

"Let us talk about your mission now, Bash."

Dorian stood behind her, his hand hurting from grasping the sword too hard.

There were so many things he desired to do for her, so many things he wished he could give her. Could he still do those things where he stood?

Could he?

The Mighty Lion

Bless of Day - Silver Grounds, Haste Mountains

Few things carried a fate worse than Death's kiss.

"Again."

He once believed he knew most of those things, especially by carrying his family's name.

"Again."

Yet at that moment Leander had realized how foolish he had been, for what could be worse for a warrior than to teach incompetent, uninspired fools to use weapons that were clearly far too advanced for their capabilities.

"Again!"

Lady Faeryl had ordered him to train the newest recruits, since with the tournaments the Order would gain more recruits and with that, they needed more capable, skilled knights. Her reasoning for that ridiculous task was beyond him especially when he was already dividing his time with the mage's apprentice and his own swordsmanship. How could three weeks be enough to teach anyone how to survive on those mountains when the best teacher was the White Mountains themselves? It was an entirely different ecosystem, as if it was another world inserted into their reality; any person who ventured through those mountains without understanding them first *never* came back. Not even the House Argyris would conduct their famous hunts on those cursed mountains and the coming-of-age ceremony which was once performed on the White Mountains had been abolished by every head of the family. With the exception of his father.

"For all the Divines, how could any of you even dream of becoming a knight without even wielding a proper weapon is beyond me. Again!"

The knights were already out of breath, their arms shaking after holding and swinging the swords after a few hours. How could an organization focused on training and molding the best soldiers be willing to accept those types of people? No desire to learn, no energy to spend, no soul to give. Worthless, all of them. Even their armor was made of poor quality leather, pieces that should've been replaced years ago. It covered the knights' chests, arms, knees, elbows—a poor armor set for training, regardless.

Worse of it all, he had seen in their storage room the "decent" armor sets with rusted gauntlets and chainmail, broken helmets and smashed breastplates. This made Leander think the *real* reason the Order made competitors bring their own armor and weapons; they couldn't even take a decent care of their own.

"So you are an arsehole with everyone, I see."

Leander held his breath, not daring to glance at his side. He knew *what* would be standing there. "I believe I gave you a task," the man managed to speak under his breath.

"A pointless task, love. Writing about the mountains environment is not only tedious, it holds no purpose." The woman was watching the knights fling and move their swords alongside him, her fragrant scent reaching him with no effort, a warm and sweetened perfume. "There are other ways to deal with me than giving me fake tasks, handsome. Other means I can use my time and skills as well." Again, her words were filled with mischief, a devious glow in her eyes reflecting her flirtatious smile.

He clenched his jaw. "I do not need fake tasks to get rid of someone like yourself."

"You mean a *mage?*"

That time Leander *did* glance straight at her, seeing the two dark braids falling way below her waist, her body covered with layers of fabric. The woman met his eyes, something passing through them like a wave, something Leander did not know what it was, and it made his skin burn and crawl.

"I mean immoral, cheap tricksters that only know how to win their battles with cheats."

Those words made the woman smile, a laugh escaping her lips like a soft bell. "Cheap tricksters, you say? You surprise me, warrior, for someone with so many resources and such a nice home I would've thought your mind wouldn't be as ignorant."

"I do not need to be of an ignorant mind when my eyes have seen enough. If you have nothing more to add, then you may leave and finish your tasks since our time is running short."

Leander did not look back to see if the woman had left or not. The Argyris continued to look at the knights with arms crossed, most of them continuing to embarrass themselves with their stances. Such a waste of time.

"Sir Argyris, my lord—if I may speak my words?" One of the knights held the sword in the air, his gaze staring at his feet.

"Speak."

The knight trembled before he could say his words once more. "May we take a small interval? Most of us are not used to this kind of training. Could we take a short break to have some water and regain our strength?"

Leander was not even annoyed—he should expect no less from *Order knights*. At that point Leander himself was tired of watching them as a sitter, trying to teach toddlers how to behave like adults. "Go at once. If you do not have the will or the determination to continue, do not even bother to return."

He saw relief spreading through their faces as they lowered their weapons and rushed away from him. The Argyris was not used to training people apart from his own kin, taking the place of his deceased uncle. His own father would often watch as Leander trained and taught the small ones, after they had passed their coming-of-age ceremony. To train an Argyris was not the same as to train a group of aimless knights who lacked motive and purpose, passion and strength. Everything was wasteful. Leander doubted even half would return to the lessons.

The man walked toward the headless training dolls, his body heating up as that memory came to the surface, taking out his sword to continue his own training.

One that would bring results, one that was actually demanding. At least, that was what he was planning to do.

"—don't even know the oath?! Now, now, that can't be true. Carlton, he does not know the steps, not even the oath!"

"I told you already—I am new! And I was quitting the Order before all of this happened, so—"

"We are new and we have never seen you before. Then you arrive suddenly, become a new Knight with a demonic pet, and get to be above us?"

"It's *quite* unfair."

Leander *was* trying to continue his own training, however he kept hearing nonsense from foolish beings. He glanced to the side, watching as a small group of knights surrounded the younger man Bash. Although, to Leander's eyes, he only saw children.

"I think is unfair that you were born with a crooked nose and you with a dying voice, yet even then facts won't change that easily, will they?" The Knight Bash spoke, his hands resting on the sword's handle with the tip still sunk in the ground. The others surrounding him walked even closer, as if they held a belief that they were threatening in any way.

"What, you think you are better than us? With that hair and those eyes?"

"That depends. Better fighter? Don't know. Better-looking? Certainly."

The others were already raising their weapons when his patience to watch that ridiculous play came to an end. Leander's shadow covered the knights and the younger Knight, their eyes widening and trembling when they saw him.

Nothing but *children*.

"Since you all cannot keep your opinions to yourselves, I might as well contribute with my own." Leander watched as they cowered, taking a few steps back while getting away from Bash. Leander pointed his sword at them, noticing the pendants with Säh's mark on each of them apart from the Knight. "You sure must think highly of yourselves for not being able to even hold a sword in a proper stance for longer than ten minutes. Not even that but you four spout foolish words toward someone that not only holds a sword better than you but was not out of breath by the end of my lesson." The Argyris lowered his weapon, locking glares with each one of them, his words filled with disgust. "Know your place if you want to put someone else in theirs."

When none of them moved, he rolled his eyes as the words left his mouth already tired from such a petty discussion.

"Begone now, you lot."

They scattered like insects, walking faster than any dignity would allow. The Knight stared at him with a lost gaze, a loose grip on the sword.

"Thank you," Bash spoke, a voice that seemed far more surprised than it should be.

"There is nothing to be thankful for. We have no time to waste on stupid, pointless arguments. Keep training."

With that, Leander turned his back and returned to where the training dolls were. Why the Knight Bash was there taking his lessons was beyond him. It was probably an order from Lady Faeryl, something related to the boy's own quest. He was certainly better than the rest, yet the Argyris knew the Knight was not skilled at all with a sword.

However, when the break was over and only a few knights returned, Leander was slightly surprised to see Bash among them.

Golden Stars in A Silver Sky

Fall of Night - Woods, Haste Mountains

She could feel the cool breeze against her skin, the warmth of the sun long gone, yet for that moment, her heart was at peace. The princess stared into the vast, dark sky with no thoughts of the Divines or the weight of her decisions. Kayden was simply admiring the night. Once Orion told her that even when the stars seem close together it's only but an illusion, for they are far from reaching each other. Yet they all possessed their own light, their own space to be the brightest in the vast sky. Even if the princess felt stars could become lonely, she envied them for their freedom. They shone and fought to be the most beautiful, even with the moon dominating them all when it was full, yet they did so with pride. At least, that was what Kayden wished for. Proud, bright stars.

A rumbling came from below, almost like a purr, and the princess smiled. "Yes, I also think it's pleasant this way."

The white dragon was resting on the grass with Kayden lying against her body, rumbling as she felt the breeze and the night's energy fill the space. Antrühriel was much like the leader in that sense, to Kayden's surprise. They both longed to appreciate the small beautiful things in a world that carried a weight they both feared to take on their shoulders, yet they had to. Albaron's princess and heir could feel the dragon's peace overlying all worries and fear that loomed over them both. Even if forced, it was good to be able to enjoy a small moment such as that. No Divines, no war, no Death.

Only stars shining as bright as the sun.

Kayden was smiling before she heard his voice, his feelings rushing through her like gelid and uncertain waves. "I heard your call, princess."

"You may call me by my name, Bash. And yes, I did call you."

After a few moments passed in silence, the Knight shifted in his place while avoiding glancing at her. "F-for what purpose have you called for me, dear leader? If Vührāh said anything against me, let me just say *I'm* the one really trying to make this thing work. He ignores me and even denied to let me ride him! *He* is the one to blame here, I swear on Säh's fingers and toe—"

"Bash." Kayden could sense the rush not only in Bash's words but in his eyes and heart. The young Knight was holding his breath, his eyes at last staring right at Kayden's. Her words were as peaceful as the night, melting the rush inside him with ease and care. "You can sit down. The Ancient Vührähkam was not the reason I called for you."

His movements were cautious even as he sat on the grass, eyes moving to the sides as if he was expecting an ambush of sorts, sitting as far as possible from Antrühriel without standing far away from his leader. Kayden could not help but think it was quite an adorable way for someone like him to react. She wondered if she had ever been like that when she was his age, even if that wasn't long ago...it felt like decades.

"If it is about my mission, your Ward already talked to me and we will meet tomorrow at Wake to—"

"Look at the sky, Bash. What do you see?"

He blinked a few times before complying with her request, although she felt like Bash thought of it as a demand. His words carried the same tone and feelings as his posture. "They must be the most bored glowing bits in the sky, not able to move or do anything at all."

"How so?" she asked, amused.

Bash put both arms on the ground, using them as a support as he looked up toward the sky with a small hint of a smile on his lips. "The moon shifts and the sun goes up and down, yet the stars never really change; they just stay there. That's a tedious way to live."

"I suppose you are also right." Yet Kayden still felt envious, tedious life or not. "Did you ever study the stars, Bash? Their constellations and the stories behind them, as well as the possible influences they might exert over our world?"

Even though Kayden fought her Sight and tried to ignore others' feelings and emotions, it was impossible not to see how the Knight's muscles tensed with her words, his own becoming detached from his heart. "I do not believe I ever had the *opportunity*, like you did, dear leader."

The princess raised her arm, pointing toward one of the brightest stars. It had a bluish tone, a bit different than its fellow kin. "That one, it is called Qirion. It is the star that gave the name to Qirion Island, in Carnarbur. The same goes for its sisters Trymion and Galmion. I always thought it was odd, how Carnarbur's faith is based on the study and power of the celestial realm. They must really believe the Divines came from there."

"I do know how much those Carnarbur folks like their stars, I think it's quite funny actually," Bash said in midst of a laugh, yet his muscles were still rigid.

"Can you see that one, farther on the left? The one with a red hue."

It took a few seconds for the Knight to reply, "Yes, I can see it. Wait, let me guess. *That's* the red star that gave the name to one of the Haste Mountains because those Orphys Knights couldn't really think of anything else at the time?"

The white dragon beside Kayden opened her eyes, looking toward her Knight. Antrühriel knew what Kayden was doing and the story the leader was about to share and she felt sad, as if the dragon had been there at the time it all happened. When Kayden thought about it, that could be since the dragon must have been alive when the Divine Order was formed.

"That star is called King's Lament. It is one of the stars that makes the Orphys constellation. If you connect the three stars close to it, in a T, and the others ahead, it almost looks like a sword. Can you see it?"

Bash nodded as he squinted his eyes, his words carrying more lies than his eyes. "Oh yes, I see them. A pretty sharp sword, if I might add. Maybe it is more powerful than the Thousand... Something that proud lion will try to find."

"The King's Lament received its name after the massacre that took the lives of all firstborns, before the Divine Order was created. It represents all the blood that was shed, all the pain and grief brought by humans' pettiness and greed. That is why it's the only red star in the constellation and the reason why King's Lament represents the sword's tip—it's where blood was shed."

Bash fell silent, his gaze locked onto the red star with something that almost looked like sorrow. "You nobles sure like to dramatize your war stories. Not only do we have Memorial Day to honor the dead, you also gave names to stars to remember it? You are odd."

Kayden sometimes thought it was weird as well. Why keep trying to remember the past? She would always hear and feel the ones who perished even more strongly on Memorial Day—feel their regret, their pain, and their deaths as her own. It was traumatic most times, something she was relieved once it passed, and days she dreaded when it came closer. Yet Kayden knew why it was important. "When the Order was created, they did not have a name for it apart from being the Divine Order, nor did the Knights have a name. Yet their leader was looking at the sky once and saw the King's Lament. He saw the tip of the sword and they gave the constellation a name. They decided to be not the sword that killed and brought grief, but one that protected and honored the ones who had received Death's cold kiss. Hence, the Divine Order of the Orphys Knights was officially created. A place to bring hope and unity, to save Tërnya from all that was evil and corrupt."

Kayden turned to face Bash, her smile reflecting the pain in her own eyes while her words carried not only the memories from the dead but their feelings.

"The Order was once a place like this and I want to bring its true purpose back. Not a sword that kills and taints but one who saves and protects. It doesn't matter who is the one holding the sword, what matters is with what purpose they hold it. Which is why I ask you now, Bash—when you hold your sword, what is your resolve behind it?"

It took a long time for Bash to open his mouth, his gaze staring deep into Kayden's eyes as if it was searching for something. "I don't really know."

Kayden knew then that Bash spoke the truth. "Then this is my official order to you, as your leader."

Bash's expression became colder, his eyes sharper and darker. It was as if he knew what she was going to ask him, yet the young Knight couldn't be more wrong.

"I want you to find your own reason to raise the sword. Not the Order's, not the Ancient's, not mine. *Yours*. Once you find a purpose to raise your weapon and fight, we will come here and watch the stars again. Maybe by then, the stars may have found a more thrilling way to live."

Something changed in Bash, the way his lines softened and his eyes reflected the stars' glow. The young man nodded once before clearing his throat and averting his gaze back to the sky. "By the way, could you try to reason with Vühräh? I really want to get along with him, but he's so stubborn and arrogant. I need to get along with him if I want to be a good knight, right?"

Kayden looked over to the stars and the moon, silver light spreading across the whole night sky. Her own eyes shone green, shivers going up and down her spine, staring at the free, bright dots that filled the night with beauty and hope. She heard Death's whispers and felt the Divines' powerful will colliding against hers with images of a future whose sole purpose seemed to mock her choices and struggles as it showed her more of the same, as if all she was trying to do was futile and hopeless. As if they were all fated to die and watch their entire world perish unless she followed Their will.

"I will see what I can do." Her words became a weak whisper, lost in the space. Kayden felt as the white dragon's peaceful emotions dimmed and disappeared, the only thing remaining in the Ancient creature and her Knight being a solid, raw feeling of desperation. "We shall train more tomorrow, all of us."

The night was, at least, only cold and ruthless.

Chapter VIII

Journal Entry, Autumn

Haze

Another sleepless night. After counting all my possessions twice, I thought it was better to go for another stroll through the halls. It has been too long since I walked Red Star so early in the day. If I closed my eyes, I could recall my first days as a rankless knight, alongside Clarice, Ritta, Felicia, Sean, and all the others. We were so happy as we went up in the ranks, becoming Ruby knights, then squad captains. Alex was the leader back then; he filled us with hope and excitement of being part of something this big.

Now Alex is dead and all the others are missing. I keep trying to figure out when it all went so wrong yet I remain with no answer. Perhaps the Divines know, yet I wonder if they would answer me.

I need to find Clarice and the others. Never in my wildest dreams would I have thought that our current leader would honor me so as to appoint me as a high commander. If I had stayed a unit captain I could still assemble a search party for this quest. This only shows how much trust Kayden has put on my shoulders, and that is not a trust I could ever break.

I managed to get two other knights to help me with the search for I do not wish to trouble Princess Kayden by taking more knights when our numbers are scarce. I think we will start with Carnarbur and try to reach Ritta and Felicia. The twins knew the arcane arts well enough to become licensed mages, but they simply didn't have enough funds to pay for their studies. If we manage to find them, Ritta and Felicia may help us find the others with the arts' aid.

Please, for all Divines, may they all be well.

Bound By Blood

Haze of Dawn - Silver Grounds, Haste Mountains

It was certainly...odd. Were royals from Albaron that much different from those of Raevich? Well, that wouldn't make much sense since he knew stories of those that carried the *mighty noble blood* from Albaron, and none were very pleasant.

Still, it was odd, wasn't it?

Bash was not someone who often mistook people's characters, at least not by the times he had confirmed them, yet Albaron's heir was beginning to puzzle him. He wondered if it was a decoy, but it wouldn't make any sense. Why would a princess want to trick him? He already had to do anything she ordered! His new leader could be saying such pretty things to him to gain his trust, yet again, for what purpose? She ruled over him *and* Bash couldn't even bail if he wanted to—and by Säh he *wanted* to—for there was not only one winged demon but three of them. Why would he waste his life like *that?* All to make a point? He wasn't an ill-minded bastard, just a regular one.

Divines and all, nothing made sense anymore. If royals suddenly turned nice, who was Bash supposed to loathe and hate?

When the young knight opened the door, his answer was right in front of him. And it looked mad.

"By Säh, you won't even give yourself spare time during the Haze?"

Leander Argyris ignored Bash's words, not even bothering to glance the other way. That was more likely. *That* made sense.

Bash didn't want to train with swords—he was not fond of them. He felt clumsy whenever he held one in his hands—it felt big and heavy. Maybe something more like a bow, knives, things he could put here and there and make a run for it in case things turned sour. He *could* run with a sword, yet for him it was something bothersome to do. Also, people used swords to fight in the front. First ones to get hit, first ones to get killed. Bash would rather stay in the back line when the big demon war happened, maybe even provide some moral support. He wouldn't be much more help in any case. His dragon could go on the killing spree to content himself, since *someone* wouldn't let Bash ride him.

CHILD.

Bash had decided to ignore Vühräh until he learned to be gentler with his Knight. Bash still had feelings after all.

"You can train with a short sword instead. It may fit you better."

Leander's words reached him from afar, the man never stopping to hit the training dummies with a furious glare. Poor dummies. Bash then looked at the sword he was about to take, the same most knights usually used when training and sparring. Was the proud lion trying to give him advice, or was he simply mocking him? He couldn't decide so Bash tried to confirm. "Why? I can use a long sword as well, also isn't that why I'm taking your lessons?"

The noble turned his cold blue eyes toward Bash for no more than one second before sinking his sword into the dummy's torso. "Do what you will."

Huh.

That was quite the uninspired reply. He could try to experiment a bit with the short sword, however, maybe then the man would criticize him for "not being a proper knight in handling a petty sword such as that flimsy one".

Yet Leander Argyris remained silent for the next few hours. Even when the Wake's light poured into the training grounds and more knights arrived, the noble had no more remarks about Bash's weapon of choice. And he hated to admit it, but it felt better to hold a short sword. He had stretched before beginning the warrior movements Leander had taught them the day before and damned be Säh's curses, the weapon felt a lot more comfortable than the ones he had held previously. It was funny how Bash still felt like a child no matter what sword he held.

YOU ARE CH—

Oh please, don't start.

The young knight moved to one of the dummies, hitting it from the side as he dashed from left to right to test his movements with the new weapon. Felt nice, good even. Though the wood was quite hard and it made his wrist hurt from the impact on every blow. He tried to jump and hit the dummy's shoulder, yet he ended up striking the head instead. Darn, he didn't want that. The sword was stuck.

"An Orphys Knight who cannot win against a dummy." The voice came from behind him, someone he did not recognize at first.

"From a Raevich *Knight,* with such dark hair, could we expect less?" Those words shared the contempt and disgust of the other one, the same group of Raevich knights surrounding him once again.

Bash smiled as he tried to remove the sword from the wood. Yes, that was more likely. The compliments he was used to hear, almost like beautiful melodies to his ears. He didn't even need to see Säh's pendants hanging from their collars to know not only were they from North Raevich; they had been quite blind to believe they were so much better than him just by having lighter hair. Apparently, Bash would have to show his amazing skills to make those snotches eat their words and prove how someone as low as himself was also worthy of a Knight's title.

Yet he didn't feel like going for the trouble. As long as they didn't bother him so, Bash was fine with laughter. He loved a good joke.

"Having some difficulties with a short sword?" Knight number one spoke.

"You still don't know the oath, do you?" That was knight number two. For some reason, Bash's eyes searched the room for Leander, not finding the tall Argyris anywhere. So that was why they found their bright courage yet again.

"I spent the entire day training with our leader. You know, the princess. She did not ask me anything about it—guess she thought it wasn't important. Maybe you all could remind her; she might have forgotten."

The three knights laughed at Bash's words, closing around him as the third knight spoke. "This dark-haired one must truly believe that he got the best out of us because he got *promoted* by chance." Bash also had a pet dragon; one could not forget that.

"You forgot the place you came from, didn't you? East Raevich gutter."

"Oh wait, now that you mention... Weren't we neighbors once?" Bash ducked the punch seconds before it hit his face, taking a couple of steps back. The second knight's fist had punched the wood dummy instead, his face a twist of pain and pure anger. Bash tried to contain the laughter in his heart. "Please, gentlemen, I thought we were all brothers under Säh's vigilant eyes."

"Not people like yourself." Number two said with burning words, the hate filling every inch of his sentence. "Those who do not carry the Divines' blessings in their blood are not worthy of being an Orphys Knight." Funny how the Divines blessed only noble and royal blood, maybe it tasted better to Them.

"You should kill yourself and give the position to someone else, that's the least you can do. Don't embarrass yourself more than that."

He clenched his fists, feeling his blood boil and rush inside his veins. For a second Bash almost thought he felt something, a hunger that did not quite belong to him. Yet the dragon remained quiet, away from his mind's touch as he simply watched the situation unfold from Bash's sight. "Wait, are we allowed to kill people here? Why did no one tell me bef—"

One knight took out his sword while Bash spoke, grazing his uncovered arm. The blade was sharp enough to cut his flesh to draw blood yet not much more than that. Bash felt the Ancient's power pulsing inside him, from some place he did not dare to reach. "Watch your mouth, rat. You already know your proper place, so own it."

Number one whispered close to Bash's ear, still holding the sword in his hand. Bash reached for his waist only to find it empty, feeling both relief and frustration as he locked eyes on the stuck sword a second later.

"Could you please step aside? Some might think you are trying to court me." It was not what he said but the way he said it that made all three knights step back, something that crawled inside his words and eyes a few moments before

Leander came back to the training grounds. The three of them exchanged a few looks before leaving Bash alone at last. After a few pushes, the young knight was finally able to recover the short sword, right on time for the beginning of the day's lesson.

There were fewer knights present for Leander's class, the man glancing over them all before opening his mouth. Somehow, Bash felt he was on a battlefield just by staring at the Argyris. "Today I will train your aim, your speed, and your resistance."

Everything, then.

"Sir Bash, come here."

Bash cursed the lion many times in his head as he walked toward the front. He *just* had gotten those snotches to let him be, yet *Lord Argyris sire* dragged the attention to him yet *again*. Was he doing it on purpose? Oh, the *nerve*!

Leander did not even bother to look at him, the man simply glanced toward the training dummy in the back, behind the knights that stood on the last line. "Attack it with your sword."

Bash blinked. "Me?"

The Argyris held his breath, his eyes lowering until they locked on Bash's. "Didn't I call for you?"

But why me?

Bash shifted the weapon in his hands, the handle feeling uncomfortable within his grasp. "I can attack in any way I want?"

Leander's eyes changed a bit then, as if their focus changed, a faint sparkle behind them. "Do whatever you will."

Bash looked at the training dummy. There were only three lines, the knights were also very far apart from each other. The distance wasn't that great either, that short sword was bothersome, but...yes, it would work.

The smile touched his lips before Bash could even think, his hand tingling as he shifted his position. The cut on his arm burned yet it made his grip stronger and his senses sharper. As he threw the sword, the weapon shot through the air in one quick motion, its blade grazing the cheek of one particular knight, the one who had drawn his blood.

They were officially cut-brothers.

The knight touched his cheek, looking back toward the dummy that had, at that moment, the short sword sunk into its chest. The knight's eyes widened and his face flustered as he shouted and pointed at Bash. "You *bloody bastard*—you could have killed me if it missed!"

"Did he miss?" Leander replied.

The knight stumbled on his words before answering back, "He-he didn't, but if he had I would have—"

"Then you would have been the fool who couldn't dodge and who died by underestimating his opponent. A true warrior does not wait for their enemy to miss, they fight to win. There is no true warrior in this pitiful Order yet the least you could do is try to behave accordingly." Leander's words were carried by nothing but an unforgiving and raw voice, making every single knight in line lower their heads to avert the Argyris's gaze. "Go back to your spot."

It took a few seconds for Bash to realize Leander was speaking to him, walking right behind his newly found brother whose eyes were too busy opening a hole in the ground for them to stare and fume at Bash. The young knight had no idea why Leander had called him and aided him to win so grandiosely the support of the other knights. It was something as odd as Princess Kayden calling him so they could simply watch the night sky. It was not something Bash could understand. Yet he did know something—he knew they were wrong about one detail regarding his throw.

He *had* missed.

Maybe Vühräh was right about him being a child.

A Warrior's Honor

Midday - Woods, Haste Mountains

PRINCESS REQUIRES KNIGHTS. TRAINING. TOLL.

He clenched his jaw, flexing his hands as he took a deep breath.

Do you reckon we still need to train together, beast?

HUMAN CANNOT HANDLE POWER YET.

You are the one who prohibits me from reaching it.

HUMAN ONE WHO NOT READY.

He clenched his fists so tight it almost tore his skin apart. *You dare say I am not strong enough?*

HUMAN. NOT. READY.

Leander scoffed, feeling the weight of the medallion around his neck. Was there anything more wasteful than trying to argue with an Ancient creature? How would Leander know himself, if he was ready or not, when the beast would not let him try? Even more, how would he know what he lacked? How to get stronger?

Ridiculous creature. Drove him to make a choice on the cost of his life, forcing *an Argyris* to aid him on a doomed mission, and the dragon would not even treat him as a proper warrior. Ridiculous. Pathetic.

I expect results.

Words from his father's letter burned in his mind, hotter even than Amträhfar's scales. Leander had written a report detailing his intention to recover the Sacred Sword, to be the Argyris to accomplish such an honor. No one in the family would ever forget his name. His father would never again be able to contradict Leander's choices and words for he would have been the one to recover their most treasured relic. Yet that was all his father wrote back, one single sentence carried by his own personal messenger bird. Leander had omitted the quest for the Ancient creature and the Sword's possible location as well as his involvement with a mage's apprentice, since he could not disclose confidential information. He loathed the position yet he was an Orphys Knight all the same. A true warrior honored their ranks and Kayden had already mentioned their actual mission—which was not the Sword—was to be known only by Knights.

Leander struggled if he should communicate this information to his father. Adon Argyris was the head of the family and the one responsible for the last scout party that had failed close to the East Kingdoms' borders. His father had invited Leander on one of the scout missions a few years back, allowing his son to see a side of him Leander did not quite expect. To see how much his father longed to hold the Sacred Sword in his hands, to put it on display on the family's house, and to show it to their ranks as they trained.

And what would he think of Leander, if he were the one to bring the Sacred Sword to their home?

The Argyris's emblem shone against the sunlight, the metal hot against the man's skin and clothes, the sword tied to his waist swinging as he walked. He could hardly find peace on the training grounds anymore, knights making the most blatant mistakes alongside their pitiful quarrels. The younger Knight, however, had surprised him in a way. He was more fit to be an archer rather than a swordsman, so Lady Faeryl insisting that Bash attend Leander's lessons was beyond him. She did not give any impression of being a blind fool on such matters, so what games was she playing? Was Lady Faeryl testing his patience instead?

The man continued with his walk, searching for an ideal space to continue his training. What he truly desired was to find a creature and train his muscles to the perils that awaited them in the White Mountains. A troll would be the perfect opponent yet where to find such a beast so far off their territory? Somehow Leander doubted one could even hunt properly in such isolated woods. To worsen the situation, any medium-sized creature would be gone from the area if they valued their lives, with three Ancient beasts surrounding the woods. The warrior could sense Amträhfar close, his dragon resting in a nest of dead, fallen trees.

Leander was ready to give up and go back to the Haste Mountains when he heard the sound of broken branches. All his senses sharpened, his ears focusing solely in the direction of the noise. His hands grabbed his sword, removing it from its scabbard as Leander walked as soundlessly as possible deeper into the woods. He could feel the breeze prickling against his neck, his heart beating in anticipation. It could be a mountain lynx, maybe even a three-horned boar. They were not uncommon in the area, yet they were becoming a rare sight. Had his luck finally shifted, the Divines and Säh blessing his blade?

When the glade came into view there was no lynx or boar to be seen, however Leander's heart continued to beat just as fast against his chest.

The woman who sat on the rock wore no clothes from the waist up, her long black hair covering her back like a shield. Yet even then Leander saw the symbols inked on her dark skin, going from her shoulders to the tips of her fingers, some following the line of her spine. His heart beat stronger, the air around him still and frozen in time. He felt like an intruder, yet there was no will on his feet to move, his eyes wide and too surprised to be closed. She still had her back to him, her hands passing something wet across her skin, covering her arms and chest.

Suddenly, her muscles tensed, her movements ceasing completely. She kept still for one brief second, returning to normal as the wet cloth went up and down her body.

"I had you for an ignorant brute, not a man carried by perverted thoughts. Should I take this as an invitation?" Her voice held no anger or shame, her words mellow and over-sweetened.

Leander felt his throat dry. "We are not in your private chambers, are we now? I came to *train*."

It should be impossible yet the man could almost see the smile on her lips through her words.

"Does the Divine Order hide dummies in the woods as well? Why, you should have invited me sooner so we could play hide-and-seek." The woman spoke with amusement, a mockery hidden between her words.

He clenched his jaw, chills going down his spine. "I came to try my luck. Find a worthy adversary, a beast to hunt. We will have to do so in the White Mountains, as you should know."

Her laugh echoed through the glaze as her fingers separated her hair and brought it to her chest, exposing her back. Leander immediately averted his gaze, baffled by the woman's lack of decency. A sweet scent reached him before her words did and he *knew* she was doing it on purpose. "Of course, forgive my insolence. I am sorry to be the carrier of such unpleasant news, but you will find no hunt here."

He put his sword away, his feet finally able to move on their own though his heart continued to beat strongly against his chest. "I realize that. You should also return as soon as possible to continue your studies, in case you have forgotten."

"Wait." Leander was already turning back when Saranm's voice managed to halt his steps. "You said you were looking for an adversary."

"Are you trying to imply that someone like yourself is—"

Leander stopped his sentence midway as he turned once again to reply to the woman's ridiculous words only to see her facing him, holding her shirt in her hands. The Argyris felt his face burning as his eyes went for the ground.

"A worthy opponent? But of course."

"A *mage?*" He scoffed. "Never."

"It is unfortunate then, great warrior, for there is no one else here to entertain your foolish desires. That is, unless I can serve you in another way." The words came out as a soft purr, blood rushing inside him as the knots on his hands turned white.

"If you believe I shall indulge myself in your fantasies, you are mistaken."

"Such a pity... I had hopes for this Lull."

The next time his eyes met hers she was fully dressed, her golden eyes null of any malice or ridicule. They felt barren, barely reflecting the empty smile the woman shared with him.

"I shall return to my *studies*, warrior. You may rest assured that I will know the name of every damned rock in those mountains."

Before she could leave the glade, Leander spoke words he was not sure he wished to have spoken. Yet there was something within him that compelled him to. "I was unaware the East Kingdoms marked their people in such ways."

Something flickered in her yellowed eyes. "What do you mean?"

"The symbols on your skin. I've never seen anything alike on your people."

Saranm walked closer to him, standing a few breaths away. Leander sensed Amträhfar as the beast opened his eyes and growled inside his mind.

"You might want to mind your own affairs, warrior. Leave me to my own."

The woman disappeared into the woods, leaving without ever glancing back. Yet what occupied his mind was something else.

KEEP AWAY. DO NOT APPROACH.

The dragon's warning resonated within him, mixing with his own emotions. The Argyris kept staring at the path the woman had taken, uncertain of what he was feeling. In the end, all he was left with were the memories of her imprudence and frivolous attitude. They would go on a mission together to recover the Sacred Sword, a mission in the White Mountains, yet someone like her could not even grasp the importance of such mission. Apparently, her priorities lay elsewhere.

I do not intend to stay anywhere near that woman until our mission starts.

WON'T HUMAN ASK WHY?

I do not need to know your reasons, beast. I have my own.

And they were plenty.

Blessed by The World

Toll of Evening - Woods, Haste Mountains

The three Ancient creatures stood with such presence it would almost seem like the trees were bowing and the wind was courting them, the stream reflecting their mighty figures with no second thoughts. To see one of them was enough to steal the breath and conscience of any living mortal, yet to have more than one dragon staring down at one's eyes was like a powerful, unbending omen. *Death will come to you soon* was what Kayden thought almost by accident as her thoughts wandered lost and amazed by the sight of the three creatures, for no person should be able to live much longer after experiencing an event such as that.

"Why is the counselor here with us?"

It was Leander Argyris's monotone words that forced Kayden back to reality—no, to *a* future. One she feared to face head-on. "Orion believes he can help us harness the Ancients' powers, or at least better explore their source."

Leander spared no glance toward the little counselor, yet the black dragon stared intensely at Orion with his bright yellow eyes. "The mage had better state his matters properly himself." By the man's tone, the leader could see that those words came not from Leander but from the Ancient one.

Something Kayden was grateful for was the fact her Sight could not peer into the bond of her fellow Knights. The Sight would show her people's feelings and pry into their lives and private moments, yet not what went between a dragon and their Knight. The princess feared what might become of her were she ever able to use the Divines' power to look into an Ancient's mind apart from Antrühriel.

"I can see the energies' flow from any living thing in this realm. It is quite likely I will be able to aid you to manipulate the Ancients' flow yourselves, if your connection permits." Carnarbur's counselor was sitting on a tree trunk with an open journal in his hands, the pen scribing without a moment's stop. "Since not one of you, apart from Princess Kayden, ever had any experience with arcane arts and the energies' flow nor did you ever tap into your core's energy, it may be hard to do it on your own when the source itself is so...vast," Orion said as he glanced toward the three dragons, his eyes tired yet focused on the creatures. "Since reaching for the dragons' source can be too risky, it is best if you three attempt to gather their energy into your own core and manipulate it from there."

Kayden nodded, her mind already seeking to get ahold of Antrühriel's power inside her in order to move her energy into her core, however one glance was all it took to realize she had been the only one who had understood Orion's words.

"I can understand the words you are saying, they just don't make any sense—Hey, you *shut* it! I have no obligation to know any of this arcane stuff!" Bash replied, at first looking straight at Orion to only a few moments later shoot a furious glare toward the gray dragon.

The young mage rolled his eyes, putting the pen aside for a second.

"I do not know how I could be clearer than that. There is the Ancients' core and your core. You don't manipulate their energy directly from their core, you bring it to your own to use it as you will—wait, what in the Divines' name are you doing?"

Bash had both hands on his temples, his eyes shut tight. "Trying to *feel* the core thing you said. But I must say, all I feel is a burning sensation in my toes."

Orion blinked in disbelief, turning his gaze toward Kayden as if asking for help, yet the princess looked at the younger Knight with torn eyes. She wondered if Bash knew and recognized what he was really feeling at that moment.

The nobleman remained still, arms crossed. "Counselor, the thing you spoke of, is it what mages do to perform their tricks?"

The little mage sighed, going back to his scribing. "Since you—neither of you—will actually comprehend a word I say, I may as well change my speech.

Yes, Lord Argyris, people who do arcane *tricks* use their core and *magic* from the realm. Would that satisfy as an answer?"

Leander ignored the mocking and impatient tone in Orion's words, his eyes locked on Amträhfar with shadows and fire crossing the man's gaze. Even from her spot, meters away from the noble, the leader could feel Leander's anger as the emotion reached her as if it were flaming waves, burning its way into her skin. From within her mind, Kayden felt her dragon's distress as the white dragon shifted her wings and showed her bare teeth toward Amträhfar.

"I shall not indulge you by learning petty tricks instead of real fighting." It took a few seconds for Kayden to realize Leander was speaking to the black dragon and not Orion. Amträhfar growled, leaning toward Leander as the heat from his body rose. Leander let out a laugh, crossing his arms. "If you won't let me touch your power myself, I shall train in my own way. Which involves neither your aid nor the arcane coward tricks."

Kayden heard Antrühriel's growl, making the black dragon avert his gaze and turn his back on his Knight. In a matter of seconds, Amträhfar was gone, the light bending and twisting in the space he previously was. Leander also turned his back, walking away from all of them yet Kayden closed their distance, reaching for the man's arm.

"Leander, wait—"

She was not expecting it—she always hoped it would never happen again, yet time and time again she felt the bitter taste of disappointment as visions from the Sight reached her, taking ahold of her mind, her breath, body, and soul. The moment she touched Leander's skin, she was blinded by such a bright and fierce light it almost made her fall on her knee. It felt like her head was being split in half by long, sharp nails. She began drowning in a sea of blood, the scent all around while the screams and the pain sank deeper and deeper into her bones and mind.

The vision lasted but a few seconds yet a few seconds was plenty to make the princess breathless, her entire body shaking as if ill.

"I will not stand as low as a *mage;* I will fight as I am. A warrior, an Argyris."

Kayden had even forgotten what she wanted to say, barely noticing as Leander let go of her hand and continued to walk away, back into the mountains. Someone touched her and for a second, she almost called Dorian's name, yet it was a pair of dark eyes that met her.

"Are you unwell, princess?" Bash's voice did share the worry in his gaze, his hands supporting her.

She smiled, attempting to conceal the exhaustion from her words. "I am fine, Bash. Antrühriel just showed me a few things, is all."

Yet even after Kayden sat down, glancing over at the white dragon as if she would have the answers the princess sought, Kayden could not let go of the feeling brought by the vision. It tasted worse than Death, a vile energy that attached to her skin and drenched her mind. Orion put his pen down as he stared at her, and somehow Kayden knew that her former teacher could guess what she had seen, the fear and worry in the mage's eyes mirroring her own.

Kayden only prayed that they were both wrong about the vision, that she had made the right choice. Yet hours later, the leader still glanced toward the way Leander Argyris had gone. And she prayed. She prayed to all Divines that a warrior would be enough.

A Kiss From The Gallows

Gallows of Night - Woods

He was, actually, impressed. He would not lie.

Not only had someone been brave enough to propose a meeting in the Gallows, of their own volition, the person themselves dared to threaten him if he didn't show up.

Oh, Dark Eye was amused. Their talk had better be one of the greatest tales and offers ever spoken by a living soul otherwise he was set to meet someone fated to kiss Death sooner than later. And why, oh, why would someone as busy as Dark Eye even dare to listen to a dead man's tales?

Because he was fond of entertaining fools. And the person who had sent him such a note was, most certainly, a fool.

If you are as smart as rumors say, you will meet me at Gallows. Otherwise, you shall forever regret it.

Oh, the audacity! Dark Eye was the subject of many rumors—he was an assassin after all, one Raevich kept doubting even existed. Dark Eye once left his name on the scene yet people thought it was someone trying to be funny. Broke his heart, it really did. The Divines and Säh cursed his curiosity right then, Dark Eye had to know how and why he would regret it. After, he would have to make amends, make some damage control. Death would sure get its lips moist.

It was saddening that the trees were losing their leaves so fast, yet the assassin could still blend well with the dark wood. It took no longer for a beam of light to fill the space, as a middle-aged man entered the dark woods. The assassin saw as the person arrived, not even daring to hide his face with a hood or mask. Dark Eye grinned. Would others believe the nerve of that fellow?

There were no clouds in the night sky, filling the Gallows with the cold moonlight, the woods as silent as they could be. If he closed his eyes and paid attention, would he be able to hear the screams of the deceased? Of all the fools who ventured in the Gallows and got caught by monsters like him, beings sent to Death's embrace before the sun even woke. Would he be able to hear the future screams of the one who gambled poorly with their luck and managed to get Dark Eye out of his comfortable hidden place?

"If rumors are truthful, which I believe they are, you are already here. Isn't that so, Dark Eye, sire?"

The mockery and insolence in those words and tone—oh, he could feel his fingers shaking with anticipation. Should Dark Eye choke that man or gut him like the pig he was? Decisions, decisions.

"Do you want some praise for bringing me here, uncle? Some nice, exotic sweets and a pat on the head?" In the assassin's hand, the dagger felt heavy and warm, a precious part of him. Dark Eye pondered if he should throw it at the person's thigh or hand when the time came.

"Nothing of the sort, sire! I am merely praising your punctuality, always arriving ahead of time. I find people who fail to maintain their appointment an utter disgrace."

Oh, the pig was keeping the *sire*? Should he be flattered?

"Why don't you rush the appointment and speak whatever words you came here to speak?" *For my patience is lacking.*

The older man smiled, the lamp's light making the shadows within his eyes shimmer and move. "I hear the famous Dark Eye owns a stolen slave."

The knife flew before the assassin was even on the ground, making the older man jump as the blade scraped his haunch. Maybe that person would be able to hear the growls that grew within the darkness, inside the younger man. Maybe that person realized Dark Eye was done listening and that Death's lips were close to touching his own.

"Wa-wait! I am not here to harm you in any way, sire! I only desire to help the boy. Lee is his name, isn't that so?"

Dark Eye still gripped his other knife, the knots on his hand whiter than snow. For the first time he did not worry if the light was revealing too much of his face as he pressed the metal against the older man's ribs—he had no problem with the dead seeing him. "Since you made me come all the way here, I shall indulge you for a minute, *uncle*. Yet you better be wary of your time; the sand is falling."

The assassin was happy to see the older man hadn't even bothered to take out his own weapon. He truly knew better than to waste both their time with foolish maneuvers.

"My name is Sean. I watched as Alexander mistreated you in so many ways. That is why I came here to give you a very precious piece of information!"

The person named Sean jumped in place when the wind howled and some animals groaned.

"Speak faster, uncle, your time is running out," Dark Eye's words were whispered into the man's ear as if they were passionate lovers ready to stay awake the entire night. He could almost taste and scent the blood in the Gallows, the beast inside him hungering for it.

"I found the boy's real family! As well as his sales certificate and ownership contract. You could free the boy and bring him back to his kin."

The assassin felt the blood in his veins slow down and freeze inside, his heart beating in an odd way against his chest. He loathed the confident smile Sean showed to him yet what he hated most were his words. "If you are simply going to lie, I will end our appointment here—"

"I swear on Säh's truth! The boy's family is alive and well. They live under Queen Shaq'Ynna's domain—five sisters and a doting mother. I can give you the sales documents if only you let go of the weapon, sire."

Was it a trick? Something inside his mind kept urging him to butcher the man and ignore those words, yet deep inside him there was a feeling that got harder to ignore by the minute. What was it?

"If you even think of running away or going for that pretty sword, you will be feeling Death's cold tongue inside your throat to claw your filthy soul out of this body, uncle. I hope we are clear."

As Dark Eye stepped away, the blade cut Sean's shirt and skin making the man flinch. Yet he replied like a good boy, "Thank you, sire."

The man named Sean searched inside his inner pockets, giving to the assassin not five seconds later a folded document. It was a bit crumpled and stained, yet when Dark Eye opened it his eyes widened and the heart that was pounding before was almost silenced by the words written so elegantly on the brown paper.

That *was* Lee's sales certificate, the document that proved he had been sold to a man in Raevich. However, that man was dead, so according to the certificate Lee was open to be bought again. One would just have to show the certificate with the money in some slave post; that was it. Without the certificate that Dark Eye held in his hands, Lee's ownership belonged to his last slave master who still breathed joyfully in the East Kingdoms. He had tried to hunt that bastard down, but Dark Eye never had enough luck.

The man always had ten trained assassins and warriors guarding him at least, from the moment he woke to every single time he went to shit. And of course, he had slaves to taste his food for poison, twice every three bites. Dark Eye was one of the best assassins in Raevich, yet he was only *one.* With the slave master alive, and with no certificate, Lee could be severely punished for not going back and Dark Eye would have to pay quite the expensive fine for "owning" a slave he had no rights to own.

The assassin tried to hide the trembling in his hands as he hid the certificate in his pockets. "What do you want me to do for the ownership contract?"

Sean laughed, his eyes reflecting the lights with pure amusement. "You *are* as smart as they say! I must admit I am most pleased to be hiring you, Dark Eye, sire."

Dark Eye smirked, holding the blade close to the man's throat. He felt his own heart pumping and making his blood flow, his fingers aching to just press the blade a bit deeper. "I hope they also said how very good I am at my work. Now speak your words so I can finish this soon."

Sean's smile managed to carry the dark insanity of the Gallows. "Tell me, sire, are you also good with undercover operations? I require your services to spy on someone."

In his mind, Dark Eye heard a warning. He knew he would not like the man's next words yet he knew he would still listen. He would still comply.

"Who am I to spy on now, uncle?"

"Albaron's sweet, daring heir. The Order's new leader."

Dark Eye could only smile in order to not explode in laughter. As always, nothing good ever came from within the Gallows, for it was Dark Eye's home, master, and servant.

Chapter IX

Ancient Ones - Close Analysis, Day Two

After a closer inspection, my theory was proved right. The Ancient dragons do carry more than one energy within their bodies in the most fascinating way. They hold within pure Divine energy while their body [recipient] is almost made from demonic energy mixed with the world's. One could almost believe the creatures would not be able to maintain a stable form if not for the demonic body that shapes and keeps their Divine power together.

Their connection with the Knights is also formi dable. If I was younger, perhaps I would be able to discern some of the flows and say if the Ancients are connected to their Knights by their cores or purely by a unique bond with each other's energy—perhaps I should've brought my glasses. If I had known Kayden's offer would bring me such a productive day, I would've accepted it sooner.

The Knights are a problem, however. The Argyris's core cannot possibly manipulate energy on its own without shattering and to touch the Ancients' Divine power [source] directly, although alluring, would be a fool's bet at best. Maybe that is the reason why Kayden let the boy be, she must've known how he is not fit to manipulate flows. The younger one frightens me, however. His core is not all bad, it has some potential—his brain is the problem. I would never allow someone of the like to step into my classroom, let alone exhaust myself by explaining the most basic of things.

Where did all the rare gems of our youth go? Maybe this realm is fated to be destroyed simply by lacking intelligent and intellectual living beings.

A Dance Sharper Than Knives

Wake of Day - Red Heart, Haste Mountains

THE HORSES WERE RESTLESS. He noticed from the way they breathed from the way the animals kept moving their legs, never standing still. It was as if they could sense the stillness in the air while knowing what was coming, what awaited them. Dorian did not know what was coming, he simply knew how to wait.

There was this space inside the mountain where the horses rested. It resembled a common stable with all the hay scattered around the floor, the saddles hanging on the walls, the water troughs, and a scent that reminded him of home. There, the animals received sunlight from the high windows, with rounds between knights to clean and feed them. Maybe once there had been more than ten horses, maybe years ago every cell was occupied by one animal and the rounds had to be more frequent. Yet Dorian had asked to be the one to check on the horses, even if they were all well fed. The Ward gave them water and brushed their manes, checked their horseshoes, and gave his own horse an apple—even though it was in season, it was getting harder to find good ones, otherwise he would have shared with the rest of the animals.

As Dorian brushed Lyon's mane, the horse still chewing the fruit, the man felt his heart shrink and coil. "What afflicts you, buddy? What are you afraid of?" Dorian asked those questions of himself every day, maybe hoping his horse would answer them instead. Sometimes he thought he had an answer, however there was no reply. "I do not know either, Lyon. I wish I knew. I wish I knew..."

Soon, the Argyris would depart with Orion's apprentice to fulfill their "sacred mission". Dorian had spent the past weeks aiding the younger Knight Bash with his own quest—on Kayden's request—and he did not feel any calmer to know that Bash was learning fast. He could not remember the last time he saw his lady genuinely smile or laugh; he watched day by day his princess waning. She was never rested, she was never content, she was never at ease. Had he known her poorly maybe he would be able to say Princess Kayden was that way. She was a woman that shouldered more responsibilities than most people would in their lives; one does not reach the top by standing still. However, Dorian knew her since they could not even reach a horse's saddle and he might not possess the Divines' cursed Sight yet even then he could see that something haunted her—no, he could *feel it.*

The air around her was always cold, distant, lost. Sometimes Dorian was afraid to touch her, fearing the princess would disappear the moment his fingers brushed her skin. He tried to be someone she could trust to share her concerns and perils, yet she was sparing him. *Him.* Her Ward, the man who had pledged his life, heart, and soul to her and her entire royal family. Kayden had the Order within her grasp, control over the Orphys Knights, knights to train, and an Ancient dragon to guard her. So where did *he* fit? Dorian had never felt more disconnected from her, had never felt so alone. He was not even attending the special trainings Kayden was taking with the Knights because he could not bear the thought that she would sense through her Sight all the horrible things Dorian felt every time he saw the Ancients and their Knights, secluded in their own world.

And he was disgusted with himself for thinking and feeling so.

So, he tried to aid her the way he still could. He was trying to contact other Wards placed on Albaron's noble Houses to grasp their positioning, to understand the current state of her kingdom. Yet he could not even share good news with his lady for Albaron's current state was *not* good. Dorian sighed, looking at his empty hands. He wondered if he could provide Kayden with the thing she wanted the most. Take her crown away, take her curse on himself, and watch the princess stay with her own happiness. It did not matter to him who would be by her side at the end as long as she was smiling. However, he could not even give her that.

The horse warned him before Dorian noticed himself, the person walking inside dragging an entire storm behind them. It took less than a heartbeat for Dorian to realize who that man was.

"Ward."

"Lord Argyris."

The men said nothing more. Dorian saw as the Argyris headed toward one of the horses, a black mare with a white spot on its forehead that stood right in front of Dorian's horse. The purebred had a long, thick mane and low-set tail that almost reached the ground, and sloping shoulders accompanied by a compact, muscular body. Dorian knew the moment he set eyes on the animal that the mare belonged to the only person in those mountains capable of raising and owning such an expensive and noble breed. When compared to Lyon, the Argyris mare was an empress, a ruler.

"Were you the one who tended the horses, Ward?"

Dorian decided not to glance toward the Knight, the glow of the jewel on the Argyris's wrist threatening to reflect in his eyes. No, his hand was focused on brushing his horse's mane. "It was I, yes."

"I shall thank you this time, for you seem knowledgeable enough to tend to their basic needs, however let me tend to my own horse in the future. She requires a special attention someone like yourself could not possibly manage."

The Ward stopped his hand for a brief second before replying with empty words. "As you will, Lord Argyris." How that man would tend to his mare's *special needs* when he departed to the White Mountains was beyond Dorian.

"I do hope your lady will be knowledgeable enough to teach someone of trust to tend to Tusäh's needs while I am gone. I will not tolerate any mistreatment with my mount, I shall make myself very clear."

Dorian finished brushing Lyon's white mane, his mouth closed shut, the words being pressed into his lips as his voice forced their way out. "As you will."

"You should state this to your lady clearly, Ward. This place's mounts may be of poor quality so most are used to a lower treatment, however I will not forgive such a thing for Tusäh. Her worth is more than any knight could imagine."

Dorian's feelings toward the Argyris were as simple as they could be. He did not like him. "I will be sure to tend to the mare's needs, Argyris."

The man stopped in place, turning his head toward Dorian. "Why would—"

"If I were to deliver this message to Princess Kayden she would no doubt put the task in my hands, so you can rest assured. I am not one to treat horses as I would their owners."

A faint smile touched the Argyris's lips, his body turning to face Dorian. "I see you share the same tongue as your lady, Ward. Has Lady Faeryl never taught you how to respect those above you?"

Dorian should have been chosen instead of that man. He should be the one to live in the same world as his lady, to possess a stone etched into his skin, to be able to aid Kayden in *every* way possible. This was his desire, the wish that made his very soul ache and cry as he saw himself left behind in that new reality that surrounded Kayden and her Knights. Why chose a man who was so adamant on not engaging and was so disrespectful? As those thoughts tried to surface in his mind, Dorian did his best to ignore and suffocate them deep inside. Emotions like those, thoughts like those... He had no right to possess them.

"For someone so keen to disrespect their superior officer, and with such frequency, has your family taught you nothing apart from being a haughty self?"

The Argyris clenched his jaw, taking a few steps ahead. "Watch your words, Ward. Do not believe you can fight against one who knows one of the true Ways of Sword with such a frivolous perception of the world."

"I know some Ways, Argyris, perhaps we should see which is better."

As the air got heavier, thicker, the nobleman got close enough to touch Lyon's mouth. Dorian hadn't moved one step from his spot. The Argyris's blue eyes ventured through him, glancing up and down his body. "There may be some honor and talent in you after all, Ward, if you truly stand by your words."

"I believe in myself, Argyris. It is one's conviction to fight and win that truly moves a battle, is it not?"

The man almost smiled, a faint hint of amusement filling his cold gaze. "It is not common to see a Färküh Ward with such *faith* in their sword, especially when facing stronger opponents. Who taught you, Ward?"

Dorian ignored his question, his words mimicking the stillness of the wind around them. "We have never fought before. I do not know if you are stronger than me."

The smile finally flourished in the Argyris's face, his body leaning closer as the noble's hand moved toward his sword. "I may have found a worthy opponent, then."

"If your eyesight was of a better quality, you would've found one sooner."

The curious and amused glow that was hidden inside the Argyris's eyes vanished, a shadow replacing its light. "Do you speak of the mage's apprentice or Lady Faeryl herself?"

Dorian spoke of many opponents. "I would not even go that far, Argyris."

The Argyris clenched his fists, already taking one huge step closer, the sword almost free from its scabbard when the man flinched, his hand going toward his temple with pain-filled eyes. Dorian watched as anger twisted the man's face, darkening his eyes and face like the Gallows itself.

"I am required in the Silver Grounds, a request from *your* lady. Maybe this is your chance to show me, Ward. This conviction you seem so proud of."

Dorian had no reason to accept the man's offer.

"I shall meet you there, Lord Argyris."

He had no reason at all.

The training grounds had more knights than he was used to. They all wore their leather training armors: their chests, shoulders, forearms, and abdomens covered by the worn-out material. Kayden had talked to him a previous day about providing new armor sets for the Order; the issue was the funds. Leander, however, wore his own dark padded armor and one glance was enough for Dorian to notice the quality of the armor; the care given to it.

Until that moment, Dorian was not sure what exactly he was doing there. In his heart, he knew he should be some place else. He was a Färküh Ward, that was the place he truly—only—belonged, so why had he accepted it? Why was he standing there in front of so many knights, getting ready to face a man from a noble House?

"Feeling regretful, Ward?" the Argyris asked while removing the sword from the scabbard.

"I pray I am not disrupting your class, Lord Argyris."

"I told them today would be a practical class. They would be smart to observe and learn."

Dorian's gaze ran across the knights, their eyes following his every movement. He was reminded of his training days then, how he and his colleagues would be obliged to watch as the veterans sparred with one another, analyzing their mistakes, their strengths, and their movements. Dorian would often be punished by his teacher for lacking observational skills when questioned after the fights. Those were actually bitter memories.

The Ward scrubbed his wrists unconsciously before reaching for his own sword. "Whenever you are ready."

The Argyris smiled with a calm posture. "I have hopes for this demonstration, Ward. Do your best to meet them." There was a genuine request in the noble's words, which made Dorian's heart beat faster against his chest.

How many years has it been since he had fought using one of the Ways? He had sparred a few times with Kayden yet she was no master of the Way of Sword taught to her. His lady only learned a few movements. His teacher *was* a master yet the man was as sly as he could be when it came to teaching his students the forms and movements of the Way he knew. There came a point where Dorian could recognize the names of the forms in a heartbeat yet fail again and again to mimic it. There were more than a few Ways of Sword and each master would proclaim their Way to be the strongest, yet Dorian had yet to meet a noble family more secretive and arrogant when it came to their Way than the House Argyris.

Their swords met with one loud strike, the sound echoing throughout the training grounds. It was odd how silence seemed to fall over them, as if the echo had stolen all noise and sound after it departed, leaving but Dorian's breathing as the Argyris's gaze sank into his own. Yet that silence lasted no more than two seconds. And from the very start, the Ward could tell Leander Argyris was not holding back. Though the man was not exerting himself, each blow was powerful enough to shake Dorian's bones as he blocked it. Every strike was aimed at vital points, and every action Dorian made was being analyzed. It made the Ward feel like he was in the middle of a battlefield.

The sword seemed to dance in the Argyris's hands, its blade cutting the air uninvited again and again, and for minutes Dorian did nothing but duck, block, and counter the nobleman's blade. The sword came toward his face, its tip barely touching his nose as Dorian leaned just a bit to the side, and in less than a heartbeat its direction changed going right for his rib cage. If Dorian focused too much on his opponent's arms, the Argyris would aim for his legs and feet. When the Ward spent too much time watching the noble's footwork, he would be obliged to block the weapon that went for his heart and neck. It was almost a dare, the Argyris's taunting way of saying that no matter how much Dorian watched and observed, he would not learn anything from that Way of Sword.

"I am most impressed, Ward," the man spoke as Dorian took two steps backward, sweat running from his temple. "I have rediscovered my hope for the skills and lessons taught to Färküh Wards. Or maybe you are a rough diamond among many fools' gold."

"You should not waste your awe this way, Lord Argyris. You will have none to spare when you finally encounter something worth being hopeful for."

Dorian changed his posture right then, switching the sword to his left hand while swinging the blade across the Argyris's arm. The sword was blocked, however there was genuine surprise filling the noble's gaze as Dorian pushed the opponent with his weight, leaning forward as the blades slid together until freeing from each other's touch. The Ward tried to punch the Argyris in the stomach with his free hand, but his fist was covered with the Argyris's own hand, being twisted to the side. Dorian struck again with his sword and as the nobleman

blocked the attack, the Ward used the impact to free his hand and step aside, creating a new distance between them.

Leander Argyris smiled for a brief second. "Indeed, I almost forgot. You fancy using your hands sometimes, isn't that so, Ward?" It took a few seconds for Dorian to understand what the Argyris was trying to imply when a single memory came to him. The night of the Blood Ceremony, he had lost control.

Suddenly his fists became gelid and rough, the air still around him. That was a memory he did not wish to revisit.

"I fancy whatever I have at my disposal, Lord Argyris." His words burned with a distant cold, something Dorian was not sure if it was still there or not. Feelings that had been brought back by that past moment, by that one night, where every thought and movement made by him was controlled by something he had no autonomy over. Fear.

"I can finally understand more about your conviction, Ward. Even if your poor attempts to mimic some of the Ways are lacking at best."

Dorian knew he could not perform a movement like his teacher or Kayden. He knew that because he was never successful in watching them fight, to truly observe and learn their methods. Whenever Dorian watched someone fighting with one of the Ways he would get bewitched. It was almost like a spell, a trance he would not be able to recover from fast enough and even at that moment, while fighting the Argyris, Dorian could feel this lure with every blow and every attack, by the way the man held the sword and moved its blade in the air. It was like a slow dance. It was an art, something that came from deep down in their hearts. It would be the same thing with Kayden and her rapier, his teacher and his polearm, Leander Argyris and his sword. A true Way master did not fight using their weapons. They sang and danced alongside their tune.

Yet all Dorian could ever hear was the wind, all he could ever feel was the air and even though he would be in awe no matter how many times he saw a master fight, he knew he could never do the same. Perhaps that was the reason no Ancient chose him, why one never would. His soul and heart were not his own, his own world belonged to another. How could he ever bond with an Ancient? How could he ever become a master of the Way? He was fated to serve.

The Ward lowered his sword, his heart aching as it beat again and again. The Argyris stopped with the blade midair, straightening his posture before speaking his words in a calm yet powerful tone, "Are you tired, Ward? Did your own movements bore you?"

Dorian wiped the sweat off his forehead, putting his weapon back in its scabbard. "It was very entertaining, Lord Argyris. Perhaps we can spar again before you depart. However, I must end our fight now."

Leander Argyris said nothing more, the man simply lowered his blade with a dim smile reflecting in his eyes. "You managed to meet some of my hopes, Ward. I thank you for the efforts. If you think you can meet them again, you can come meet me here. Bring your lady as well, perchance."

Dorian did not bow as he left nor did he say anything else. His gaze fell on the beautiful jewel on the noble's wrist, its color pulsing and glowing like never before. His eyes met the youngest Knight, Bash, and it reminded him he was supposed to give more lessons to Bash about the castle later that day. Bash smiled and waved at Dorian as he left, the stone on the young Knight's wrist staring back at him before he reached the doors. Both his wrists burned cold, a pain echoing inside his heart as his eyes were filled with guilt.

Should he feel pity for himself for wanting to be one of them or should he simply feel disgust toward the desire? Would it make any difference? That was the only question Dorian knew the answer to, and it gave him neither reassurance nor peace as he walked through the mountain's halls searching for that one person who could ease the weight in his mind. Even if briefly, even if for a foolish second—it would be more than enough. And it did not take long for him to find her.

Dorian's heart missed a beat when his eyes met Kayden's. She looked smaller, somehow. Thinner, paler, more tired, her eyes darker. He wanted to ask if she had eaten yet, even if Dorian knew better than to ask. She was talking with Orion, the little mage holding a teacup in his hands as the words poured out of him like an arrows' curtain descending to the ground. Kayden was listening with a chilling air surrounding her, a gaze covered in shadows and wariness yet when she met his eyes some of those shadows were gone and the air got a little warmer.

Just a little.

Dorian bowed without muttering one single word, for he feared his own voice and words would betray him, speaking things he could not ever say, even if he could not hide them from the Sight. The Ward remained silent, right behind Kayden, feeling for the first time wrongly placed—even if the one thing he knew was that there was no other place for him to be.

Feral Darkness

Wake of Day - Silver Grounds, Haste Mountains

Holy Säh and blessed lights.

Leander-man was an animal.

Worst of all, it was not even a ferocious, disgusting animal. As Bash watched the spar between Grumpy Ward and Proud Lion, the knight saw something shine in Leander's eyes, something he never thought he would be able to see, while breathing, in an Argyris's face. Fun. Fun that did not involve humiliation, torture or defamation. Bash was *impressed*. It almost seemed unreal how both men fought, as if their swords were actually having a conversation. He really wasn't used to something like that. In East Raevich conversations were made with old and boring fists, curse words, and occasionally some small and sharp blades one could conceal under their coat and shirt to keep things thrilling and going. Though Sir Ward did use his hands here and there, their fight was something... almost beautiful to see.

Bash even got chills up his spine. For real.

When Dorian started to leave, Bash was so lost for what to say as they locked gazes, he just waved. He wanted to compliment the Ward, to be truthful, yet he could see how anxious the man was to go back to his dear princess... Bash thought a wave was good enough.

"Everyone, form pairs. I will see how you behave in an actual fight and if there is any hope; I am not wasting my time by teaching you."

The door hadn't even closed when Leander started to speak. Bash then realized he had been wrong about the Proud Lion being in a good mood—and the young knight cursed the nobleman five times before cursing himself.

Hey, buddy, want to pair with me? I can give you some nice treats. Apples, you like apples?

The gray dragon did not even bother to reply. The Ancient was far too busy doing what he did every single hour of the day. Sleeping. Bash let out a laugh, his fingers twitching as his eyes scanned the room, watching pairs forming everywhere. Yet he did see some hope after the third time he counted the knights and confirmed they were an odd number and he would be left alone. Bless Säh's heart and robes.

Wait, he wouldn't have to pair with flimsy Proud Lion, would he? He would rather choke on a blooded boot.

"I can spar with you."

It took a few seconds for Bash to find the source of the voice and a few more for him to process who was talking.

"I don't really do arcane...things, you see." Bash raised the short sword in his hand, gaining no reaction from the woman.

"I know. You can still use me to train your attacks." After a few seconds of Bash staring at the child's apprentice, the woman gave him a half smile as she spoke with a hint of amusement in her words. "I know how to avoid a sword, Knight."

Bash was more worried about her sending him flying, making him catch fire or something of the like. "Well...then yes, of course, we may pair up. I appreciate your kindness, dear lady."

The woman, Bash couldn't recall her name, positioned herself in front of him. It was odd to see a woman from the East Kingdoms, especially one with those gold eyes, wearing such clothes. It was oddly cold for autumn—he recognized that—however women from the East loved their dresses and fancy fabrics. Women from the West enjoyed the East fabrics as well, but it was almost something rooted in the East Kingdoms' culture. The way they dressed, their inks, and jewelry. However sweet apprentice there, she had the eyes, the hair, the fabric, and the braids.

Yet she did not give any impression she *was* from the East. If Bash thought it was possible, he would even consider the woman as some noble from the three kingdoms who bought a pair of golden eyes and had a mage attach them to her face while she spent some time in the burning sun to get her skin peeled again and again until she got the right tone.

"Does sword-fighting often involve this much staring, Sir Knight?"

Bash smiled with embarrassment. "Forgive me, lady, you just remind me of a friend. Let us start before our angered lion comes to spoil our fun." That got her laughing, which quite surprised him at first until he remembered that the poor woman was obliged to have private, tedious lessons with the man. Oh, that poor, poor soul.

Bash was happy to see that they made quite a nice pair. The woman defended his attacks and matched his speed with ease, slowing and speeding up here and there as if she truly wanted to help him get used to a sword. It was nowhere near as intriguing as Grumpy Ward's fight, however it fit what Bash wanted perfectly. A distracting and effortless spar.

"You will also depart on a mission of your own, isn't that right?" the woman asked as she evaded the sword's attack on her right. It took a few more strikes for Bash to be able to speak his own words.

"Yes. Though it will take a bit longer for me to depart. You and Leander leave in a couple of days, correct?"

"Yes."

He gave a brief pause. "You think you will be able to find the Ancient creature? With your *arcane senses*?"

"I believe so, yes."

It took seven strikes for Bash to open his mouth again. "Are you anxious about the mission?"

"Professor Orion trusts me, so there is no reason why I should feel anxious."

Professor Orion. The child. Of course. "How much do you trust the chil—Professor Orion?" It took less than a heartbeat for her to answer.

"I trust him with my life."

And just like that, the remainder of their friendly spar was filled with nothing but sounds of Bash's sword cutting through the air. And Bash was quite fine with that, gave him some time to ponder and wonder about the "private mission" he was so enthusiastic and glad to be part of. His heart could barely contain his excitement and joy. Truly. Really. *Overwhelming happiness.* Bash could have spent the entire training thinking about his positive and cozy feelings regarding his mission, with ease, yet Leander spoke words so bright and courteous it made his heart skip a beat.

"Everyone, stop. Get in line. I will call your name and one of you must step forward to fight, it cannot be the one you were previously paired with." Leander stared at the woman, some long seconds if someone asked Bash, before speaking again. Bash was actually amazed how that man managed to shout without raising his voice. "Get in line. *At once.*"

He wondered what the other knights thought about Leander's lessons, the ones who had given up. And if it was so different from what the ones that still took the Argyris's lessons thought. Bash was not sure why *he* hadn't given up yet—it was quite unlike him. Maybe part of him would be sad to not be taunted and provoked every day by his Raevich fellows. Maybe he should ask a mage to remove their light eyes and replace them with black ones, like Bash's, so their friendship would go beyond their appearances.

That was actually quite poetic of him.

"Who wishes to go first?" Leander asked with a clear yet distant voice, his words lacking his usual furious thunder. Yet Bash saw with his pretty dark eyes a flimsy lion looking at a fair, dark-skinned lady for more seconds than he would stare at any living creature in that space. Oh my, oh my—*the scandal.*

However, Bash committed a mistake then as he tried to control the smile on his lips by watching the proud Argyris's love affairs; he completely ignored everything else that was happening. And in normal circumstances, that wouldn't be so much of a problem.

Yet it had become, quite quickly, a problem.

"Bash."

The why was quite simple. First, by Leander's voice and glare, that was not the first time the man was calling his name.

"Yes, sir!"

"Will you accept?" Second, the young knight hadn't the faintest idea what the Knight was talking about and he would not even dare to ask.

"Yes, of course. It is fine by me."

Maybe Bash should have caught something from Leander's expression when he accepted, something that would make him confess his lack of attention and question what in Säh's cursed light he was accepting.

Yet Bash's final mistake was just that. He did nothing.

"What are you waiting for, then? True warriors do not leave their opponent waiting."

Bash was not a genius or a brilliant man. There were very few things he could say he was actually good at—one of them being the ability to realize when he had fucked up. His newly scarred brother was out in the front, glaring at him with so much contempt the young knight almost smiled. Someone was still sour with the whole sword-throwing incident, it seemed. However, Bash finally realized what he had accepted and dear Divines—how he regretted his life choices.

"You shall be put in your place," the other knight muttered those words in shallow, burning whispers as Bash walked past him. He would not tell any lies, those were some adorable words. Maybe Bash could give the knight another scar, something to remember him by? If he chose to strike a blow, that was. Or maybe he could have an utterly, humiliating defeat so that his fellow Raevich friends would leave him be. As Bash tried to decide which one was the best approach, their spar dragged on.

His opponent, someone Bash had never bothered to recall his name, was quite diligent in expressing his anger through the sword. Each blow possessed its own raw, brute strength yet there was neither impatience nor impulsive movements. Bash sometimes chose which attacks to dodge, which ones he would pretend to block, and some he actually had to defend against. He was still pondering if he should try his own luck—maybe Säh was feeling charmed by him that day to bless him for a few brief seconds—and try to make a mark on the knight's left cheek or if he should just trip on his own feet and eat some dirt so the knights could "make their point". On one side, his Raevich companions were already quite bothersome to deal with so it would be pleasant to see some fear in their eyes.

On the other hand...

It could bring him more problems to act against them. None of them possessed blue, green or gray eyes and their hair was nowhere near blond to mistake them for people who carried royal blood. Yet they could still have connections or be prestigious ones from some gold-plated scum. If word got out, not only Bash would hear a mouthful from the flimsy lion but from his leader as well. It was yet too soon to get on the bad side of those nobles. Also, the thought of Princess Kayden being reprimanded for his petty vengeance made Bash feel bad for some reason. Maybe their secret stargazing was planned precisely to gain some sympathy from him.

Then, that left Bash with only one option. Make a fool out of himself and be done with it all.

Minutes into their fight and his adversary's anger was still as palpable as the flames that burned in his eyes. Should Bash start to lose? The young knight was about to accidentally drop his sword on his next attack—like a proper fool—when his feet suddenly got stuck. Bash tried to move his legs, take a step to anywhere, yet there was a pressure, some force that would not let him move. It took him a few seconds to find the culprit in the line, the man's hand moving discreetly by the side. Who would've thought that one of Bash's Raevich friends knew some arcane tricks?

"What is the matter? Is your fear so grand that it froze your legs?!" the opponent shouted while the blade cut to the side, coming straight at Bash's face.

In the angle he was stuck, it was hard to block. He did not have his legs in a proper position, his back bending as he struggled to protect his face. Those little bastards played dirty. Maybe they were nobles after all, from the lowest cattle.

"What happened with your tongue? No comebacks this time?"

The sword came at Bash again, toward his testicles that time. He almost burst a vein to move his feet, managing no more than one step each, enough to defend his cut-brother's attack. That was a tiny bit unfair.

I CAN HELP.

The dragon's voice flowed into his mind, the Ancient's words mocking and condescending.

Oh, *have I become worthy to share a bit of thy power?*

They both knew that Bash had no intention of ever borrowing the creature's power for a spar such as that one. However, things were starting to get a bit dangerous. The opponent's sword rose once more yet the moment Bash was about to block the attack the short sword in Bash's hand became heavier than a boar, as if the air was pressing the weapon down again and again. By glancing at the line, he could see the same knight with two hands moving at his sides, blood trailing down his nose.

Bash would not be able to block.

Before the blade came in contact with Bash's body, its metal froze completely with pure ice covering its blade from tip to handle. His opponent cursed, dropping the sword at the same time. The accomplice who still stood in the line furrowed his brows, the force on Bash's feet and sword vanishing as the man lowered his hands and cleaned his nose.

Before Bash could take advantage of that situation, the child's apprentice came toward them with such an intimidating gaze it sent shivers down his spine. And she wasn't even looking at him.

"*Fools.*" It was only one word, yet Bash saw the knights lose any color that existed on their faces. They both exchanged glances, silenced, however if there was any fear they were trying to conceal in their eyes it soon became visible with their trembling knees when the man himself came rushing toward them. The only true noble in that room, his blue eyes piercing their very skin.

"What have you two done?"

Bash never thought he would see such a face on the Argyris. Living in Raevich, he had heard the stories. About the cruelty of the House Argyris, their mercilessness, their rage. He had heard stories of men pissing themselves with one single glance, workers who had lost their tongues and fingers for the pettiest reasons. And maybe because Bash had gotten used to seeing Leander usual angered face, the man's daily complaints and words about the Order's incompetence, about a warrior's way, he had forgotten about those stories. *Now I'm part of one of them.*

"I-I do not know about what you are speaking, Lord Argyris. I was simply—"

"Have you any idea of what *you both have done*?" Leander did not shout, but his words made the air bleed and their eardrums blow for in those words there was not only rage—

There was pure bloodlust.

"We-we just wanted to show... We wished to prove to this lowlife his proper place—" Bash's opponent could not mutter his words without stuttering and trembling and the one who had used the arcane powers could not even look straight. Next thing they all saw was the back of Leander's hand striking the knight who had not succeeded in finishing that sentence.

"You do not deserve to speak. You two do not even deserve to breathe. Performing such trickery, in *my* class..." Leander grabbed them by the collars, his voice nothing but a whisper yet the rage that poured out from every word was as loud as thunder.

Bash could not speak. He glanced over to the others, eyes widened and sweat dripping from their temples. Bash knew right then that he had been the only one to have forgotten the stories.

"Forgive me, my lord. I shall repent on my actions."

"Never will I touch the arcane again while I am breathing."

The knight who had battled Bash was entering a catatonic state. The other one was crying.

The mage looked over to Leander with a certain worry filling her eyes, looking like someone who was about to get sick or pass out. Before she could open her mouth, Leander threw both knights to the ground, their faces hitting the dirt first.

"Repent? You wish to *repent?!* You should pray for all Divines' mercy and pity! I spent hours, days teaching you unworthy lot to be proper warriors and what am I *obliged* to see?!" When there was no answer after a couple of seconds the Argyris

screamed and Bash could not describe the nobles' expressions better than ones filled with insanity. *"Answer me!"*

Both knights on the ground groveled on their knees, their words incomprehensible. Bash could see veins bulging on Leander's skin, his muscles so tense he thought they would rip the noble's shirt. Throughout his life, he had seen plenty of different people in East Raevich. Bash had seen the nastiest betrayals, the most scandalous love affairs, passionate vengeances, and incredibly ill-minded people. Yet he had never seen an anger going that deep into one's soul. A hatred whose words burned that fervently.

"You believe this is what a true warrior is supposed to do? Think this is how a *man* acts? How an *Argyris fights*?!"

It was as if the world had slowed down. The woman widened her eyes the same moment Leander took out his sword. Or he already had his sword free in his hands and Bash had only noticed when the man moved his arm. Bash was so confused by what was happening—the young knight only realized what the Argyris was doing when the sword sank deep into the wrist of one of his fellow companions on the ground. Both Bash and the woman shouted Leander's name at the same time and Bash did not even know why he did so. He was not feeling sorry for any of the knights who cried on the ground. Yet it was their shouts that saved his opponent's hand.

When the world went back to normal, blood was pouring from the almost severed hand with such speed it made three knights pass out right then. Bash could feel the stone in his wrist burn and pulsate, urging him to do...something. He did not know what.

Leander dropped the sword and took three steps back, his legs staggering. The scent of blood was strong.

"You must be such an honor for your family, *warrior*." There was pure contempt in the woman's voice as she knelt by the knight's side, her face paler as the knight's screams almost overshadowed her words. "You truly put *my kind* to *shame*."

It took almost an entire minute for Leander to speak again and even then the man did not seem to have found his voice. "Lessons are over. Any word of what happened today to any of your families...those outside these walls will suffer. I mean this."

Bash was, likely, the only person who saw. As the woman tended the knight and the others watched from afar, Bash was only a few meters away from the Argyris. He had never stopped looking at Leander because there were so many similarities his eyes could not avoid—they made his heart slow down and *listen*.

When the noble put his reddened sword back into its scabbard, he saw the noble's shaking hands. When Leander spoke, Bash saw the man's lips tremble and pale. When the noble turned his back to them all, Bash could almost smell the sweat. Most of all, what Bash could not only see but feel and hear was the fear and the utter despair displayed on the man's face. It was something he could have died without ever catching a glimpse of, without ever knowing it to be a part of Leander Argyris's story. For Bash knew that despair and fear all too well and it hit too close to his own stories. Everything he had just seen, he had once lived. And he knew he did not like that at all. He would rather listen to the Argyris's cruel stories. He would rather have just a noble monster, and nothing else.

Echoes From The Abyss

Bless of Day - Haste Mountains

He did not know where he was. His feet simply took him somewhere while the mountain's air currents made his body colder, the sweat drenching his shirt.

He was trying to ignore the scent. He was trying to ignore the blood. Yet the sword weighed on his waist, its metal burning through the scabbard into his own flesh.

At some point he left the mountains, yet he only realized when he stumbled into a dry wood and fell on the earth. The images kept flashing in his mind again and again, without ever stopping, his own words echoing inside his head louder each time. He raised his hands, the golden sunlight reflecting the red that also shone on his own sword.

A knight's blood. No—

It was the blood of a boy. Memories from the past overlapped with the ones from the present, but they were the same. *He* was just the same, there were no changes. Nothing had changed over the years, not himself, not those words, not even the outcome. It had ended with blood, it always ended with blood.

you are weak you will always be weak you will always be a failure

No no no he was strong; he *was*! He simply did not wish to see so much blood anymore. Yet choosing so would make him a failure. It would make him weak once again.

The jewel on his wrist never felt colder and suddenly he could not breathe anymore, the world was collapsing under him, trees were bending to kill him, birds were staring at him, staring at his failure and the sky kept showing all his mistakes and his disgrace and he was going to die he was dying the air was not filling his lungs anymore. The air entered his body and crushed his throat and even though he knew it would not make a difference he prayed and prayed for Death to spare him because he did not wish to die not yet he wanted to thrive he wanted to fight however the entire world was crumbling and burying him underneath it and the darkness was covering his eyes and that would be his end—it would be the end of everything and dear Divines he was so afraid of that darkness—

A roar burst into his mind, a sound so intense and loud it made all his thoughts vanish into nothingness, bringing a beam of light into his surroundings. His chest went up and down so many times the man lost count of how many seconds, how many minutes it took for his breathing to return to normal. For the air to fill his lungs without suffocating him. When he saw the world around him standing still, the trees in their place, the sky frozen with clouds moving around, some birds flying far away while some stood closer, he managed to calm his heart enough to look straight. The Ancient creature stared deep into his eyes, its yellow glow bringing an odd comfort to him. There was no judgment in those eyes for the creature, he could sense, understood.

"He can never know—" His words were weak, his throat dry. There was no reason to speak out loud yet even then he spoke. He spoke for otherwise he would fall again and die again and the darkness that watched him from that abyss would try to grab him one more time, the blood would follow him once more. "My father can never know. He can never know I am not like him." His voice failed.

Leander tried to make his body cease its trembling. He tried to soothe his body by holding the silver lion that hung on his chest.

He failed.

Chapter X

"The existence of creatures from another realm, commonly and perhaps mistakenly known as Demonic Lands, was brought by many studies and scholars throughout the past few decades in a futile attempt to justify the demonic war and previous inexplicable events. Though many know about the existence of demonic creatures, and that Ancient dragons also carry such a title, Tërnya has yet to see other creatures crawl from such cursed lands to prey on mortal flesh."

- *The Divines' Truth on The Demonic Lands*, Ibha Kaminer

"Some theorize that demons are not only intellectual creatures but that they possess a hive mentality and connection where their ranks are separated according to their size. Yet one of the most acceptable theories is that demons are common carnivorous beasts unleashed by the Great Divines before humankind settled on this world and that their sole mission is to be a reminder of the punishments men and women may face when defying the Divines' true will."

- Through the Divines' Will, Parson J.H and Parson Willoughby

The Misery of Those Who Know

Haze of Dawn - Ice Draco, Haste Mountains

Kayden's skin was still drier than the East deserts, her lips cracked with a few bleeding cuts while nausea came and went like violent waves. The princess had been locked in those chambers since the day before, when the incident on the Silver Grounds occurred. She was barely on the same mountain as them yet her Sight did not spare her. At first, she began to get light-headed, her skin burning and itching as if someone had scrubbed poison leaves on her body. Neither Orion nor Dorian were able to do anything before the Sight struck her, showing her their pain, their despair, their blood. Kayden did not want those images, did not want to know, yet the Sight showed her everything nonetheless.

Leander Argyris's emotions were so grand it made her kneel and vomit where she fell. Orion visited her a few times during the day and once before the Gallows to help soothe her stomach yet so far she still could not get up from bed.

"He should be punished, Kayden."

"Orion and Saranm managed to tend to the knight's injury, so he shall be fine. We should be more concerned with the White Mountains mission—they depart soon."

"Kay—"

"I ask of you, Dorian, to please trust me on this."

Her Ward had not left her side the entire time since she had gone to those chambers and that was one of the few things that was actually making Kayden feel a bit better. The man sighed, pacing by the bed. "I trust *you*, my lady. Yet I do not trust the Argyris. He nearly cut the boy's hand off for no justified reason!"

Dorian's words were carried with a low and powerless voice yet they stung. She did not need the Sight's reminder of her friend's concerns, of his fears, of his pledges. She could feel them all through his voice alone.

"I may know you saw something that can somewhat justify your Knight's behavior but the rest of the Divine Order does not. You are their leader, you must—"

"I *know* what I must do." The moment Dorian met her eyes was the moment Kayden regretted her tone, her voice. She averted her gaze, drinking the water in the glass as if she was drinking her own guilt, making it disappear. Her next words were spoken with care, a soft and weakened voice that she wished did not belong to her. "I felt their pain, Dorian. I *know*. I can also feel all the anger, all the fear—it's sickening, it's poisoning the air. You must be feeling it too for I also feel your restlessness, I feel and sense all of this all the time. And each time I attempt to open that door it worsens, as if They are mocking my mortality, my fragility." A laugh escaped her lips. "For I am no Divine, I am not even their only puppet. How many people carry the Sight throughout their lives, fearing Death and darkness, praying for the Divines to show Their mercy? I can sense their despair too. I live through that despair."

"Kayden—"

"That is my problem, Dorian." The knots on her hands were whiter than snow as she held the glass tight in her fingers, as if she was holding her own miserable fate. "I know a lot of things, forgotten things from the past, secrets buried in the future, shackled moments in the present—They show me all of those. All the moments I need to see and all the things I want to run away from; They show me *everything*. And with those, I *know*. Yet what good does this knowledge bring me when the means and ways I can use it are so useless and pathetic, for I am nothing but *one* person who cannot even open the door without losing my standing!"

The glass flew from her hand, crashing into the wall. Kayden watched the water as it splashed into the carpet alongside the broken glass and though she touched her own cheek and felt no tears, her voice and soul betrayed her.

"Kay..." Dorian took both her hands and the woman saw all the tears she hadn't the strength to shed falling from his eyes, his pain so close it resonated with her own. Again, Kayden sensed his sorrow as a punch and kick in the ribs, a blade filled with melancholy piercing her lungs and stealing her breath. "What have the Divines shown you? Please, *tell* me."

Kayden could do nothing but smile, she could feel nothing but a hopeless happiness that Dorian knew her so well. The sentences left her mouth without direction, trying to find their way amid her own confusion and loss. "If I tell you what I know and what must be done, will I be forgiven? Will I please the Divines and save us all from all the darkness that surrounds our world?"

The Ward's gaze kept fighting to find an answer, searching deep in her own eyes and Kayden knew he would find no answers there. She wiped his tears away, placing her lips on his wet cheek and even with the sadness that fell from him, he was still warm.

"Let me be the one to carry this knowledge, Dorian. All you must know is that what we seek is in the White Mountains and that as long as the Divines are right, we can still hope."

It took a few seconds for Dorian to process her words. She saw as his eyes lost focus for a brief moment right before his hands tightened their grip on her own, his words ripping their way out of his throat with a hoarse, wounded voice. "Let me stay by *your* side, Kayden! Let me bear this pain with you, *please*." His hands went for her shoulders, the cracking sound of his words loud enough to make her own heart crack and break as Dorian begged. He begged with his voice, with his hands, with his eyes. "You can rely on me, Kay. I *can* be part of it all. *Please*." He begged with his entire heart, and it crushed her.

Her throat ached, her eyes stung, and she spent far too long searching her own voice, trying to mutter words she knew would break him. "Forgive me."

Dorian closed his eyes shut, his grip losing strength until his hands fell in his lap. The Ward stood up and it was as if time had stopped. Dorian's eyes tried to reach her one last time as his fingers tightened around the sword's handle at his waist. Yet time was still running and as the seconds passed the man bowed and walked away without uttering a single word. The sound of the door closing was strong enough to keep echoing inside her head yet it was low and fading like the seconds that she had already lost. As she watched the closed door, Kayden wept. The words she ached to say were so different, the seconds would've turned differently, her skin would be warmer and their hearts would be closer. Whole. Yet she could not and would not say those words ever, even if she had to waste all her seconds in that cruel and ruthless world.

For she loved him far too much to make him suffer alongside her, and she would not give anyone else to Them.

Gallows' Red Sun

Wake of Day - Red Heart, Haste Mountains

"Must I really bother on memorizing so many names? Most of those people won't even be at the castle."

Sir Ward was in a very precarious temper that day. He was not even looking at Bash. He kept sharpening swords and writing letters as if Bash was not even there. That actually hurt a little.

"Due to the circumstances, we can never know when a House may visit the castle. It will be helpful if you at least know who you are watching in case these scenarios occur. Read their names again."

Bash thought Leander was the one who spoke cold words yet the Ward talked as if he was looking at a grave trying to decide if it belonged to him or a pup. The young knight sighed, forcing his eyes to look down at the scribbled papers once again. There were so many names and short descriptions it gave him a headache. Why was he wasting time doing something so useless? He knew he wouldn't recall half of those people. He felt better when they were studying maps, secret routes and passages, best hiding locations, places he would more likely find blades and weapons—*that* was interesting. Those things he remembered.

The names of all the noble Houses' families, daughters, heirs, chiefs, and prestigious ones? He would rather write their full names and just burn those papers in a fire to warm his room. Bash knew how to recognize a gold-plated and he already knew their Houses colors and emblems. What more did he need? Apart from a huge pay, that was. Dear Säh—how *much* could he receive if that was an actual paying job? Infiltrating Albaron's castle and spying on its king should earn him high quality meat for at least three entire months.

A thought suddenly crossed his mind, making Bash purse his lips before opening his mouth again.

"Did you hear any news from Leander? Princess Kayden had asked me to participate in his lessons, but now I am not sure there will be any more of them."

All Bash could hear for an entire minute was the sound of the blade being sharpened and when it finally stopped, the knight wondered why the sound of silence was still so similar. "Leander will be leaving the Divine Order for an undetermined time."

Bash furrowed his eyebrows. "But won't he be leaving for the White Mountains with the child's apprentice?"

It took less than a minute for Dorian to answer that time yet he did not stop sharpening the blade. "Yes, he will."

It took a few minutes for the knight to understand, and when he finally did Bash smiled. "Kayden never really disclosed this mission to the rest of the Order, right?" It was less than a question.

"That is correct."

So their favorite and deranged pet lion was being punished without being punished. Bash thought he would be angrier about it, the injustices of an unfair system that bowed to nobles and let common people like him rot for their mistakes—yet he wasn't. Maybe because he somewhat knew the things that awaited Leander Argyris in the White Mountains, maybe because he simply did not care enough about the man or...maybe he was still trying to forget the things he saw.

By Säh's cursed eyelashes, why had Bash even bothered to follow the man that day? Why had he bothered to pay attention, even? Of course the noble wouldn't be sane! There were no sane people living in Raevich especially with a king such as theirs. If Bash was to feel pity or sorry for a troubled nobleman, he would first have to feel pity and sorry for all the troubled poor bastards like himself and, with all due respect to the poor bastards of Raevich, Bash hadn't time to do so. He was occupied being sorry for humanity as a whole. Then why wouldn't his bloody mind stop thinking about that day?

"I...am not sure if Leander is well enough to go on that mission."

Wait, was that his voice? Was he the one who had spoken? Dorian finally turned, after hours of showing nothing but his back and shoulders, his eyes at least revealing something more than pure stagnancy. "Why would you say that?"

Fuck me twice and let it rot, why *would I say that?* "I just... Well, you clearly weren't there that day. If he reacted like that with one of his own students imagine what it will be like when it's just Leander and the mage. It could be the spark that man needs to really lose his mind and create a licensed mage genocide." The smile died on his face, memories fighting to resurface even after burying them in the depths of his mind. Some things just wouldn't be forgotten, apparently.

The young knight touched those names on the paper, feeling the written marks beneath his fingers almost in a trance.

"You may call it a feeling... Both you and the princess know I am no proper Knight and that this is no place I belong to. The place I belong, there is no simple way to explain and see things. Most people end up facing the same situations in predicable and miserable ways, so believe me when I say that no good may come from someone who reacts to their situation like that. It only brings more predictable outcomes."

For the first time since they had met, Bash felt that Dorian was looking at him, truly looking *at* him. The young knight was not even sure why he was saying such words, maybe he had been traumatized by almost having his balls cut off in a petty spar and the event messed with his brain. He had received that threat more than once after all.

"The one who made the decision was my lady, and I do not believe she will turn back on her words." Was that sadness in the Ward's words? It was almost grief, and for what Bash had no clue. Yet nonetheless, those words made his heart throb for just a brief second before letting it beat at its own pace.

"Well, since it's your lady the princess, we should believe that was the right choice. We need to wake the Ancients after all, bring them a nice feast for breakfast and treats to appease their empty stomachs, isn't that so?" Bash laughed even though there was no soul in his joke, no enthusiasm to fake the tone in his voice. And when the Ward said nothing else it only made it worse, as if the young knight was actually right to be uncertain about the mission. As if Bash was right to be afraid.

Divine Strings

Haze of Dawn - Ice Draco, Haste Mountains

"THANK YOU FOR MEETING with me, Saranm. I owe you my gratitude for tending to one of my knights."

The woman did not sit, her eyes wandering the space with an absent gaze yet there was still a smile on her lips. "There is nothing to thank me for, Lady Faeryl. Also, it was Professor Orion who aided the boy the most. It is thanks to him that your knight will be able to hold a sword in the future, although whether he will be able to use it as well as before remains a mystery."

Kayden felt a strain on her heart, the tip of her fingers going numb as her Sight threatened to strike the leader once again. She had already seen, felt, and heard the events that led to the knight almost losing his hand and she had no desire to relive them once more. Orion must have used time manipulation to heal the boy's injury yet that was extremely risky. Kayden knew only two licensed mages in the entire West Kingdoms that were skilled enough to manipulate time flow and of those two, Orion was by far the most proficient. Yet time manipulation was only that—playing with time. If a wound is not supposed to heal, no matter how much time passes, it cannot be treated by any arcane art in the realm. At least not by human hands. If Orion succeeded—no, if the mage used time manipulation that meant he was confident there would be no great infections and illnesses to befall the knight were they to try to reattach his hand by normal means.

"You still played an important role in his recovery, so I thank you."

The apprentice was closer to the door than she was to Kayden's table however the princess could almost touch her distress. "If that is all you would like to discuss, Lady Faeryl, I need to return to Orion's side. Creating a portal to the White Mountains can be quite demanding, even for my professor, so I wish to aid him—"

"Actually, I also carry orders from your teacher."

That was the first time Saranm showed any emotion on her face, weariness and surprise blending within her eyes as her body took a defensive stance. "Why couldn't he tell me himself?"

"Orion left a couple of hours ago while you slept. He received some news from Carnarbur and had to make haste. He did all the preparations for the portal beforehand as well."

The woman's face was drained of blood and color, her fear reaching Kayden like daggers and melting needles, piercing deep into her skin.

The princess smiled, softening her voice while attempting to control the sickness that came over her. "Orion left you a few supplies, saying you should carry them on the mission. He was also very apologetic that he was not able to bid you farewell."

Saranm's fear subsided a bit. She crossed her arms, a single braid falling from her shoulder all the way to her thighs. "What orders were given to me by Professor Orion?"

Kayden took a few seconds to answer. In that brief moment when silence fell upon them, the princess wanted to scream and cry, cut out her own tongue and burn it, or perhaps simply get rid of her eyes and Sight all together. She hoped the Divines would be as forgiving as They were cruel. "He told you to avoid using fire manipulation the best you can, no matter how small and insignificant the energy."

Saranm's muscles tensed and she clenched her jaw while the grip on her own arms got tighter. "Did he happen to mention why I should avoid fire? It would be most beneficial for the journey on the mountains."

Kayden's voice continued to carry a kind, soothing tone. Yet the person she was trying to soothe was not the mage's apprentice. "Orion did not go much into details, yet he was very certain about it. He also said in the case of any crisis you should contact him at once, I believe you know how to communicate with your professor—"

"Yes," Saranm's reply was almost desperate, cutting Kayden's words so fast it surprised the apprentice herself. "I meant to say, yes, the professor and I share a way to communicate in case of...urgencies." Her figure was smaller, cornered. The silence between them stretched for a few more seconds before the woman opened her mouth again with a weakened smile, her words faint and lacking strength, "We will depart on this Bless, correct? If so, I must apologize and leave now, Lady Faeryl. Where did my professor leave the supplies?"

"He left them inside the chest in his chambers, right before he left. No one touched them, so you can rest assured that your private affairs were respected."

The woman nodded slowly, her gaze lost and out of focus. "That is perfect, Your Highness, thank you kindly." Saranm gave one small bow, her long braid turning slowly as she went for the door. Kayden continued to stare at the knob as if the door would open again with Orion waltzing into the room as he had done so earlier that Gallows.

"Are you certain about this? Shouldn't you at least bid her goodbye?"

"It is better this way. I am not fond of partings." The fact that Orion spoke as if he would never again see his own apprentice made the leader's heart shrink and wither. The mage's gaze gave nothing away of his concerns, not even his voice.

"Is the situation back at Galmion so dire as to force you to depart during the Gallows?"

The mage's gaze did shift then, the light color of his eyes becoming darker and somber. Orion had received an urgent message from King Gregory, requesting him to go back to the capital as soon as he possibly could. Her former teacher had not disclosed the full contents of the message yet even without her cursed Sight, Kayden could tell Orion was definitely not pleased. "I always believed the Gallows, although the time should not be underestimated, was overstated with its numerous rumors and tales...however there were some unexpected casualties that will require my undivided attention. If I was to share the news with Saranm it would only disrupt her mission, so it is better that things remain as they are. Only promise me you will notify me if you see anything, Kayden."

Kayden swore she would fly herself to Carnarbur and pick Orion up if she had to. After all, she was not as knowledgeable about transportation flows as the small counselor. The princess could only rely on the white dragon for emergencies.

Hours after their last meeting, she was still staring at that handle waiting for it to open. Might it be Orion, Saranm or even Leander across the hallway, Kayden felt the strings of the Divines pulling her very core, burning and numbing sensations that never fully spread yet never disappeared. They were waiting, just as she was, for the Sight to be fulfilled. For the hands of fate to choke them all.

For Kayden to succeed and carry Their will.

A Secret From The Gallows

Gallows of Night - Woods

Dark Eye was *NOT* happy.

In his head, Sean-man had died by his hands several times that day alone, let alone the moments when the pig was actually in front of the assassin. No more than two months, that had been their agreement. After the end of these two months, he would give Dark Eye all documents and certificates related to Lee and Dark Eye, on his honor, would leave Sean-man alone. The assassin had no honor as a person, yet he was a somewhat faithful businessman—even if it pained him deeply, he would honor that deal.

Which was why he was praying to all Divines that Sean would break their agreement before the two months, so he could have an excuse to butcher him like a spoiled fish. The thought made the monster in his heart smile like a joyful child.

"What news do you bring on this fine Gallows, sire?"

Oh, he was still *sire,* was he?

"Now, now, uncle, you better pay up first," Dark Eye said with a laugh, his hands already reaching for the goods. Sean gave him a guilty glance, removing the parchment from his pockets.

"Please, do forgive my manners. My contractor and I are mostly anxious about your report. I gather it was not difficult to infiltrate the Divine Order again, correct?"

Dark Eye did not like the look in Sean's gaze when the man said that, didn't like it at all. "You and your contractor can both rest assured about my ways." It was almost impossible to contain the poison in his words as the assassin reached for the parchment, carefully checking its content. It was letters and news from the East Kingdoms regarding Lee's real family. He did not spend a second more glancing at them before stashing them in his own pockets after confirming what he wanted. So far, Sean had also been somewhat of an honorable businessman.

To Dark Eye's *enjoyment.*

"Apparently, one of the Orphys Knights got himself into a bloody mess. Nearly cut out the hand of some random, useless knight during a lesson."

"Which Knight did such atrocity?"

"Gold-plated, the son of Adon Argyris. I was hoping I could get that hand as a nice souvenir to give to you yet it is still attached to the human, unfortunately."

Sean smirked at the mention of the hand. "Anything else?"

"Her Royal Highness sent him to some contemplation, somewhere."

Sean-man raised his eyebrows. "Is that so? What more can you tell me about our sweet, dear princess? After all, your job is to keep her under your watchful eyes."

Dark Eye gave a strained smile that made every single muscle of his face hurt. "I am well aware of what I was hired for, uncle. The princess has barely left her chambers after the incident with the Argyris and whenever she is seen it is either talking with Carnarbur's counselor or locked inside her office. There is not much to tell."

The older man crossed his arms, shaking his head while filling his voice with layers of disappointment. "I was hoping you could have brought more for me, sire. I am really doing the best I can to help you set your friend free, back to his dear family. You could be doing more for him—"

Dark Eye grabbed the man by the collar, showing not only his teeth but his fine dagger, pointing the blade toward Sean's eyes. "Listen here, *uncle.* I don't really care about you or your benefactor and I'm starting to care less and less about my friend since you are bothering me so much. Maybe I can kill you and be on my way as if our nice agreement had never happened."

Sean's eyes widened, his face reddening as the man stuttered his words, "W-wait, please try to understand, sire. It is not our wish to upset you!"

"Then stop telling me how I should do my job," the assassin muttered under his breath, putting his dagger away, and fixing Sean-man's clothes. "I am a professional, uncle. Isn't that why your contractor chose me?"

The man smiled in the most uncomfortable way, grabbing his shirt with white knots showing on his hands. "I beg your forgiveness, sire. It was not my intention to offend you. It is just that my benefactor is worried about the Divine Order! You see, Princess Kayden is withholding *so* much from those poor knights, we only wish to shed some light on the truth."

Dark Eye laughed, putting his hands on his waist and feeling the weapons beneath his clothes around his waistline. Should he use one of them just for the fun of it? "Is that so? A leader—no, a *royal*—hiding things from those that stand below them? Oh, I am *shocked*, uncle! I may not even sleep this Gallows."

Yet Sean's eyes glowed as they reflected the flame's light, revealing something else behind them—a spark, a desire, moving alongside the lit fire. "You fail to see the depths of her deceit, sire. If my contractor is indeed correct, Her Highness Kayden Faeryl is setting the entire Divine Order for its damnation. You may take my words as nothing but a humble suggestion, sire, but maybe you would like to know what the princess is hiding behind her closed doors."

Dark Eye loathed the fact that he was wasting his time with this man, let alone listening to his words. Yet what he despised the most was his own curiosity and the fact that the one he was most intrigued by was Sean-man's contractor. Wasn't it funny how that person seemed to know so much yet refused to share even a little? There was a low rumble, a murmur caressing Dark Eye's mind as he pondered what to do.

"Who is your contractor, uncle? Why does he care so much? Let the Order burn, isn't that what others often say? Even these days with the return of winged demons people do not trust the Order still, so why care? This makes your contractor the suspicious one in my eyes."

Sean softened his expression while opening his arms with a smile so sweet it could give him cramps and diarrhea. "My contractor is truly a special being, Dark Eye, sire. I dare you to find a benefactor kinder and more diligent than that person in this entire realm. The only thing that motivates my benefactor is the opportunity to make this world a better, loving place to all living creatures."

Dark Eye could not even blink.

That was maybe the most utter bullshit he had ever heard in his entire life. He *was* going to be sick after all.

"Sure, uncle, whatever words you speak." The daggers on his body became colder as the minutes of that cursed meeting stretched, making his skin itch.

Everything about Sean-man and his unrealistic contractor stank worse than burning decay and rot, and that was really bothering the assassin. One does not live long in Raevich by being a brainless fool and doing every job that pays well. Dark Eye knew the jobs that paid and the ones that were just impossible. He knew the difference between an ill-minded person, an idiot, and a vengeful kin. He would deal with idiots and people seeking vengeance to fuel their hate—he would not deal with those who did not possess a sane mind. And the more Dark Eye listened to Sean and heard about his mysterious benefactor he felt a weird taste in his mouth.

Taste of pure shit.

"You should try to go inside the princess's chambers and her office, Dark Eye, sire. I am sure you will be delighted at what you find."

He was *sure* he doubted that. "Whenever you wish to meet again, you know how to contact me."

Even after he was far away from their meeting place, with the wind howling in the distance, Dark Eye was not happy. The assassin loved the Gallows for he knew the wretched hour better than he knew himself. Yet he knew nothing about the people who were so intent on blackmailing him into doing their will. He did not like that, he did not like them, and he did not like doing those things while being put in such situation.

So maybe it was time to try to find out some things about that humanitarian benefactor of Sean-man.

Chapter XI

Journal Entry, Autumn

Bless

We left before the Knights departed from their mission. It feels odd to be called high commander, at best.

Our leader, Kayden, made no special request, however I felt it was best for us to leave without disrupting the Knights' preparations and the arrangements for the tournaments. Someone in our party is acquainted with Ritta and Felicia's family so we shall begin our search in Carnarbur. The sisters have some relatives on the Narturers' island, so we will probably reach the kingdom in the next couple of weeks.

I attempted to contact the others' relatives one more time as well. So far there was either no response or my fellow comrades never came back home. Since I never received a confirmation from the twins' family, they are now our best chance.

I only pray to our Divines that they are all well. That they are all safe. That Clarice is safe.

Otherwise, Sean, I will come for you and deliver Death's sweet kiss straight to your lips.

This, I swear.

Will of The Wind

Bless of Day - Haste Mountains

An Orphys Knight and a licensed mage were departing to the White Mountains at last. Dorian did not know where they were in the Haste Mountains, he just followed Kayden as he always did, his feet guiding him with a mind of their own as if they were afraid Dorian would get lost if left to his own thoughts. It was the first time the Ward was seeing Leander Argyris after the incident and, as far as he could see, the nobleman was behaving like he always portrayed himself. However, Dorian sensed, felt deep in his skin, how something about the air around the warrior was not usual. The younger Knight's words would not leave Dorian's mind no matter how hard he tried and with Kayden pushing him away, the Ward was left completely in the dark.

If there was something to show him—give him a taste—of the kind of environment the White Mountains were, all he had to do was look at the apprentice and Knight's armor. Leander Argyris had a big pelt on his back on top of his gambeson armor, a thick white fur covering his boots, while darker sets protected his wrists and the hood that covered his face.

As for the mage's apprentice, she wore a dark set of padded armor and a heavy black cape that almost touched the floor, with fur coming out of her boots, gauntlets, and hood. The Ward had never stepped into those cursed mountains, and seeing that made him feel grateful for that fact.

His lady often kept her Sight to herself and Dorian knew better than to ask. He saw how painful it was to her, how Kayden would sometimes cry herself to sleep when Memorial Day came, and how that curse would overwhelm her with nothing but grief and pain. So, Dorian never asked, he just listened—to her concerns, her crying, her hopes, Dorian always listened with open arms. Yet that day, he *saw* Kayden. The princess was crumbling piece by piece by herself, yet she assured him she was holding all the pieces alone. That she would not let them fall. But Dorian felt the air around her, so cold, so *distant...* It was as if Kayden was not even there in the real world with him. She was being kept by the Divines, by her Sight, whatever it was—his dearest friend was creating a wall to keep all her suffering inside, away from him. How could she do that? After all they have been through, after all the pain they bore together, how *could* she?

Then it came to him. *They* had shown her something. Something about the mission, something about the Argyris and the mage, something Kayden refused to talk about. Something she would carry alone to her grave. And after Bash's warning about the Argyris's state, Dorian could do nothing but wonder and wait with tied hands. For he would not pray to the ones responsible for his lady's suffering.

"Most of the preparations were done by Professor Orion, so we have little to do," Saranm explained while carrying the bags filled with supplies inside the circle. It reminded him of the circle Kayden had made the Order create on the night of her Blood Ceremony. The symbols, the pattern—only the size was different. This circle was much bigger compared to the one that Kayden used that night. "My core's energy is enough to transport the two of us and our belongings, so you do not need to engage as well, Lady Faeryl."

By Kayden's state, Dorian was unsure if his lady even *could* help. From all he had heard about the arcane arts, about the cores, energies, and manipulation, a mage's strength and reliability came from their state of mind and body. *The more well rested, the more control over their manipulation a mage has*, those were words that Kayden had spoken to him once. How "well rested" one had to be was what he really wished to know.

They were in a wide room where the roof opened through a mechanism that Kayden operated by pushing a lever on the wall as soon as they entered. The sky was fully exposed to them, sunlight pouring into the room alongside a chilling breeze. It was a bit colder than Dorian expected. The leader told him as she watched the question filling his eyes. "The sun is a powerful source of energy, which is why we are doing this in an open space."

"Would it not be easier to fly there?" When all eyes shifted to Bash, the boy let out a weak smile as if to justify his question. "Please, tell me you *at least* considered the idea. So far that's the only thing we can do with them." By "them", Dorian assumed the Knight was speaking about the Ancients.

The Argyris was silent for a brief moment before locking eyes with the circle in front of him, his arms crossed with the lion pendant shining fiercely on his chest.

"Amträhfar refused." It was all the nobleman replied.

"We must use the strongest light of the day, so let's make haste. The circle will take you both to the destination of your choice, Leander, since Saranm has never been in the mountains." Kayden's voice echoed through the room, pointing toward the circle. "You must keep a clear image in your head. Visualize the place you want to go in your mind and in your heart."

"How does one *visualize* something in their heart, Lady Faeryl?" His reply was dry and cool.

"Someone like yourself would not know, warrior. It is an art too advanced for you, perhaps your Ancient can guide you," Orion's apprentice spoke with a smile playing at her lips and reflecting in her gaze as she stared at the Argyris from the side. The nobleman barely met her gaze as he lingered outside the circle, eyeing the bags and the symbols marked on the floor.

"I only need to think about a particular spot, correct?" he asked while shifting the sword at his waist.

Kayden met his eyes and in that moment, Dorian saw almost as if time itself had halted. The faintest of glows passed through her eyes, a shiver that made the princess hold her breath and clench her fists, a pain that reflected in her eyes for the briefest second.

Then she smiled. "Correct, just picture yourself back in the White Mountains. Saranm will aid you with the rest."

Dorian walked toward them before his mind could think of a reason. Maybe deep down he needed to see the man for himself, look into the Argyris's eyes and try to find lies in Bash's words. Try to find a hole, a fault, anything that could hinder the Divines' plans for that man and for that mission, something to prove that Kayden did not need to be so afraid. That things would all be fine. The Ward met the Argyris at the border of the circle, opening his mouth to say whatever words that came to him.

Yet no words were spoken.

"What is it, Ward?"

Dorian could not breathe.

He tried to inhale and gather all the air inside him, tried to fill his lungs again and again, yet nothing came for there was no air. His eyes were lost for a few seconds, meeting Leander Argyris's gaze one last time before the man turned his back on him out of patience, walking into the circle. Dorian gasped, choked, he could hardly move as he watched the nobleman and the apprentice inside the circle, the symbols glowing and shining as fiercely as the sun itself. The Ward took steps back and only when there was distance between them did the air come back to him, his lungs aching and burning as if someone had a lit torch inside them. Dorian felt his heart race as he looked at the Argyris one last time, the words finally reaching his lips.

"*Wait—!*"

In a blink they were gone as the light and space bent within them, embracing them both with a loud snap. Bash looked at him with an odd gaze, glancing back at Kayden with doubt in his voice.

"Was there something wrong?"

The princess would not even look at Dorian as she answered her Knight, "No, all is well, Bash. Let us leave this place—you have training of your own."

Bash glanced back at him, as if the Knight was unsure. The Ward took a deep breath, his emotions hitting his resolve and heart like turbulent waves, his thoughts in complete turmoil. He knew, deep in his soul, he would some day regret that moment. However, if he let things be, Dorian would not be able to live with himself.

"Bash, you may go to the Reliquary. I will meet you there shortly after I talk with my lady."

Both Kayden and the Knight widened their eyes, yet only one stayed. Even after Bash left, it took several minutes for his words to leave his mouth, the sentences carrying the weights that had been corrupting and tainting his heart for days, weeks.

"I never doubted or disproved any of your choices, Kay. Even when I could not understand them, I trusted your judgment."

The fact that Kayden still refused to meet his eyes, that his lady still attempted to dismiss his concerns—it hurt him. "I thank you for your words, Dorian, yet there is still much that we must do and—"

"Who are *we*, Kay?" His words bled and his voice mirrored his pain, yet even then he did not stop. "You and me, you and your Knights, you and the Divines, who? Because you are making sure that everyone around you stays clueless about your plans."

Anger flashed in her eyes, the princess walking closer to her Ward with closed fists. "You know pretty well those are not *my* plans, Dorian. *Nothing* about this situation was in my plans."

Dorian's grip on his sword was strong enough to break his fingers.

"Be the plans of those damned Divines—you are the Order's *leader*! You should know better than anyone that Leander was not in a stable state of mind to go on that mission, yet you still sent him to that place—"

"Because we do not have a choice!"

"There is no we!" His shout made Kayden hold her breath, her lips trembling. "For this entire month there's only been *you*, Kay! Ever since the ceremony you have refused to share *anything*, even with your own Knights! If you were to lie to them and say you received visions through the white dragon, you could still bring them close to you, yet you keep pushing everyone away from your problems—you keep pushing *me* away!"

Kayden stood breathes away from her Ward, their arms almost touching; to Dorian, she could not be more distant from him.

"Do you think I ever wished for *this*?" Her whispers carried not only thorns that pierced his ears, but sorrow and grief. A voice that whenever he listened to it, it felt like a wail that never found its place. "To be the one responsible for leading an army—one that we do not even *possess* yet—to a battle we will most certainly lose? To be the one responsible for every life in the realm, the one people can blame for their salvation or utter destruction?"

To hear his princess say, with such certainty, that she thought they would not win the battle... It sent shivers down all the way to his bones. To know that his lady *believed* that...it destroyed him; it broke his soul. However, he could not bring himself to stop, to let his words be buried within his heart again. So he spoke. He spoke words he knew would come back to haunt him, for he had no other choice at that moment.

"The people around you also carry this same burden, Kay!" Dorian grabbed her shoulders, trying to contain the desperation on his words, trying to not let so many emotions escape from him, for he *knew* it would hurt Kayden. "Your visions and your fate, they do not affect only you! They affect me, the Orphys Knights, the Order, Orion and his apprentice, the kingdoms—every single person related to them! And you *know* this." His voice broke, tears threatening to escape his eyes as he saw Kayden crumbling away, the pain and misery flooding from her eyes stabbing him like daggers.

"I already told you, Dorian. My Sight, this knowledge, it is mine to bear. The Divines' Will is absolute, something we mortals could never comprehend."

"They are hurting you, Kay! And by pushing everyone away, you are not condemning only yourself, but all of us. The Knights deserved to know the fate that awaits them; Leander shouldn't have left for this mission."

"Our fate depends on that mission." Her words were like thunder and the air that surrounded them turned ice cold, so distant Dorian thought Kayden spoke from another land, another world. She took a few steps back, pulling herself away from his grasp, her gaze meeting his eyes. Yet it felt cold. "I am not the one that shall challenge the Divines and neither should you. If They wish to curse us mortals with Their Sights, so be it. If I have to carry Their will in order to save us all, so be it. If I must suffer in order to guarantee our victory...so be it. Neither you, nor anyone else, should have a say in this matter."

He saw as her eyes trembled, her voice carrying not only anger and frustration but pure anguish and mourning.

"If you excuse me, I must go back to my duties; I will leave you to yours." The words left her mouth against their will, their presence fading and weak. And as Kayden turned and left the space, Dorian could not help himself but weep. Not for his own hurt and pain, but for his lady's. The Färküh Wards' insignia shone in his chest, reflecting the sunlight with pride. Yet to Dorian, the shackles that bounded him to his fate, the chains that weighted in his soul did not share that pride. They sunk deeper and deeper, into a fearsome darkness the Ward was afraid to face. He had forgotten his place, and he paid the price.

As Färküh Dorian, his fate was always to serve.

Yet even after he was all alone in that space, watching nothing but an empty circle basking in sunlight, Dorian could still not forget that feeling. The moment when the Ward met the Argyris eyes, he knew. There was no spell, no trickery that made the air simply vanish—it had been him, Leander Argyris himself. It was at that moment that Dorian not only realized the fact, but he felt deep inside his skin and soul as if he had the Sight himself.

Bash was right. And worst of all, so would be Kayden.

A Warrior's Duty

Wake of Day - White Mountains

Twenty-Nine Nights Before Memorial Day

The wind was brutal, icy, and harsh yet it was not the wind that woke him. Leander's own body knew where he was before he opened his eyes, the memories flooding him all at once, making his heart race. Pain was what made the warrior sit up, his head fazed and troubled. He felt nauseated and his muscles were sore and rigid, however what was truly unsettling was all that snow. It was as if he had turned back time, the White Mountains unchanged after all those years. They had been transported to the exact place the man had pictured in his mind, the spot where he had stayed and known for months when he was younger. Three months he had stayed in those grounds after his eleventh birthday. Three months that felt like one's lifetime, a time that made it possible for him to return as a true warrior, a legitimate Argyris. And those three months were all it took for that place to be burned inside his memories forever.

"You finally decided to stand, handsome?" Saranm's words reached him with ease, her face standing not even a meter away. "You should stay put for a few minutes, until the sickness comes to pass. For someone with such a small core, to endure an energy this strong, it can be a burden on their bodies." Her words were masked with mischief and scorn yet the woman's smile and gaze whispered words on their own.

Leander could not decide what he dreaded more, the cursed mountains or that woman so near him. He raised himself, his stomach turning over while shivers ran through his spine and skin. "We shall not make any delays. Can you feel the Sword's presence from here?"

Saranm said nothing at first, her eyes analyzing him with a chilly, fierce stare. "There is a faint source, up north."

"We must secure our supplies first. There is enough for two weeks. However, one can never know in these mountains. We must prepare a strong heat source and find a good shelter in case the storm worsens." Leander had brought enough for an entire month the first time he came to the White Mountains. All supplies were ruined during the first two days. In those lands, safety and comfort were not what protected people, it was what got them killed.

The woman started to laugh, the devilish grin filling her lips alongside a charming gaze. "Aren't you a precious little man, handsome. Here I was asking myself when you were going to start giving orders and I must say, I thought you would be giving them before we even landed, if that was possible."

Leander closed his fists, fighting himself so that annoyance would not stain his words. "I believe I am here to make us survive through this mission and because Lady Faeryl judged me to be the best *guide* to secure our lives. Warmth, food, and shelter; that is how we will live to see the next Bless."

Saranm shifted her long braid, her eyes searching for something on the landscape. He had no idea what the woman wished to see—there were only trees, snow, and rocks surrounding them. Nothing else. Leander recalled one cave nearby, a place they could stay when Fall came, and it would not be difficult to start a fire. He could only pray that the Sword was not located at one of the mountains' peaks. If that ever came to be the case, they would need food and pelts with urgency.

They had to start hunting soon.

"Come this way," the mage suddenly spoke, accommodating one of the bags on her back, walking within the trail.

"Is that the direction you are *sensing* the Sword?" That time the warrior did not hide the contempt in his voice.

She laughed with amusement, the sound coming out of her mouth almost as a purr. "It would do you good, warrior, to not question what you don't understand. Yes, this is the way."

Before his feet could move, Leander felt the stone in his wrist pulsate and sting as if it was a warning. Amträh was close, yet the dragon refused to be anywhere near the mountains. It was the beast's stubbornness that forced them to take such ridiculous measures to go to that ice prison, the reason why Leander was feeling nauseated that same moment, and why they had to use wretched *magic*. When Leander tried to pry into the beast's mind, all he could sense was the strong aversion the creature felt regarding the mage, which Leander would not even dare to question. However, the warrior did find the dragon's feelings odd. Though he did not care the slightest to pry further.

Not only that, but Amträhfar showed a great contempt for the White Mountains and their freezing, harsh weather. He would not come closer to the location, his presence was far in the west and away from all that cold. Deep down Leander was envious, for he too wished to be as far as he could be from that place, yet the image of the Sacred Sword shone in his head. The Argyris could picture himself holding the artifact in his hands, bringing it back to his household to his father's grasp.

How would the family praise his name, his feats? How long would they bask in his glory and success? The promises brought by that bright future, one filled with prestige and honor, was enough to make Leander clench his teeth and march forward deeper into those accursed mountains.

DO NOT ENGAGE DANGER. I WILL NOT AID.

I would never ask.

That had been the only exchange of words between the warrior and his dragon. There was no concern in the creature's words and if the beast hid any other emotion, Leander never attempted to pry. He kept following that woman, his gaze every so often wandering to the sides and over his shoulder.

Something felt...odd. A feeling that he could not dispel no matter how many times he attempted to ignore it. What *was* it? Was it something in the air? Leander felt strange, this unsettling cloud getting thicker and heavier in his chest.

Wait, no. That was certainly a mistake. It was thoughts of the black creature tampering with his own, the dragon's own superstitions and fears getting in his way. Leander knew those mountains better than he knew his own home. The air was warmer than it should be, the wind harsher and angrier, yet there was nothing to be noted as uncommon. Leander would neither indulge his dragon's fantasies nor feed that woman's futile *magic senses.* There were six senses the Argyris counted on, the only ones that truly mattered; only one was born from battle. And *that* was the one sense he trusted the most.

As if the Divines had intruded his own thoughts, the warrior heard something within the trees. It was a low, faint sound that the mountains were glad to swallow whole, yet his ears knew better than to let such a sound pass by. His ears, his nose, his own skin—they had learned well from all those years. Especially the months Leander lived on those same grounds. On the White Mountains every sound missed was one step closer to Death's kiss. He did not stop walking, yet his hand closed around the sword's hilt, waiting. The wind tried more than once to cover the sounds, cover the movement within the trees. It failed.

Still, they were both ambushed.

"Don't move!" Leander shouted as the seven wolves jumped and surrounded them. Their front teeth were long, two tusks that were as sharp as daggers, their tips a bit curved. Their bite was strong enough to crush bones, and their black claws could tear human skin off as if it was nothing but thin paper.

"Not moving won't make them go away, handsome," the woman whispered behind him, her words stiff and restricted like their movements. Leander responded with a low, firm voice trying to keep his heartbeat steady.

"I thought you had studied all there was to know about the White Mountains."

"Which is why I'm *stating* this fact to you."

Leander scoffed, his fingers starting to remove the sword from the scabbard, calculating inch by inch. Those wolves were not keen to hunt in large packs, five was already a great number for them. They would not sneak up on their prey and chase it, they would surprise it and surround it to attack all at once. The moment any of them moved the wolves would attack. Leander had three of them locked in his sight, however he was not sure if he would be able to avoid all three if they decided to attack together. Which he was almost certain they would. All the wolves growled, saliva dripping out of their mouths while baring their teeth. There was this hunger, this ferocity that filled their bright yellow eyes that made his muscles stiff and tense, even heavy. *Pathetic*. Leander had faced stronger, bigger animals during the Argyrises annual hunts—his body should know better than to respond in such a way.

"You can stand aside, witch. I can deal with them." Any properly trained Argyris should do that much. So, he had to do more. Maybe try to beat all seven by himself.

However, Saranm only laughed behind him, the sound making the creatures tense their legs as if they were getting ready to jump. "I would rather die, warrior, than leave all the fun to you."

Two of the wolves moved at the exact same second, one aiming higher at Leander's neck while the other went straight for his ankle. The sword's blade swung in a single arc, hitting the animal's body as if it was made of rocks. That *damned* fur of theirs. Yet even though the blade did not cut through the wolf's coat, the warrior's strength was enough to send its body away. As for the other wolf—

Its mouth closed around Leander's leg, the man feeling the pressure of the teeth trying to sink into and penetrate his skin. He was wearing fur boots, made from a troll's coat, and it was the only piece of clothing he wore that had not been frozen and damaged by the White Mountains' heartless environment. The wolf kept chewing his leg, its tusks almost reaching his skin when the Argyris hit it in the head with the sword's pommel. In the next second, the first wolf, the one Leander had hit with the blade, came at him once more, a third jumping at his chest and another at his arm. An ice shard came flying to his side, hitting one of the beasts right in its face. The Argyris wanted to look back, his eyes aching to watch what was happening behind him, what that woman was doing. His lips pressed themselves together as the man dared her once again to intervene in his fight.

Blood boiling inside him, the man raised his sword high toward the sky while shifting the weight of the weapon in his hands, its blade swinging in the air, fending off the creatures that came at him by striking them with the iron blade again and again, feeling as the metal hit their bones and limbs until they winced and whimpered. The Way of Sword was with him, a real strength feeding his movements as his body moved and dodged just as it was trained to do—a pure, heated battle. That was how an Argyris and true warrior fought. How he would be remembered.

He heard another wolf come from behind him, its mouth already closing on his head bringing with it the rotten scent of death and blood. Leander began to spin his whole body, moving the sword to attempt to block the attack, when suddenly a huge hole opened in the beast's head. A piece of ice, unnaturally white and clear, had burst from within the wolf's head, its shards dripping with the animal's blood and insides. The wolf fell dead on the ground, the snow turning red below it, causing a chain reaction on its fellow pack members. The creatures became more agitated and aggressive, and Leander had the time to glance at the woman before returning to his own fight, her hands raised toward him as she fought for breath, a strain marking her golden eyes.

"Do not interfere with my enemies, woman," he spoke with frustration building up within his words while he kicked a wolf in the snout and broke the leg of another. The mage's apprentice snorted, the sound of shots increasing behind him.

"That one was *mine*, love. You still have your toys to play with, so let me play with mine as I see fit."

Playing with dirty tricks. Disgust was all he could truly feel, the sword becoming hotter in his hands as it finally pierced the wolves' hides. Within him, a warm sensation began to spread and, for a split second, Leander could swear he was stronger, faster. The Ancient's presence was unmistakable in his mind, the dragon's grasp seeking and searching for something inside with a gaze that burned the Argyris with its intensity.

Why are you prying, beast? You made it clear I would receive no aid from you.

I NOT THE ONE AIDING.

The dragon's presence got weaker until it became nothing but a fading flame inside his head. The warm feeling the man felt began to disappear as the seconds stretched, even when the sword's metal burned in his hands. Although he could not comprehend the dragon's words, Leander felt relieved. To receive the creature's aid to beat only a pack of wolves—he would *never* dare to stoop so low. He was an Argyris, a true warrior, a carrier of the Way of Sword. His achievements should belong to him alone.

Then it happened.

He distracted himself for a brief second, the sharp pain in his head worsening for a moment; that was all it took. The wolf with the broken leg jumped at his back while another one closed its mouth on his thigh, two long tusks sinking deep into his flesh. Leander *felt* the tusks moving, grinding inside him, the wolf's teeth brushing beside his bone. The Argyris screamed, the sword protecting his neck while he punched the wolf that had its mouth on his flesh with his free hand. On his back, the other beast kept using its black claws to tear his skin yet it hadn't been able to pierce through the fur hide the man was wearing. But it would soon.

That was when he felt that wave, an energy that made him feel weightless for a split second before throwing him meters away in the snow. The energy was warm, like a summer's breeze, however it made the wound on his leg throb and pulse as if it was aflame. Leander could feel the snow covering him like a gelid, unwelcome embrace. His mind raced while he tried to get ahold of reality. When he attempted to stand, pain shot through his entire being, a pain so sharp it made his vision darken and his mind light. Leander clenched his teeth, using the sword to support himself, searching for the creatures around him.

He found none. Not alive, at least.

When the Argyris finally got on his two feet, Saranm was giving the final blow on the last wolf, the snow around her fluttering and moving before becoming a pure ice spear that went into the wolf's mouth, sticking the creature into a tree. The woman's arms fell loose beside her, her breathing heavy and uneven as she fought for air. When she met his gaze, the mage smiled.

"Forgive me, handsome, you were taking your sweet time with them and my patience was running short. You will do better next time, I am sure."

He wanted to scream and shout at her. Yet before he could open his mouth the man saw his own body tumbling to the side, his mind beginning to slip away.

It was as if all that snow was inside him, freezing every inch, every corner of his body. Leander glanced at his thigh, blood gushing out of the wound like water in a stream.

Fuck.

He needed to cauterize it, no—he had to get his bag. There was a tool that would aid him in the bag.

Leander felt a hand touch his cheek. It felt so warm he almost closed his eyes to simply relish the feeling.

"Open your eyes, love. Otherwise, I will kiss you."

His eyes were closed? The Argyris forced them open, his eyelids heavier than rocks, seeing a face that it took him a few seconds to recognize. How she was there, so fast? Did the hand that touched him belong to her? If so, he would rather cover his entire face with snow.

"Bag..." He tried to speak, unsure if he succeeded. Saranm glanced behind her shoulder before meeting his eyes again. There was something in her eyes, a glow of sorts, something that made Leander feel uncomfortable. Yet apart from that there was this thing, a feeling that filled the woman's gaze entirely, however Leander could not say for sure what it was.

"You can curse at me later, handsome. Right now, please be still."

Saranm grabbed his sword with her warm hands. Someone like her should not even touch his sword let alone hold it. How dare she taint a true weapon—*his* weapon—

The metal touched his skin.

The scent of burnt flesh came to him first, followed by the sound of his own skin burning.

Pain was the last thing he felt.

Challenged By The Gallows

Gallows of Night - Silver Grounds, Haste Mountains

Twenty-Nine Nights Before Memorial Day

It was late. People would, wisely, avoid the Gallows be it by their own superstitions or by bedtime tales that went too far on scaring children. Even when most of those stories were real, Bash could always find scarier things to fear apart from the Gallows. It was not hard at all, in fact all he had to do was think about *where* he was, *who* he was, and what was being asked of him. There, he almost pissed himself again. Especially after the dream that woke him that night. A red sun glowing in the Gallows' dark sky with dead bodies rising from the ground, as if they were all answering a call. Maybe that was the real world and Bash was dreaming about the end of theirs and being responsible for it when truly he was just another corpse digging through dirt to watch the pretty sun shine.

I need you to go undercover.

Those were Kayden's words to him weeks ago after giving to sire Leander the dangerous White Mountains mission. Wasn't that ironic? His sweet and kind leader wanted to send him on an undercover mission, in her own kingdom, to spy on her own father. *Him*. Like a rat creeping the sewers. Should he feel honored or ashamed for giving himself away? Maybe no matter how clean his clothes were Bash would only be able to live in that one reality, the one filled with death, dirt, and Gallows. And Princess Kayden Faeryl knew it, that was why she asked *him.*

Dorian had spent hours of their days teaching Bash all about Albaron and its Houses, the castle, and the important places and spots. Bash was baffled that the castle did possess—no joke—real secret passages. With all due honesty, Bash would sell himself short for secret passages especially if he could open them with a torch lever. *That* would be the childhood dream he never knew he had, coming to life.

However, even when all the young knight could do about his current situation was joke and laugh at it, a bottomless pit grew in his stomach as the day for his mission approached.

"The House Vam'Dammes has a very close relationship with Carnarbur, since they receive their precious stones from the kingdom. They are also very keen to hire servants whenever they need instead of opting for prestigious ones."

"On Memorial Day, all Houses will gather at the castle to celebrate. That will be your chance to infiltrate the castle as a Vam'Dammes' servant. Orion has already written a recommendation letter that will reach Klaude Vam'Dammes. You remember who Klaude is?"

"The head of the family—"

"So, when you get hired by Klaude, you know where you have to go and what you have to do, correct?"

Both Dorian and his dear princess had spent hours going over the *plans* with Bash, about the Vam'Dammes, about Memorial Day, about the castle, about King Felix, all the while bringing such a tension and pressure into the room, Bash thought he would suffocate. If they weren't talking, why teach him *together?* Better yet, why not make their peace in a bed and be done with it? Share less heated words and more heated bodies—everyone knew sooner or later Grumpy Ward would be the one apologizing. Unless he was gravely mistaken about their relationship; he was willing to bet on it.

Bash thought he would become another ill-minded bastard before the day ended. He didn't mind about infiltrating the castle much less about pretending to be a gold-plated's servant to spy on a rotten king. In all honesty, the whole idea was entertaining to him. The young knight would make fools out of them all, listening to their secrets and devious plots. That was, maybe, one of the most humorous and amusing things he would do in that entire year. The princess even convinced Vührähkam to let Bash ride him in order to reach the location on time! There were only wins in that situation for him, *nothing* to complain about.

Then why did Bash feel so...anxious? Troubled, even. Was it because he would be used as a tool by a noble—a *royal* for that matter—to spy on another royal? Was it because the entire realm was doomed and even as a *chosen Knight* all Bash was good enough for was to spy on an old man? Deep inside he was happy, probably, to do the boring stuff for he was not fit to be one of the heroes at all. He was born and raised in East Raevich, under Säh's shameful gaze—if there was something he was good at, it was the shady side of business. He should be thrilled to be able to swim in such warm, known waters. Yet he was not. Bash could not focus, could not sleep, and was wandering the dark halls inside the mountain with so many thoughts running through his head, the young knight was having serious trouble making sense of a quarter of them.

What could Kayden possibly want from her father to *forcefully invite* Bash on an undercover mission to spy and report on the infamous king? How far he could go in order to keep his mission and orders a secret? Was he allowed to silence other servants? Kidnap a Vam'Dammes? Murder someone? Things could get a lot darker quite fast, so how much control was Bash allowed to have in those scenarios? Since no answer would simply wander into his mind, Bash decided he could force himself to grow tired and exhausted in those haunting Gallows by training alone at the Silver Grounds. There was no more flimsy lion to get under his skin, no more Raevich "brothers" to keep pestering him about his unworthy blood and above all else—

He had the secrecy of his dear Gallows.

Imagine the irony when he saw the moment he opened the doors, swinging a sword in the middle of the room, none other than his dear leader Kayden. *Princess* Kayden. Their Grumpy Ward needed to learn more about courting; things would go nowhere this way.

"If you wouldn't mind, Bash, could you close the door behind you? The winds travel fast inside the mountains." Her voice was calm, her words soothing, and yet all he could feel was a chill running through his spine. He really did not wish to meet her at that sour moment, when his weak heart was wavering and his occupied mind was far too confused. The stables were quite close to where they stood, after all.

When he closed the doors realizing he was still inside the training grounds, Bash knew he had lost his chance to perform the most insane yet amazing horse escape ever to be witnessed by mankind. Or at least, by the princess.

Such an escape could only be surpassed by a *dragon* escape, however what could he do if Leander got the cool one?

Bash took a few steps inside, looking around as he swung both arms. "If you desire, princess, I can come back at another time—"

"Nonsense. Grab a weapon, let's train together." Kayden barely looked at him as she spoke, completely focused on the way her sword moved in the air. It was interesting to see how her movements resembled Leander's more than her loyal Ward's.

But train together? Against the bloody Tournament winner?

What a *spectacular* idea.

The training grounds were almost haunting with so many candles lit, the fire's light providing little more than the minimum amount one would need to see more clearly. Even with the leader's gaze focused on her own weapon the knight could feel its weight, his heart beating faster and heavier in his chest. That could be an opportunity, if he was to be honest. He went for the short sword, however he stopped for a brief moment, pondering, thinking, considering the possibilities until his fingers finally reached the longsword. It had been some time since Bash had used one so maybe he wouldn't be so terrible at it, with some luck. It took only a few minutes for him to be staring at Kayden's green eyes, all of her attention focused on the young knight himself. She had her hair loose and was not wearing any armor, which to him was the most unfamiliar image of her. However, she did look paler than usual.

Had she lost weight? That only made Bash feel like an intruder, a dark shadow creeping behind a pretty and sick princess who was training in her nightgown in hopes to be alone. Why would the princess ask him to stay? Showing her bare arms and legs—well, that was actually quite a long gown so one-fifth of her legs—made the knight wonder how many scandalous rumors could be born just by that fact alone. *A shadow and a princess in the Gallows*. Maybe his heart would explode and send his entire head flying before any scandal came to be.

"You attack and I defend, then we switch."

It took five seconds for his brain to understand that her words were not a question.

"Oh, sure enough! Yes, we can do that."

Kayden did not smile or laugh, she simply put her guard up and waited. He should not be feeling shy, much less uncomfortable to attack, but here he was. It took Bash a few moves to understand and get the sword's balance again and a few more for him to find the strikes he was looking for—neither too weak nor too strong. He doubted it would make that much difference anyway. Kayden kept blocking every single strike with such ease, it made him feel bad enough to push a bit harder. Yet as he listened to the metals hitting and resonating together in a constant rhythm, his heartbeat slowed down, becoming steadier. Calming down due to the sound of weapons, that was one of the only things that actually made some sense.

"Princess—"

"You may call me Kayden, Bash." The leader cut him with a smile, her eyes glancing toward him from time to time.

The knight let out a weak smile. "Forgive me for that. So, Kayden...I—it is pure curiosity, mind you, so I hope you will not feel offended by my words—but why would you want to spy on your king?"

He saw her eyes getting darker, and as the princess blinked, a shiver went through her body the moment their swords collided as if she was ill. However, there was still warmth in her voice. "Even if you are from Raevich, you must have heard the many rumors and fame surrounding my father. I worry for my people, that is all."

Bash was also smart enough to know that the princess would not say much more regarding that subject. Even then, he tried. "King Felix sure made a name for himself, yes—I just thought it was odd. For another royal, especially one in your position, to create such an elaborate plan when there are more pressing matters."

His sword went flying, the impact so strong that Bash lost all his grip on the weapon. He let out a small cry, his wrist aching before looking at Kayden once again.

"You better go and retrieve your blade, Bash." There was some warmth in her voice yet there was none in her eyes.

He did just that, biting his lower lip. Had he pushed too far? Turning back to her, Bash raised the sword again, uncertain if he should attack or defend this time. The princess answered for him, swinging the blade inches from his face. Apparently, he had hit a nerve.

"Perhaps I am only a fool doing foolish things. Perhaps, in the end, that's all we can be." Kayden's words carried such a sorrowful tone, a distant voice that was maybe just as lost as himself. He met her eyes then, afraid of what he was seeing reflected within her gaze. "Yet all I want is to try to do better. Be better. What about you?"

The young knight stopped his movements for a moment, feeling a knot tightening in his chest. Maybe all he could ever be was a childish fool.

"Any reason why you are awake at the Gallows? Worried about your mission, Bash?"

He was half relieved that the leader changed the subject, for the other half was still bothered by where she had taken the conversation. The knight could feel his hands freezing against the sword's handle, his mouth dry.

"There would be no reason for me to be worried, princ—Kayden, my dear leader. I've performed similar missions countless times myself."

Why...?

No, he meant... *Why?* Why, for Säh's fucking sanity, would he even *say* something like that?

The princess smiled as she rested her sword on the ground, staring at him with her deep green eyes. "If that is so, how come you are so nervous?"

"Who said I'm nervous? I am calmer than a soothing breeze!" He literally choked as he answered, cursing his tongue some hundred times for its uselessness and incompetence in performing the simplest tasks—not embarrassing him. It was one of its *only* jobs.

Kayden's blow came almost as a surprise, aiming at his stomach. Bash jumped in a heartbeat, blocking the princess's blade with his own. Bash blinked in shock, watching as his leader's movements got faster and more...fatal, for lack of a better word. Glad to know his body still remembered how to keep him alive. However, being a good and disciplined body or not, Princess Kayden was taking their training in quite the serious tone. She was not rushing her attacks, each strike was precise, fast, strong.

Cheers, cheers for the Tournament grand winner.

"Have you thought about it?"

He furrowed his brows, hesitant on how he should reply. Fake it or be honest? "I...am unsure of what you are talking about."

The princess's smile was faint. "Your purpose. The reason to raise your sword, your reason to fight. Have you thought about it?"

Suddenly the sword became heavier in his hand, its weight demanding most of his focus and strength. The question that permeated his mind was a completely different one. *Why should I even raise it? Why* should *I fight?* He was not a Knight, not really, much less the world's savior. Even Princess Kayden had to be aware of that, otherwise she would not have asked him to play the dirty spy. Did someone like him possess any right to find a rightful purpose?

"I am working on it, princess."

Kayden stopped briefly in the middle of her attack to look into his eyes. Bash felt a chill that went all the way thorough his spine then deep inside his body, spreading its cold shivers. The leader's gaze locked onto his, glowing as they reflected the candles' light on the space.

"Why not give your all, Bash?" And with those words, she turned her body to the side and kicked him hard in the stomach, sending him a good few steps back as the knight bent over and dropped his sword.

The words fought their way out of his mouth, battling the pain. "That...was a bit harsh and uncalled-for, princess."

He would not barf in front of the princess. Not. *Ever.*

"Why? Are we not training seriously?" There was annoyance in her voice, her words fierce and sharp like the very blade she carried. "Do you believe your enemies would go soft on you, or that in Albaron your words will be believed if you are ever questioned? Why are you so afraid to try? Is it because I am your leader? Or is it because I am *royalty?*"

Bash barely had the time to pick his sword up to defend Kayden's strike on his neck. She could decapitate him with that blow. Holy Säh, she was trying to *kill* him. "I never said I was afraid! I am trying, princess, I swear on Säh's good grace—"

Kayden's sword brushed his nose, its tip touching his skin. "My name is not 'princess.' I am Kayden, the leader of the Orphys Knights. You will address me as such."

Shit. He had pissed her off—that was bad. "Forgive me, Kayden! Truly, I am very sorry. Could we pause the training? My throat is a bit dry." Blocking the leader's attacks was getting more troublesome by the second and all Bash wanted at that moment was dear solitude.

"We stop once you disarm me." It was then that Kayden struck and closed their distance completely, her face a few inches from his. "Show me how much you are *trying,* Bash."

He could not even hear his heart anymore, that was how he was going to die; a heart attack.

Yet nothing he did was enough. Every muscle in his arm ached, his breath uneven with sweat dripping from his face. Disarm her? He was busy enough trying not to get killed.

"Do you know what I truly think about you?" Kayden's words were like a dark ice, frigid and obscure so that Bash would never know what hid beneath. Did he wish to know? All instincts he had that still worked were screaming a solid no. "To me, you don't try or give your all, for you do not believe you are worthy."

Her sword collided with his and for the second time it sent the weapon flying from his hand. That time Bash could not even feel the pain that spread through his hand and wrist, the princess's words sinking inside him within a ruthless darkness. She let out a sigh, removing the hair from her face before meeting his eyes again. That time the kindness had returned to her voice, the leader's words warm and caring.

"The power that was bestowed upon us, the Orphys Knights, was not given for our worthiness. We were chosen because there was no other option for them."

"I am quite aware of this fact, Kayden," Bash spoke almost to himself, feeling the dragon's presence in his mind almost as a mockery. It was as if the knight could hear the Ancient's rude laughter.

Kayden shook her head, closing her eyes briefly before continuing with her words. "No, Bash, you are not. This means that from everyone they saw, you were the only person that could really help them. The *only one* that could save them."

Before he could take any step back, the princess placed her hand on his shoulder and to his surprise her hand felt warm. Why did he think it would feel cold?

"What matters is not the sins from our past but the purpose of our actions in the future. Remember that."

His mind imploded and his eyes burned. All around him, the air was disappearing from the room, making him suffocate and choke yet even then Bash managed to smile and touch the leader's arms briefly before pulling away. "Thank you for the kind words, dear leader. This session was a real adventure, one could say too much for me to handle in one Gallows. I pray you will find yourself more comfortable without my presence here, so I shall bid my good night. See you when the sun wakes, Kayden."

He gave her a short bow, leaving the grounds with a steady pace. The moment he closed the doors, both his hands kept pressing it together as if to prevent the princess from leaving. Not that she would come after him, why would she? Yet after a few minutes Bash turned his back to the door, sliding his body against the dark wood until he touched the cool floor. The young knight bared his face in his trembling hands, trying to collect the pieces together deep within his mind, trying to keep the cuts clean and the broken pieces as close as he could.

What am I to do now?

Not even Vührähkam gave him an answer to mock the knight and, somehow, that made it all worse.

A Witch's Call

Bless of Day - White Mountains

Twenty-Seven Nights Before Memorial Day

"TELL ME, FAIR WARRIOR, how is life on Raevich? I never dared to visit."

"Why would that be? Afraid your so-called *arts* would be ridiculed for their shameful true nature?"

"I possess a very delicate nose, you see. That foul stench would damage it beyond salvation."

The warrior scoffed, "You claim to possess many things, woman, and how great you excel at each one of them. One would have to start doubting which ones are actually true."

"I saved you and your leg, warrior. I believe this would be proof enough of my skill." Saranm turned to face him with a devilish smile playing on her lips and a gaze that made the Argyris shiver. "Also, some things must be shown so you can experience yourself how skilled I truly am, handsome." Her voice was soft and within her mellow words Leander could almost feel a heat. Something that could burn and mark him if he listened too much, if he stood too close. If his touch lingered longer.

It had been two days since the wolves' attack. He could sense as the air froze his nostrils' hair, his eyebrows and eyelashes. Leander woke up earlier that Wake with pain shooting through his leg. He was not wearing any trousers and his skin was patched with wet leaves, with a repugnant smell so strong it almost made him sick.

"Give it a few more hours, handsome, and you will be able to at least walk on your own. Unless, of course, you prefer some help."

"You are a fool to believe I would give you any excuses to touch me more than you already have."

Saranm smiled when he said that, yet there was something hidden behind her eyes that he could not interpret in any way. Leander wanted to wash that smell from his leg and get rid of any ominous concoction that could affect his body. He was strong enough to heal on his own. He had enough marks to prove that, enough memories. His body was that of a true warrior and he had no need to cheat his way to recovery. Yet the thing that stopped him was not the pain that made his flesh throb, but time. It could take days, perhaps even weeks, for his leg to heal itself and Leander had no desire to stay longer than necessary in that place. They had to find the Sword as fast as they could and leave, and *he* had already spent two days lying around, wasting precious time.

"Shouldn't you be focusing on finding this source of yours instead of speaking gibberish?" the warrior mumbled, clenching his fists as he walked. With every step his body protested, the injury on his thigh demanding rest, stillness, and attention like a stubborn child. The Argyris limped as he adjusted the wolves' fresh hide on his back. He wanted to start tawing them as soon as possible. At least they had more food and a way to block the mountains' wind.

"You better not rush me, warrior dear. I might leave you to the trolls."

"They would make a far more entertaining company, I assure you."

She laughed, a sound almost melodic that held a low and warm note to it. Like a soft purr. "I can be far more entertaining, warrior. I would just require a night."

Before Leander could reply, a sound echoed through the mountains. It was far, far away from them. Yet something inside Leander recoiled briefly, an invisible grasp closing around his heart while drowning it in a gelid, dreadful water. It made him sick, a dizziness befalling him for a brief moment.

"I might have joked about the trolls too soon, I see."

The warrior did not catch a glance at the woman's face, yet he could feel by the way her words weighed in the air that Saranm herself had studied enough about the cursed mountains to *know* what that sound implied. The creature was still far from catching their scent, yet its roar often meant it was on to something. And that whatever it was, it should stay away. He pressed his eyes closed long enough until the dizziness stopped, until his sickness disappeared from his body. Then he continued his walk.

After minutes with no words spoken between them, the woman glanced toward the horizon with a shadow crossing her eyes. "I can *feel* it, but it's faint. I am not sure why—it seems like it's hiding its presence on purpose."

"How can a sword hide its power?" the warrior asked with irony dripping from his words, yet there was no reply. The grasp around his heart tightened. "Can you at least say if this presence is close?"

"I do not think it is *too far*, yet we would have to walk for a few days. It is deeper within the mountains."

Leander felt the air disappearing around him for a few seconds, the grasp around his heart and throat until he forced himself to breathe. He was an Argyris, his body should obey him. "We must find a good place to rest before the Fall, then. A cave would be ideal, as long as we make sure there are no—"

"No threats or creatures roaming inside," the woman finished his sentence, smiling his way with a flirtatious gaze. "As you can see, love, I made my research as promised. Should I receive a reward?"

The man averted his gaze, trying to stay ahead of her by dragging his leg by force. "Your reward is staying alive. Now let us move; daylight ends faster in the mountains."

Time and time again Leander could feel the Ancient's touch inside his mind, as if the creature was checking something. Making sure his Knight was still breathing and progressing with the mission before pulling away. That was beginning to get under his nerves. He had no need for a wet nurse. If there was anyone who needed assistance, it was the woman. She kept staring at the distance with a distracted and lost gaze and it seemed that every time he looked at her, she had lost more color to her skin.

You see this? This is what we call weakness. Remember that, Leander.

His headache returned as his father's words echoed in his mind, a sharp pain strong enough to make his head throb and pulse. The Argyris glanced around, searching for any familiar terrain, any familiar spot. It was almost Fall, they had to stop. There should be one around that place—

There.

"Stop."

The woman stopped after a few seconds, turning her head in a slow motion as her gaze shifted its focus until it found him. It took a few more moments for her expression to change again, a sly smile blooming on her lips.

"Did you get tired from admiring me from behind, handsome? Wish to take the lead?"

He ignored her useless words. "It is getting late. We should stop for today and replenish our strength. I located a cave that we can use for this night—it is just a few meters ahead," Leander said as he motioned toward the cave with his head, shifting the weight of his injured leg.

The woman sneered, coming a few steps closer to him. "Weren't you complaining hours ago how we should not waste any more time? How I should have woken you before, how I almost spoiled the wolves meat by not cutting them properly. Yet now you wish to rest *again?* I know other things we could do on our spare time at Fall, handsome."

Leander clenched both fists, his heart racing. "One does not venture through the White Mountains at night, unless they are searching for Death's kiss. If you studied these mountains as you claimed, you would know this."

She walked closer to him, her eyes reflecting the sun's light too strongly for a brief second. "Are you afraid, warrior? I can protect you from the monsters, worry not." Her voice was like a low rumble, making his skin crawl and his hair rise, yet nothing changed her ridiculous statement.

“If you tired yourself from speaking nonsense, you can start walking faster. The snow is piling up, it will take us longer to reach the—”

Saranm turned her back to him, raising both her hands. The air shifted, swirling around her as the snow parted ways into one single trail that went straight to the cave. Leander held his breath, for once appreciating the chilling wind that blew on his face. When the woman turned to face him again, she had a victorious smile brightening her face.

“Now we can take our sweet time, handsome. You can thank me later this night.”

He was about to scream and shout at her, his nails already sinking into his hands, when he saw a trail of blood running down her nose. Even her dark skin was getting paler, her gaze waning. The Argyris let out a shaken breath, focusing on the cave ahead of them. “You should spare your energy for things that matter. If we encounter another pack of wolves or any other creature, you’d better not become a liability.”

She only laughed, shaking her head as she got another hold of the supply bags around her, continuing her way.

When they arrived at the cave, Leander was relieved to see the location was empty and that the cave itself was not very grand. There was plenty of space for them to gather their belongings, arrange some beds, and also a space for the Argyris to start tawing the hides. He was relieved when Lady Faeryl was able to provide the proper materials for him, although they probably would not compare to the aluminum owned by his family.

While the woman started to set the fire, Leander removed the rest of the skin from the hides with his hunting knife. His leg burned and throbbed, the pain reaching from his toes all the way to his waist, however as he cared for the animals’ hides, he felt at ease. As his mind focused its attention on washing and cleaning them, to later melt the snow and warm the water, the headache that had been haunting him the past few days started to fade. The sounds of the world became muted and all Leander heard was his own breathing.

Until he felt a touch on his shoulder.

The Argyris jumped, his hand already reaching for his sword when he met those golden eyes staring deep into his own. Though his muscles relaxed, he felt a hint of annoyance escaping his mouth. "Yes?"

Although the woman did not hide her smile, there was something in her gaze he could not interpret. "I need to change your bandages, otherwise they can cause an infection. I am certain you wouldn't want that, warrior."

With the mention of his injury, all the pain came back to him at full force, strong enough to make his head weightless. "Will you wrap my leg with plants once again?"

Saranm's grin got only wider, her voice lower. "Unless you wish me to wrap it with something else. I do have things in mind."

The lack of prudence of that woman managed to make his own bones crack in distaste. "Just do it with haste. I still need to prepare our meal."

"The meal is prepared already, warrior. Keep searching for excuses; the outcome will be the same."

Leander glanced back, surprised to see at that moment the fire heating the pot, the smell reaching his nose. It was a familiar scent, cooked meat blended with vegetables in the hot pot. Yet it was that scene that made his eyes tremble and his heart throb, the image of one lone pot on top of the fire bringing the memories of a child he did not want to meet again. *I am stronger now. I am a true warrior. An Argyris.*

"Handsome, could you spare us from the pointless anger? It brings a foul scent to the air."

He furrowed his brows, turning to face the woman. "Whatever do you mean?"

Saranm's laugh filled the air between them like a slow and warm melody, her golden eyes glancing toward him. There was sweat running down her face. "Please, being angry and pissed is your thing. I do not think I ever saw you at peace, not even in your sleep."

The arrogance and ridiculousness of her words almost made him laugh. "You hardly know anything about me, woman, to proclaim such a ludicrous thing."

She stopped for a moment, shaking her head as if she had been caught in a dizzy spell, her smile becoming even wider in the following seconds. "I do not need to *know* you, handsome. Your family's fame is far too loud for me to ignore. All I ask is that you keep your anger in check."

Even with his leg throbbing, he closed their distance, unable to control the hate and the fury that cracked in his voice. "You know *nothing* about my family or what it means to be an Argyris, so keep your mouth shut."

The fire went out. Rather than seeing it happen, the man felt it—a sudden chill on the back of his head, a primal instinct warning him of danger. Though he looked around the cave, seeing nothing but stones, that feeling did not go away. Yet the moment his eyes met Saranm's, his body froze. Leander felt his temperature rising, his skin breaking into a sweat in a matter of seconds while the pain that spread through his leg was utterly forgotten. His vision began to blur and his senses became twisted and confused, yet even then the warrior felt hands grabbing his face, a fierce and fiery glow filling the woman's golden eyes.

"You are a child." Her words were filled with pity, a sorrowful gaze penetrating his eyes. "You are a child who believes to be far too great for this world. Not better, *greater*." Her hands traveled down toward his chest and with every touch Leander felt hotter, weaker, like a fire starting from within his organs. He felt himself losing his senses, one by one. Leander could not move.

"Wh-what are you doing with me...?" He spoke his words without knowing if he had spoken them out loud. All he could see and know for sure was the touch of Saranm's hands traveling down his chest, his arms, his neck.

"You exhale such strong and shining light others would mistake you for a Divine." She chuckled, her grip on his arms intensifying. His head started to hurt. "But you are no Divine, Leander Argyris. You're nothing but a noble fool who was blinded by your own miserable glow and got trapped inside the tragic illusion that you are a worthy human."

"What are you even saying, witch—"

He felt suffocated, as if there was an invisible hand choking him. The woman's golden eyes shone a deep crimson red as a terrible smell hit him, his body feeling as if it was melting. Once again, her hands covered both sides of his face, as if he was a weak child being comforted by a mother.

"In this reality, Leander Argyris is nothing more than a pathetic existence fated to go by unnoticed."

"Let go..." The warrior tried to pull her hands with his own, but his muscles felt numb.

"I am tired of your existence in this realm, *human*. I shall kill you now."

The woman Saranm closed their distance, sealing his lips with her own.

And then everything was completely swallowed by a ruthless and cold darkness.

Chapter XII

"Many royals and affluent nobles seek to bring more prestige into their homes and lands by acquiring ancient artifacts, which are nothing more and nothing less than trinkets that survived the perils of time somehow, while carrying the fame of their dead owners. It is foolishly believed by many scholars that the artifacts carry not only their fame but mysterious powers that could be linked to demonic forces, created solely to lure the ordinary man toward their fall. The fact that one would pay obscene amounts of gold for old objects that are supposedly haunted is beyond insane and idiotic."

- *The Divines' Truth on Ancient Artifacts*, Ibha Kaminer

"The dangers that surround ancient artifacts could not be stressed enough, for the common people seem even more unaware of the implications of stumbling upon an artifact that has been corrupted by evil. While many artifacts were created in Ancient times, ancient artifacts are the ones that made a name for themselves through their powers given by arcane arts. Yet what many still fail to see is how the powers that some artifacts may carry does not come from the arcane nor from our Great God Divine Säh but from the vile creatures that haunt and prey from the Demonic Lands."

- *Through the Divines' Will*, Parson J.H and Parson Willoughby

A Witch's Lament

Unknown - Unknown

?? Nights Before Memorial Day

It was as if he was floating in the ocean. No, not floating—

Sinking.

He felt weightless, the world silenced. Oddly enough, he felt at peace. Whenever he tried to move, however, it would be as if the weight of the entire ocean was upon him. A thousand mountains crushing his bones, water filling his lungs, blood being forced out of his body.

Yet if he remained still, he felt nothing at all.

He enjoyed that sensation.

Yet after a while, a sound reached him from the depths of that darkness, a sound he was sure he recognized even if it was unknown to him at the same time. It was, he realized, someone weeping.

He still did not know why he chose to bear that pain, to carry that weight only to open his eyes but he did. And as he opened them, the image he saw was something that got buried deep inside his mind.

There was a woman with symbols on her skin and long, dark braids. The symbols glowed, making her golden eyes shine while reflecting its light on the tears that wet her face. The woman wore no clothes apart from a blanket that covered her from the waist down and her hands rubbed her arms, her chest, and her neck with such aggression he could sense the desperation coming from her frame. And all the time she rubbed the cloth on her skin, passing some liquid into the glowing symbols, she cried and wept.

At some point, her golden eyes met his.

She froze.

Then she smiled at him and said something he could not hear. Not in the depths he found himself in.

Yet as she spoke, no sound reaching his ears, he found himself sinking even deeper, his eyes closing yet again.

The world became still, weightless, painless once more. From afar, he could hear a roar trying to reach him. It was almost a desperate cry, furious and powerful. For a moment he felt a presence alongside him in those depths, sinking at his side, urging him to do...something.

However, he soon sank deeper into that blackness, the roar getting more and more distant until there was nothing else to be felt or heard.

An Old Star's Lost Glow

Lull of Afternoon - Ice Draco, Haste Mountains

Twenty-Two Nights Before Memorial Day

"THE DATE OF YOUR departure has been decided, Bash. You shall leave tomorrow at Fall in order to meet the Vam'Dammes at their state." The princess was actually relieved. She feared that due to the crisis in the kingdom and within the Houses the family might not consider hiring new servants for the journey or even worse, might not even attend the Memorial Day ceremonies. However, Orion's letter had arrived that same Bless, explaining with brief words that Alain Vam'Dammes had hired four servants through Carnarbur's recommendation on his father absence, Bash among them. All that was left was for the Knight to fly to Albaron and meet the family in the north.

They were at the leader's office, the wide window behind her basking the room with the sun's light that had begun to fade. Kayden was seated on her chair, books and scrolls open on the dark wood table with a few closed demanding her attention. Orion had left so much to aid her with her own studies, his own research journals from years to date, reports from different kingdoms and territories, letters exchanged within Carnarbur's islands, and so much more. With everything she read her fear hid deeper in her soul, her mind trying to calculate and make things work yet failing every time.

Their realm was dying, there were cases and signs everywhere, however there were almost no clues about the Ancients' resting places. Apart from the one at the White Mountains, Kayden hadn't received any other Sight that could aid her on their quest. The fact that the Divines kept taunting her with information, sparing her from the ones she needed most while haunting her with others she feared was beyond a cruel joke. Yet she was only a recipient, the spokesperson of Their vile, cruel messages. She could control nothing when it came to the Divines and that killed her a bit every day.

"*Tomorrow*? As in...this very next day?" Bash widened his eyes, his words stumbling over each other. The boy's anxiety was almost like poison to her, sickening her stomach and making her light-headed. Kayden cursed her Sight, digging her nails into her legs as if to force her mind to focus and her Sight to disappear.

"Precisely. Dorian is also aware." Mentioning her friend hurt. Although Dorian, as her Ward, would still remain by her side and follow her...he behaved only like a servant. During the past days, she missed and wanted her friend; not Färküh Dorian. Yet maybe it was for the best. "He will review the mission with you one last time before we begin the preparations tomorrow. I am sure neither Alain nor his father will bother themselves in questioning you about your background, however we must be prepared for anything. There are also the specific locations inside the castle that I need you to keep watch over, as well as the king's current schedule."

Bash was silent for a very long time, his eyes looking down at his feet, his mouth closed tight. "Meet Dorian, go through the plan, meeting the nobles—yes, everything is quite clear."

Kayden tried to meet his eyes, yet he would not look at her. "I understand it can be stressful, Bash. But you have been preparing for weeks and I trust your abilities and skills—you *will* succeed on this mission."

Something in his eyes shifted, a smile blooming in his face. "I thank you kindly, my dear leader. To have the very princess believe in my skills to spy on her father the king—it humbles my soul."

She almost got up from her chair, yet the fear she could sense within his eyes was what made her stop. How could she talk him through it? How could she make him *see?*

There was a shy knock on the door, to which Kayden was somehow grateful for. Perhaps that could be an opportunity. "You may open the door."

The doorknob turned in one slow movement, the knight entered without leaving the door with one of his hands fully covered with bandages. "I heard you called for me, Princess Kayden?" His voice was weaker than his gaze and she noticed Bash's surprise when the knight spoke.

"Call me Kayden and yes, I did. Please, come in and close the door."

The knight showed no emotion at seeing Bash as he stopped at his side, however Kayden could almost taste them, even if faintly. The knight was nervous.

"I heard from Saranm before she left that she and Orion were able to save your hand."

The knight blinked a few times, licking his lips before answering, "Yes, it is healing nicely."

The princess smiled, glancing toward Bash for a second before continuing, "I'm truly glad to hear this. Also, I am deeply sorry about this incident, Rick. The behavior of my Knight is inadmissible, that is not the message I desire to leave for my knights in training."

At the mention of Leander the knight got paler, shifting his weight as he shook his head. "Nothing happened between us. We can all just forget about it. It was nothing, truly. I am fine, I will be able to hold a sword, that mage said so." His words were as shaken as his eyes, his fear reaching her with the stench of rotten meat.

Bash chuckled, turning his head the other way. The knight clenched his jaw, whispering something to her Knight that Kayden could not hear yet it was enough to make Bash's body stiffen.

"Well, if you feel this way there is nothing I can do about it. However, I called you here for another reason. Sir Rick Quentin, as of this day you are no longer part of the Divine Order of the Orphys Knights."

Both men widened their eyes, the knight Rick raising his voice and taking two steps closer, almost reaching her table.

"What do you mean? Are you *insane?* You cannot do this—"

"I am perfectly sane and I am the leader of this entire organization. There is only one person who can do this, and it is I."

The knight's face reddened, fear being replaced by anger in a matter of seconds as his words became bitter and twisted with spite. "Your bloody Orphys Knight almost cut my hand off—I deserved payment from you!"

She stood up from her chair, raising her voice while locking her glare with his. "What I heard from multiple sources is that you and your colleague kept assaulting one of my *Orphys Knights* and used arcane arts during a training session without your instructor's consent, putting his life at risk only to indulge your petty egos. Your friend Calvin confessed you orchestrated the whole thing, and all he did was act as you instructed after you threatened him."

The knight kept his mouth open, one of his eyes twitching as no words came out.

"Am I wrong, Rick Quentin?"

Bash did not move from his spot, staring at Kayden with pure shock. Could he see it? Were words like those enough to make him realize what she was trying to say to him? Deep down Kayden was still unsure.

"We were not going to kill him! We just wanted to teach this bastard his place—"

"Sir Bash's place is at my side as an Orphys Knight and worry not, I am teaching him just fine without any aid from you." Her words were like thunder echoing in a storm, her voice fierce and strong enough to make Rick Quentin coil as she spoke, making his fear surpass his anger for one brief moment. "Through your actions you dirtied the name of the Order and tainted what we stand for and by doing so, you proved to yourself and to me that you are no knight from this Divine Order."

The knight hit his hand on the table, shouting in her face while pointing directly at Bash. "He is a *fucking nobody*! Admit it, you are protecting only the Argyris because he is from a noble House and you are Albaron's fucking princess—"

Bash's fists struck the other knight right in the left eye, sending him meters to the side. Before the knight could even react, Bash struck again, this time on his nose, making blood spurt like a red fountain from the man's face. With only one hand to attack, Bash dodged the knight's punches with ease while hitting Rick in the face again and again.

"Stop!" The moment she spoke Kayden reached for her own core, touching the energy around them. It was like a wall of wind spreading between the two men, separating them with one single powerful burst. Bash almost fell while the other knight ended up kneeling on the ground staring at their feet. His face was a terrible mess with tears falling from one of his eyes and blood running from his nose and hand, as he tried to cover it.

Kayden walked around the table, stopping by the knight's side with nothing but pure contempt in her words. "Not only do you insult me, but you dishonor my Knights and this organization. You are nothing but a disgrace, Mr. Quentin. I hereby declare that you shall never again step inside these mountains and reach for a knight's title while I breathe. There will be a horse waiting for you outside and that shall be the last courtesy I show you. I bid you farewell."

It took almost minutes for the former knight to stand up and reach for the door, his face pale as snow. When the door finally closed, Kayden felt her shoulders relax somewhat, a bit of the tension leaving her body. The princess shifted her attention to Bash, who still watched the closed door with pure disbelief in his eyes. She went to his side, taking both his hands with ease, noticing the new bruises that appeared.

"Forgive me, I should not have let the situation escalate this much. Still, thank you, Bash."

It took the younger Knight a few more seconds to shift his gaze and meet Kayden's and even more for him to notice that she was talking to him and holding his hands.

"Why?"

That question could have so many different meanings. Why had she stopped him? Why did she not punish him? Why had she allowed him to hit the other knight in the first place? Why thank him? Yet to every possible meaning that question had, Kayden found herself giving the exact same reply.

"I told you before. I want to bring our true purpose back—to be better."

Bash never replied, never spoke back. He only took a few steps away and went through the same door he was watching before. And as always, the Divines did not show her what she wished to know.

They showed her scenes to haunt her.

By A Cold Night

Fall of Night - Ice Draco, Haste Mountains

Twenty-One Nights Before Memorial Day

When he appeared at her door, Kayden was almost surprised. She was actually expecting him to come see her days before, after their quarrel. However, Dorian had maintained his distance, which brought a sad comfort to her. She missed him, yet it was better that way. But what really astonished her was to see her Ward without his armor. His black cape, the Färküh Wards insignia, the silver armor, all gone. Kayden had appointed her childhood friend as her Ward as soon as he graduated, almost seven years ago. In all those seven years she could count with ease how many times she saw her Ward without his armor, without his insignia. And it did not surpass ten.

"Dorian, it is almost Gallows—"

"Which means you should already be resting, my lady."

When Kayden took two steps back, Dorian walked into the room closing the door behind him. It was his first time in her chambers and by the look on the Ward's eyes, she could see his contempt and disgust. "Why did you choose *this* room?"

"It is the leader's chambers. There was no other room for me." The leader's chambers had a nice fireplace, two wardrobes made of dark wood that could almost fit five people each, a beautiful canopy bed with sheets made from satin exported from the East Kingdoms, and the most amazing view from the window, occupying almost the entire wall. Not only that but the many tapestries and the blue carpet gave it a lovely look. It was not a bigger room than her own back at Albaron however she almost felt more at home here, as if she truly belonged in that space.

"It was *his* chambers. I can still sense the stench of his vile thoughts in the air." Dorian almost spit his words, the hate drenching them like poison. Kayden could still feel that man's presence there—how could she not? Her Sight showed her the former leader's obsession and spite like a cold coat made of thorns and rotten flesh that would embrace her every time she entered the room. That was how deep Alexander had fallen into insanity, his mind ill and perverted. It was one of the reasons why Kayden sometimes preferred to sleep in her office instead and why she stayed in other chambers when she fell ill with the Sight days before. It sickened her far too much. However, she *was* the new leader and as such, that *was* her chambers.

"I am fine here, Dorian. What do you wish to speak with me about?"

She did not need her Sight to know the man did not believe her, nor to see the conviction filling his eyes. "Do I have permission to speak candidly, my lady?"

The power in his voice was so strong it made her heart race for a small moment. Such a serious tone, carrying words that were as much desperate as they were pleading. It was different from that day—to begin with, he had asked first. "Yes, you may, Dorian. Speak your words and I shall listen."

There was a brief relief that passed through his eyes before he nodded in silence. He crossed the room, removing the sword from his waist and placing it on top of the bed. She wondered how much Dorian was trying to conceal from her Sight, how much he was succeeding and how much of it he was aware of. How much he resented her. Kayden could see even from where she stood, a few meters behind him, how his hands were shaking. The princess focused on the vile and sickening feelings attached to the room rather than her friend's emotions for she had no desire to know what he was feeling. Once had been enough, and he deserved his privacy more than anything.

He turned around to face her, his eyes locked on her as he approached bit by bit. He stopped a few steps away from her, his arms loose beside him. In that moment,

Kayden realized she was only wearing her nightgown. For the first time in years, they did not feel like a princess and her Ward—they were simply themselves.

"I am terrified, Kay." His words shook the air between them, the fear within being enough to raise the hair on her neck. "Ever since you won that Tournament, I've been watching you wither, languishing day by day without being able to do anything—"

"Dorian, I—"

"No." He cut her off, his voice practically commanding her silence. "Let me finish, please. I must say this."

Kayden closed her mouth, feeling a knot forming in her heart. When she said nothing else, Dorian took a deep breath, letting out a long sigh.

"You are killing yourself, Kay. You are not sleeping, you are barely eating, and I see you carrying all this weight *alone."* His voice broke as he spoke and the feelings that poured from those words made her heart bleed and cry. "I cannot be a Knight to aid you, I have no bond with an Ancient, I cannot fight by your side without slowing you down, I cannot play a role big enough in this war to ease your worries—and that is *fine*. I will not ask you to smile to soothe my mind nor will I ask you what the Divines showed you that frightens you so much, much less demand you to share with others. If you wish to take the curse of the Sight by yourself, I will respect you, for I cannot fathom the pain you go through. Yet what I am about to say, I speak not as your Ward but as someone who loves you." Dorian choked on his last words, closing the distance between them while grabbing Kayden by her shoulders.

As she stared into his eyes, she fought with all her strength to not be swept into all the hurt and suffering in them, to not drown in his pain and sorrow and above everything else, to not let her tears fall from her eyes for they would only hurt him more. Kayden focused on the room, on all those feelings and emotions Alexander had left behind, even stumbling upon emotions she had never felt until that moment. Betrayal, confusion, and anger pouring so strongly that it should be all her Sight focused on apart from Dorian, anything to keep her soul and heart from being torn apart. Even then, even though she fought that accursed Sight,

Kayden still felt Dorian's words cutting her skin and crawling into her bones, tearing them apart.

"Please, Kay, *do not* push me away. I cannot stand idle any longer, watching you destroy yourself this way."

"Dorian..." A tear escaped from her eye yet it felt like blood. It hurt—it hurt *so* much.

"Use me however you want, *I do not care!* Send me alone in a quest to find another Ancient, order me to find more clues about Kih Nähsur and the demonic realm, use me to cook your favorite meals, and brew your favorite teas every day so you can eat. Just *please, please* let me help you! Let me stay *at* your side. I am not weak—I won't crumble if you lean on me."

Her friend was not fighting his tears as his hands grabbed her shoulder, his grip strong and desperate. What could she say? How could she protect him and shield him from her sins, from all the horror and desperation They were showing her if by doing so she was hurting him that much? Kayden opened her mouth yet no words came to her, they were stuck in her throat choking her. Dorian pushed her for an embrace, caressing her hair again and again as she sobbed, feeling as hopeless as she could be.

"I do not know what to do, Dorian...I swear I don't."

"Just let me help you, Kay. Do not keep yourself in the dark alone."

But how could she ask him to stay there with her when there was no way out of such a place? When all the Divines showed her was death and damnation, how could she let someone so precious to her walk into that horrible place to help her stand?

Yet how could she not?

A Sight from the Gallows

GALLOWS OF NIGHT - WOODS

Twenty-One Nights Before Memorial Day

THE ASSASSIN TRIED TO ignore the growl that came from within. Tonight he would not heed the beast, he would only heed the monster. To the Gallows. His emotions were in disarray as he rushed to their meeting place and, for the first time ever, Dark Eye was late. Worst of all, the man named Sean *knew*. One could see it in his face, the way he flashed that stupid grin as the assassin approached. Dark Eye did not even bother to hide in the trees, to sneak behind, to use the shadows as a sweet and pretty cover—no, he was too furious for that. As the assassin walked toward Sean-man, who was almost laughing through his teeth, the daggers found their way into his hands in the most comfortable way. The beast inside was feeling his rage but above all else, it was feeling his bloodlust. The monster demanded answers and death while all the beast wanted was blood.

That was something he could come in terms with. After all, corpses can also bleed.

"At last you appear, Dark Eye, sire! I was almost afraid I would be left alone after such a long journey myse—" The man choked and dropped the lantern, the thing almost breaking as it fell to the ground. One of the assassin's hands closed around his throat while the other pointed the dagger close to the man's eye.

"I will be the one asking the questions tonight, uncle. As you can see, I found myself in a foul mood." Dark Eye's words were like acid dripping from his voice, the smile reflecting only the anger that grew inside him. "Wait! Let us make this even better, why don't *you* bring me to meet this benefactor of yours? I am *dying* to meet them."

The man Sean struggled to speak, his hands grasping the one closed around his neck. "I would love to answer your doubts, sire, yet I cannot stress myself enough for you to set me free."

Before Dark Eye could ask, he heard the sounds coming from all around. They were hidden among the trees and the bushes, some carrying arrows while others had blades—at least eight people. He began to laugh, losing his grip over the pig that started to clear his throat. Look at that, pig Sean-man had prepared—he had made *plans!* Wasn't that adorable?

"Oh my, I thought our reservation was for two! Had I known more people would come, I would've dressed better."

Sean massaged his neck, the smile frozen on his face like the stiffness of a corpse. "Forgive me, sire, it was my benefactor who insisted that I brought some...insu rance to today's meeting. I hope we can still finish our negotiations peacefully, however."

Insurance. Dark Eye's blood was on the point of boiling and turning into acid, melting his veins, bones, and skin together just to get to that man. From the beginning, he must have known the things that Dark Eye would find or at least had some idea. He had been playing in that pig's hand like a fool from the start. The growls inside him increased, the demand for blood was almost resonating with his anger. Yet the assassin had some business to do before inviting Death's sweet kiss to their celebration.

"Of course, uncle, I am an understanding man. Can I ask my questions now?"

Sean picked the lantern up from the ground, sending light closer to Dark Eye's face. The assassin instinctively took a few steps back, making sure there were shadows covering his face. "Ask away, sire. I am but a humble man requiring your services after all."

Your fucking arse, you are.

"First of all, the ownership contract. Do you have it or not?"

The man's eyes shone with malice for a second, their dark glow reflected by the lantern's fire as Sean-man spoke with sadness and pity touching his voice.

"Forgive me, dear sire, my contractor did not feel satisfied by our previous encounter to give me the contract. I do have some precious information to compensate you for your troubles!" The excitement and joy that poured from his lips, as if those words were something Dark Eye should feel most grateful to hear, sickened him to his core. Yet in that moment, for the first time, the assassin did not have the upper hand. He was surrounded and outnumbered in a very bothersome, disadvantageous situation with no actual power to negotiate. What he would do to be knowledgeable in the arcane arts to choke them all to their deaths or at least fry their eyes.

"Why would your contractor be unsatisfied? I brought precious information about the princess's routine and things regarding the Ancient beasts your contractor was so eager to know. And none of these things were easy to find."

"Yes! And my contractor was glad you managed to find all of that classified information, sire. However...we must change our deal somewhat." From his left, Dark Eye could hear someone loading a crossbow. Either of two things would happen, Dark Eye was certain of that, and both scenarios involved Death.

Scenario number one, by all Divines' grace, the pig Sean-man would try to kill Dark Eye. In that case, he had one last trick up his sleeve. However, what the assassin truly feared was scenario number two.

"What do you want for the ownership contract?"

Sean's eyes were filled with a certain hunger that Dark Eye recognized all too well. "We want you to finally complete an unfinished job. Kill the new leader of the Divine Order and the contract is yours, Dark Eye, sire."

His heart almost came to a full stop while the monster and the beast fought inside him. One demanded blood and the other demanded death, but he could only heed one. "In case you forgot, not only does the leader know the arcane arts, but she also has in her possession three winged demons that could make our fight quite unfair. Why do you think this job remained unfinished?"

Please, may it end with scenario one.

"That is why my contractor is such a great person! They provided us with the perfect tool to end the princess's life with the minimum of risks." The man named Sean whistled and at the same time two figures came out from the woods. Dark Eye raised his hands immediately, daggers already in aim, however the robed figures paid him no mind. They simply carried a small metal chest to Sean's feet and disappeared the moment the thing touched the grass.

The growl inside him became louder. "What is this?"

Sean's smile only grew wider, insanity touching his lips. "A special artifact. Bring it with you when you face the princess and the fight shall be just in every way."

Dark Eye stared at the chest, feeling for the first time in his life that maybe the Gallows could not protect him. "But what does it *do?*"

The other man shrugged. "Not of importance. You will be the one to actually kill the leader."

Dark Eye's smile grew as he tightened the grip on the daggers. "What if I say no? Maybe the idea of risking my life on such vague promises may not suit me."

"Then, sire, I will feel obliged to share some precious information with you." The man took two steps forward, lowering his voice so it would be nothing but a lost whisper in the Gallows, a whisper that brought nothing but forgotten promises and foreboding deaths. "I can bet my own heart and soul that Princess Kayden Faeryl knows *exactly* who you are."

Those words made all his blood freeze inside him and created a pit inside his stomach, deep enough to make him drown forever in his own despair. "How could that be possible?"

Please, end with scenario one, he prayed.

"Because, Dark Eye, sire, our sweet princess possesses the Sight." That whisper was carried between them with nothing but the haunting promises that came from the Gallows.

Nothing good *ever* came from the dark, beautiful Gallows.

And so it ended with scenario two.

A Warrior's Scars

Unknown - Unknown | The Past?

?? Nights Before Memorial Day

I'm cold.

He could finally feel the warm sun on his skin again.

I'm hungry.

That night they would feast on the creatures he had hunted himself.

I do not wish to fight the monsters anymore.

He was on his way to becoming one of the greatest warriors.

I feel so alone.

People kept greeting him in every room he entered, picking up his belongings and carrying them to his chambers.

I miss my mom.

From upstairs, he could hear a woman screaming.

I miss my mom.

She screamed as if someone was ripping her heart out with their bare hands.

I want to go back to my family.

After some time, he heard a baby crying.

I do not want to stay on these mountains anymore. I'm cold.

People rushed up the stairs.

I'm hungry.

The baby continued to cry.

I do not want to be alone anymore.

He did not want to climb the stairs.

I want my mom.

The woman was not screaming anymore.

I want to go home.

Suddenly the house was quiet.

He did not climb the stairs.

He could not.

A Warrior's Blood, A Witch's Poison

Wake of Day - White Mountains

?? Nights Before Memorial Day

The first thing Leander felt was a knot tightening within his heart, carrying memories he had no wish to recall. The second thing he felt was warmth, a pleasant feeling that spread across his chest, leg, and arm making that frozen grasp around his heart melt away even for a moment. It made him feel so relaxed, it almost lured the man into a slumber once again. However, the last thing he felt made everything else fade into the back of his senses, a soreness and fatigue overtaking his entire body, making it feel like all the energy and strength had been drained from him.

Within his mind he could hear something buzzing, a low alarm yet Leander was too exhausted to formulate thoughts, to process and attempt any kind of understanding. The Argyris continued to feel that warmth, a comfort in a dark and confusing world he did not want to face yet. However, it did not take long for Leander to realize that warmth had its own weight. His head ached and throbbed as he tried to process, to *feel* the shapes without opening his eyes. A sense of dread and horror flooded through him as the warrior opened his eyes, shame battling resentment and pure incredulity.

Neither he nor the woman were wearing clothes. Not even the smallest piece of fabric covered her breasts, much less her thighs, legs, or her genitalia that touched his leg. Saranm's breasts were pressed against his chest and Leander found his arm across her shoulder, while his other hand laid peacefully on her waist. He commanded his body to move, to take back his hands and get ready to stand up in one single desperate movement, yet the moment he moved his head the Argyris almost got sick, his vision darkening and weaving.

The pain was so grand it was as if someone was trying to split his head using poisoned fangs that burned their way into his skull. He could not even retrieve his arm before meeting her gold gaze, piercing through his own with an intensity the man had never seen before. Yet as Leander blinked away the dark spots from his sight, something within the woman's gaze made him feel somewhat distressed. Was it relief? Fear? Before he could interpret it that thing was gone, dissolving into a smile he had seen too many times before but carrying a new meaning, a new memory.

"What a pleasant view to have such early in the Wake. Have you slept well, o my handsome warrior?"

Leander swallowed hard, his mouth dry all of a sudden. The confusion that filled his mind began to twist and blend itself with anger and shock. Reason and clarity kept running away from his grasp as the man tried to make sense of the situation, tried to fill in the blanks in his memory, yet the more he forced his mind to remember, the more it hurt. When he finally found his voice there was no way to hide the cold rage that echoed within his words. "Tell me what you have done to me. Now."

Saranm's smile grew even more, the malice and deviousness dominating her entire face as she sat without ever taking her gaze away from him. "I believe you mean what *you* have done to me, which I would have to reply...a lot of things, dear warrior."

Her breasts were inches away from his face, her hand almost touching his penis and the man simply knew she was doing that on purpose. He tried to move away from her, grunting as his entire body ached and shouted in protest. It was unrealistic to think that one night of sexual activities had made his body feel like that—it simply should not be possible. More than that, the mere thought of him lying down with that woman was beyond madness.

"I am trying to ask in the politest manner, so you had better answer me, woman. What. Have you done. To me?" he asked while trying to catch his breath, his lungs burning as if he had run without rest for days. Leander managed to back away, his naked back touching the cave's gelid wall and even the touch between the rocks and his skin made him shiver and ache. He had been well the day before so how come his body had fallen with such strange sickness in such a short time? How come his body would not obey him?

"It was not in my knowledge that you were so moody in the Wake. And why ask me, I'm sure you must remember yourself," Saranm replied while moving her long dark hair from one shoulder to the other, standing up and stretching her arms and neck right in front of him. Although he averted his gaze, even through the pain he could feel his skin heating up, his body reacting on its own.

Leander was about to open his mouth with annoyance filling his eyes and words when the images began to flash inside his head. Images of Leander grabbing and touching the woman's skin again and again, her arms, legs, and breasts, not only with his hands but with his mouth as well. He could see her hair falling on top of him like a deep black waterfall, caressing his skin, her mouth playing with his chest and if he closed his eyes, if he focused hard enough, Leander was almost able to *feel* it all once more, the feeling of being inside her, the touch of her fingers, her scent, her voice, her taste—

A shiver went down his spine as Leander forced the memories away. No, not memories—images. Trickeries. He tried to stand up once again yet his legs failed him, not allowing such a move. "Those things did not happen. It is not possible." His words had little to no strength and it hurt to breathe. Had she poisoned him while he slept?

She laughed, picking a wolf hide from the floor and throwing it around herself. "You must be tired, still. Let me get something for you to drink, handsome."

As she walked away, the Argyris tried to make sense of his surroundings, glancing around the cave, searching for his belongings and clues, *anything*. He had never given in to meaningless carnal urges, much less to a being of her *kind*. Yet how could anyone deny the state he was at that moment, memories within his own body and images that permeated his mind like a plague? Even if he wished to reject the idea, their clothes scattered around the cave were the weakest proof about their shared night. Yet Leander knew for a fact that whatever had been done, had not been done in a sane, sound mind.

"Here it is," a voice called him. It was soft, strong, inviting, and while it seemed to reach him from afar, the woman was already by his side.

"What is this?" The man did not even spare a glance to whatever it was that she was holding. Had she said the same words to him before? Was that liquid she carried in her hands responsible for weakening his body?

"You must be tired. Drink; it will make you feel better."

Leander did not throw the cup from her hand because his arm would not move, yet when he turned his head away Saranm grabbed him by his hair and yanked him, forcing his mouth open while she poured the liquid into his throat. He almost choked. Worst of all, Leander felt too weak to fight back, making the anger boil his blood and drench his bones like acid. The liquid had a strange consistency, being completely flavorless, resembling no alcohol, herbal tea, juice, or anything else the man had tasted in his entire life. He was about to curse her when he felt the strange liquid going down his throat and...it alleviated the pain. As if a terrible weight had been lifted from his muscles, some strength returned to him while the air entered and left his lungs with no difficulty.

"What did you give me?" There was no need to hide the suspicion in his voice.

She smiled, her finger tapping the glass cup she was holding. No, that wasn't glass—it was ice. "I told you that it would make you feel better."

A thought suddenly surfaced in his mind as he glanced toward the hide she was wearing, his mind working once again. "It should take weeks to finish the tawing process. How could they be—"

"I accelerated the process." Saranm cut his words off far too quickly.

He clenched his jaw, beginning to stand up. "You used your *petty* tricks on my hides—"

"We can discuss this later. You should rest a bit more now."

He frowned, a sarcastic smile playing on his lips as his words dripped with unbridled rage. "For what reason? So you can bewitch me once again and avoid answering my—"

"Sleep." The command in her voice was so strong it made his head vibrate. He saw her eyes glow again before his eyelids began to get heavier and heavier, his consciousness fading away.

Leander woke up with two roars, one coming from the outside and the other echoing inside his mind, however it was the one that came from outside that made his stomach drop and his body freeze.

A snow troll.

It had caught their scent. But so soon? If it was with a pack, it would be hard to defend themselves against so many. Snow trolls were nothing like wolves—they were nefarious, bigger, stronger—Leander had to ensure that the troll was alone and eliminate it before it could warn others of their location. That time he managed to lift himself without pain spreading through his entire body yet he still felt lethargic, slow. Saranm was nowhere in sight and he was relieved to find himself wearing clothes that time. He found his sword and axe close to the fire, feeling a wave of shock and disbelief when his arm almost failed to carry the weapons due to their weight. How could that be? Why was his arm trembling as if forcing itself? A weight like that should be nothing to him.

Why was he so *weak*?

Another roar echoed through the cave, closer than ever before, followed by the sound of trees crashing and falling. The ground beneath his feet trembled, making his skin crawl as memories flashed before his eyes. Leander bit his lip hard enough to make it bleed, the taste soon spreading into his mouth. He was not that child anymore—he was a full warrior—there was no need to be afraid. He was *strong*, he knew the Way of Sword. *I* am *a warrior.* The Argyris grabbed his sword, his arm crying and complaining with the little strength it had left, as the man walked toward the cave's entrance seeing nothing but snow in his sight.

He managed to take one step outside the cave, where the howling wind blew against his face with vicious force, when something flew before his eyes, clashing against one of the trees, breaking the wood in half. Leander watched as the top of the tree bent and cracked backward while a human body fell weightless to the ground. It did not take long for him to recognize that long braid and those golden eyes, the woman meeting his gaze with panic and horror.

A trail of blood ran down her mouth, yet she still shouted at him, fear and anger battling against each other within her voice. "For Divine's sake, man, *go back inside!*"

Before anything could be said or done, another roar erupted behind her, the enormous creature raising both its arms before hitting the ground with pure sheer strength. Saranm had the time to roll to the side but Leander could see the troll's fist almost grazing her back, the snow trembling and jumping from the impact. The Argyris tightened the grip on his weapon, his foot already taking another step toward the creature—

And then it saw him. The snow troll met the nobleman's gaze, arms thicker than tree logs, a dense and thick grayish fur covering its entire body with two long tusks coming out of its mouth. The fists were like gigantic human hands with long sharp blackened nails yet it was the creature's eyes that made his heart stop. Four eyes that, although small, were strikingly blue; a color so vivid it seemed to glow even in bright daylight. Leander remembered those blue eyes, the heinous energy that emanated from that gaze. It was all the same as the one he met years ago.

The troll opened its mouth and roared at him, a horrific blend of rot, blood, and death reaching him from meters away yet he could not move. His legs were stuck, his arms powerless and deep down something inside Leander wanted to run away and hide. *I am a warrior not a child. Move.* However his body refused to obey even when the troll approached the cave, one of its hands grabbing the roof. Instinct told Leander to raise his weapon and take a defensive stance, nothing else.

Attack. I must strike first.

The troll raised its fist, its gaze never leaving the man's eyes.

I am *a warrior. Move.* Move.

The creature suddenly let out a cry, turning its back to the Argyris. He saw blood trailing down the creature's back, something hidden within the gray fur yet only when his eyes focused on Saranm was he able to see the ice floating around her like crystal fangs. Her face was paler than he had ever seen, sweat dripping from her chin while the blood on her mouth had been wiped.

"I hate foolish men the most."

Leander was not sure how he was able to hear her words with the wind crying and moaning between the trees. Maybe his mind made up her words while his ears pretended that was what she would've said, with the smile touching her lips and her eyes staring at him that way. Saranm shot the ice crystals toward the troll with one hand, moving her fingers in the air as if she was caressing it as the crystals hit the snow troll with an insane speed. Three crystals missed but two hit the shoulder and chest of the creature without piercing its fur. With her left hand the woman raised her arm toward the sky as if she was pushing up a mountain, pain spreading across her face while the snow in front of Leander shook and moved on its own.

He was a second too late to realize what was happening, unable to do anything but jump backward as an ice wall rose between him and the troll, blocking the cave's entrance completely. Although it was not swarmed in darkness, the cave became colder, filled with shadows. The man could hear the fight happening outside, the forms moving behind the ice wall. The first thing that Leander felt was a sense of betrayal, a battle being stolen from him right under his feet.

However...

The anger that rose within him soon vanished, the wall staring right back at him, the shadows whispering and grabbing his legs and arms. There was no more exit, the entrance blocked. No more light, no more escape. And he tried, for all the Divines that could watch his miserable state, he tried to push away the memories, to forget and focus on the anger, on his pure desire to break that wall and fight.

Leander Argyris could not.

His body began to tremble while the sword slipped from his grasp. The warrior's heart was beating so fast the man felt it would explode in his chest as air failed to fill his lungs. From the other side of the cave, Leander could see a boy coiled against the wall. The child was crying, screaming, and shaking while a giant snow troll kept banging against the cave, making more and more stones fall. The boy was certain that he was going to die, that the troll would get and eat him, certain he was never going back home. But the snow troll went away, leaving the cave and the child imprisoned by stones that blocked every ounce of sunlight from the outside world.

Leander buried his face in his hands, feeling his face wet. From the other side he heard the woman scream, the ground shaking as the snow troll moved and attacked with its powerful fists.

No, that is not me. I am not a hopeless child.

"Cease your vile acts, witch! Free me at once!" Leander banged his hands on the ice wall, his own voice betraying him by its shaking and weakening. He did not know what was colder, the wall or his own skin.

This is no behavior of a worthy Argyris. Where there is no worth, there is no man.

Leander heard his father's words as if they were spirits haunting his very soul, shivers running through his entire skin as the man continued to bang on the ice wall in hopes it would break soon. The child kept staring at him, bruises across his body, his face whiter than snow. No! That child was *weak*, he would have never survived the White Mountains—Leander did so because he was an Argyris. He broke every nail on his hand but he dug his way out of that cursed cave and felt the sun warm his skin. He was *strong*.

Then why wouldn't his body stop shaking?

I'm a warrior. I carry the Way of Sword for I am worthy of such.

He banged once, twice, then again and again and again. "You cannot slay the troll with your petty tricks, woman! Dissolve this wretched wall *now!*"

Something flew across the wall, breaking and shattering it completely before hitting the farthest wall of the cave. Ice shards exploded everywhere, some cutting the man's face while others almost hit his eyes. Leander looked behind him, seeing the woman defeated on the ground. A fetid smell made the Argyris turn his attention once again toward the outside, giving him just enough time to pick up his fallen sword before a hand closed around him, lifting his body. Frozen, harsh wind blew on his face and clothes, stealing every ounce of warmth he had managed to save.

The world surrounding his eyes was pure white, covered in snow yet cruel and savage. There were fallen trees everywhere, markings and holes on the ground showing more than enough. The troll opened its mouth showing all his teeth and tusks, roaring at Leander's face as it squeezed the warrior in its grip. All the air left him as if it was running away from a promising death and all Leander could do was try to pierce the troll with his sword. But it was so heavy, his arm felt so tired, and weak—

Yet the child had survived his encounter with a troll. That weak child had returned home. Leander was stronger, faster, smarter. He had proven his worth.

I'm a warrior I'm a warrior I'm a warrior I'm a warrior I'm a warrior I'm a warrior I'm a warrior

For a moment he felt that same presence in his mind, that familiar and ancient touch. Warmth spread within his body while pure strength filled him, a new power running within his veins. Leander screamed, raising the sword and its blade and sinking it deep into the troll's wrist. The creature let out a cry so high it almost deafened him, throwing him inside the cave. Leander hit his shoulder hard against the wall, feeling the rough rock ground graze his skin as his body slid toward the far end wall. The Argyris felt every muscle on his body bellow, denying his control over them as tears burned his eyes. He could not die in such a shameless position. He could not call himself a warrior if he could not raise himself right at that moment. He would not be worthy of carrying the Argyris name if he could not come out victorious in that fight. Not in *that* fight.

So why wouldn't his body *obey* him?

The whole cave shook and trembled as the snow troll crouched to look at them, four blue eyes drowning in rage as it hit the cave's walls and roof again and again. It wanted to bury them inside. His heart almost gave out, ceasing its beating at once. *Not again.* Leander kept hearing the small rocks falling, cracks appearing, yet he could not even move a finger. The boy was just below the troll, appearing and disappearing from his sight like a ghost. The child had his black hair and his blue eyes, yet he was not a warrior, not yet. However, Leander could feel his mind slipping away, failing to stay awake even with the sheer panic that was grasping and cutting down his heart and bones.

Something lit up the entire space, warmth spreading and reaching Leander in a hot embrace. Leander turned his head just enough to look at the source, for he had no strength to move farther. Perhaps his weakened state had corrupted his mind as well, for he saw arcane symbols and the first thing that came across his thoughts was how beautiful they were. The woman's marks glowed like small contained suns while flames poured from her very skin as if they were scales floating in the air. Saranm's eyes were gold no more—an eerie yet mesmerizing red filled her pupils as if they were also aflame. She stood still, arms resting beside her body with her braid undone with the dark hair flying above her shoulders. For a brief second, and it was very brief, Leander thought he was seeing someone like him.

A warrior.

The woman moved her hands and arms as if she was dancing alone, with no rush to her movements. Yet as the air became hotter, Saranm became faster, her motions more rapid and defiant. When she screamed and threw her hands forward a blast of fire shot right toward the troll's face. The creature howled, letting out a grinding cry as its face melted and burned, the scent filling the entire cave within seconds. Saranm continued to pour the flames out of her body, the fire glowing almost as much as the marks on her skin. Only when the snow troll tilted to the side and fell with a loud thud, making the entire cave shake as a grotesque face stared at their direction, did the woman stop and lower her arms.

Saranm fell on her knees with an uneven breath, sweat dripping from her temples and neck with her hair falling down her back in dark waves. The woman turned around, spotting the warrior and opening a bright, victorious smile.

"You are fucked now, handsome. I saved your pretty arse with my *devious magic* twice. You owe me now. Warrior's shitty moral code, right?"

Leander felt a small burst of rage go all the way to his mouth, ready to give his reply, however the words never left him. The last thing he felt was Amträhfar's touch inside his mind, a desperate warning aiming toward the woman.

Beware human.

As his consciousness faded, Leander saw one last time the boy crying against the wall. Scared—

And alone.

Twenty-Six Nights Before Memorial Day?

Chapter XIII

Something That Could One Day Be My Journal, First Mumbling

Haze

I have never done this before. Write my secretive thoughts, my inner feelings, my fears and hopes. Maybe the reason is because I never truly hoped for anything and was too used to my fears being a cruel, harsh reality of who I am and who I will be.

...But I do not know anymore. Who I am supposed to be. What I am supposed to fear, what I am supposed to hope for, there is no more clarity or purpose in my life. I know nothing. I feel *like nothing.*

I have never been so lost.

Maybe the reason I'm writing this here is because the only thing I hope for is that someone will read it and write down an answer. For I have been asking myself the same thing over and over again, and I feel worse each day.

Who am I? Who am I, truly?

Please, anyone, answer me. Answer me and tell me that the answer I came up with is wrong.

Please, tell me I'm wrong.

A Witch's Penitence

Haze of Day - White Mountains

Twenty-Five Nights Before Memorial Day?

WITH EACH STEP THE warrior took, half his stamina seemed to vanish into thin air as if he had spent an entire year laying sick in bed. With every passing hour, that woman would oblige him to drink her "teas" either by forcing it down his throat or not allowing him to move. Worst of all was that it *did* make Leander feel better as the day progressed, as if it was returning little by little the strength that had been, somehow, stolen from him.

Ever since the snow troll attack, they had been silent. The man could feel the Ancient attempting to communicate with him from time to time however their connection seemed to be getting weaker the farther they went into the mountain. There were many things the Argyris wished to ask the mage; things that, whenever he thought about them, he would feel the anger rising inside him like a vile beast, turning his blood and muscles into acid and poison.

Yet she had saved his life.

"I believe we are getting closer to the source," Saranm said with a weakened voice, although her eyes seemed alert enough. They were taking advantage of the current weather to cook some of the troll's meat, since the wind was hardly moving the snowy trees around them.

"Good. We should not waste so much time here." Leander watched as the woman's hand stopped briefly as he spoke, continuing to put the meat into sticks.

"Can you get the bag beside you, warrior? I have my hands full." Her words were filled with honey, that same smile placed on her face like all those other times. Images of their shared night began to surface, but Leander burned them within his mind.

The bag was not even a meter away, all he had to do was lean over and stretch his arm out, however the moment he did so the warrior felt a sharp pain in his abdomen, strong enough to make him flinch and curse. The woman's smile faded faster than a wet torch.

"What is wrong?"

He would not meet her gaze. "There is nothing wrong. Keep your focus on the meat. We will need it for the next days."

Leander clenched his jaw as he grabbed the bag, feeling like his abdomen's skin was tearing apart. Before he could turn around and give her the bag, hands grabbed his arm, forcing him to look up. Those golden eyes stared down at him, nothing but concern being displayed on her face. That almost made him laugh.

"You are hurt. The troll—You said *nothing!* How dare you?"

The Argyris could not understand the hurt within her eyes much less the betrayal in her voice.

"How dare I...? I owe you *nothing*, witch. My injuries are but my own responsibility, especially those I gain from my battles. I have tended to the cut properly, now I just need to wait for it to—what do you think you are doing?"

Saranm opened another bag, taking out the plants and mixtures she had applied on his leg. "I will aid you, warrior, what else would I do?"

There was something about her words, about her reactions... He could not place a word for it yet, however it was odd. "You need to do no such a thing, woman. Just focus on what you were doing before—"

"If we encounter another troll or more wolves, how will you defend yourself? Better yet, why don't you lure them here with your open wound?" Anger flashed in her eyes for a mere second before it dissolved into an ironic gaze. He clenched his fists, holding his breath while he opened his shirt and removed the bandage he had made. There was one cut on his side, not deep enough to threaten his life but enough to hurt and make him weaker. For once the cold was welcome on his skin, numbing the pain for a while.

Within a few minutes Saranm was already on her knees, the herbs and plants in her hands, however before she could apply the nasty thing to his cut she stopped. Her eyes widened as if in shock, yet when Leander followed her gaze she was not looking at the injury.

She was looking at his scars.

"Could you please make haste? There is nothing important to see—"

"That is why your core is so shallow." Her words echoed like the dead's whisper, something forgotten and far away. She raised her hand, her fingers touching the scars in the middle of his chest, two parallel straight lines. All the others were marks he had gained from battles, from victories. They were proof of his path as a warrior, marks he got from fighting creatures and sparring with others. Yet not those two. Those scars, he could not remember.

"What are you talking about?" A part inside him was afraid to ask, afraid she would give him an answer. Yet the words left his mouth almost on their own, seeking a truth he had always desired to know.

Saranm's eyes filled with tears, her voice carrying a grief and sadness he could not comprehend or empathize, something that should not belong in him. "I have heard stories of noble families that would remove their children's energy cores whenever they started to develop too much, grow too much... Your own family *violated* you. They crippled your core so you would never be able to manipulate energy."

At first, he was shocked. He desired to say those were lies, yet deep down his heart knew she spoke the truth. Leander wanted to say that was good, that his family did the best choice they could have. Arcane arts were nothing but petty and immoral tricks and he was better without them. However, there was something in the way she looked at him, the way she cried for him... It made him wonder if what he had lost was something that precious.

"Why are you crying?" was all he could ask.

"Because it is one of the saddest things someone could have done to you, warrior. They took away something before you could even understand it, before you could even remember you had it." The way she spoke her words, the way the sorrow filled every space between them, the way the tears fell from her face, it did not seem like she was speaking those words only to him. Her fingers traced the two lines while trembling, her touch freezing yet warm and gentle. He remembered her touch then, her hands caressing his skin in so many places it made the cold go away—

Then a thought crossed his mind. "Why are you acting as if you never saw them before?"

It took two seconds for Saranm to process the warrior's words. He knew that because he saw the exact moment her eyes changed, when she recoiled her hand. "What do you mean by that?"

"We shared a night together, did we not? You ravished me, I tasted you, again and again. You should have touched all my scars, known all their locations." His body was heating up once again, but that time it was not caused by lust or unreliable memories. It was pure rage.

Saranm smiled again, her voice mellow and passionate while touching his shoulder yet that time she could not hide the shame flooding her eyes. "How could I know them all when it was so dark? A mere flame was not enough to do your body justice, handsome."

Leander grabbed her hand, his own gaze burning while staring down at her. He placed her flat hand on his chest, making her feel every inch of every scar on his body. "You tell me you were not able to feel them in the dark? Their texture, their shapes—I remember you placing your *tongue* above them, witch, now you tell me you didn't know?"

Saranm pulled her hand back, standing up in one quick movement. When Leander stood up, she took a few steps back and at that moment he finally understood what was wrong with all her reactions, with her voice, her side glances, the way she would look at him. It was not fear, or desire, or pity.

It was guilt.

"What did you do to me? You just made it very clear that all those memories are nothing but lies, so why I am feeling so weak?" When she did not answer, he pointed toward the wolves' hides around them, some on top of the wood they were sitting on while others rolled beside the bags. "There was no way to finish tawning the hides in just a few days. Even if you used your bloody *magic* on them, you said yourself only your teacher knew how to perform those kinds of *time spells*. How much time has passed?"

The woman averted his gaze, her hand touching her arm as if she was soothing herself. When no answer came, Leander grabbed her wrists, forcing Saranm to look only at him, to feel the anger in his eyes, to listen closely to the burning in his words.

"Speak, *you devious witch!* For how long have I been pining away in that cave, having all my forces drained and sucked dry by you?!"

"Fucking three weeks!" Saranm shouted at his face, her smile finally gone with no trace left on her lips. Within her eyes there was only hurt, tears still falling but that time they carried not only sadness but anger as well. "You were out for more than three weeks. I kept tending your leg, making you drink my tainted tea while cursing you from Wake to Gallows. Is that what you wish to hear, o *brave* warrior? Your hides were done after those three fucking weeks and as long as you stay away from me, your strength shall return. Now let me *go*."

Leander blinked a few times, releasing the woman with a laugh stuck in his throat. Mages were nothing but worthless, corrupted souls—how could he have ever thought otherwise?

"I will finish cooking the meat. Focus on finding the source." He could feel his fingers shaking, his heart beating faster, his own mind racing as different thoughts crossed his mind. If he killed her, would he regain his strength? How stupid had he been to be deceived to such an extent? If she had been the one responsible for his sudden weakness, then why help him recover? Why save his life?

"As you wish, *warrior*," she spat the words, almost spitting on the ground as she turned her back and left the space with her braid barely moving, as if frozen with disgust and rage.

Leander picked up the herbs and mixtures from the ground, glancing toward the injury on his leg that did not hurt as much. He felt his muscles ache, his fatigue winning over as he moved and breathed, glancing toward the path the woman had taken alone.

Why was she crying?

Why feel guilty?

The Argyris tried to reach for the dragon for the very first time, yet there was a wall separating them. He could feel the beast somewhere within his mind, their connection and bond still present and alive but intangible and dim. Leander should just focus on doing what he always did after all. Being a warrior.

A worthy Argyris that would bring the Sacred Sword back.

Two Nights Before Memorial Day

Entrapment of A Star

Lull of Afternoon - Leader's Office, Ice Draco

Twenty-One Nights Before Memorial Day

"What did you say?"

Kayden's voice mirrored Dorian's own state of mind. At that point he was not sure of what to think, much less what to do.

"Bash has disappeared. I cannot find him anywhere, neither me nor the other knights. No one has seen him the entire day." Dorian could not stop blaming himself for noticing far too late. When he did not see Bash at Wake eating his morning meal as he did every day, the Ward though the young Knight had decided to indulge himself in his sleep a while longer. When Dorian did not see Bash training at the Silver Grounds, he gave it no grand importance. It was only when the man waited almost an entire hour for the Knight at the Reliquary Room to review his mission one last time that Dorian had a desperate thought, reaching his mind from the depths of his body.

Bash had run away.

But that could not be. He, above everyone else, should know how much Kayden depended on him. Not only that but Dorian was certain that Kayden could locate the young Knight no matter where he was through the Ancient's bond, so it would simply make no sense for the boy to try to run away.

"Did you search his chambers?" Kayden asked as she stood from her chair, the air around her becoming agitated and chaotic. "Was there anything out of the ordinary?"

Dorian shook his head. "You can find him, isn't that right? You can communicate with the white dragon and find Bash."

The princess closed her eyes, her expression becoming more strained as the seconds passed. When Dorian met her gaze again, he saw only panic flooding inside her green eyes. "Antrühriel cannot reach Vührähkam. It is as if there is...a dense fog blocking us from them, as if they were worlds apart. I cannot feel them anymore, neither can Antrühriel."

It was as if they were all staging a play. The moment Kayden finished her sentence there was a knock on her door and all she did was look at Dorian for him to rush to turn the knob, one knight holding a single scrolled paper in her hand. When the knight saw him she immediately saluted him, making one short bow. "Färküh Dorian, I was told to deliver this note to our leader at once."

"Bring it to me." The only reason there was no more urgency to Kayden's words was because it wasn't possible. The scroll was sealed with wax, yet what made Dorian widen his eyes was the insignia stamped into the red wax. When he gave the paper to his lady's hands, she too saw the emblem, pressing her lips tight together before opening the small parchment.

That insignia stamped on the wax was the Orphys constellation, the Divine Order's emblem. Dorian glanced toward the table, seeing the stamp right beside a pile of books. Whoever sent that had not stolen the stamp. They used it there, inside the leader's office, before Kayden arrived. Last night the princess stayed in her room and as far as Dorian knew, she only came to her office at Wake. The office was always locked whenever Kayden was not present, and the only window in the room could only be opened from the inside. In that short time, how had someone managed to come in?

His thoughts were cut short when he heard his princess's low gasp, the color fading from her face with such speed it made his heart freeze in his chest. "What does it say?"

The leader said nothing.

She gave him the open note with cool, unmoving hands. Dorian grabbed the paper and it took him less than seconds to read its content, but he did so, again and again, as if his eyes were searching for clues, hints, anything that could tell him more of the situation that was about to unfold, anything that could help him prepare for such an obvious trap. Yet the more he read the more he felt himself staring at an abyss that kept laughing at him, waiting for him to fall.

I stole something that belongs to you and I am dying to give it back.
Meet me at Fall. You know where.
From your dear friend,
D.E.

It was all the note said.

"Do you remember who gave this to you?" Dorian asked after he was able to find his voice again, shifting his gaze toward the knight who still stood at the door.

The young woman appeared to be taken aback at his question before replying, "I do not know—it came attached to a messenger bird. It was labeled as urgent and the instruction said it should be delivered straight to our leader's hands."

Dorian could swear he felt his own heart shake and tremble as he crumpled the paper in his hands more for fear than anything else. That was the assassin hired by Alexander to kill Kayden—Dark Eye. It could only be him. But why contact them after so long? Why capture Bash at all and most important, *how* they were able to do such a thing? If the assassin kidnapped Bash, he had to have some way to fight Kayden, to nullify her bond with the Ancients. Who was to say Dark Eye was not accompanied by a small army? Who was to say they would truly meet her alone? Even worse, how could they have any guarantee that Bash was still alive? After all, Kayden was not successful in communicating with the Knight nor his dragon. That note could very much be just an empty promise of a rescue, something to lure the princess out of the mountains straight to her demise. The next moment he looked at Kayden, she was staring at the ground with an absent gaze, her mind away from their reality.

"He was there... Last night, those feelings I felt... They were not Alexander's, they were *his*. He was *there*."

Confusion filled his words, his voice almost hoarse. "Kay, what are you saying? Was Dark Eye *in* your chambers last night?" It was impossible to omit the panic as he spoke, urging Kayden to reply to him as fast as she could otherwise his heart would fail. The thought of an assassin inside her chambers, no—of an assassin anywhere near her—going unnoticed to him was enough to make Dorian want to rip out his own eyes and heart and set them on fire.

Yet she did not answer him. Kayden had her eyes focused on something, a memory, a plan, a thought. He recognized that expression. "Dorian...do you trust me?"

He never enjoyed that expression.

"More than I trust myself, my lady." But the certainty that the princess was about to do something that would set his entire soul aflame would not be shaken away.

Kayden turned her head toward the knight, her eyes burning with a faint glow. "Prepare a horse at once. Tell the others I have a meeting to attend."

He grabbed her hand almost by instinct, by pure fear. As if Kayden would never come back if she left those mountains that day. And even when her eyes met his with warmth and a pleading gaze, his heart was not soothed. His mind was not relieved from its damned and desperate thoughts.

"Prepare *two* horses. I will come with you." It was all that he answered as he let go of Kayden's arm.

He did not allow himself to look back for he was afraid she would make him stay, or worse. That he would not trust her enough to let her go.

To Reach A Lost Star

Toll of Evening - Woods

Twenty-One Before Memorial Day

A few Minutes Before Fall

IT WAS FINE. *YET he had heard us.* She could still succeed. *Yet he* knew *about the Sight.* She had been preparing for that moment for days, trying to steer things into the best outcome and at last things were set. Just as the Divines' will had dictated.

But the Sight works toward the Divines' goals and not my own.

And he was not supposed to know about it.

The two horses ran through the woods with tremendous speed, the sound of their hooves hitting the ground echoing between the trees. Above them the sun was almost gone, the last rays of sunlight fading away as the minutes passed.

"You said we should not worry about Dark Eye anymore, Kay. I trusted that the Divines had showed you enough to make you certain of that, but now...that fiend has one of your Knights," Dorian said with clenched teeth, his hands gripping the horse's reins with a slow burning rage.

Kayden did not even know what to say to him. "We can discuss this another time; for now we must make haste."

But Dorian had more to say. "We must double—no, triple the guards within the mountains, maintain watches for your chambers, your office, all entrances—"

"Dorian, we can discuss that later. For now—"

"No, Kay!" Dorian shouted, surprising her.

He glanced toward her for a brief second, his eyes flashing with anger and frustration. His emotions were like a tempest, agitated and turbulent waters alongside howling winds and a black sky where Kayden felt herself inside a small boat.

"With all due respect, my lady, I will *not* let this pass or make no deal out of this situation. A professional assassin managed to not only get inside the mountains, but inside *your* chambers and your office. If the Divines do not care enough about you to show you a Sight about your life being threatened, *I* do. My sole purpose is to make sure you stay protected and alive, Kay. Do you really think I would be able to forgive myself if something had happened to you?"

On his last sentence the words got stuck in his throat, almost choking him. Inside that tempest, Kayden could feel his sadness and fear like a never-ending rain, pouring so heavily against her it was enough to make her drown. "Forgive me, I did not take you or your feelings into consideration. I *am* sorry, Dorian, and we *will* discuss this further when we get back. I promise."

Dorian clenched his jaw, keeping his gaze on the path ahead. "Dark Eye set this trap in order to kill you, Kayden. You must know that at least, Sight or no Sight."

"He will not be able to harm me, Dorian." And that was the only thing of which she was almost certain.

"Why contact you again, after so much time has passed since his contract with Alexander? Why risk his life to kill the Divine Order's leader with three Ancient creatures guarding you? Not only was Dark Eye able to kidnap Bash right under our noses, but he made it so neither you nor the white dragon can find him. I can only pray that Bash is not dead."

"He is not dead," Kayden answered so fast and with such conviction pouring down from her words, it made her Ward look at her once again, doubt filling his eyes.

"Is that you talking or your Sight, Kay?"

She did not answer, only watched as the sun disappeared on the horizon. The princess knew they had arrived at their location before her eyes found the place because Antrühriel roared inside her mind, causing a pain so severe it almost made her head split. Kayden had to bite her lip to prevent herself from screaming, pulling the reins in one movement and bringing her horse to a halt. Dorian stopped only a few meters ahead of her, climbing down off Lyon with a concerned gaze as he searched their surroundings.

It took him less than one minute to find the right spot. "The air around here is completely wrong, Kay." Fear dripped from his words like blood from a deep wound, neither stopping nor slowing its flow. That only made it harder for her to convince him.

"Dorian, listen to me."

It was her voice that made the Ward flinch, making his muscles tense and rigid before he turned to face her. He knew that whatever Kayden was about to say was not a request or a plea. It was an order he was obliged to follow as a Färküh.

"My connection with Antrühriel is already weak from where I stand, the moment I cross over she will not be able to communicate with me. There might be traps or other people surrounding the area. I want you to guard the entrance and stay alert for any suspicious activities."

If Kayden could not hear his heart stop, she could see it happen by looking at his face. "My lady, the chances of you getting hurt or worse are extremely high—I cannot allow you to go by yourself. Even if it is your own orders, if there is any real threat to your life, as a Färküh Ward I have permission to act of my own volition to protect you and guard your—"

"Dorian."

She could almost hear the scream stuck in his throat.

Please, don't. It was what his eyes seemed to cry to her.

"Do you trust me?"

He shook his head, staring at his feet while gripping the handle of his sword. "Kay, I don't think I can—"

"I *must* go alone." Her voice was soft and that time, it was a request. A fact, a promise. It was enough to make him meet her gaze, enough to make him concede.

"I *must* save Bash. So please trust me, Dorian. I swear I am not pushing you away this time and I promise you I will explain everything when we are finished, but for now just place your trust in me. I need to do this by myself."

Dorian said nothing. He tied the horses to the trees, he checked his armor and his sword, and he tried more than once to control his emotions. So, when he finally stood in front of her, at least in his eyes, there was no fear nor concern. He took her hand, taking it to his lips for a warm kiss before touching her fingers to his forehead.

"Promise you will stay safe, Kay. *Swear* to me and I will go."

She pulled him in for an embrace, whispering the words in his ear, "I swear and you must also do the same."

When they parted, the sun was completely gone.

There was no more light.

It was a smart decision, to have their "trade" at a cave. That way, even if her connection with Antrühriel came back the dragon would not be able to help her directly. The entrance was too narrow, only a small fissure in the rock, and the passage itself was troublesome to get through with her sword, making Kayden glad she had chosen to wear her leather armor.

Dark Eye was indeed a very smart person.

Kayden did not walk far until the cave opened, revealing itself completely as she left the narrow passage and entered the huge open space that was lit by candles and torches, making her shadow dance and tremble with the weakest breeze. There seemed to be some spaces and deformations above her and the bones spread around the space made Kayden realize that the cave could actually be the nest of some animal, probably having another entrance. However, if there was one, it was nowhere to be seen. The path continued on the other side, with a wider passage but small nonetheless. She was glad the ground was mostly plain and solid rather than unsteady and filled with holes and different levels. But with every step she took the sound reverberated through the cave, a constant dripping sound from afar.

"Welcome, princess."

His voice was deeper than she would've thought, yet there was a raw emotion inside it that made her skin crawl. "I appreciate you lighting up the place for our meeting. It would be unfortunate if I could not see you properly."

As he chuckled, Kayden looked around trying to figure out where the sound was coming from, yet it came from everywhere, even his feelings permeated every stone, pebble, and bone. "It took some time, yes, but I am glad you like it. I did it *for you*."

His words burned her, made her eyes tear and her throat dry. Yet she had to hear them, she had to take them all. "So, not everything was Sean's doing, I see."

There was a long pause. Only the dripping sound could be heard and Kayden's own breathing before a laugh exploded inside the cave.

"But *of course* you would know! How could you not?! You have the Divines' pretty Sight, have you not, *princess?*"

She said nothing yet as her hair rose from her neck she grabbed her sword, waiting.

"I could barely believe it when I first found out. It just could not be true—you feel me?"

Kayden felt the air moving behind her, however when she turned there was nothing.

"Even when Sean-man told me you *knew,* I could still not believe it. But after you came here, I guess uncle was speaking the truth after all. You *know* who I am, do you not, princess?"

Some rocks fell a few meters in front of her, their shadows moving on the cave's walls. The betrayal that poured from his words worked like poisonous daggers, cutting away her skin and bones. It made her sick, made her dizzy. Yet even with all those emotions punching her left and right, she could still discern something hidden underneath all that anger and frustration. Shame.

"How can you be so sure of that?"

Dark Eye laughed one last time but when he did, Kayden felt her hair move. She turned as fast as she could, the blade protecting her face and the moment she did two daggers collided with her sword, aimed directly at her head. The hood slipped from the assassin's face, his smile sharing the same hatred from his gaze.

"Because not even once did you mention your precious Knight since you stepped into this cave. Guess you knew I didn't need to be rescued, isn't that so, dear leader?"

Bash spat those words as he pushed the daggers closer, making Kayden take two steps back. He was wrong about that.

She *had* come to save him. And that was what she was going to do.

Chapter XIV

The star glanced down below, yearning for a place to belong
The lion stared above, longing for the cosmic glow
The star, entrapped by the never ending night, wept
The lion, cursed by the land's mortality, craved
The lion leaped toward the skies, eager to swallow the light
The star bled, its glow blinding
The lion roared, its existence forgotten
Then both descended into Death's embrace, away from the Divines' Bless
Pulled away from their wishes and shackled by their yearnings
Such was the fate of the lion and the star
Falling forever into nothingness

- *The Curse of Yearning,* poem written by an unknown author.

Betrayed By The Gallows

Fall of Night - Woods

Twenty Nights Before Memorial Day

Even after he confirmed with his own eyes, Dark Eye could not believe it. There was neither shock nor surprise on Kayden's face, not an ounce of astonishment, dismay, confusion—*nothing.* Even worse, she looked at him with pity.

Fucking *pity.*

Bash was not furious. He was not sure how he felt. Maybe he could start by saying he was, perhaps, somewhat frustrated. How could he not be, after all? Not only had he found out his leader could hang for possessing a whole forbidden divine power—by spying on the princess inside her own wardrobe no less—he also discovered that she knew all along he was a professional assassin.

The one that had been hired to kill her, speaking of it.

He simply could not understand *at all* what in Säh's name the princess was even thinking, nor who was the stupider one. "Tell me, princess, did you enjoy yourself? Was it *fun* to see me try to train and do all that Knight bullshit for you?"

The sound of the daggers sliding on the sword's blade was like a sweet tune to him; it made his black heart come alive.

"All I ever wanted was for you to see your true potential, Bash, nothing else. I *never* lied to you." She managed to push him back, swinging her sword close enough to his face so the blade's tip almost touched his nose, forcing him to lean back. *Oh*, his leader did have some nerve.

"My *potential?* As what, *a worthy Knight?!*" He shook his head, smiling so hard it hurt his face. "Look at me, princess. I was never fit to be a knight in shining armor and never will be." *I belong to the Gallows.*

He ran at her, hitting her sword with the left dagger while aiming for her rib cage with the right one. Kayden moved her body to the side just enough to make him miss, hitting Bash with her head. He staggered, a sharp pain going all the way to the back of his head. Dark Eye always knew the princess would not be an easy target, which was why he had planned the perfect assassination for her, twice. Fair enough, he did not know she was a princess the first time before she won the Tournament. Still, a lot of thought was put into making the assassination a plausible reality. Bash was, after all, a professional.

"Did Sean order you to kill me this time?" Her voice was a blend of contempt and confidence; she *knew.* Just as she knew his identity, just as she knew probably everything about his fucking life.

"If you already know the answer, why ask, princess? You realized who I was because the bloody Divines told you, so why keep playing games with me?"

Dark Eye charged at her again, yet that time Kayden began to fight back. She reminded him of Leander and the way he used the sword—the power and the assertiveness of each strike as their blades collided in the air. He tried to pierce her eyes, her neck, and her chest but her sword always met his daggers, her body always swiftly moved away.

"Be truthful, leader. For how long have you known about my interactions with that man? Weeks? Since the moment we met? Is that why you went to the Silver Grounds so late in the Gallows, so that I could 'break into' your office and have something to report?"

He said those words half expecting her to deny, or at least counter him to some extent, yet she stayed silent. Bash almost stopped his arms midair, disbelief flooding him for a brief second before he clenched his teeth. Wow.

Just...wow.

Ha, it was *unbelievable*. He was baffled, he *really* was. "So everything I did, everything *you* let me do, was for a purpose. *Is that it?!*"

Her expression changed a bit when she looked him in the eyes—her lines softened, her gaze fell. Their duel had reached another stalemate, with Kayden blocking his weapons and not letting him move forward. "Bash, listen to me—"

"No! You listen!" He broke free from her sword, slicing the air with the dagger as his words tore their way out of his mouth. Inside him, something burned and hurt.

There was a ghost touch inside his mind, a presence that he had grown more and more acquainted with for the past weeks but that was, at that moment, practically gone. He was overjoyed to be the only occupant in his mind again, for not having to share everything with an ancient demonic beast that would only laugh at his dismay. The stone on his wrist felt frozen and distant, as if whatever glowed inside it had finally perished. For once in a long time, he felt free.

Still, it *hurt*. "I asked myself *every* single day—why *me?* Why choose a killer? Why pick *Dark Eye* as a Knight? But he would never answer me, he would only laugh and ignore me—and honestly, I was fine with that. It only seemed *fair*."

Actually, Bash could even understand Vühräh after some time. The big fella enjoyed some bloodlust, that was why the dragon did not say anything when Dark Eye went to meet with Sean, he was waiting for some action! The assassin could feel the beast's bloodlust as if it was his own—no, it even blended with his own. Maybe that was why he was chosen, then. He could provide with ease something the Ancient wanted and get richer in the process. It was a promising partnership. All Bash had to do was ignore all the rest about him saving the world, being a hero, and pretending to be a knight and simply focus on doing the thing he did best—being a blooded monster inside the Gallows. That was all.

But apparently, he had been sorely mistaken and the reason why moody Vührähkam was tagging along was because Albaron's princess was taking her sweet time using Dark Eye to fulfill her needs—*fucking free of charge*.

Bash pointed one of the daggers toward her, his face twisting as the words left his mouth, leaving a bitter taste behind. "Say, princess, would you tell me to kill your father after I gathered his dirty little secrets and passed them on to you?

Would you let me continue with my secretive escapades as long as it brought you closer to Sean-man? Or did you really want to meet his contractor? I would be lying if I said I wasn't curious myself." Bash made his daggers collide, the metallic sound echoing and spreading throughout the cave. "Oh, maybe you already know who the contractor is! You have the Sight, after all."

"That is not how it works."

For the first time the princess showed something beyond pity toward him, her voice rising with anger. *That* was better, it made him smile.

"Oh? Did I hit a nerve? Is the whole *'Sight'* thing a sensitive topic, princess? Why, do not tell me you *actually* hate being able to pry into everyone's life with the Divines' seal of approval?"

Something in the air changed, even Bash was able to feel it, as her hair suddenly moved to the side. She was trying to use the *arcane*. Dark Eye saw the exact moment when she tried to do that whole core and energy thing and failed, a strain appearing in her eyes, her face twisting in confusion. Bash took that chance, throwing the two daggers in his hands at her chest. As Kayden blocked, he ducked to her left taking out the short sword that was tied on his waist. Every time he raised the sword and hit, his grip on the weapon increased, along with his rage.

"You have no idea what you are saying, nor how the Sight *truly* works. I never intended to know about your secrets, Bash. All I ever wanted was for you to trust me."

"Oh, I am *sure* I know nothing of your hardships and perils, princess. *How could I?!* I am *nothing* but a gutter rat, an assassin for hire! What can I know of the pain and struggles you *fucking nobles* go through. You gold-plated fuckers are *all the same!"*

He hit her again and again, and every time the short sword only met Kayden's blade. On every strike the weapons met and recoiled with such aggression and power, it made his arm tremble.

"Bash, why can you not *see*?! I've been trying to help you since the beginning—"

"You have been using me since the beginning!" His shout made her flinch and widen her eyes. "You *pity* me, letting me think you actually believed all the lies

I told in an attempt to *belong* with you all, saying all those things about destiny and making the Order a better place, trying to convince *me* I belonged—"

"You *do* belong with us!" Kayden sped up, her movements becoming more oppressive and merciless as her sword moved alongside her, her strikes sending Dark Eye back bit by bit. "I chose you to watch my father because I know you are the best for the job. I chose to let your secret stay hidden because it was never my choice to learn about it. *I told you*! I do not care about the sins of your past."

He felt his lips tremble and his eyes burn.

Why?

How could she not care? How could she let a person like him walk inside those mountains as if he was any other knight? As if *he* deserved to be a *Knight?* She should be just one more princess, one more noble to look down on him, treat him for what he really was. A rotten, spoiled thing brought by the Gallows. A nobody, a monster.

Yet she helped him.

But I am Dark Eye.

She, *a princess*, treated him as an equal.

I am a monster born from the Gallows.

She, *the leader*, defended him against another knight.

My sole purpose is to bring Death's kiss whenever I'm paid.

She, Kayden *herself*, believed he could do some good in the world.

And during all that time, as she helped him, believed in him, and protected him, she had known who he *truly* was.

And she was still fighting for him. Because *she* believed he was *worthy.*

Kayden stopped her sword in midair as he felt something warm running down his face. He knew why Vührähkam let him do whatever he wanted, accept Sean's proposal and even the artifact. He also knew why Kayden agreed so easily to meet up with him. They both knew, all too well.

He could not bring himself to kill her. Not even if he wanted.

"I do not know why you still care for me...after all the things I did, how could anyone trust me?" How could anyone believe in him?

Kayden dropped her sword on the ground and threw her arms around him, pulling him in for an embrace. He could barely feel her touch as his body shook, his skin so cold it hurt.

"Can you see it now, Bash? I *did* come to save you." Kayden's whisper in his ear was warm and kind, and it broke him. It destroyed everything he stood for, all he was, and all he cared for.

He kept touching his face and rubbing his eyes to make it stop, make all those fucking tears stop and go back to where they came from because Dark Eye *did not* cry. He was ruthless, merciless, cruel, a Gallows' servant. Bash never asked to be saved, he never asked for a savior, and he loved the Gallows more than he loved his own life. All those years, he never regretted his choices, never regretted becoming Dark Eye and killing all those gold-plated trash, he *was* happy.

"Let us go back now, Bash. To where *we* belong."

He dropped the weapon onto the ground, the sound of its fall echoing inside his heart. He never asked to be found. Never wished to be saved.

Then why did he feel so relieved?

A Warrior's Cry

Bless of Day - Glacial Mountains

Night of Memorial Day

"Stop. It's here."

They were in a space where there were no trees, almost like a glade with the mountains' rocks closing the space in front of them. The only thing he could see was snow and the sky and nothing else. There were no caves, no holes, no craters, no anything. Above all else—

No Sword. No Ancient.

"If this is your idea of a joke..."

The woman laughed, gazing up to the sky while turning toward him. "I don't expect someone like *yourself* to find any joke I shall ever tell entertaining, warrior. The source comes from here, there is no place else."

Was she making a fool out of him? Tricking him once again? Who was to say Leander wasn't in a deep slumber, all those scenes being projected by the woman just like she had done before. However, there was something in that area that even the Argyris could sense, a feeling that did not come from petty magic but from his own experience as a warrior. It was something unsettling, something...wrong.

"Let us start searching, then. The faster we find the Sword and the bloody Ancient the sooner we can get back." Yes, that was right. No Argyris had ever been so close to the Sacred Sword before. If he brought it back to them, he would be remembered for generations—*a legend*. No one would ever be able to doubt his worth, his abilities and proficiency, his place within the family. Even more than his current disgust toward the mage's apprentice, finding the Sword was more important.

Saranm closed her eyes, a frown appearing on her face. "The energy is so scattered... I cannot place its exact location, it is almost as if they were below the ground."

Below...? Would they have to enter a cave and venture into the depths to find the resting place of the beast? Leander's heart began to race, a cold sweat breaking on his neck as chills made his skin crawl.

He clenched his fists, feeling the nails dig deep into his skin and forcing his mind to focus. "Then we must find an opening, if they are below there must be an entrance of sorts."

Yet no matter how much he looked around, there seemed to be only snow. There weren't even trees or rocks near. It could not be that the entrance was below all that snow, could it? Saranm held his arm as Leander started to move, her lips pale and cracked yet holding the same confidence and malice as she smiled.

"You stay here. Let the evil witch do her part."

"What, are you planning to use your *talents* to levitate all this snow?"

The woman ignored him, walking into the center of the glade and raising both hands in the air. The seconds passed one after the other yet nothing happened, the look in her eyes changing from focus to one filled with pain and frustration. The man could see her arms beginning to tremble as her face became more and more ill, blood trailing down her nose. He was strong enough to be able to close their distance with no great difficulty, his legs dragging him down every three steps. From time to time the snow below their feet trembled and shook as if being charged with a weak electricity, only to fall silent after a couple of seconds, the cycle repeating every few moments. When Leander finally reached the woman, the blood was almost touching her lips, the smile long gone from her face.

She glanced at him from the side, changing her posture while wiping the blood off her nose. "Got tired of watching from afar, handsome? I shall succeed in no time."

At that point he should know better than to care enough to ask. "You used your arcane skills quite well before, woman. Why are you struggling now?"

Saranm laughed again, however that time the sound was hollow and distant. "For someone who had their core broken you sure seem quite versatile in the arcane arts to spout such words."

Leander watched her struggle in vain for a few more minutes, seeing the snow tremble and move even weaker than before, until his feet stopped right in front of her. He grabbed her hand, her skin so hot it almost burned him. He squinted his eyes, taking his face closer, staring deep into her eyes. "I do not need to know such wretched arts to *see.* This magic is making you ill."

The woman scoffed. "I am simply struggling to manipulate the energy here in the mountains, the source of your *sweet Sword* is hindering the flows. My *magic* does not make me ill."

His eyes widened briefly before he could control the shock in his voice. "You've been straining and forcing yourself since we arrived here, is *that* what you are saying?"

"I am not that weak, handso—"

"If every time you used your energy caused you pain, *why?* Why steal my force only to save me weeks after?"

She tried to pull her hand away, yet Leander did not let go, not yet. He had to know, had to understand. Saranm's eyes were filled with tears but none fell, the smile on her face being nothing more than a cheap illusion.

"You tell me, warrior. Apparently, you have everything figured out. Perhaps I wanted you weak to make it easier to assault you later on, and all I did was show you how our night together would be."

Anger boiled inside him and the words that he shouted burned with it. "Stop with this *frivolous act!* You *really* believe I am a fool to fall for such blatant lies, when you make it obvious how hard you are trying to play this part?"

She finally managed to free her hand from his grasp, taking a few steps back, her golden eyes trembling with rage as she shouted back at him, "You know *nothing* about me!"

"How can I know anything when all that leaves your mouth are *lies?!*" Leander closed their distance, grabbing both her shoulders while feeling the heat of her skin. "Tell me at once—what were you doing with me?! What are you even planning?"

Her voice broke, tears finally rolling down her cheeks. "I was fucking *saving* you."

The ground started to shake.

It was as if there was a giant asleep beneath their feet waking up with nothing but wrath, a low rumble that kept growing and growing, making the snow tremble violently above it. And almost as if it was mocking the golden-eyed mage, all the snow around them began to levitate as if there was no end to it, rising meters above the ground and surrounding them as a huge, colossal wall around the glade. The snow then started to solidify, getting harder until it became pure crystal ice clearer than the cleanest glass.

Even with a vast area surrounding them, Leander could feel the air failing to enter his lungs, his heart beating in madness against his chest. It felt like the tallest ice prison, one that had no doors nor windows but an infinity of sky to gaze upon in a hopeless wish that the walls would one day melt. Within him a child kept whispering, crying, screaming—*this is going to be my grave. I will* die *here.* However, there was one sight within the ice walls that made the panic inside him go quiet, silent for a moment.

All around him the man could see as if spirits had been frozen within the ice, as if their souls had been trapped with their vague silhouettes and haunting eyes, arms and hands desperate while they reached out for something that seemed to be far beyond their reach. All souls, all spirits looked and crawled in the same direction. As Leander followed their stretched hands and gazes, he found himself looking straight into the object they all seemed to ache for. Even though Leander had never seen it or touched it, the man knew exactly what it was. The Sacred Sword, deep inside the ice wall, calling out to the spirits within the ice from all directions making them swim, crawl, fly, and drag themselves to get a glimpse of it. Even though they were all frozen, their eyes seemed too much alive, too much alert.

Leander was afraid to blink, to move, to breathe in fear the Sword would disappear from his sight. It held such a stunning beauty as if it had been made to be wielded by the Divines Themselves, a blade so pure and white as if made of hardened snow with dark red jewels on its hilt. A single crystal on its pommel seemed to possess its own glow, its own light, and even from afar the warrior felt the immense power that emanated from the weapon.

Then he took two steps back.

It was something he could not explain, that his mind could not understand even as his feet moved backward, something his body did of its own volition. That Sword, that place—it *reeked*. It was such a vile stench, something he had never felt before and somehow he *knew* did not come from something tangible. For a moment it was as if Leander was borrowing the senses of his Ancient, even if the dragon's voice was muted to him, for he knew *that* was the stench of evil and malice, a stench that was not only in the air but on every crack, every particle, every snowflake piled in the corners.

The warrior felt a fear he had never felt in his life, not even when he was almost buried alive by the snow troll, when he faced a giant boar alone, or when he met Death for the first time. No, that fear made every organ and every limb in his body coil and tremble. He dared to turn his head, searching for the woman who had been far too quiet, and when his eyes found hers something inside him broke. Saranm's face was twisted in pure agony, her eyes bulged as if they would jump out of their sockets with her mouth open as if she was screaming her soul out of her body. The symbols on her arms were glowing stronger by the second, so much he could see them beneath her clothes and Leander could feel the heat coming out of her like a hot wave expanding.

For years I have been longing for the taste of fresh souls to enter my domain. It has been long nights and days since I last tasted men's blood, dragging them into my lair as they themselves sought riches, power, and moments of grandeur.

The voice itself opened a hole inside Leander's chest. It felt like falling into a black and endless pit, his body feeling Death nearing as he fell endlessly into its darkness. It brought this primitive and animalistic thing inside the warrior, something the Argyris had banished from his body and soul for there was no place for that thing inside him, no place for such weakness. *Despair*. Leander turned around, searching for the source of the voice and that overwhelming fear that kept trying to take control of his muscles and mind. Yet all his eyes met time and time again was the Sacred Sword, calling for the entrapped souls within the walls.

HAVING SAID SO, I SEARCH IN MY MEMORIES RECENT DAYS WHERE I ENCOUNTERED MEN WHO DID NOT SEEK ME FOR THEIR GREED AND IGNORANCE. I HAVE FOUND THAT I CANNOT RECALL SUCH DAYS. YOU ARE THE FIRST TO FOLLOW MY PRESENCE WITHOUT FULLY KNOWING WHAT WOULD BE MET.

"Reveal yourself, monster!" Leander forced his fingers to pull out his sword, the weapon still weighing in his hand. His face twisted in horror when he saw his own hands shaking, and not from lack of strength. He glanced toward Saranm, seeing the woman frozen in the same pitiful position as before. "We seek only the Ancient and the Sword. The sacred artifact does not belong to you. I am an Argyris and this weapon is our birthright." He should not be proud of himself that his voice was not trembling, that it still possessed strength. He should not be. Shame ran over him like an unstoppable snowstorm, freezing the warrior as he was overwhelmed by denial and disgrace of his own self. How dared he act in such a way? Leander's grip on his sword got even tighter. "If you do not comply, beast, I shall be the warrior to bring Death's kiss to you." His words did not betray him, did not weaken nor were filled with despair. His words showed his real self, one not controlled by shameful fear, words that belonged to a worthy Argyris. A *true* warrior.

MONSTER, YOU SAY?

From inside the wall, the Sacred Sword seemed to project itself away from the ice as if it was moving on its own. Leander Argyris could not believe his own ears but the haunting voice was coming from the weapon itself. It floated on the air, mere meters in front of him, an eerie aura exhaling with such strength it made the man's skin numb and cold, as if it was carrying Death's kiss by its own white blade. At that moment, a dark aura started to surround the Sacred Sword as if calling him in, luring Leander to touch it, to grasp it.

SHOW ME HUMANITY'S ANGER AND I SHALL GIVE IT A SHAPE. THEIR DESIRE FOR VENGEANCE, THEIR ACHE FOR HATE, THEIR CRIES THAT MELT WITH FURY AND BURN IN A BLAZE OF FIRE, IT ALL BELONGS TO ME. THEY ARE MY KIN, MY FLESH AND BLOOD. I FEED ON THE THINGS THAT MOVE YOU AND MAKE YOU FEEL ALIVE. TRAVEL THE DISTANCE OF TIME ITSELF AND YOU SHALL FAIL TO FIND A MORE POWERFUL BEING ON THIS MORTAL PLANE. I AM WHAT MAKES MAN THRIVE AND I AM THEIR UNRAVEL. WHO IS AN ARGYRIS BEFORE ME?

As it spoke, the dark aura grew and surrounded the Sword even more, an ill feeling spreading inside Leander's body. Whatever was inside that weapon, his mind could not process, could not fathom its existence. The warrior clenched his teeth, gripping his sword with both hands as he stared at the Sacred Sword. *I am worthy.*

"My words shall not be changed, creature. Reveal yourself so I can slay whatever taints our sacred treasure, otherwise I cannot promise you a peaceful death."

Laughter was all Leander heard in response and even though the sky was clear, light was stolen from within the ice prison. Only a faint source of light remained, coming from Saranm's glowing marks. As light vanished and turned Bless into Gallows, Leander felt his will to fight fail him while the primal instinct to run and secure his life began to dominate him. *No! I am a warrior, I will retrieve the weapon and leave this place. I* will *survive.*

The dark aura grew and grew until it was shot into the air, disappearing from sight as the Sacred Sword fell on the ground, the sound of its metal echoing within the prison like Death's own whisper.

Then there was a scream. It was as if Saranm was tearing her own throat apart with her bare hands while her limbs began to bend in the most unnatural angles possible, the sound of bones breaking and muscles ripping apart haunting his ears with every movement the woman made. He almost dropped his sword in pure shock, his feet stuck in a dilemma of risking to approach and rescue the poor woman or stay where they were. Saranm fell on her knees the moment her arms and legs went back to their usual places, hands sinking into her head as if she was trying to crack her skull open, screaming as if she was going through the most unbearable pain.

She is dying, Leander thought. *Somehow the beast is killing her without even making an appearance, without even touching her.* This mere thought was frightening and infuriating for it meant his fate would be the same. He would have a miserable death without being able to fight. Finally, he attempted to take a few steps closer, raising his sword as a final merciful act toward the mage who had, more than once, saved his life. He would cease her suffering in a painless way, it was the last thing he owed her.

The Argyris blinked, just once.

Before he blinked, he was standing in front of the woman as she screamed in pure pain with his sword raised high, images of his blade cutting that knight's wrist threatening to appear in his mind. He hesitated and blinked. The next second the hand that was once holding the sword bled without control, its bone completely shattered while the weapon laid on the cold ground. He could not breathe. The pain took its time to come, perhaps due to his mind not being able to process what had happened fast enough. Suddenly he was being held in midair, as if he weighed nothing, with fingers closed around his throat, fingers so hot he could feel his skin burning like coal as they blocked his airway. His vision began to darken as the warrior suffocated, making pitiful attempts to free himself from his aggressor. Saranm.

"For years I struggled against those petty tricks to take control of what is *rightfully* mine. I was not yet whole, my power scattered among a few treasures..."

The left side of her face was blackened, the darkness spreading in a slow pace as she spoke with a voice that did not belong to her. While her left eye was filled with blood, crimson tears falling from it, her right side was still human and showed a golden eye that had too much sorrow, too much pain to even compare to the wickedness and cruelty its other side expressed. Leander's hand, the one that was still usable, desperately searched for a weapon on his belt.

"It's been too long since I tasted such a nutritious meal. Such a strong *emotion*. One weak breath and one can already tell how deep runs this hate."

The woman opened her mouth, the skin on her face ripping apart as it opened more than it could, a slick pure black tongue crawling outside and reaching Leander's face. The tongue licked him until it reached his eye, leaving a trail of dense and sticky saliva that felt like acid against his skin. Leander felt a dagger's handle at his waist, his fingers closing around the weapon. In one swift and desperate movement, the man pierced the dagger in the woman's arm, a loud cry echoing through the space.

Leander barely had time to take a deep breath to fill his lungs after he dropped onto the ground. The kick to his chest sent him away with such insane brute force, it made the ice wall break and crack behind his back as he collided against it. Once again, the man lost his breath with blood pouring from his mouth. The world was suddenly painted in pain and confusion. Even in a daze he sought his weapon on the ground as the creature that controlled the woman's body approached. Yet *control* seemed too weak a word to describe what was happening with Saranm.

"Yourself would make my satiety poor and scarce were you not able to fight at least this much, human."

Leander took three deep breaths, feeling his chest burst and strain with every attempt. Dark dots filled his vision, yet he saw the weapon ahead of him, feeling the fatigue from the past days enter his bones and muscles. It was hard to think and focus. Before he could even take two steps, Saranm's body was beside him with the long dark tongue licking her blackened lips, as if savoring a favorite meal.

"Would you like a spare hand, warrior?"

The monster picked Leander up by the collar, its words dripping with mockery, throwing him in the direction of the weapon. He covered his face during the fall, rolling thrice before his body stood still on the hard ground with the sword only a few inches from him. Leander could not move his right hand, not even his fingers, without severe pain running across his entire arm.

The warrior crawled, grabbing the sword's hilt with his left hand as he tried to get up. When he raised his gaze, the image of that woman crying blood stood right in front of him, her body floating on the air with legs crossed as if she was sitting on the floor, the blooded eye staring at him with boredom. The man first felt all his blood freeze and dry inside his veins before it began to pump and run like melting flames inside him, urging him to attack.

"Do you not think about your fragility, your weakness? You humans believe it is best to let fancy words about honor and pride be spoken before the moment of your deaths, as if they would actually do something for your fates. Why do you lack so much intelligence while being such a widespread race, mortal?"

The Argyris bit his tongue as he swung the sword with all his strength, yet the blade hit nothing but air. Less than a second later he felt teeth sinking into his neck, warm blood gushing from the wound as Leander let out a furious cry throwing his head backward, feeling it collide with the woman's. That thing released its teeth from him and as the Argyris turned around to face the damned creature once more, he saw his blood dripping from her chin, a wide and evil grin covering her entire face as the long black tongue licked the remains of blood.

"Your blood is old, human. It carries plenty yet still lacks substance. Your hate, however, remains *delicious.*"

Every single instinct warned him of the outcome, showed right in front of him the immense and insane power that a mere human like Leander could never reach, told him in every possible way he had no chance to ever survive. The invisible hand closed around his heart, burning pure cold inside it. Yet there was this thing, deep inside his mind. It felt like a voice, his *own* voice, calling forth all the frustration and dissatisfaction he had felt throughout the years. A voice that showed all he could conquer with the power of a warrior, that dared his weaknesses to appear in front of him. *You are Leander Argyris. You are a warrior. You are worthy.* Indeed, he was a warrior, no, he was a *true* warrior. And that vile creature dared to defame his own name, his own family, while speaking ill of his own values?! *Preposterous.* Ridiculous.

He would put that monster in its place.

With every step taken, Leander Argyris felt his whole body aflame as if he was burning at the stake. His pain was numbed by the wrath he felt growing and dominating his every motion, the fury escalating every time he missed and saw the woman's tainted face. No words were strong enough to describe how vast was his anger. The warrior was slapped in the face, his body thrown inside the wall by the creature's force. He cleaned the blood from his lips and from the cut that kept bleeding into his eye, feeling no pain. He had never felt so great, so *powerful.*

He charged again.

And again.

And again.

Never striking, hearing his bones crack and his muscles tear with every kick, hit, and slap the being possessing the woman gave to him.

He felt no fatigue, he had no weakness. He was a warrior. He was an Argyris.

He was *Leander Argyris.*

However, before he could raise the sword one more time, something caught his eye, something made his arms stop in midair—the child, trapped inside the ice wall.

Leander felt his heart shrink and ache, trembling more than it ever did. The boy stared at him, shirtless, showing all his bruises with swollen, reddened eyes. However, that was himself before the White Mountains, before the snow troll and the cave. That was Leander when he was eight, when he was with his uncle. Adon Argyris's brother, the one who taught him how to gain the worth and respect of an Argyris, the one who gave him the family's pendant. A mighty lion whose roar could swallow the sun itself. Yet that child was not deserving of that pendant, that boy was weak. Pathetic.

The warrior ran toward the wall, swinging his sword as the blade cut the ice in one clean hit, making but a single scratch in its surface. When he looked into the wall again, it was empty, reflecting only himself.

Then he heard a baby's cry. The Argyris was suddenly alone in the ice prison, not even the spirit of the dead within its walls. From the other side, the crying intensified as if it was demanding his attention, his focus. Leander Argyris walked closer, his body still burning from the inside out, until he saw a woman lying in bed. For a moment, that invisible hand held his heart with such a strong grip, it felt it had crushed it. Burst it. Then it was gone, the anger boiling quietly inside him.

"Mother..." Leander heard his own whisper, even though his lips were sealed. There was too much blood on the bed, the woman's face weak and pale, but the crying continued even when the woman herself was gone. Then there was a little girl sitting on the bed, with clear blue eyes and curly dark hair, wearing a white dress and the Argyris pendant. However, that was not right. Leander Argyris never saw his sister growing up—he only saw her twice. The last time in a coffin, days after her birth. Yet the girl still looked at him, stared right into his eyes, into his soul.

"You know who killed me, do you not, brother?" He had never heard her voice, so then why did it sound so familiar? Why did he miss it so much?

"You are not real. My sister has already received Death's cold kiss." He was not sure he managed to whisper those words.

"But you do know, brother. You know why Death took me. You saw." The little girl's eyes became two black holes, a circle of fire burning the skin around her neck. "Why do you keep protecting him, old brother? Why have you never avenged me?"

As the bed caught on fire he heard another voice, and saw that same boy beside the little girl. That boy had more scars, more bruises, and possessed a gaze even more hopeless and tired while holding a bloody pendant in his hand. It was his fourteen-year-old self. "You never avenged her for you are just like him. You and that man are the same."

"I am nothing like my father!" he shouted, words cutting their way through his throat and sealed lips. "You shut your mouth! You are not worthy to speak to me!"

"I am." The new voice came from behind him and that time, it was an adult. A man who shared the same hair and eyes as him, a man who had more power and respect than Leander could ever imagine. Adon Argyris himself. "You *want* to be like me, do you not? No, you want to *be* me. You should, in fact. Otherwise, how could you even call yourself an Argyris?"

"You are the same, aren't you?" the children said again, that time holding hands as they spoke together. "You are the same as that man. The same as our father. You are an Argyris."

"No...I am not the same—I am not!" His voice was losing strength, his sword losing will.

They started to cry while the flames consumed them within the ice, their flesh melting and burning. "Then why have you forsaken us?"

Because you are weak.

"No...you are..."

Weak.

The voice inside his head kept speaking louder, angrier. The image of his father appeared within the flames, his body untouched by the fire, his hands closing around his sister's neck. Crushing her.

"You are the weak one, Leander. You are the failure, can you not see?" His father looked at him with arrogance and contempt, his words cold and rough. "You could not even punish that knight for his mistake. A true Argyris would have cut off both of his hands, you *know* this. You saw it happen before and you failed once again."

His father snapped the girl's neck, the skin and flesh breaking due to the fire's heat, her head falling into the boy's hands. Soon enough, there was nothing more for the flames to consume.

The warrior clenched his jaw, his teeth almost breaking as he crunched them together. Leander cut his father across the chest, his blade only meeting ice. "Bastard." For the first time, Leander felt his own lips moving, the grip on the sword getting stronger as the warrior screamed and shouted at the reflection inside the wall, the anger and the hate drenching and filling his words with fury. "You low piece of trash! *You* are the weak one! *You murdered her!*"

The warrior began to hit the ice wall with the sword's pommel, with its blade, with everything it had, not even noticing as his own blood dirtied the wall even when there was nothing more to be seen inside. No reflections, no memories, no flames, no promises. Yet Leander kept hitting the wall as he screamed, hitting faster, stronger, more desperately. He suddenly caught its sight, then, a swift shift in his gaze as it fell upon the sword's pommel. There was a crystal on it, tainted. Leander's eyes widened as pure horror filled his eyes, the white blade vibrating under his rage. The Sacred Sword burned his hands as if it was made of pure fire.

FEED ME, HUMAN.

Leander dropped the Sword on the ground with shaken arms, his body crushed under all the injuries, all the cuts, bruises, and blood as pain spread like venom. Since when? Why would he...?

"What ails you, human? Why stop now when there is still plenty to be shared?"

As the warrior turned, he saw the woman once again, yet he could not be sure if she was still alive at all. Her whole body reeked of rot, her skin was black as coal with only a small area around her right eye untouched. A golden eye that looked at him with grief, shame, and sorrow as tears fell and evaporated before ever reaching the ground.

"I finally know what you are, *demon*. I shall not be part of your games." How could he have been so blind? How could he not have felt it until that moment? The old memories from the last Knight were so vivid at last, he could only curse his own stupidity. He tried to reach for Amträhfar, but the dragon could not touch his mind, could not communicate with him even when the creature felt Leander's desperation. Something blocked their bond.

The creature laughed with a distorted voice. "You truly know nothing, human. What could possibly be known by someone such as yourself, who has yet to live and explore the realms?" The Sacred Sword flew toward the demon's hand, a dark light pulsing around the weapon. "Real demons live *inside* you. Inside every mortal who dares to breathe in this world there is an evil while their feelings and emotions pave the way to *our* ascension. In honesty, there is little to be done for your race. *You* are the ones with tainted egos and wounded hearts and beings such as *myself* only revel in the nourishment that comes after your fall. Such is the destiny of you mortals."

"You are wrong." The words left his mouth as a growl yet that only seemed to entertain the demon even more.

"Demons cannot *lie, mortal. Humans* are the ones who lie. This foolish woman, who you nourished with so much anger and hate, lies constantly." One of the eyes was filled with contempt and disgust, while the golden one closed as if in pain. "Her desires, her true powers, her reasonings—*all lies*. She covered herself in deceit in order to weaken me, afraid I would take control, afraid I would awaken inside her. Yet it was all for naught."

He felt his heart trembling inside him, the question being forced out of his mouth. "What do you mean, demon?"

The smile the creature gave him was enough to make him ill. "I mean what I said. This foolish girl is rightfully mine."

Leander felt neither anger nor rage. He felt sadness and grief. He felt frustration. He did not even know if he could walk anymore let alone fight, however that was not to be decided. There was only one choice to be made since Leander knew for certain three things.

The first being that he had to kill the demon.

"Why have you become so silent, *o great warrior?* Lost the will to fight, at last?"

The blackness had almost covered the woman's body entirely. The stench of rot was practically unbearable while the hot waves made Leander dizzy. Saranm's golden eye never left his gaze, never stopped begging and crying to him. That was all that was left of her, one eye.

He had one last weapon with him, his axe. It was a short axe, strung on his waist, yet it had to work. When it saw the man grabbing his axe, the creature started to laugh madly, the slick black tongue licking the blood that fell from its left eye.

The second thing Leander knew for sure was that, in the end, he and Saranm were the same. They were not warriors, they were not powerful—

They were prisoners.

"You truly wish for death, *human*?! Wish to fight *me* for it?!" The dark aura surrounding the Sword shifted for a brief second as if the demon had breathed in the dark glow itself. For that brief moment the air got colder and Leander felt in his very core that Death was not only near, it was holding his face. "Why even try so hard?"

The words that left his mouth tasted like blood and sweat. "Due to a certain shitty moral code."

The demon smiled.

Saranm mourned.

"I am glad to have crossed paths with you, *Argyris*, although our encounter was brief."

The last fact the man knew for sure was that he would die trying to free at least one of them that day.

It took less than a few minutes. Leander waited, for his legs couldn't move on their own, while the demon closed their distance in a blink. It was pure instinct and reflexes that made the man block the Sword from cutting his head off and even then, his arm almost gave out. He was lucky the attack hadn't lasted a second more. The demon gave him a sick and cruel smile, its tongue licking and curling up on the Sword's blade.

Leander pushed the creature back with his axe, knowing with certainty that the demon let him, reversing his grip on the weapon. Every single assault, every time the man tried to strike the beast, he would fail, hitting only the hot air that remained in the spot while the demon shifted its weight and body with such dominance and speed, it almost looked like the creature was dancing alone as Leander aimlessly tried to attack it.

Sweat dripped from his face as the man started to crumble. When the demon's smile faded, it came from the left, grabbing Leander's arm with both hands. It made a single movement so fast the only thing the man saw was his arm bones sticking out as the blood fell without effort to the ground, breaking his bones the same way one would break a stick. As his axe fell Leander screamed, unsure if he would pass out or get sick. The next moment the demon was raising him by his face, a bored and angry look in its blooded eye.

"I am done playing with you, human."

Leander felt the pain as the woman's blackened hand went through his chest and he could swear he actually felt the fingers brushing his heart before feeling their pierce. A tangible, hot grasp around his heart.

"I shall watch as Death kisses yet another failed man."

There was no pain anymore. He felt his whole body relax and his whole world darken. The last thing he saw was that golden eye and deep down he was glad to know that someone in that wretched world had shed tears for him.

"Forgive me, I failed you..."

The man did not know if his last words were truly spoken.

For Death's kiss had sealed his lips.

Chapter XV

Let us pray to our Divines, on this sad reminder. Let us pray and pledge that all deaths shall be remembered and recalled, that every tragedy shall be retold and forsaken, that every kingdom shall be awakened and wary of the ruins that still haunt the West and their blooded history. Let us all pray and ask our Divines not only for patience but wisdom, not only strength but humility for forever Tërnya shall remember its dark times when its three kingdoms from the West shared nothing but casualties, famine, and terror, when they engaged in nothing but battles, destruction, and calamities, when Albaron, Carnarbur, and Raevich lost not only their beloved people but their future and their peace.

Let us pray to our Divines to bless our West and their lands, to let us bask in Their glory and bestow upon this realm not only harmony but the ability to right our wrongs, so that the children and the young shall never witness such dark times again, so that our elders may rest with sane minds, and so that our future may keep prospering within the light.

Let us pray to our Divines.

Let us honor those who passed and those who fought.

So that they are never called again to haunt the Gallows.

So that they may find peace.

- *A Prayer for Memorial Day*, written by various authors.

Rise of A Star

Gallows of Night - Woods

Twenty Nights Before Memorial Day

Only when Dorian entered the cave and found Bash sobbing against Kayden's chest did his muscles relax. He had waited for more than two hours and, in the end, he could not force himself to wait any longer. He was already preparing his heart and soul to find his lady injured or worse, however the truth was something he could hardly fathom. Even as his mind raced, trying to piece things together, he still looked for the assassin.

When Kayden confirmed the absurd thoughts that kept crossing his mind after they left the cave, Dorian tried his best to maintain his composure. He had been teaching and spending time with the very person who tried to assassinate his princess not once, but twice. Someone who killed for money, a professional. However, the young Knight could not even meet his gaze, his eyes swollen and red, so even if all Dorian wished to do at that moment was punch Bash in the jaw just once, he could not muster the strength to do so. It felt like he would be hitting a wounded child.

"Here. This is what Sean-man gave me to...you know, *block* things. I thought you would want it to study whatever creepy arcane energy it has. Could be useful in the future." The Knight gave a dark metal disk to Dorian, something inside him screaming how wrong that thing was. As if it should never belong to their world.

"When we return, I will send a letter to Orion asking if he would look into this artifact. In the meantime, could you keep it inside the chest?" When Kayden finished her sentence, looking toward Bash, the boy widened his eyes before jumping from his spot and running away from them. It took a few minutes for him to return, carrying an ornate chest. Dorian knelt in front of the object, touching the metal and the marks engraved on it. Upon his touch, an electrical current ran through his fingers, making him recoil at the same moment. What *was* that?

"Are you well, Dorian?" Kayden touched his shoulder lightly, glancing toward the chest with furrowed brows.

"Yes, my lady. I will put the disk inside."

The current did not occur again, even when the Ward opened the chest and placed the metal artifact inside. The very moment he closed the chest it was as if all the air in the area had been replaced, as if they were inside a bubble that suddenly burst, the energies and sounds returning to the place. Bash began to scream, placing his hands over his ears while falling on his knees yet Kayden had a beautiful smile on her face.

"Do not worry about him, he is being reprimanded," she whispered her words almost as a secret, her hand still touching his shoulder.

"Believe my words, Kay, I could not worry less about him at this moment."

"Please, do not be so strict with him. The Sight did not show much, but I believe he was being manipulated by Sean—"

"How long have you known?"

Kayden took a few seconds to reply. "The Sight showed me some things about Leander's and Bash's pasts when they bonded with the Ancients. It was never my secret to tell, so—"

Dorian turned his head to face her, not trying that much to hide the anger and frustration swelling in his words. "Kayden, he attempted to *murder* you—"

"He did not, Dorian." There was so much compassion and kindness filling her eyes, it melted any ill feelings he was mustering inside him. "You know that Bash possesses a noble heart, *you* told me so. I believe he has a friend that needs his help, he was only going along with Sean's plans in order to help his companion."

The Ward averted his eyes, glancing toward the young Knight who still screamed and cursed on the ground. That did make him feel a little better. "That does not justify his previous actions."

The leader smiled, resting her head on him. Dorian forced his heart to calm down, forced his hands to remain beside him even if all he wanted to do was to pull her closer. "He is but nineteen, Dorian. Another child that suffered more than he should. Bash could use more friends like yourself. Perhaps you can help him after his mission, to find whatever Sean was promising him."

He sighed, somehow pitying the Knight who rolled on the forest ground. "Perhaps I can."

"For Säh's fucking eyeballs, *I am sorry!* I swear I won't cut you off like that ever again, just *stop* shouting in my head, you smug bastard!" It took only a second for the Knight's body to relax, pure relief spreading across his face. "Was that such a hard thing to do, bloody winged demon—*ouch*, hey! Do not dare to start again!" Bash pointed in front of him, Dorian seeing nothing but trees and the dark night sky. Then the light and air bent, the dragon appearing a few meters away from them as if it had always been there.

Kayden laughed when Dorian jumped from the scare. She walked closer to Bash and gave him her hand. "I am glad to see you both getting along, Bash."

The Knight's eyes bulged, pure horror on his face as he accepted the princess's hand to stand up. *"Getting along?!* Vühräh hates me! He just said he will make me fall on purpose—Kayden, my leader, I know I did a lot of awful, nasty stuff. I will repent. Just make him promise on his fucking soul he will not drop me from the skies. I have no wish to die yet, have to spy on your sweet father first, right?"

Dorian glanced toward the gray dragon, the horns making it seem more menacing than the look in its eyes. Wait, had the dragon just smirked?

"Vührähkam cannot harm his Knight, Bash, do not be concerned. However, you both need to depart at once. You cannot be late to your meeting with the Vam'Dammes."

Bash passed his hand through his hair, his gaze going toward his feet. "Yes, all right...I shall believe in your words, princess. And about the whole Sight thing...I will not tell a single soul."

Dorian's body became stiff, but Kayden's smile grew brighter, warmer. "I know. Now go—and do not forget to write your reports every week. I must know how your mission goes."

Bash nodded only once, turning his back to them and walking toward the great Ancient. He stopped only once, looking back toward his leader with something crossing his gaze. A glow, almost. "Thank you for what you did for me, Kayden. I will not forget." The young Knight then rushed toward the dragon, climbing on top of him. Although Dorian could not understand from where he stood, Bash seemed to be talking with the creature while twisting his face, the stone glowing on his wrist.

When the dragon opened its wings, Dorian almost fell to the ground, the sheer force of the wind moving every tree in the area. The Ward watched as the Ancient's legs left the ground, going higher and higher into the sky until it completely disappeared into the Gallows's night, flying away into the east. Toward Albaron.

He approached his lady, standing beside her while holding the sword's handle with a firm grasp. "Do you believe he will do well, Kay? The Vam'Dammes are not easy nobles to be dealt with, for someone like Bash to pretend to be their servant..."

He heard as Kayden held her breath, he saw her closing her eyes. Whether she shivered from the chilling breeze or from a Sight he could not tell.

"He will do fine. He is a professional after all."

To that, Dorian had many doubts. Yet once again, he chose to believe her.

Just like he always did.

Twenty Nights Before Memorial Day

Nineteen Nights Before Memorial Day

Seventeen Nights Before Memorial Day

Fifteen Nights Before Memorial Day

Ten Nights Before Memorial Day

Four Nights Before Memorial Day

Two Nights Before Memorial Day

The Curse of The Sight

Fall of Night - Ice Draco

One Night Before Memorial Day

When the war between Carnarbur, Albaron, and Raevich finally came to an end, the founders of the Divine Order of the Orphys Knights proposed a day to be celebrated by all three kingdoms. A day to remember all those who had fallen, all those who had lost their loved ones and served their kings even in an unreasonable war. On that day, all three kingdoms of the West would pay their respects to the deceased as well as to celebrate the end of a desperate era. That was the meaning behind Memorial Day.

Yet for Kayden, that day held another weight. There would be a feeling looming over her, as if there was a vengeful spirit with her with every step she took, haunting and cursing her. However, that day had been different. From the moment she woke up, Kayden could feel that something was not right. It was almost Memorial Day, for that reason the feeling was not completely strange to her. There had always been this energy on Memorial Day that would stick to her, like a gruesome and foul stench that would not leave her skin, that would penetrate her pores and spread farther inside her until the day was over. Too many dead, too many whispers and long-lost emotions, too many memories.

Sometimes she was able to see them, the ones who died in the wars, and their wailings and moans would echo inside her ears for hours, Wake till Gallows, making her insane. It was harder for her Sight on Memorial Day, yes, however after decades the princess was used to it. Just like the monthly bleeding, the princess expected the pain, the suffering. She still dreaded and feared it as the day approached, the whispers of the dead getting stronger by each Gallows. She would only be at ease when Memorial Day was long passed.

It had been Falls since Kayden had been able to have a sound night of sleep, however there was something on that morning, something different from all the other years. The dead still whispered, the feelings still loomed over her like a plague, yet that was not all. There was this sensation one would have in their body right before falling sick in their bed, something that would tell they were not fine, that they were getting ill. The sudden coldness of the skin, the dampness of the hands, the hollow and nauseous hole in the stomach, a light head. Kayden felt like Death was licking her lips but not daring to come any closer. As the day progressed, those symptoms worsened and when night came at last the princess was hardly able to focus on anything.

She was going through all the applications they had received in the past weeks for new recruits, overjoyed to see that the tournaments in Carnarbur and nearby kingdoms brought more licensed mages to the Order. Although recruits from Raevich and Albaron were scarce, smaller kingdoms and villages showed more interest in the Divine Order. Perhaps things would change from that point—the Order would finally get back to what it once was. Fight for the things it once stood for. However, before that, there were pressing matters that weighed on her mind.

"My lady, you are pale. Is everything all right?" Dorian's voice reached her, yet she could barely fight the cold shivers that took over her hands and arms.

The princess was relieved that their relationship was back to what it was; perhaps it was even stronger. However she had yet to receive a message from Bash, her mind in turmoil. Kayden hadn't heard from him for days and she was worried. In his last letter, Bash had mentioned how he should be able to write before Memorial Day and her anxiety would not let her rest.

"It will soon come to pass, Dorian. You should not worry."

Even with her words the Ward did not leave her side nor did he lose the concerned and pained look that dwelled in his eyes. Dorian came closer, kneeling beside her with his sword by his waist. He offered to take her back to her chambers, yet Kayden refused. The man stood up with one quick movement, his words harsh and cold as if he was almost giving her an order.

"Kayden, your lips are blue as a wolf's-bane rose and you can barely stop your body from shaking. What good will do you if someone comes and sees your glowing eyes? The moment we receive a letter, I swear I will take it straight to your hand, so let me take you back to your chambers. *Please*."

Normally, Kayden would have argued. That day, she did not. Her Ward knew all too well the things she had to endure when Memorial Day came, and it was not so rare the times Dorian had to stand guard in front of her chambers to prevent anyone from entering. It almost made her smile, how familiar that situation was. At last Kayden nodded while raising her hand, letting Dorian hold it while she used his arms for support.

The pure relief that washed over her friend was almost like a soothing wave and a calm breeze in her mind.

"I appreciate it, my lady. Do you believe you can still walk?"

She was not sure, however she walked anyway. To be seen by any knight in such a frail state would not bring any good to her at the moment. However, the walk to her bedroom was quiet and painful, her vision coming in and out of focus throughout the entire time. Kayden felt her Sight numb her fingers and strike her eyes only to fade away seconds later with a cold shiver. It was different than the past weeks. As if she had finally lost all control toward her Sight, not able to manifest in its rightful way. Kayden suddenly stopped, her entire world weaving, turning, and dancing all around her.

"Dorian," she whispered with a weak voice, the word tumbling out of her mouth.

"Speak your words, my lady."

"I'm going to be sick."

Dorian kicked open the first door in their sight, an empty room on their right. She was unsure if minutes passed or if it was mere seconds, but suddenly there was a bucket in front of her and Kayden felt something burning its way through her throat. Kayden did not know when it finally stopped and at what point she started to scream—it felt as if her insides were turning into scorching coals burning her body from the inside, melting her flesh and bones, and vaporizing her blood. Kayden's eyes began to hurt as if there was someone squishing them to make them jump out of their sockets. Pure white light flashed inside her mind while images passed so fast they burned like melting iron being poured inside her head.

There were so many flashes, the light was so bright Kayden could not say if what she was hearing was her actual voice or the screams that were trapped within the visions. From somewhere she seemed to hear Dorian's voice, yet it was so far away. Everything was so far away and that pain would not stop, the images would not stop, the screams and voices would not stop, and Kayden just wished for Death's kiss to come and take her soul at last, take everything from her.

The next moment, it was as if her body had been thrown in the middle of the ocean. Kayden felt a gelid embrace dragging her down to a pitch-black darkness, hitting the bottom with a soundless drop. She could smell the blood from every possible direction and as Kayden tried to stand up, the princess saw her own reflection on the ground. Yet it was not the ground, it was a sea of blood. In the blood Kayden could see hundreds—no, thousands—of bodies with their gazes resting on her as if they were waiting for her next movement, waiting to see what she would do. Their eyes were the only thing that could make one wonder if they were alive at all for their skin and flesh had no color, their bodies were twisted in the most horrible ways, and that sight alone made the tears fall from her eyes, a silent pain grabbing and taking control of her heart.

What is all this?

The blood started to get colder, thicker. A few meters away from the princess a tall, grand chalice stood made from a silver that somehow seemed to possess its own light, like a star. Kayden glanced back toward the bodies, their restless eyes never leaving her, their anguish never hidden from their gazes. With her body trembling, the leader walked slowly toward the chalice, the blood getting thicker and heavier with each step she took, as if it was a viscous mud or something worse. The foul iron stench was making her sick yet it was the dead's eyes following her that left Kayden unsettled. When she finally got to the chalice, the object only reached her waist and its glow grew even brighter.

Its light felt cold and distant.

All the eyes inside the blood had their gazes burning with urgency, as if they were pressuring Kayden to act with haste. Deep down, the princess knew that whatever the dead wanted her to see inside that chalice, it was not something good. It was something that would tear her heart apart and destroy her, something that would create a pain greater than anything she had felt before. Yet their gazes would not leave her. Their pain was beginning to enter her, stab her legs, and crawl their way up her body. Kayden would not be able to bear all their pain, all their suffering.

She had to see what they wanted her to see—she had to in order to make them all look away, take their ails and sorrows away. So, the princess got even closer to the chalice, pressing her waist into the cold metal, and looked inside it. For just one moment there was nothing, only its cold and distant light being reflected in her eyes. Then blood started to fill the chalice like a torrent and even though the blood kept spurting, gurgling, changing its direction like waves in the sea, Kayden was able to watch what the dead wanted her to watch.

Kayden watched every piece, every scene, every detail. And as she watched she could not only feel the dead's pain and suffering climbing on top of her but her own, a wretched pain that could as well kill her from the inside. That blood could be hers just as much as it could belong to the thousand dead bodies around her, to the body inside that chalice. Her mind could not believe it, would not believe it. Yet in her heart Kayden knew it was *true*.

The princess gasped with tears falling from her eyes without ever stopping, seeing Dorian's gray eyes staring back at her. Kayden's eyes burned as if they had been open for far too long and even so, the leader could not close them. The fear of going back there, going back to the dead and their gazes as she watched the past unfolding right before her eyes was too much, that pain was too much.

"How long was I gone?" She spoke her words yet they had no strength. They tasted like blood, thick and viscous.

"Far too long for my own good, Kay. If not for your beating heart, I would swear for all the Divines that you were long gone."

Only now did she notice his red eyes and wet face, a horror that made his words tremble and shake as he spoke. Kayden raised her hand, caressing Dorian's cheek with a faint smile made only for him.

"Forgive me, my friend, for causing you such distress."

Dorian chuckled, holding the hand that touched his face with a strong grip as if he was afraid to let go. "Your distress seemed far greater than mine, Kay. Yet I must ask, do not do this again. Ever."

He pulled her close for an embrace, his warmth slowly spreading to her, breaking the coldness that was making her shiver. Yet her heart still wept, her tears still fell. She knew she was bleeding, she simply didn't know from where.

"Dorian, we must go to Albaron at once."

The Ward did not part their embrace, but he did push her back enough so he could see her face and look Kayden in the eye. His fingers wiped away her tears, even though they would not stop falling, and the sadness that welled inside almost made her choke.

"Was that what it was? The Sight, it showed you something? Is it about Bash?"

Kayden nodded once, afraid that the moment she spoke what she had seen it would become real. However, the princess knew the moment she saw the scenes that what had been shown to her inside the silver chalice had already happened, that it was nothing but a fragment of the past. Something she would be able to change no more, not even if all Divines allowed, and Kayden knew They would never.

The princess stared at her Ward, forcing the words out of her mouth and even then they could barely be heard. There were so many emotions and feelings dwelling inside those small words, Kayden wondered how they did not sink back into her throat. However, she did manage to speak to him, that sentence cutting its way out of her lips.

"King Felix has been murdered."

The tears would not stop, the bleeding would not stop.

However, the pain, it was slowly fading away.

Interlude

Journal Entry, Winter

Gallows

They are all dead.

Every single one of them.

How could I let this happen? I was their leader, their commander. I was the one responsible for them, yet I let them all perish, and in such a way... Forget finding my former colleagues, forget finding Clarice, how can I even continue the search in this situation?

I can only pray to the Divines for one thing. I pray that Sean finds this before I find him. I pray that he reads this before I set my eyes on him.

So find and read this, Sean, so my words can haunt you until the end of your days.

I will kill you with my bare hands, Sean. I will hunt you down and I will make you pay.

Even if it's the last thing I will do with my life and soul, I will make you regret. For what you did to my friends, for all of those knights, for my dear Clarice. You know quite well why *I am known as the Red Knight, and you* know *I always honor my promises.*

So wait for the Red Knight in the Gallows. Wait for me in fear. Wait as I become Death's lips and bring your end. I will come.

That, I swear on my soul.

He Who Brings Darkness

Gallows of Night

Two Nights After the Blood Ceremony

Those were lands that for decades had not seen the sun or been touched by light of any kind, for the Divines could never reach a place so heavily drenched with the demonic. The living had no business there and the few creatures that were brave or fool enough to crawl into that tainted soil would soon be forgotten by the world. The air was almost unbreathable, so dense and harsh that it alone was enough to kill any who came uninvited. On the Unhallowed Graves, there was no green, no forests or rivers. Only the putrid scent of the rotten decay, a blood trail leading any wanderer into the ruins of its Lorn Castle, sharp and rocky stones that were long destroyed and abandoned. However, it was never empty.

One could hear the pleas and screams of those who had died, black birds flying above the blackened lands. Within the ruins, a frozen air howled between the walls and halls, a darkness tainting every inch and space. Inside the throne room even the coldness and silence of Death were vanquished, creatures and beasts coming out of paintings, cracks, walls, floors, ceiling, pieces of broken glass, and even through the remains of a long dead rat. Demons, in every shape or lack thereof, moaned and growled the most disgusting and guttural sounds. They were not only restless; they were famished and in a frenzy after decades of being dormant.

"They kaaame...!"

"Our mazter was right."

"We kil' again."

"Bak, bak, 'ey r bak."

The creatures could barely speak human language, mixing letters or prolonging the sounds too much. Rotten flesh weighed in the air as the stench impregnated every inch and stone. The throne appeared to be empty, no more than shadows and pure darkness could be seen from the seat. The demons' eyes glowed as if they were carrying infernal flames within them, at least the ones that had eyes.

"Silence, fools. Our master shall wake." It was the demon that dominated the human speech the most, Natür. The monster hid and blended into the shadows with the smoothness of a snake, its five eyes never missing a blink. Natür too felt the euphoria and excitement of those lesser demons. It too felt drool accumulating inside its mouth, shivers going through its skin, the promise of blood and flesh too real to ignore. "Bring food. He will hunger."

A pack of low demons dispatched, trampling and running over themselves as they shrieked, growled, squeaked, and grumbled. Natür rolled two eyes, those lackeys were not worthy of its other three. A smaller demon came jumping in Natür's direction, it had a distorted face and a body like a fat frog, with its one big eye blinking thrice before dragging its words.

"How....Master....wake....soon?" That voice was too deep and hoarse, being almost inaudible. Natür only smiled, revealing its black teeth.

"He must felt the power before us have. He will wake and he will hunger. You go and find more food. Good food. Others only bring the untasty."

The other demons began to jump and move with trembling bodies, some engaging in small fights and spars, biting off each other's flesh, stepping on each other's blood and fluids. They were all too excited, too ecstatic. Their master was waking. Natür felt waves of pure pleasure and satisfaction wash over it, making its own body twist and shake.

Soon. He wakes soon.

And soon, it came. There were small, subtle changes; the room got colder, the air went still with not even one passing breeze going between cracks and holes, the walls seemed to recoil while the ground shook weakly. They were very small and subtle changes, but they all meant the same thing. Their king had awakened. Their king was waking to rule them all once again. On the throne one could see the pair of eyes, almost as if they were hanging in the air like Death's, watching and waiting.

"You are too loud. If I did not understand the words you speak so disgustedly, I would almost say you were pestering me about something of grave importance." His voice was deeper than an underwater cave, it carried more power than a beast's roar; it demanded subjugation. All demons lowered their heads, the ones that were able touched the ground with their faces, the ruins filled with their joy and euphoria upon hearing the man's words.

"Our...king...!"

"Bak, bak!"

"Em.Pe.Ror."

Their voices, moans, and sounds got louder and louder, some even spilling saliva while they struggled to pronounce mortal words. But Natür knew its king, it knew what pleased their emperor and what enraged him, so Natür bit down its long tongue and waited while bowing its body enough to feel the cold stone floor touch its head.

"Silence!" The man hit the throne with his fist, the sound echoing through halls and walls as if it was running away from the man. The creatures shrieked, bowing, and lowering even more, coiling and begging, hiding and weeping.

"For...Gave...."

"Have uz in merzy."

The man raised himself from the throne and Natür could swear upon its thousand lives that, from the outside, dead trees bowed toward the man together with the entire land. There was a strong obedience that emanated from him, as if his presence demanded every ounce of will from the living as well as the dead. Natür's smile grew so much it hurt its face. How strong and powerful their king was. The world was recognizing their king once again, it would bow to their king once again. All humans would bow to his desires, once again.

"You all must have felt them. They have returned to this plane," Kih Nähsur spoke with eyes filled with a melting fire.

"Saw. Saw."

"In boneyz, in flezh."

"Air got changed. We see with our eyes the light change, when they woke. But just light change, nothing else," Natür spoke, its five eyes looking down as the man walked past it, his steps echoing as rocks, chills running down its skin when the king's scent filled its nostrils.

"Did it, now? I guess they are weaker than before." Nähsur walked toward one of the ruined windows, looking past all the anguish and sorrow the Unhallowed Graves possessed. "Which is truly a pity. It is not in my interest to replay our last battle, to only take another puny victory to show Them our power. Time is of the essence now—I will not tolerate the same plays, the same ruses, the same fights. They have to feel threatened by us." It was like hearing poison drip from the man's mouth, a delicious and alluring poison that only made the demons laugh and moan, some choking and gagging on their own drool while rejoicing in memories of the feast brought by the last war.

As they all recalled the taste of human flesh, the many flavors the mortals' blood had to offer, the demons began to spiral out of control. Even Natür almost succumbed to its own desires, yet Natür was superior. It was its king's best servant. "What shall we do? Do we seek more food? Taint more lands?"

The ruins trembled and started to crumble, the air vanishing completely from the throne room and Natür was one of many who could feel in its flesh and bones the menace and bloodlust coming from their king.

"You will leave the humans and their pets alone. They must grow stronger if we want to show Them a better play, in a greater stage." The man still faced the window with his back facing the creatures. None could see his eyes nor his expression, yet they all could taste the death their king promised were they to do some foolish act. "You have my permission to watch your ancient kin and nothing else. For now, we shall wait for a while. And after we wait, after they grow stronger—"

Natür did not need to hear the rest of the sentence. None of the creatures did. Kih Nähsur turned around and one look in his eyes was all it needed. The answer was there, like so many others, making Natür smile and lick all its teeth and blink all its five eyes again and again to contain its pleasure and joy.

The human realm should prepare itself.

Death was coming. It was coming to them all.

Acknowledgments

WHERE SHOULD I EVEN start? I believe the best is to thank all the people who supported me with the appropriate style. Which is, with a poem (for I believe poems are, in their own right, very stylish).

Though this story began almost 10 years ago
At first, with no direction and no real home
I had my sweet parents to let me know
That I could do this, no matter how many years I had to roam
The journey was indeed long, not easy at all
There were trolls, insecurity, and procrastination along the way
Yet there was this grand witch Triz that I always would call
She not only would hear the tales but made characters that in the end just had to stay
Though generations and culture would set us apart
My dear grandparents acknowledge it, would even make them proud
Without understanding much about plot, they would say it was art
They would share it to whoever would pass, no matter the crowd
Some years went by with the story untouched
There was not much motivation, time, or drive
Yet may it be fate, chance, or the years that rushed
I met you, Robert Jordan, and your words made my imagination thrive
And on that same year, October 2020
I formed new friendships, as precious as they were brand new

I'm talking about you, Writerly Conglomeration of Cats Wizardry—as if there were many
It is WACHOW for short, and you were the guys that made me go through
From WACHOW, there is a special someone
Who I call xixister at times, who is nothing but a dear friend
My very first reader, kind Difa, who spoke words brighter than the scorching sun
I owe you way too much, and I shall owe you until the very end
And along the way, I met some other brave soldiers
Special readers who gave this tale a chance
One aided with editing, the rest lifted weights off my shoulders
With all kinds of words, shapes, and sounds; they were like instructors to my wild dance
At last, but never at least, I must thank
To the one with not only the investment but also the brains
To one of my oldest friends, dear Victor, who I first thought was pulling a prank
Without you, there would be no book, no joy running through my veins
So really, thank you. From the bottom of my heart.

And to give some specific credit...

I must thank all my dear beta readers (especially my dear friends Rodrigo and Janine), who helped me through numerous drafts and made it possible for me to shape this story—this novel—into something I was actually proud of.

Anne-Marie Rutella, who was just as much a reader as she was my editor, writing the best D&D related comments ever

My dear mom, who would love the characters like sons and daughters and hate whenever I wouldn't write.

My caring father, who always believed in my dream and continued to support me and celebrate my accomplishments alongside me.

My dearest brother Peter, who brainstormed with me and was just as invested.

To the amazing and talented voice actors that brought the characters to life: Brandon Stone, Sarah Kisko, and Kyle Quibell. I am very fortunate to have found you among many, and even more grateful that you chose to participate in this project (and a big shoutout to Kyle for helping me so much with my weird sentences.)

To Lya, who created such amazing illustrations not only of the characters and the scenes but also the cover for this dear story of mine.

Finally, to my best bae, my sweetest hubby. You never read it, and probably never will. Yet you aided me still, through your support, your love, and by simply being you. You are way more creative than you give yourself credit. Thank you, my love, for everything and more.

And of course, to every single reader who gave this story a chance, I am eternally grateful. You are the reason I write, the people that truly make my story and characters come to life. I wrote this story for you, and I shall continue to do so (I have HW books 2 and 3 written, and more on the way).

Shit, almost forgot—

Thank you, Google-sensei. You were useful, and a real hero. Cheers to you, mate.

Many happy blessings to you all, from this witchy and odd author.

C'EST ÇA

Arcs Guide

- Beware of the Gallows
- The Legend of Kih Nähsur
- The Sound of the Realm
- He Who Brings Darkness

ARC OF DIVINES

- Ties Shackled by Blood
- A Sight Too Bright to See
- A Divines' Call
- Ten Stars in Clouded Skies
- The Great Demonic War
- Winds that Flows Adrift
- A Sight Too Blind to Miss
- Curse Through Ancient Blood
- Three Realms, Three Pillars
- Stigma of a Red Knight
- Golden Stars in a Silver Sky
- Blessed by the World
- The Misery of Those Who Know
- Divine Strings
- An Old Star's Lost Glow
- By a Cold Night
- To Reach a Lost Star
- The Curse of the Sight

ARC OF STARS

- Talk in a Haze
- Decaying Freedom
- Reawakening
- A Fool's Covet

- Bounded by Blood
- Feral Darkness
- Gallows' Red Sun
- Challenged by the Gallows

ARC OF WARRIORS

- Blood and Stones
- Reawakening
- The Weight of Choice
- The Lion and the Snake
- The Mighty Lion
- A Warrior's Honor
- Echoes From the Abyss
- A Warrior's Duty
- A Witch's Call
- A Witch's Lament
- A Warrior's Scars
- A Warrior's Blood, a Witch's Poison
- A Witch's Penitence
- A Warrior's Cry

ARC OF WINDS

- Stale Winds
- Influx Winds
- In a New Tomorrow
- A Sight Too Strong to Hold
- Child's Play
- Promises of the Wind
- A Dance Sharper than Knives
- Will of the Wind

- Entrapment of a Star
- Rise of a Star

ARC OF GALLOWS

- A Dark Eye from the Gallows
- A Pretty Punch in the Jaw
- Farewell, Great Gallows
- A Kiss From the Gallows
- A Secret From the Gallows
- A Sight From the Gallows
- Betrayed by the Gallows

Manufactured by Amazon.ca
Bolton, ON

55800143R00243